ON HIS MAJESTY'S SERVICE

www.**rbooks**.co.uk

Also by Allan Mallinson

Fiction featuring Matthew Hervey

A CLOSE RUN THING
THE NIZAM'S DAUGHTERS*
A REGIMENTAL AFFAIR
A CALL TO ARMS
THE SABRE'S EDGE
RUMOURS OF WAR
AN ACT OF COURAGE
COMPANY OF SPEARS
MAN OF WAR
WARRIOR

Non-fiction

THE MAKING OF THE BRITISH ARMY

* Published outside the UK under the title
HONORABLE COMPANY

ON HIS MAJESTY'S SERVICE

ALLAN MALLINSON

BANTAM PRESS

LONDON · TORONTO · SYDNEY · AUCKLAND · JOHANNESBURG

TRANSWORLD PUBLISHERS
61–63 Uxbridge Road, London W5 5SA
A Random House Group Company
www.rbooks.co.uk

First published in Great Britain
in 2011 by Bantam Press
an imprint of Transworld Publishers

Map on pix by Tom Coulson, Encompass Graphics

A CIP catalogue record for this book
is available from the British Library.

ISBN 9780593058169

Addresses for Random House Group Ltd companies outside the UK
can be found at: www.randomhouse.co.uk
The Random House Group Ltd Reg. No. 954009

The Random House Group Ltd supports the Forest Stewardship
Council® (FSC®), the leading international forest-certification organization. All our
titles that are printed on Greenpeace-approved FSC®-certified paper carry the FSC® logo.
Our paper procurement policy can be found at
www.rbooks.co.uk/environment

Typeset in 11/15pt Times New Roman by
Falcon Oast Graphic Art Ltd.
Printed and bound in Great Britain by
Clays Ltd, Bungay, Suffolk

2 4 6 8 10 9 7 5 3 1

CONTENTS

PART THREE: THE PURSUIT OF VICTORY

MAPS

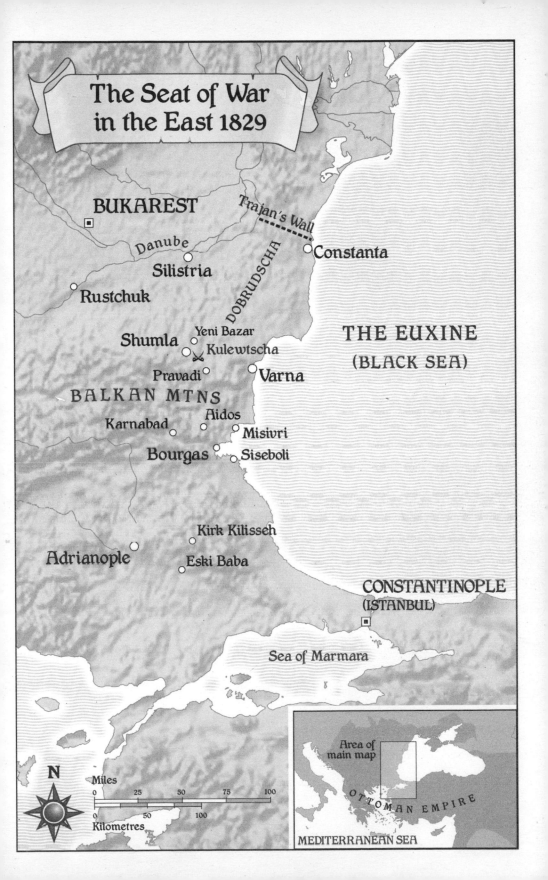

The Seat of War in the East 1829

BUKAREST

Trajan's Wall

Danube

Silistria

Rustchuk

Constanta

DOBRUDSCHA

Yeni Bazar

Shumla

Kulewtscha

Pravadi

Varna

THE EUXINE
(BLACK SEA)

BALKAN MTNS

Karnabad

Aidos

Misivri

Bourgas

Siseboli

Kirk Kilisseh

Adrianople

Eski Baba

CONSTANTINOPLE
(ISTANBUL)

Sea of Marmara

N

Miles

0   25   50   75   100

0   50   100

Kilometres

Area of
main map

OTTOMAN EMPIRE

MEDITERRANEAN SEA

FOREWORD

The past is never dead. It's not even past.
William Faulkner

In the first edition of *The Spectator*, 5 July 1828, there is an article describing the topography of 'the theatre of war in Turkey'. Russia had fought the Ottomans no fewer than eight times in a hundred and fifty years, but in none of these wars was Britain directly involved, nor, indeed, very indirectly. There had been a close shave in 1827 when a combined British, French and Russian fleet had – incredible as it may seem – *inadvertently* sunk a sizeable Turkish fleet which lay at anchor in Navarino Bay (the battle which features in the ninth Hervey tale, *Man of War*). By deft diplomatic activity, however, war was averted – one of the Foreign Office's finer moments.

In that *Spectator* article, quoted at length at the beginning of Part Two of this latest Hervey adventure, there is a statement with sinister echoes: 'The truth is, that the Danube debouches in a very obscure portion of Europe, and, except in the case of a contest, like the one commencing, there is very little reason why we should trouble our heads with its geography.' For is this not reminiscent of Neville Chamberlain's speech in September 1938 during the Czechoslovakia crisis, in which he referred to 'a quarrel in a far-away country between people of whom we know nothing'? War came but a year later for Chamberlain's Britain; in the

Russo-Turkish quarrel it would be another twenty-five before Britain found herself embroiled (in the Crimea). But in both cases the British army, sorely neglected in the preceding years, fared badly at first, and only survived by the innate strength of the regimental system until it could variously pull itself together. *On His Majesty's Service*, the eleventh volume chronicling the military life of Matthew Hervey, a cavalryman in the pre-dawn of the Victorian era, is not written as a tale for our times, but the reader might occasionally feel that there is a certain contemporary resonance. It is sad to relate, for example, that publication sees the army at its lowest strength since the eighteenth century, and facing even further cuts. Sad because the army's expertise has been hard won; its 'operational heritage', giving it that intangible winning edge, reaches back to Hervey's day and beyond. Quarrels in far-away countries between people of whom we know nothing have in the past become *our* quarrels, and although Plato never actually wrote what is attributed to him on a wall of the Imperial War Museum, it nevertheless reflects the wisdom of the ages: *Only the dead have seen the end of war*.

But Colonel Matthew Hervey is a professional soldier. War is his business. And the events in which he now takes part 'in a very obscure portion of Europe' actually happened.

HANSARD
28 July 1828
THE KING'S SPEECH AT THE CLOSE OF THE SESSION.

After the royal assent had been given, by commission, to several bills, the following Speech of the Lords Commissioners was delivered to both Houses by the Lord Chancellor:

'My Lords and Gentlemen, we are commanded by his Majesty to acquaint you, that the business of the Session having been brought to a close, his Majesty is enabled to release you from your attendance in Parliament.

His Majesty commands us at the same time to return to you his warm acknowledgments for the zeal and diligence with which you have applied yourselves to the consideration of many subjects of great importance to the public welfare.

The provisions which you have made for the regulation of the import of Corn, combining adequate protection for domestic agriculture with due precaution against the consequences of a deficient harvest, will, in the confident expectation of his Majesty, promote the inseparable interests of all classes of his subjects.

We are commanded by his Majesty to acquaint you, that his Majesty continues to receive from his Allies, and from all Foreign Powers, assurances of their friendly disposition towards this country.

The endeavours of his Majesty to effect the Pacification of

Greece, in concert with his Allies, the King of France and the Emperor of Russia, have continued unabated.

His Imperial Majesty has found himself under the necessity of declaring War against the Ottoman Porte*, upon grounds concerning exclusively the interests of his own Dominions, and unconnected with the Stipulations of the Treaty of the 6th July 1827.

His Majesty deeply laments the occurrence of these hostilities, and will omit no effort of friendly interposition to restore peace.

The determination of the Powers, parties to the Treaty of the 6th July, to effect the objects of that Treaty, remains unchanged . . .'

* The 'Sublime Porte' is a figure of speech for the Sultan's court and government of the Ottoman Empire, or for the empire itself. It derived from the practice of receiving diplomats at the *porte* (gate) of the headquarters of the Grand Vizier (prime minister) at the Topkapi Palace in Constantinople/Istanbul. Later 'Porte' came to refer to the foreign ministry.

From the Princess Lieven, wife of the Russian ambassador to the Court of St James's, to her brother, General Alexander Benckendorff.

3rd/15th July 1828

Dear Alexander,

. . . While I was writing to you, the despatch from Karassou of June 12/24 announcing the surrender of Hirsova and Kustendji arrived. Bravo! Bravo too for having managed to make mention of Wellington's regiment in the account. There was never a cleverer bit of irony than this; all Europe will be laughing at his expense. He will be the only person to take the matter seriously; that is to say, he will be quite flattered at seeing his name associated with glory as far away as the Black Sea.

I was unable to finish yesterday. There will be arriving with you shortly an English officer, Lord Bingham, who will pass for being an officer in Lord Heytesbury's suite. He is a weak little man, a trifle stupid, to whom this favour has been accorded because he is pro-Turk – it was refused to Cradock because he is pro-Greek. The truth is that Lord Bingham will be anything you wish, and will probably become enthusiastic about the Russian army. He will be a peer some day. His departure was quite kept secret by Wellington's orders, who had the idea that mothers here had designs upon his happiness or his fortune . . .

PART ONE

GREAT EXPECTATIONS

I

HOME THOUGHTS

Tuesday 13 January, 1829

Hervey had rarely seen water come with such force. It was that of the falls in Canada, near Fort York (if an infinitesimal fraction of the volume), which a decade past he had observed for himself in their icy midwinter trickle. And the enveloping steam was like the mist that had shrouded him in safety on the heights of Esi-Klebeni as the warriors who had assassinated the Zulu king pursued him with like intent.

'Remarkable,' he said, shaking his head.

His friend Edward Fairbrother took the cheroot from his mouth and frowned at its dampened glow. 'I confess I am astonished that you wonder at such a thing after all you have seen,' he replied, blowing the end of the remaining three inches of best Indian leaf. 'We have come here twice by steamship, have we not? And I fancy the Romans bathed with scarcely less luxury hereabout in centuries past.'

Fairbrother's practised insouciance almost invariably amused. Indeed Hervey thought of his friend increasingly in terms of

3

indispensability – not as jester but (since it was he that had spoken of the ancients) more as the crouching cautioner in the triumphant procession: *Respica te, hominem te memento* – 'Look behind thee, and remember thou art but a man.'

Not that Hervey saw himself as the man honoured in triumph, for although he had saved what remained of his troop in the desperate fighting at the kraal, he had not been able to save the Zulu king's favourite, Pampata (his ward in their flight thither); but he returned now to London with commendations for resource and bravery, and in the prospect of command at last of his regiment. This latter, whatever his regrets – above all the slaughter of men under his authority – was ample cause for satisfaction. But first, before any *triumphus*, or anything remotely resembling it – before, indeed, reading any of the letters, official and otherwise, that awaited him – he was determined to bathe.

'And by this 'andle 'ere, sir, the water is regulated,' said the valet, first slowing and then stopping altogether the surge. 'And then you can 'ave it as 'ot or as cold as you will by this other 'andle 'ere, sir, which regulates the cold water in like manner.'

'Admirable, admirable,' replied Hervey. 'Thank you, Wilkes.'

'The steward says as the valets must draw the baths, like afore, but I reckons it won't be so long as members'll be able to do it for 'emselves,' opined Wilkes, surveying his remarkably effortless work with satisfaction. In the United Service Club's old premises it would have taken him the better part of half an hour to fetch water for a bathtub a quarter the size. And almost as long to empty it again. But now, as he pointed out, by merely lifting the brass cylinder which acted as a stop to the drain as well as ingeniously permitting the outflow of water if the level in the bath rose beyond a safe level, or perhaps a level necessary for adequate ablutions (for the heating of water was not without considerable cost; best Tyne coal was now thirty-three shillings and sixpence per double chaldron), the contents of the bathtub were conveyed effortlessly by leaden pipes to the cesspit beneath the building, and thence – he knew not quite how – to the Thames.

'Well then,' began Hervey, certain he was now tolerably well trained in the United Service's most recent advance in its members' comforts, 'perhaps you will permit me to draw my own, and attend on Captain Fairbrother, who may take his.'

'Very good, Colonel 'Ervey,' replied Wilkes, with an approving nod: he was confident enough that if there were any mishap, the hero of the Cape frontier would be able to subdue the steward's ire. 'Is your groom to stay, too, sir?'

Hervey explained that he was not, that Private Johnson would not return until the day after tomorrow, and that he would be glad of Wilkes's services in the meantime. Then he returned to his room to slough off his travelling clothes.

The United Service's new quarters in Pall Mall (on which site until a year ago had stood Carlton House, 'Nero's Palace' as it had irreverently been known, the residence of the former Prince Regent) were greatly to his liking. And there was the added advantage that not far hence was the Horse Guards, the headquarters of His Majesty's Land Forces – so perfectly convenient for him to present himself later in proper fettle. He did not know Lieutenant-Colonel the Honourable Valentine Youell, whose signature was on the summons to attend the commander-in-chief (with its unspoken promises of reward and further duty), but he supposed him to be no less capable than his old friend Lord John Howard, in whose temporary absence (he had remained at the Cape, whither he had lately travelled in the hope of seeing action at last) Youell acted.

Of course he would be capable; it was unthinkable that Lord Hill would have any other on his staff; but undoubtedly he would be less inclined to intelligence a mere officer of light dragoons as faithfully as had Howard. Hervey had always counted himself fortunate in having rendered valuable service to Lord Hill (and, for that matter, to the Duke of Wellington) in the field, for it was by no means every officer who could enter the Horse Guards on terms of familiarity; but to have such a friend as Howard at court had always been a double fortune indeed.

When he was out of his travelling clothes he put on a dressing robe, gathered up the towels and other appurtenances of his toilet, and then returned to the baths like a Roman at his ease. 'Thank you, Wilkes,' he said as he handed him the robe and stepped into the joyously hot water – carefully, so as not to disturb any of the elements by which so perfect a bath was drawn. 'Captain Fairbrother is equally comfortably served?'

''E is, sir. 'E asked as for me to bring 'im a glass of port as well. Shall I bring one for you too, sir?'

'No, Wilkes – no port, thank you. I'm merely inclined to close my eyes a while and contemplate the luxury of the club's new arrangements.'

Wilkes bowed gravely: who indeed could begrudge a little luxury to the man who had battled with savage warriors in that most heathen of lands (he had read of Hervey's exploits in the *Morning Post* when the newspapers were taken from the smoking room at the end of the week)? He would tell the other valets that they must not disturb the colonel: let him take his bath at leisure; the other gentlemen would have to wait.

As the door closed, Hervey let his shoulders sink below the water. That he could do so without bending his knees was remarkable. 'Capital,' he said, smiling and shaking his head. In India, where everything was worked on a voluptuary scale, the bathtubs were not one half the size. His head, even, was below the top, so that the outlook was solely a white-painted ceiling, which now served as a sort of canvas on which to picture the events past that gave him pleasure, and in the future that promised likewise – a vivid fresco, a tableau of people and places that few men were given to know.

Yet almost at once the pleasurable recollections were displaced by darker ones. He had lain in his cot aboard the steamer many a time, or dozed in a deck chair, yet not once had such thoughts come – or else so fleetingly that they were gone before they made any true impression. Perhaps he had banished them, but was now ready to let them come? For come he had always known they must. Once, as they cruised off the Ashanti coast, he had woken from a dream of the whitening bones of the dragoons he had left behind. And yet the bones had not rebuked him, nor even in truth disturbed him – only puzzled him, for he had left many bones to whiten in distant places in the service of the King, and never before had they appeared before him, in his sleep or otherwise. Afterwards he had pondered on it, asking again what more he might have done to save them, but the dereliction that had led to the ambush at the royal kraal had not been his. Everyone knew it – and he knew it himself, of which not even scrupulosity, had he been inclined to suffer it, could have dissuaded him.

It was not bones that paraded before him now, however, but the faces of the living – though momentarily, as if to remind of what he had turned over in his mind during the leisure of his passage home. Serjeant-Major Armstrong, his NCO-friend of many years, new-widowed, father of five (was it?) – what now might his prospects be? Armstrong might find a wife, if he could overcome his grief for the sake of the children – as he, Hervey, had done – but that would take many months, perhaps more. Were Armstrong an officer he might elect to go onto half pay until his arrangements could be regularized, but an enlisted man had no such option. Had he, Hervey, been taking the lieutenant-colonelcy at once instead of, first, the mission to the Russians (he wondered if he really wished for this mission, now), he could have approved indefinite leave, having Armstrong's duties performed by a serjeant with temporary rank ... Perhaps he might prevail on Lord Holderness, the commanding officer whom soon he would succeed, to do likewise?

But these things were ever perilous. It ought, after all, to be considered no singular thing for an NCO to conduct himself in the manner that Armstrong had in that desperate fight with the Xhosa; as Lord Hill was wont to say, it was the duty of the officers to show their men how to die, and that of the NCOs how to fight. He must trust therefore to Lord Holderness's good sense and consideration – which he had after all shown in ample measure during his command – or, at least, to a certain disinterest, for within the year Holderness would be major-general, and the regiment's regulation therefore no longer his concern.

He slid further into the bathtub, his head went under, and, as if it were the Jordan, he surfaced purified of dark thoughts. For there before his eyes was Georgiana – eleven years old. Yes, he had been absent for many of those years, but that did not matter now with the prospect of happy reunion and ... re-acquaintance. Their last time together (he now understood) he had not admitted her years. He smiled at the thought of buying her 'Mrs Teachwell's' *Fables in Monosyllables*, despite her having told him – in the same breath, almost – that 'I know what are nouns and prepositions, Papa. And verbs and adjectives – and all the other parts of speech. Aunt Elizabeth has taught me.' He knew now that he could not make up lost years by treating her as if she were still in the middle of them. When last he had seen her, six months ago and more, he had been struck by how tall she was grown, and how like her mother – the large, happy eyes, the raven ringlets. In six months she would perhaps have grown even more like her, and he was surprised to find himself perfectly contented with the prospect.

'Aunt Elizabeth has taught me.' He smiled to himself again. At first he had been inclined to think of the words as a rebuke, albeit unintended. He owed more to his sister than he could repay – and perhaps always had – but that must not prevent his now repaying what he could, if only in treating her with proper sensibility. It had been for her sake, though, as well as for Georgiana's (he told himself) that he had in large part been so determined on marriage.

And yet Georgiana had remained in the protection of Elizabeth, for that was evidently where she found things most agreeable. That, of course, must change (he meant that she must find living other than with Elizabeth agreeable), and he was sure it would just as soon as he could make some proper establishment at Hounslow. Well, sure *enough*. For with Kezia, his wife of but six months, he could not see his course with anything like the same clarity. Kezia, lately Lady Lankester, whose husband (then his commanding officer) had been killed at the siege of Bhurtpore these three years past, had taken him in marriage with unexpected readiness, and yet she showed such little inclination to embrace all the purposes (as the Prayer Book had it) for which matrimony was ordained . . . Well, he checked himself: there had been so little opportunity to live as man and wife. There were a dozen or so years between them, but so had there been between Kezia and her first husband, with whom there had been issue. Yet there was between them a gulf of incomprehension that . . . well, he had not the power to comprehend. She had followed her first husband to India, but had been unwilling to come with him even to the Cape – and had said very plainly that she would not go with him to Canada if he were to accept command of a regiment there when command of his own at Hounslow had looked increasingly remote. He understood perfectly that her music was to her a very considerable matter, that she was possessed of an excessively fine voice and a rare skill at the fortepiano, and yet . . .

He sighed, as he had many times during the passage home, and steeled himself: it did not serve to make any comparison, however remotely, with what there had once been, for his late wife – it was now more than ten years – had been so wholly different in spirit.

For there was Georgiana to remember. It would all be regularized, put on a proper footing, resolved, just as soon as he could make a proper establishment at Hounslow. November was the month indicated, when Lord Holderness would be made major-general and the lieutenant-colonelcy would pass to him – or certainly that was what Lord John Howard had told him at the Cape was the commander-in-chief's intention.

If only this assignment in the near Levant, in Bulgaria, could be foreshortened and Hol'ness promoted early. The Turkish war was hardly one in which the King's ministers had the remotest intention of becoming engaged, especially not after the debacle of Navarino – the 'untoward event', as the Duke of Wellington had called it. Untoward indeed: three squadrons in concert, one British, one French, one Russian, had sent the pride of the Sultan's admiralty to the bottom in the Bay of Navarino, and then His Majesty's government and that of France had expressed their utmost regret, leaving the Russians, their erstwhile ally in the romantic crusade to unyoke the Hellenes from the tyranny of Mahomet, to make true war with the Turk – and to do so ashore. What a mazey way to conduct affairs of state!

So why was the Horse Guards so eager to have an observer at the ceremonies? Lord Hill could not believe there would be any novelty of strategy revealed? And, if truth be known, he, Hervey, was not a little affronted at the thought of relieving Lord Bingham so that that new-come officer (Bingham had not even been in uniform at the time of Waterloo) might take command of the 17th Lancers, for which he had paid an unconscionably large sum. He wished Lord Hill had not asked him to be the relief. He wished Lord Hill had not suggested it in such a way as to make it seem that it was by way of their former association, a sort of favour indeed. Except, of course, there was something undoubtedly thrilling in the prospect of observing the clash of armies on a scale not seen since Waterloo.

He sighed, and ducked his head under the water again: he would travel to Hertfordshire, to where Kezia lived with her people, as soon as the Horse Guards gave him leave, and thence to Wiltshire to see Georgiana and his own people; and then he would ready himself for the assignment with the army of the Tsar.

But thoughts of Navarino made him break surface almost at once, for in that battle his old friend Peto – cruelly disappointed in his betrothal to Elizabeth, who had (though with great resolution and with sound reason, he now conceded) broken off the engagement, to marry instead a former officer of the King's German Legion – had suffered the most grievous wounds in command of his ship. What life lay ahead for Captain Sir Laughton Peto now? To be sure, he was well tended in Norfolk, his native county, where the Marquess of Cholmondeley had made Houghton Hall an *Invalides*. But with no prospect of sea service again, and scarcely of a wife, how might that estimable man fare? He swallowed hard: Houghton – it had been by Kat's hand, Lady Katherine Greville's. In her letter, which he received just before leaving for the Cape again, she had written of her expectation of some improvement in his old friend's condition (though how that could be with such grievous wounds he found hard to understand): 'And George' (the new, young Marquess of Cholmondeley) 'has most eagerly contracted to attend to all dear Captain Peto's needs until such time as he is able to return to his own house.'

How he wished to banish all thoughts of Lady Katherine Greville.

Well, so let it be, he prayed. He would go and see his old friend too, after Hertfordshire and Wiltshire, just as soon as he was able.

But Kat: she would *not* be banished, no matter how hard he willed it. If only she had dutifully followed her husband, agèd though he was, all would now be different. Lieutenant-General Sir Peregrine Greville, for nigh on ten years the military governor of

Alderney: he had occupied that martial outpost without (as again the Prayer Book had it) the mutual society, help, and comfort, that the one ought to have of the other – of a wife, indeed, and one whom he had elevated, if not in rank, then certainly in material condition, from the penury of a crumbling Connaught mansion, her father's, an Irish peer. It was strange, to be sure, that so many years after the Peace, Alderney had not been reduced (in its dignity, that is; the actual garrison was long dismantled). It might even be supposed, mused Hervey, that a staff officer at the Horse Guards, lately asked what might be done with General Greville, had replied that, since he was anyway fast approaching 'the days of our years' (full threescore and ten), it were better to let things take the natural course. For although Sir Peregrine stood high in the gradation list, no exigency of the service would have induced the Horse Guards to appoint him to any active command.

But then Hervey smiled wryly, and soon shamefacedly: that same staff officer, had he heard the news, would now be pondering on the late-revealed virility of this general, this *senex amans*, for Lady Katherine was with child. In two months' time – Hervey knew the date well enough – Kat would present Sir Peregrine with a son and heir, or perhaps a daughter, but the paternity would not be that which was entered in the register.

He closed his eyes once more and slid under the water, as if to wash away the sins, and the remembrance of them.

II
AN EMPTY COMMAND

Later that morning

It was snowing again. And Fairbrother delighted in it, the first he
had ever seen, the flakes caught in the light of the post-chaise along
the turnpike the night before, and then this morning from his
window, the white carpet that was Pall Mall. He was fascinated by
the sound of it beneath his feet as they walked to the Horse Guards,
not yet feeling the chill he knew must be its consequence.

'And so this is how you marched to Corunna?' (thinking that at
last he might understand what hitherto he could only imagine).

Hervey smiled. 'But a twelfth part. What's this here – three
inches? There was never less than three feet on that march.' He
turned up the collar of his greatcoat as they came to the steps at the
end of Carlton House Terrace. 'My blood has evidently thinned at
the Cape, though; I confess I find it damnably cold! Do not
you?'

But Fairbrother was like the schoolboy, and would have taken to
snowballing had the decorousness of uniform not forbidden it. He
declared that he did not in the least feel the cold this morning, and
proceeded to descend the steps at break-neck speed, all but sliding

across the Mall, which was no longer the muddy avenue of his earlier acquaintance but a broad, white highway, before recovering an appropriate enough composure to cross the parade ground of the Horse Guards.

'See yonder fellows at their drill as if the snow were nothing!' (nodding to the company of greatcoats at the far side of the square): 'Such men! Such incomparably fine men!'

'Admirable,' replied Hervey, feeling chastened by his friend's heady appreciation, and trying to repair his inattention. 'The First Foot Guards. I recall seeing them come into Sahagun after we took the place from the French. They held their bearing even then, though we were knee-deep in snow.'

'I rather think they are the Coldstreams, the grenadier company – the officer's white plume?'

Hervey's brow furrowed beneath his forage cap as he peered at the guardsmen in greater scrutiny. And then he nodded somewhat abashed. 'You are more eagle-eyed than I. I saw the bearskins and nothing more. I'll gladly pay a sconce at dinner.'

'*Salut.*'

Hervey recovered himself a little. 'Mark, they would jib at the "s"; they will answer to "the Coldstream" or to "Coldstreamers" but never "the Coldstreams". Though do not ask me why.'

Fairbrother smiled. '*Touché.* But I fancy they need no reason. And it is, I suppose, regimental weather?'

'Regimental weather?'

'Did they not march in snow all the way from Coldstream when Cromwell died?'

Hervey nodded again, his friend's eclectic knowledge ever diverting. 'And where did you come by that?'

'I read it in Bishop Burnett's history.'

Hervey shook his head in part despair. 'I confess I have not read him, but my good and late departed friend D'Arcey Jessope was always inordinately proud of the march, which he somehow placed on a par with Bonaparte's on Moscow.

'"A cold coming they had of it. The ways deep, the weather sharp, the days short, the sun farthest off in *solstitio brumali*, the very dead of winter".'

Fairbrother inclined his head, his turn to be impressed.

'A sermon on the Nativity,' explained Hervey, 'by another bishop. My father is wont to preach a deal of it each Christmas.'

'Which bishop?'

'I don't recall. Is it of any moment?'

'Everything is of *some* moment, is it not? You yourself have said so in matters of soldiery.'

'I concede. But I can't remember.'

They were half-way across the parade ground before Fairbrother voiced his doubts about their destination once more. 'You are sure Lord Hill would wish to see me?'

Hervey shortened his step only very slightly. 'If he wishes to see me then there can be no doubt that he will wish to see you. He is a most affable man, and besides, your repute has gone before you in those despatches from the Cape.'

Fairbrother had saved the life of the lieutenant-governor in the desperate skirmish with Mbopa's warriors. Hervey was sure that this alone would secure him entry to any drawing room in London.

Fairbrother made no reply.

They walked a few more yards in silence. 'And it was Bishop Andrewes. Lancelot Andrewes.'

'I shall make enquiries of him,' said Fairbrother in all serious-ness. 'What fine words, they: "The ways deep, the weather sharp, the days short". I only wish I might hear them from your father's pulpit.'

Hervey smiled. 'I'm sure you shall. The parish is very fond of the sermon. They would have him preach no other at Christmas.

Perhaps we might resolve here and now that if we do not Christmas next at Hounslow then we shall do so at Horningsham. There; does that serve?'

'It does most assuredly.'

'And you shall come with me to Wiltshire as soon as we are finished here and wherever we must – to ride the Plain again, and shoot bustard. Just as I promised we would.'

'Agreeable in every respect.'

Fairbrother felt a warming in his breast that no brandy could induce. In truth his studied nonchalance and contrary passion masked a great want of companionship, which Hervey had come unexpectedly to supply, and which Fairbrother by return supplied in like manner, though in Hervey's case the want arose not from birth on the other side of the blanket but by the steady falling away, for good reason and ill, of those with whom he had seen service.

It was more than that, however. In Fairbrother, Hervey recognized a quite exceptional aptitude for the sabre and the saddle, a sort of 'sixth sense' for the field. He himself had been taught a good deal as a boy – in a boyish sort of way – by Shepherd Coates, who had lately been trumpeter to General Tarleton. But it seemed to him that Fairbrother's talent was not merely acquired; there was something that came with the blood – and he was sure it must be that part of the blood which came from the dark continent of Africa. Fairbrother's mother was a house-slave of a Jamaica plantation, and therefore but one generation removed from the savagery of her tribe – the savagery *and* the wisdom. When the two friends had faced that savagery together, at the frontier of the Eastern Cape, it had been Fairbrother who had known, unfailingly, what to do. But more: he had then been able to execute his own advice, to take to his belly to out-savage the savage. And yet, too, such were Fairbrother's cultivated mind and manners – which his father, the plantation owner, had seen to as if Fairbrother had been born in the great house rather than one of its cabins – that his company would be sought by gentlemen of the best of families. When first Hervey had introduced him at Hounslow, Lord Holderness had expressed himself delighted: 'a fine-looking man', with a 'gentlemanlike mien'.

Only a certain weariness with life on Fairbrother's part (although not so much, perhaps, as when they had first met eighteen months or so ago) stood occasionally between them. Yet so erratic was it, for his enthusiasm for knowledge seemed at times to know no bounds. But then Fairbrother never admitted himself to be a willing soldier in the way that Hervey was; he had not thought himself a soldier from an early age. His father had purchased a commission for him in the Jamaica Militia, and thence in the Royal Africans (a corps which more resembled the penitentiary than the regular army), and then on Hervey's recommendation and entreaty Fairbrother had quit his indolent half pay at the Cape to accompany the Mounted Rifles to the frontier as interpreter. Their first meeting had indeed been unpropitious; Hervey had very near walked away in contempt. But now this handsome, half-caste, gentlemanlike, disinclined soldier was his paramount, boon companion.

The clock began striking eleven as they walked under the arch of the Horse Guards – in step, for Fairbrother had picked up Hervey's as they approached (which amused his friend since Fairbrother had always affected an unmilitary air) – and Hervey returned the sentry's salute as they made for the oddly unimposing door into the headquarters of the commander-in-chief of His Majesty's Land Forces. Inside, an orderly showed them to a waiting room. Hervey took off his greatcoat, bidding Fairbrother to do likewise, and moved to the fire to warm his hands.

Hervey was now revealed in the undress uniform of a lieutenant-colonel of the 6th Light Dragoons rather than of the Cape Mounted Rifles, which hitherto he had been assiduous in wearing, for his substantive promotion on the regular establishment had only been lately gazetted. He wore no sword, as was appropriate for an 'interview with refreshment appropriate to the time of day', but carried, wrapped in leather, an *iklwa* taken at the fight at Ngwadi's kraal, which he intended presenting to the commander-in-chief. Fairbrother, in the green serge and black buttons of a captain of the Rifles, appeared unmoved by his proximity to power and glory – which was exactly as Hervey would have it, since it was his design to have his friend impress their 'host'.

'I thought that it bespoke history the last time I passed through the arch, but did not remark on it,' said Fairbrother, watching through a frosted window the change of mounted sentries below. 'Why is it, do you suppose, that the videttes stand on this side and not at what is manifestly the front of the building?'

'I may tell you very precisely,' replied Hervey, nodding his thanks to a porter who had brought them coffee, 'because I asked the same question of John Howard some years ago.'

But before he could give any explanation the orderly returned to take him to his call. He nodded to Fairbrother – he would wait here, as 'arranged' – and then walked along the familiar corridor, spurs ringing, to the antechamber of the commander-in-chief's office, where sat Lieutenant-Colonel the Honourable Valentine Youell working at his papers.

Hervey saluted as he entered, a courtesy rather than a requirement, the custom on entering an office, no matter what the rank of its occupant. In like fashion the staff lieutenant-colonel rose to acknowledge the salutation with a military bow, if perhaps more stiffly (reckoned Hervey) than would his old friend John Howard.

'I have brought with me Captain Edward Fairbrother of the Corps of Cape Mounted Riflemen,' Hervey explained as he took the proffered chair. 'I wish to present him to Lord Hill on account of his service there.'

Colonel Youell looked doubtful. 'I am not sure that without due notice the commander-in-chief will receive an officer, Colonel Hervey. And a captain at that.'

Had Youell simply voiced his perfectly reasonable reservation as to the propriety of an unscheduled call, Hervey would have taken no offence, but disregard on account of mere rank vexed him. He had the highest estimation of the Foot Guards, but occasionally their officers could show excessive attachment to form – especially when they had not been shot over. He could not check himself in replying truculently, 'We shall see.'

The remark brought a stifled groan from Youell: for his part, he never failed to be astonished by how little officers at regimental duty had regard for the difficulties under which the Horse Guards laboured. 'Wait here, Colonel Hervey, if you will,' he replied, with some weariness, gathering up a portfolio and moving to the door of the commander-in-chief's office.

Inside, Lord Hill was coming to the end of a memorandum from the chief secretary for Ireland. He looked up, took off his spectacles and said, with an appreciable sigh of relief, 'The chief secretary is of the opinion that there is no need of reinforcement.' He rubbed his eyes. He had been bracing himself for days in the expectation of having to find more troops for Ireland. 'Leveson-Gower's a most excellent fellow. Few in his place would have expressed themselves content, even knowing how damnably in want of men I am at this time. I would that the duke hastened his Relief bill and have done with the business. Or else vote me supply enough.'

Colonel Youell considered that it was not his to reply. The Duke of Wellington, for a decade and a half the prime soldier of Europe, and for a year the prime minister of the United Kingdom of Great Britain and Ireland, was no longer the bulwark of the old order. His bill for 'the Relief of His Majesty's Roman Catholic Subjects' – which, not long before, he and his home secretary, Robert Peel, had

19

so steadfastly set their face against – was daily expected on the floor of the House of Commons; as was disorder the length and breadth of the realm.

'And for that matter I would that Peel hastened his Police bill. It's all very well for the Secretary at War to be disbanding regiments of dragoons, but if Bow Street insists on patrols every day, how's it to be done. Eh? And dragoons sent all over the country to keep the peace: what the deuce are those Yeomanry fellows about that they can't scatter a few labourers?'

'Indeed, my lord.' Lord Hill's question, Youell understood from experience, was entirely rhetorical. The commander-in-chief knew as well as he that the Yeomanry were all too adept at scattering labourers, as well as hand-loom weavers and even passably peaceful citizens of Manchester deluded enough to want to listen to Orator Hunt. The problem was that the yeoman seemed incapable of giving the flat of the sword rather than the edge. It was ten years since 'Peterloo', but they had not been ten years of any marked progress.

Lord Hill shook his head, and sighed. 'Very well, Youell; send Leveson-Gower my expressions of appreciation. Is that all?'

'Colonel Hervey is here, my lord.'

Lord Hill brightened at the sudden prospect of diversion. 'Splendid. Where's that despatch from Lord Bingham? I don't recall reading it.'

'I placed it on your table yesterday, my lord.'

'Ah. Bingham is well, then, do we suppose?'

'He is well, my lord. Quite recovered, it would seem from his despatch. But that we knew already.'

Lord Hill became agitated. 'Quite so. I do consider it high-handed of him to return to his estates in Ireland without presenting himself here first, no matter how turbulent the situation of his tenantry. And, indeed, so I understand, finding occasion to attend various drawing rooms before posting to Holyhead, telling all and sundry of his eastern sojourn . . . And not to render a complete account of what has transpired other than to refer us to his despatches, which appear to travel very much more slowly than does his lordship.'

Colonel Youell could only sympathize; trying to regulate the Earl of Lucan's elder son was, by all accounts, a fool's errand. 'Indeed, Lord Hill.'

'Do you recollect the despatch? Are you able to give me its import – until I have opportunity to peruse it fully?'

Youell, anticipating the request for a summary, had underlined the salient sentences in the copy made for the record. He had done so, too, with a certain distaste (which would have come as a surprise to Hervey): he had not met George Bingham, but what he had heard did not dispose him to think at all highly of an officer so improbably rich and assured of his right to command. For though Bingham was not yet thirty, with the wealth of his father's Irish estates at his disposal, he had been able to purchase, for a sum, it was said, approaching £22,000, the lieutenant-colonelcy of the 17th Lancers. But there again, to his credit he had travelled to the seat of war between the Tsar and the Sultan so that he might be shot over – officially, to accompany the Russian army in their campaign against the Ottomans in Bulgaria, and to relate what he observed to the Horse Guards – for although wealth might buy the Seventeenth smarter uniforms and better horseflesh, it was no substitute for some schooling in other than mock battle.

He took the fair copy from his portfolio. 'It is written off Varna, my lord, aboard His Imperial Majesty's ship *Pallas*, whither Lord Bingham had been taken by stretcher, and is signed the seventeenth of September. I fancy it must therefore have come by St Petersburg. We had the ambassador's despatch a full month before, by Constantinople.' He read aloud the underlined passages:

21

To the Commander-in-chief of His Majesty's Land Forces
Horse Guards
London

My Lord,

I have the honour to report that I accompanied His Imperial Majesty, Autocrat of all the Russias, and His Excellency the Ambassador to the seat of the War at Varna, where by His Majesty's order <u>Count Woronzov took command on the 29th of August from Adjutant-general Menshikov</u> who had been wounded in one of the Turk sorties. <u>The approach to Varna by His Majesty's forces was first assayed on June 28, but the Russian avantgardes were met by considerable Ottoman forces, and the siege postponed. The appointment of Count Woronzov was signalized by a sortie made in force during the succeeding night, against the right of the Russian trenches</u>. The Arnauts entered the redoubt sword in hand through the embrasures, but were repulsed, after a determined struggle, by the efforts of a regiment called after His Grace the Duke of Wellington. <u>The 31st was then remarkable for a considerable number of attacks and counter-attacks by the besieged and the besiegers, who alternately attacked the flank of their adversary. Towards the close of the day, the Turks mastered some strong ground near the enemy's right, on which they planted five of their standards, but during the night General Woinoff regained this position, though with great difficulty.</u> A Turkish lunette was carried at the same moment, but it was retaken next morning by a storming party sent for the purpose from the garrison.

    <u>Between the 1st and 8th of September two additional redoubts were constructed by the besiegers</u>, and a second parallel was attempted by flying sap, under cover of fresh batteries. These

played directly on the guns of the fortress, instead of the more usual, and I might say scientific, ricochet fire.

On the 8th of September, the Emperor Nicholas returned by land from Odessa with reinforcements, sixteen battalions and as many squadrons which, in addition to the guards and sappers, gave an effective force of more than 20,000 men before Varna, exclusive of the corps detached to the southern side of the fortress to intercept any relief force, and of another which occupied Pravadi.

The enterprising spirit of the people of Varna, I venture to say, was elevated rather than daunted by the hosts which now threatened their walls, and perceiving a regiment of Cossacks rather in advance, covering a reconnoitring party, 500 Delis made a sudden dash and drove them back. It was on this occasion that my horse was shot from under me and I was rendered incapable.

Between that time when I was taken into the charge of the surgeon of His Majesty's own flagship and this day, the explosion of a considerable mine effected a breach in the bastion at the easternmost angle. Still the Pasha, who was yet faithful to his trust, indignantly refused to receive a summons to capitulate. At this point, however, the difficulties attending the transport of heavy guns through Bulgaria had been at length overcome, and the siege train arrived from Brailow to replace the guns landed by the fleet. At the time at which I write, additional batteries have therefore now opened to render the breach more practicable, and I am myself to rejoin Count Woronzow's suite presently . . .

Lord Hill raised a hand. 'I'm obliged. As you say, its intelligence is somewhat in arrears: this much we knew from the ambassador. See that Colonel Hervey reads it. You know, I was not minded to send anyone to observe this affair – Bingham can be deuced unrelenting – but I am certain now that it can only be to our advantage to see how these armies fare. The reforms in both are said to be considerable, but I wonder to what end? With a man like Hervey observing, we might have answer.'

'Indeed, my lord. Will you see him now?'

'I will.' The commander-in-chief pushed aside his papers with an air of relish. 'At what time is the levee at Prince Lieven's?'

'Twelve, my lord.'

'Capital. I would not wish the interview to be hurried.' He smiled. 'I might even be able to impart some information to Lieven. He pressed me only yesterday at the Austrian ambassador's to know who would replace Bingham, and when.'

'Some might speculate on whether the inquiry were on the Princess's behalf, my lord.' Youell's wryness was all the more for its being infrequent.

'Indeed. Hah! What schemes Princess Lieven has to her name.'

The door was opened, and Hervey ushered in. He put his feet together noisily in the Prussian style and saluted, a confident presenting to the man who disposed the future of every officer in the army.

'Daddy' Hill, as he had been known throughout the Peninsular army for his attention to the comforts of his men, looked for all the world like an elderly cleric, his coat dark, his pate bald and his form somewhat portly. The contrast in appearance with the previous occupant of the commander-in-chief's office could not have been more profound.

'My lord.'

'Hervey, I am excessively glad to see you,' declared Lord Hill, rising and extending a hand. 'Nothing warms the heart better on a day such as this than to see an old friend return safe from the fray.'

Hervey was taken aback, but agreeably, by the appellation 'old friend', for although he had galloped for the general at Talavera (and Lord Hill was not one to forget a service, especially one so capable as his had been that day), to be admitted to such a sphere, if in words alone, was honour indeed. All he could manage, however, was 'Thank you, my lord.'

'I have read your despatches with careful attention, and Sir Henry Hardinge likewise. I dare say there'll be a ribbon in it.'

The attention of Sir Henry Hardinge, the Secretary at War, and a soldier of some distinction himself – this was recognition indeed, let alone the ribbon ('C.B.', with which he had been honoured after the storming of Bhurtpore two years before, was already notable for an officer with so recent a half-colonelcy). 'I am glad to have been able to do my duty, General. As did others in that expedition – for one, Captain Fairbrother of the Cape Rifles, whom I should very much wish to present to you, sir.'

'By all means, Hervey. And stand easy.' He turned to Colonel Youell. 'Have Captain Fairbrother's name entered for the next levee, would you?'

'Certainly, my lord.'

Hervey cleared his throat. 'My lord, Captain Fairbrother has accompanied me from the Cape, and indeed he is here with me this morning. I had hoped you would receive him.'

Lord Hill frowned. 'That is most irregular, Hervey. I stand not on great ceremony but I cannot have the business of the Horse Guards conducted with a complete absence of it.'

Hervey felt suddenly discomposed; he had evidently misjudged matters – overreached himself, even. 'I beg your pardon, my lord.'

Colonel Youell now cleared his throat. 'There is time before Prince Lieven's, my lord.'

A smile displaced the commander-in-chief's frown. 'Very well. We shall receive your Captain Fairbrother. But first sit you down, Hervey. Take some Madeira.'

Hervey removed his forage cap, took a glass from the tray which an orderly brought, and sat in an armchair half-facing the commander-in-chief's desk and the windows which looked out on to the parade ground. Snow was now falling so thick as to make St James's Park at the far side quite invisible.

Lord Hill observed it too. 'You were not with us on that blessèd trudge to Corunna, were you, Youell?'

'I was not, my lord.' Youell did not add that he had been fevered on Martinique with General Maitland, a gentleman volunteer not yet seventeen.

'Damnably cold, and the army behaved ill – not every regiment, not by any means, but too many. Badly served by their officers, some of them, and scandalously ill-provisioned. But that was no excuse.'

None of this could have been unknown to Youell, reckoned Hervey; and he wondered at Lord Hill's purpose. 'All of them fought well at Corunna, though, sir,' he tried, risking rebuke in speaking unbidden, and seemingly to contradict.

But Lord Hill better than most knew how well they had fought that day, for he had commanded the brigade on the left flank, astride the road to the town. 'The point is, Hervey, if the retreat had continued another week we'd scarcely have had an army left to fight with at Corunna.' He looked out at the snow again. 'Look here, you will dine with me this day week, and we shall speak then of your duties in the east. There's nothing arising from your Cape despatches of which we need speak now; they are admirably clear. But I have to tell you one thing – and though it is not for me to do so, I feel the obligation since it was I who selected you to command of the Sixth.'

Indeed it was, Hervey knew – and without purchase. 'I have not had opportunity to thank you, my lord.'

Lord Hill looked uneasy. 'Yes, yes, that is all very well – and I do not need thanks for doing my duty – but matters are not as they were. I am fighting a damnably bloody war of retrenchment. I have had to give orders for the Sixth and two other regiments to be reduced, to be placed *en cadre* – a depot squadron, a hundred men, no more.'

Hervey felt his stomach turn as badly as it could before a fight. 'For how long, sir?'

'Indefinitely. They're supposed to be disbanded: that is what Hardinge asked, but I've managed to persuade him that the economy in placing them *en cadre* is almost as great, and the general situation too uncertain to risk complete disbandment – far easier to re-raise than if they had been wholly struck from the list.'

Hervey was now on the edge of his chair. 'But, sir, why the Sixth? Our seniority, our late service in India, our—'

'Colonel Hervey,' warned Youell, firmly but with a note of respect nevertheless.

'Forgive me, my lord, but it makes no sense to reduce a regiment which has acquired such expertise in its trade. Why cannot those late sent to India be recalled?'

'Colonel Hervey, remember your place, sir,' repeated Youell, though more as entreaty than command.

Lord Hill huffed, but with the air of a man challenged reasonably enough. 'Hervey, let me explain to you the very grave situation the Horse Guards finds itself in.' (By 'Horse Guards' Hervey knew that Hill meant he himself.) 'The army estimates are in course of preparation as we speak. They require a reduction of eight thousand men. To this end I have it in mind that every battalion is diminished by fifty men, that four companies of one of the penal corps are disbanded as well as the whole of the Staff Corps – some twelve hundred men – though I believe we might transfer a thousand of these to the Board of Ordnance.' He smiled grimly at the ruse.

Hervey could well appreciate the Horse Guards' difficulties, for if such sleights of hand to overcome a reduction in supply were being employed, the situation must indeed be disadvantageous. But all the same, if there were not troops enough for every call on them, why reduce the cavalry when they possessed the greatest celerity of movement?

Lord Hill appeared to read his mind. 'And yet the calls on the army are no less insistent, not least in Ireland and in Canada. I need hardly point out that the cost of a regiment of cavalry is twice that, and more, of infantry. There are one hundred and three battalions of the Line, and seventy-four of these are abroad. It is His Majesty's government's policy that troops in foreign stations should be relieved every ten years – that is to say, at the rate of seven battalions a year; but where are the reliefs to be found if there are only enough battalions at home to last for four years? Ministers, as is their wont, put forward makeshift after makeshift. But it will not serve.'

Hervey was about to ask why the prime minister himself, with all his experience of organization, was unable to suggest other than makeshift, but thought better of it and returned instead to the wisdom of reducing the cavalry. 'But if two or three regiments are recalled from India they may be replaced effectually by native ones – or by regiments raised from the Europeans there, of which there is growing number, as your lordship will know.'

Lord Hill shook his head. 'If all I were obliged to do is reduce the number abroad I might consider such a proposal, even against the advice of the Board of Control, which is ever anxious as to the *relative* number of native to King's regiments. But let me remind you that these regiments do not trouble the army estimates; it is the *Company* that pays for them.' He raised his hand as Hervey, further emboldened, made to speak again. 'You are about to argue the requirement for aid to the civil power. It is the argument that I myself made with the Secretary at War. Mr Peel's Police bill will soon be before parliament, and calls on the army thereafter should be the less – three regiments less, Hardinge calculates; do not ask me how. I prevailed on him to await the outcome of the bill, and even its implementation, before we make any irrevocable reduction. Hence the placing of three regiments *en cadre*. I trust I have made myself plain?'

Hervey shifted a little in his chair. 'Really, my lord, I am discomforted as well as honoured by the pains you have taken to explain this to me. I—'

Lord Hill shook his head. 'No, it is the least I could do. And lest you suggest that in a year or so we send the Sixth to India and disband the more junior regiment due return, let me disabuse you of the notion: we must show the saving in this year's estimates. The matter has been discussed with Lord George Irvine, and that must be the end of it.' He raised his hand again to stay one last attempt. 'But, of course, quite apart from the future of your regiment is the future of you yourself.'

By no means had this been absent from Hervey's own thoughts, but it had not been uppermost. In any case, if matters had been discussed with the colonel of the regiment – Lord George Irvine – there really did seem to be little more to say. 'You mean I am not to have command, sir?'

'No-o, I did not mean that. You may certainly have command of the regiment *en cadre* if that is your desire, but frankly, Hervey, what satisfaction is there to be had in such an appointment? You'd be little more than a troop captain. I want you to have command instead of a Line battalion.'

Hervey's face registered disappointment.

'It is beyond my power to appoint you to any other cavalry regiment since none is in want of a lieutenant-colonel. I wish you to have command of the Fifty-third.'

Hervey swallowed. Lord Hill was himself their colonel – the 53rd (Shropshire) Regiment of Foot; everyone knew it. He could make no remark that appeared either deprecating or ungrateful.

But Lord Hill was not yet finished. 'They're posted to Gibraltar later this year. With the situation in Portugal promising so ill, there are bound to be repercussions in Spain, and Gibraltar must remain on the greatest alert. You would have much to engage your talents, and Sir George Don you would find an agreeable garrison commander.'

None of this Hervey could possibly gainsay; Kezia, even, would find the posting pleasing – would she not? And yet it was so far from what he had wished for himself – from what he had been given to understand would be his – that he could not summon the will to embrace it.

Lord Hill came to his rescue once more. 'I do not expect you to decide at once, neither am I minded simply to order you to duty there – though I half believe it would save the both of us a deal of trouble if I did. You may think on it a while and give an answer by and by – before setting out for the Levant at any rate.'

Hervey smiled appreciatively, and bowed. 'Thank you, my lord.'

'Very well, let us now meet your Captain Fairbrother.'

Only after they had left Lord Hill's office did Hervey remember the *iklwa*. He thought of asking Colonel Youell to send it in, but then thought better of it since he was anyway to dine with Hill in a week's time. He retrieved the swaddled weapon with his greatcoat, thanked Youell for his consideration – indeed, he was a little ashamed at his earlier presumption – and the two friends left as the clock atop the headquarters struck twelve.

Walking back to the United Service Club, with all the appearance of snowmen by the time they reached the corner of the Admiralty, Hervey gave his friend a full account of his meeting before the commander-in-chief had in turn received him. Fairbrother said little by reply; he knew perfectly well how dejected was Hervey. And yet so affable, humane a man had Lord Hill seemed to him that he could not but think his friend ill-served in the extreme by any notion other than to accept the offer of the infantry command. But he knew it, too, to be futile to attempt a persuasion when Hervey was in a mood such as this – and with the thermometer evidently fallen while they were indoors, his earlier delight in the white blanket was turning into something more akin to Hervey's shivers.

'A good chop and some warm burgundy, I think, would assist the cognitive process,' he suggested.

Hervey nodded. It would be for the best. Better to think about these things when his breath did not freeze.

But it would have to wait. As they reached the top of the steps by the scaffolding that was the building site of Carlton House Terrace, they were witness to a most savage smash. Down the lower Regent's Street skidded a four-in-hand dray-van, the driver on his feet at the box and hauling desperately on the reins. Had the team come straight on at the bottom of the hill and into Waterloo Place he might have halted them amid the builders' stores, but with collective terror counteracting his frantic efforts, and the stables in St James's Market seeming to beckon, they turned instead for Pall Mall. The speed was too great, the road too like a sled-run, and the corner too sharp: over went the van, slewing into the scaffolding of the new Athenaeum club, dragging the screaming horses with it in a tangle of kicking, thrashing legs. Standards, ledgers, transoms, boards – all the bits and pieces of the builder's frame – collapsed on the wreckage of carriage and horseflesh, and with them a dozen men working on the new stone.

The two raced across Waterloo Place as passers-by in Pall Mall stood aghast or rushed to tend the injured, along with labourers from all corners of the building site that was the old Prince Regent's palace. Hackneys and chaises pulled up, their occupants descending to help – or to faint at so much blood made redder by the snow.

Hervey looked about for how he might take command in the

confusion of horseflesh and timber, but hard against the Athenaeum wall he saw the driver motionless and at peril of both the crazed horses and more, teetering scaffold. He pulled off his greatcoat and threw it over the head of the off-side leader, the worst kicker, Fairbrother throwing his over the off-wheeler, subduing both horses just enough to get at the traces. Hervey pulled the *iklwa* from its sheathing and began cutting at the leather while Fairbrother tried to unfasten the chains. They got the off-leader free soon enough – it managed to scramble to its feet and away, to be caught by one of the ostlers come up from the market – but the wheeler took longer, for both near legs were tangled in the traces, and Hervey had to slice more than once at the same strap until they were free. The gelding sprang forward, fell again, almost on top of him as he tried to subdue the near-side leader pinned by the carriage pole held fast by the pile of scaffold. Then it was up again, landing a shoe hard on his arm before bolting through the circle of labourers and off down Pall Mall. Mercifully the off-wheeler lay still, pinned yet faster by the pole, with the driver half under him.

Then he saw how its near hind was twisted – the cannon surely broken? 'Has anyone a pistol?' he called.

A cabman answered, offering his caplock. 'I'll do it if you will, sir. It's primed, ready.'

Hervey, for all his experience of the grim trade, reckoned the man had at least as much expertise as he, and so was content to stand aside. Almost before he was clear of the litter of harness, the cabman's shot ended the wheeler's ordeal, the crack loud even amid the general commotion, sending pigeons aloft the other side of the street.

A crowd had gathered, with enough strength – Hervey reckoned – to haul the van's broken axle from the wreckage so that they could detach the pole and haul the wheeler clear and at last get at the driver. Labourers, costers and gentry alike answered to his orders willingly, only too pleased that someone in the authority of a military hat would direct the rescue. Rope was got from the builders and lashed to the axle beam, and then to Fairbrother's word of command a dozen pairs of hands began hauling on it until Hervey was able to reach the pin and disengage the pole. Now it was a matter of dragging the horse clear any way they could. But that was dealt with expeditiously by a market carter who unhitched one of his hefty drays and began tying one end of a chain to its collar. Hervey told two of the labourers to tie the other end to the wheeler's collar, and in a minute more they were able to pull the dead weight to the middle of the street.

'I am a surgeon, sir; allow me to pass.'

Hervey retrieved his greatcoat and gladly stood to one side. In his service he had seen sights still shocking to recall, but there was a particular wretchedness in a man going peaceably about his work in the streets of London and having his brains beaten out.

Fairbrother had been speaking to a foreman meanwhile. 'Five dead. And two that don't look as though they'll see morning again.'

Hervey grimaced, and looked about. 'We must get the wounded away. Where's the foreman?'

'Here, sir,' answered a man with bow legs and few teeth.

'Go and have these cabs and carriages take your men to hospital. To St George's, isn't it?'

'St George's can't take these many, sir, cos she's being builded again. Guy's is best anyway: they knows 'ow to look after falls – all them steeplejacks they see.'

Guy's hospital was a deal closer than was Brussels after Waterloo (whither they had taken the wounded), but it would be a haul nevertheless. Hervey nodded resolutely. 'Well, there's nothing for it but to get them to Guy's. The dead as well. Go to it!'

He took a lighted cheroot from his friend. The officer's art lay in determining what must be done, and the NCO's in executing it.

Hervey could only trust that a foreman of building labourers would possess sufficient of the latter's.

'Perhaps I should engage them instead?' said Fairbrother.

But there was no need. Between the beneficence of the private owners and the rough, authoritative manner of the foreman, there were at once four chaises at his disposal – and to some cheering from the other labourers, who perceived that the 'quality' were not passing on the other side of the street.

'There is nothing I can do for him, I'm afraid,' pronounced the surgeon at last, rising from beside the prostrate driver and rubbing reddening snow between his hands. 'Have a tarpaulin cover him,' he said, nodding to one of the labourers.

Hervey asked him what was the procedure now that the injured had been attended to. Was he at liberty to go about his business, or must he find a magistrate to make a deposition? 'I confess I am strange to this. There's not a watchman to be seen.'

The surgeon assured him that he need not detain himself: there would be an inquest in the usual way, but the coroner would not require him. 'Though he would wish to commend your address in trying to save the man's life,' he added, pulling on his gloves. 'We must pray that Mr Peel's men, if they are come to our streets, will have seen service.'

Hervey nodded; the compliment to the uniform was well made. 'I bid you good-day, then, sir.'

He made to leave, looking for Fairbrother and seeing him in amiable conversation with a knot of labourers, and was taken once more by how easy his friend was with such men – as he was with men of rank. When first they had met, at the Cape, he had seemed possessed of a resentful disposition, as well as of indolence. He, Hervey, had been inclined to attribute this to mixed blood, for no matter how fine was that of Fairbrother's father – by Fairbrother's own account a kind and worthy man – that of his mother had been confected in the unknown regions, before her people were abducted (and Jamaica, from all he had heard, was an easy-going sort of place too). But, strangely, once his friend became animated by some undertaking, there was no end to his capability. Indeed he could not own that he had ever served with a more capable soldier, whether officer, NCO or private man. And Fairbrother's learning the product, he claimed, of ample hours on half pay – was so prodigious as to make his company ever a revelation. In fact he now counted that company the equal of all. He had never formed so close an understanding with any in the Sixth (even as a cornet the care had been for the day-to-day of campaigning; there had been so little opportunity for true intimacy), and after Henrietta's death he had positively sought to distance himself from any sensibility requiring intimacy, except with the opposite sex, in whose company alone he had seemed able, or willing, to let slip the mask of command. He had looked forward greatly to their serving together once more (Fairbrother had readily consented to leave the comfort of his summer hearth to accompany him to England and thence east), and he had even entertained hopes of his coming with him to the Sixth as, perhaps, a gentleman volunteer. But how could he possibly induce him to go to Gibraltar and play the part of sentry, for that was what the garrison there amounted to, no matter with what consequence Lord Hill might try to endow it?

He hailed his friend, bid the labourers and other bystanders thanks, and then the two of them struck out together across Waterloo Place for the United Service, collars turned up, peaks pulled down, leaning resolutely into the snowy billow.

'The ways deep, the weather sharp, the days short,' said Fairbrother, his voice muffled but just audible.

'The sun farthest off,' agreed Hervey. 'What will you, then?'

'O for a beaker full of the warm south!'

'Gibraltar?'
'Too distant. I'll settle for burgundy.'
'Burgundy?'
'At your club!'

III

PISTOLS AT DUSK

Later

The coffee room – as the United Service called its dining room (for a reason Hervey was never quite able to explain) – had been unexpectedly full by the time they returned, and so with little prospect of a timeous meal they decided to seek one elsewhere. 'I know a good chop house,' declared Hervey confidently as they stepped once more into Pall Mall, only hoping he could find it again.

In the short space of their time indoors, it had all but stopped snowing, and so the two friends struck out briskly for the Strand, heads high, though soon they were having to sidestep the street vendors at the bottom of the Haymarket, resisting the temptation of hot potatoes and spiced gingerbread (and even coffee, now that the tax on beans was next to nothing), then beyond the assorted stalls and barrows, striding out again across the white piazza before the old King's Mews, newly cleared of its eyesore huddle of shanties (and with so fine a view of St Martin's church in consequence that they stopped to remark on it), and then beyond into the Strand itself, strangely silent without horseshoes ringing on the metalled road. Finally they turned up the alleyway of Bull Inn Court, and right into the cul de sac of Maiden-lane, and to number thirty-eight. Hervey was gratified that his memory and instincts had not failed him, for the work of the demolition men was changing the face of these parts by the day.

But 'chop house' hardly served: the sign read *Rule's. Porter, pies and oysters.*

'And deuced fine they are too. Shall we go in?' he asked, giving up trying to see through the frosted windows.

It was middling full, but they found a table near a stove in a window booth which let in the light and kept out the draught, which Fairbrother was glad of, for he confessed that the cold had begun to chill his blood. And he owned to being fair famished. Hervey, also feeling the cold, had regained his appetite too, dulled before by his disappointing news. They ordered whitebait at once and asked for time to examine the rest of the bill.

It was Fairbrother who at length broke silence. 'I do believe I could eat a whole steak and oyster pudding,' he said, having scoured the list, which was long by the standards of the United Service.

Hervey nodded, but as yet was unsure of his choice. 'I recollect that I had some fine mutton here once . . . But I shall join you in a pudding, and if it is insufficient then we may order another. And burgundy.'

Fairbrother smiled contentedly. The waiter took away their order.

The burgundy came in no time at all, and the friends had drunk half of it in even less. With both constitution and judgement restored by the time the whitebait was brought (in prodigious quantity), Hervey was expansive once again. 'You know,' he said, with a shake of the head and a satisfied sigh, 'I doubt I could live anywhere truly content without the prospect of a whitebait dinner periodically. It is Old England.'

'Indeed?'

'Indeed. Did you know the cabinet has a whitebait dinner each year before parliament's prorogued?'

'I did not,' replied Fairbrother, making an even larger pile of the fish than did his friend.

'Yes, at Greenwich. They sail down there and eat whitebait at the Old George. At least I *think* it's the Old George. We should do so ourselves.'

'Admirable custom. Capital idea.' Fairbrother had already taken up knife and fork.

'I doubt there's whitebait in Gibraltar,' said Hervey, frowning.

'We could enquire.'

Hervey nodded. 'I suppose we could,' he replied, not very enthusiastically.

The whitebait was consumed hungrily and in silence except for appreciative asides.

And then the burgundy was replenished, a sturdy steak and oyster pudding was laid before them, and a dish of Savoy cabbage, and Fairbrother could at last begin the serious business of interrogation.

'Where do you suppose one might buy a pistol like that cabman's? I'm resolved never to go on campaign again without a capped weapon.'

Hervey smiled knowingly. He owed his life to the percussion cap – at Waterloo, possibly the only capped carbine in the field that day. Yet the Board of Ordnance saw no reason, still, to put it into the hands of the rank and file. 'Flayflints,' he said, with a sardonic smile at his pun – and to Fairbrother's mystification. 'There's a gun-smith's in Leicester Street, the other side of Covent Garden – Forsyth's. We might visit there later. Did the cabman say who was the maker?'

Fairbrother inclined his head. 'In truth I found him difficult to comprehend, for he said several times that it was *dirigé*, but I could not understand *dirigé* by whom. It is French, we may suppose?'

'It's possible. Forsyth's will know.'

Fairbrother helped himself to more burgundy, and became contemplative. 'But let us suppose we return from this war twixt Turk and Russian sound in wind and limb; what then? Shall you put on a red coat, for it seems clear to me that a blue one will scarcely be worthwhile if all you shall have to command is a hundred dragoons?'

The matter was unconvivial, but Hervey welcomed the opportunity to rehearse aloud the arguments he would otherwise have to make to himself. 'I confess it is a bitter blow. And if the die is cast, then so be it, but I have a mind that there's much water yet to flow under this particular bridge. Lord George Irvine may yet make his weight felt. I shall go to see him as soon as may be.' The colonel of a regiment, although no longer the proprietor he once was, carried nevertheless a deal of influence, with the King especially; and Lieutenant-General Irvine, a Waterloo man and now entrusted with command in Ireland, was not an officer whose opinion could be set aside lightly.

'But if all else fails and your regiment is indeed reduced, what then? You surely wouldn't wish to preside over a squadron?'

'I would not wish it, no, but I might bear it,' answered Hervey cautiously.

'But what would it profit you, in both satisfaction and advancement? I'll wager it would profit you nothing in either.'

Hervey took a deep breath. 'There would always be some satisfaction in the proximity of men with whom I'd served long years.'

Fairbrother nodded, almost spilling his wine. 'That, I grant you, but you wouldn't wish their captain to be forever looking over his shoulder? And might not you and they tire of the proximity, confined to Hounslow, even with an occasional calling to clear the streets of "tumultuous assembly"?'

'I think, were that to threaten, I should seek a temporary assignment elsewhere – as this mission to the Russians.'

Fairbrother nodded again. 'That might serve. What, though, would it do for your prospects?'

Hervey thought especially carefully before answering. There was nothing base in the desire for promotion; it was woven, so to speak, into the fibre of every officer's coat – or ought to be. 'Sir George Don would be, no doubt, an agreeable commander at Gibraltar – as Lord Hill said – but he is a man of fortifications and suchlike. He spent the whole of the war on Jersey. I am not a man of fortifications. What do you suppose I should do to distinguish myself there? In which case, what would be the difference if I were to stay at Hounslow?'

'That, I grant you.'

'And besides, would I persuade you to serve at Gibraltar?'

Fairbrother smiled. 'Its climate, I fancy, might suit me better than here; I should not wish to grow pale!'

Hervey scowled. 'But does the thought engage you sufficiently? You agreed to come with me to the Levant, and then to stay awhile at Hounslow.'

Fairbrother's brow furrowed; he was much bemused. 'Hervey, I am excessively diverted by the notion that I should have any determination in the matter. But are you quite sure? I would not wish you to calculate for any preference on my part.'

Hervey did his best to make light of it (how he envied his friend's easy way with matters): 'I should value your . . . company . . . advice . . . and so on.'

Fairbrother reached for the burgundy again. 'And what of the distaff side? Would Gibraltar be agreeable?'

Hervey checked the movement of any muscle that might convey an unhappy inability to speak for his wife. 'I very much hope so.'

Kat had once followed him to Lisbon; his own wife might

41

reasonably be expected to travel the few miles further. It did not occur to him that his friend's answer might be consequent on it.

'In principle I have no objection to service – however unofficial – in Gibraltar, nor in proximity to men in red,' his friend replied, smiling wryly. 'Indeed, I have no principled objection to anything after service with the Royal Africans!'

Hervey reflected the smile. 'Quite. Just imagine had Lord Hill appointed *me* to a penal battalion!' He took another good measure of burgundy, and signalled a change of course. 'This pudding is uncommonly good, is it not?'

Fairbrother understood at once. He invariably did. He did not always heed the signal, but he recognized it, and on this occasion he was happy to oblige. 'What did you make of Youell?'

And Hervey smiled the more for his friend's understanding.

They left the warm upholstered comfort of Rule's just after four o'clock, and set a hopeful, if indirect, course for the gunsmiths. It was darkling, but the streets were well lit, the gaslight made brighter by the snow, and the builders were still at work in Covent Garden, where the plan of the new market was now manifest – a great classical temple on a scale Hervey had seen only in Paris.

Fairbrother remarked again on the ubiquity of London masons.

'The King is a great builder, I believe,' said Hervey, slowing to admire the work on a section of Corinthian pillar about to be hoist. 'Or so he was when regent.'

'*Urbem lateritiam invenit, marmoream reliquit,*'* declaimed Fairbrother magisterially, if a shade slurred.

Hervey looked at him with an approving smile. 'My old cornet-friend Laming was fond of quoting Suetonius – and any number of

---

* 'He found a city of bricks and left a city of marble.' Said of Augustus Caesar and Rome.

others whose words seemed apt to our predicament. You would have liked him – a very excellent fellow. But then so are you; Gibraltar would be the duller place without you – brick instead of marble!'

His friend merely inclined his head.

'I lay emphasis on the conditional, mind. I might add that so would Hounslow be – the duller place, that is.'

Indeed he was certain of it. He did not doubt there were agreeable officers in Gibraltar, and he supposed there would be too at Hounslow – though he fancied that no officer of spirit would stay in a depot squadron, which is what it would amount to if the regiment were placed *en cadre*. But with Fairbrother he knew he might speak his mind, and in turn receive unvarnished opinion. He had never felt the want of that resource before, but he had lately, at the Cape, felt its beneficial qualities keenly, and he did not wish to be done with it now.

'I am greatly flattered.'

But Hervey intended no flattery, only the truth. 'Fairbrother, let me speak plainly. I should esteem it the greatest good fortune if you accompanied me either to Hounslow or to Gibraltar – or, frankly, to anywhere else His Majesty is pleased to post me.'

Fairbrother, for once inclined to cast off insouciance, clapped a hand on his friend's shoulder. But there was increase in his sportive humour nevertheless. 'Might we *conditionally* visit the Fifty-third's tailor then, and lay a swatch of red cloth across your breast?'

Hervey was inclined to enter the spirit of archness. '*Scarlet* cloth.'

Fairbrother smiled, conceding the point. 'Ah, yes – scarlet. It seemed to me in the Royal Africans that the distinction lay solely in the fastness of the dye. A private man's red coat was a pale affair after a good soaking, whereas an officer's scarlet remained true – an allegory, as it were, of devotion to duty.'

'The burgundy makes you excessively poetic. I have no intention of visiting the Fifty-third's tailor. A red coat's a red coat, and I fancy I can imagine what a button with "fifty-three" on it looks like – as opposed to one with "fifty-two", or whatever it might otherwise be.'

The calls of the flower sellers – which with little other than greenery to sell were more importunate than those of the costers – were now intruding on their conversation, so that both men had to raise their voices to continue. 'Even so, what a world apart are those two buttons. Would not the Fifty-second tempt you dearly?'

The Fifty-second – the 'Oxfordshire Light Infantry' – had been with Moore and the Light Brigade at Shorncliffe, and then Corunna; they were (they considered themselves, at least) an elite. Hervey was certainly tempted to agree with his friend – if only for the purpose of silencing him on the subject of red coats. 'The Fifty-second would tempt anyone.'

A flower seller, pretty, Italian-looking, in a cloak with the hood thrown back, stepped in front of Fairbrother, bringing both men to a halt. 'Buy these snowdrops from a poor, frozen flower girl, captain,' she said, in a curious mixture of the accent of the streets and somewhere more distant. 'It's bitter cold, captain, and I needs buy a hot supper.'

Fairbrother reached instinctively inside his coat for his pocket-book, before realizing that coin was more appropriate.

Hervey wondered why the girl had made his friend the object of her entreaty and not him. Was it the affinity of a similar complexion (for he observed that hers was not much lighter than Fairbrother's), or did his friend possess a more generous countenance? More susceptible, even?

'How much?' asked Fairbrother, purse in hand.

'Sixpence, if you please, captain.'

'*Sixpence?*' said Hervey, astonished.

The girl turned to her questioner. 'Why, sir, they're picked this morning and brought a good long way,' she replied disarmingly.

'Here's a shilling,' said Fairbrother, taking no notice. 'Two bunches, if you please. That will buy a hot supper will it not?'

'It will, captain. God bless you.' She handed him the snowdrops with a smile that might have been genuine.

He took them and then gave a bunch back to her. 'Put these in a window to brighten it.'

'Oh, thank you sir,' she thrilled. 'And a very good evening to you.'

Fairbrother raised his cap as she stood aside to let them pass.

Hervey said nothing until he was sure they were out of earshot. 'I will say that I have been similarly done to in the past, but never more charmingly. I dare say we'll be lucky to make it from the market without having to give a shilling to every girl. She'll be telling them all this very moment.'

'Oh, I'd reckon not,' replied Fairbrother, in a knowing sort of way. 'She'll wish to sell us a bunch tomorrow if we're passing. Why tell others and spoil her trade?'

'Upon my word, you are reading London keenly!'

'Not London, not especially. I observe it as universal nature.'

'Well, she was bold and it was nicely done by both sides.'

'None but the *fair* deserve the bold!'

'That is very droll. The cold evidently neither dulls your brain nor cools your heart. I am all envy. Or is it the burgundy again?'

Fairbrother smiled. 'You make matters easy for me. Recall the rhyme? – "Drinking is the soldier's pleasure/ Rich the treasure/ Sweet the pleasure/ Sweet is pleasure after pain."'

Hervey nodded. 'I allow that you are in excellent form. London agrees with you.'

'Oh, indeed,' his friend assured him, as if the contrary notion were impossible. 'My heart swelled as soon as we landed and began posting for here. Did not you see?'

Hervey had not seen. He had been far too preoccupied with his own thoughts. It was not London that swelled his heart, but what bounties London could bestow – at least, what the Horse Guards could bestow. For the rest . . . too much was changed for him to throw himself into the arms of the city as readily as Fairbrother seemed able.

And not a minute later they were reminded of the welcome those arms could take.

'Would yer like a nice time, dearies?' came the familiar invitation from beneath a gaslight as they turned into (of all places) Bow Street.

Hervey glanced across the road at the two swaddled doxies, and felt emboldened to sport. 'Oh, girls, desist; I am a married man!'

But they were not to be played with by a couple of tipsy officers. 'Begging yer pardon, I'm sure, but we're only after yer money!'

In Leicester Street, which they found quicker than Hervey thought they might, the cold air sobering them, Forsyth's was barred and bolted, though otherwise the shop was open for business. As they were let in, Hervey expressed himself surprised by the precaution. The presiding gunsmith, a corn-fed man with beady eyes, was in no doubt of the necessity, however: 'Popery, sir! This popish Act of Parliament. Gordon, sir; riots!'

Hervey was a deal taken aback. 'The Gordon riots are fifty years gone!'

'Ay, sir; but memories are long of these things!'

Fairbrother was surveying the shop's formidable contents, faintly bemused. 'Might you not put your trade to use rather than barricade the premises?'

The man looked offended. 'That, I believe – the public order – is *your* business, gentlemen. I should not wish the occasion to fire on staunch Protestants, however misguided!'

Hervey judged it better to withdraw. The sooner the Police bill was enacted, the better (although it was undeniably to the interests of the regiment that it was not). 'Speaking of guns, we saw today a coachman with a very handy capped pistol. He said of it, we believe, that it was *dirigé*. I am not acquainted with the term; are you?'

The gunsmith thought a while, then shook his head, until suddenly the furrows in his brow disappeared. 'The cabman did not say, perhaps, that the pistol was made by *Deringer*?'

Hervey looked at Fairbrother, who shrugged his shoulders as if to say that he might have.

'Deringer of Philadelphia, in the United States of America, sir. He has of late made an art of travelling pistols, but they have not so far been imported in any quantity. We have a pair of capped pistols by Hetherington of Nottingham, sir – a very capable maker.'

'Might we see them?'

The gunsmith pulled open a drawer beneath the counter and took out a polished case. Inside were two cap-lock pistols, the walnut fittings finely worked. 'Handsome weapons, think you not, gentlemen?'

'"Handsome is as handsome does",' said Hervey, taking one from the case and handing it to Fairbrother.

'Quite so, sir. They are most do-able pistols, Birmingham-proofed, forty-bore.'

Hervey weighed the other pistol in his hand. It was about eight inches from butt to muzzle, shorter than the barrel itself of the regulation flintlock – handy enough, but still not as compact as the coachman's. Yet 40-bore was certainly right for his purposes: the ball would weigh about half an ounce, which would do the business at close range. He cocked the hammer – it was a simple replacement of the frizzen, the pistol a converted flintlock – checked there was no cap fitted, brought it up to the aim and pulled the trigger.

'It would serve, certainly, though the trigger guard is close for a glove, and there's no safety lock.'

'They are *travelling* pistols, sir.'

Hervey nodded. He could not expect them to be as robustly made as those for campaign service – and yet if the pistol were to be carried on the person rather than in the saddle holster, and loaded, he did not relish the idea of the hammer's free movement. 'I fancy it would not be beyond your workshop to fit one?'

'By no means, sir.'

Hervey looked at Fairbrother. 'What say you?'

'I think the pistol will serve, but I too should want a safety lock.'

Hervey nodded again, this time decisively. 'Very well, we shall take them – with a safety lock that may be worked with the thumb. I ought, I suppose, to enquire the price?'

The man thought for a moment. 'Eight guineas, sir, to include the modification. A further fifteen shillings for horn and bullet former – and, perhaps, two dozen bullets and caps?'

Hervey glanced at Fairbrother, who nodded. 'That will be in order. A week, then, shall we say? And if you have hearing of a Deringer weapon, perhaps you will alert me?'

It was full dark when they left, and the glass had dropped five degrees – so marked that they pulled up their collars as high as in the morning, and hastened step to that of the Fifty-second. All earlier thoughts of the theatre were banished in the contemplation of a good fire at the United Service, and an easy supper. In any case, Hervey had work to be about – letters to write, campaigns to plan; and Fairbrother, though thinking how agreeable might be the company of the flower girl who had so charmingly importuned them in Covent Garden, said he was more than content to return instead to a decanter of port and the latest *Edinburgh Review*.

Quickened further by the gradient of the Haymarket, they overtook all before them. Two recruiting serjeants saluted from the steps of a public house below the Theatre Royal as they forged past, prompting Hervey to say then what he had been keeping for the United Service – that his thoughts had returned to 'family', though not to Hertfordshire, nor even Wiltshire.

Barely opening his mouth, so bitter now was the cold, he announced plainly: 'Tomorrow we go to Hounslow.'

IV

THE DIVIDEND OF PEACE

Next morning

Hervey slept little, and even then without rest. As soon as he nodded, unwelcome dreams began shivering him. Each time he woke (and he was scarcely conscious of sleeping at all) his mind was full of the images of estrangement. What had possessed him to visit Holland Park, slipping from the United Service after supper without telling his friend, only to find it barred and shuttered? The cabman, mute until he had seen that there was no one at home to admit him, told him that Kat was well – it was the common knowledge of his trade – that she and the household had gone to Ireland a month and more ago, and that it was only that he supposed his fare to have intelligence of her return that he had carried him to Holland Park in the first place. And so Hervey had returned to his silent club and restless bed, and there, half-sleeping, half-waking, had counted the hours to reveille; and the barring and shuttering which, he knew full well, was only what any prudent household would do on exchanging town for country, became a sort of dreamy symbol of what there had once been but which was now gone and could never be again.

Nearing four o'clock, he rose and put on his dressing gown, and over it his greatcoat (the fire was long out), lit the lamp on the writing table and took up a pen. Yesterday, before going to the Horse Guards, he had written to Wiltshire, expressing some hope that he would be able to return for Georgiana's birthday, but that it would be consequent on his marching orders (had it ever been otherwise?). He had written to Hertfordshire too. Now he must write to Kat, if only to tell her that he had been to Holland Park.

Some force stayed his hand, however. He found it impossible to write even the salutation. Each time he dipped the pen in the inkwell, carefully draining off the excess on the rim of the glass bowl, he found that no words formed in his mind. Or rather, that several words formed themselves, but none of them he judged apt. He could not begin 'My dear Kat', and certainly not 'My dearest Kat' (as once he would), nor simply 'Dear Kat'; and most assuredly not 'Dear Lady Katherine'. But without a beginning, how could anything follow? The salutation was indeed the encapsulation of his predicament: what now was his connection with Kat? It was not even that of last summer, when she had told him she was with his child. There had been an interval of full six months; feelings might intensify or abate in that time, but they did not remain as they had been. What indeed *were* his feelings? What were the proprieties to observe in his peculiar circumstances – a new-married officer and the wife of a general who secretly carried his child? He put down the pen, sick to the pit of his stomach.

There was, he knew from long years (the debilitating contemplation of Henrietta), one antidote to this condition – activity, *any* activity. It did not cure, but it did relieve. And sometimes the relief continued long after the activity ceased, by placing the demon-cause out of mind's reach. He dressed quickly, slipped silently from his room, descended the stairs of the sleeping club, and stepped out into an empty Pall Mall. A horse, a gallop, would have been his natural support, but in its absence the most vigorous walking – marching – would suffice. He would imagine himself a cornet in Spain again, dismounted, forging through snow which the infantry had not yet trod. And beneath his frosty breath he would keep repeating the line of scripture: *For I also am a man set under authority, having under me soldiers*. It would call him to duty. It never failed.

He set off towards St James's Palace, hastening past the watchmen's braziers and the guards, through Milkmaid's Passage and into the darkness of the Green Park. Here, shortening step, he broke into a double, clenching his gloved hands to his chest and matching his breathing to the four-pace rhythm. With the snow underfoot, the moon was bright enough to light his way once his eyes had disaccustomed themselves to the gas lamps of St James's, and he doubled confidently to the wall which enclosed the gardens of the King's new palace at the other side of the park, except for running into a goose-girl whose terrier then snapped at his heels for twenty yards, the geese honking noisily as if in encouragement. At the wall he turned right and lengthened the step to challenge himself the more on the grade to the Piccadilly-bar, where gaslight once more lit the scene – a few empty cabs plodding east, and night-soil carts passing both ways. He doubled on the spot for a while, taking in the torch-lit façade of Apsley House, where first he had met Kat. It had then been the residence of the commander-in-chief, and now it was that of the prime minister. He would not see its inside again; what there had once been was now gone, and would never be again . . .

He doubled across the road at a cinder crossing, giving the lonely sweeper a penny without stopping, and on into Hyde Park, wary now of footpads, then along the New Road, where poor Strickland had met his end when his chariot ran into the Oxford Mail, then turning off south down an interminable rutted path to the Royal

Military Asylum, and thence along King's Road, catching the
toll-booth napping, and back round the south side of Buckingham
House into the Mall as far as the Duke of York's Steps, which he
took two at a time into Waterloo Place, where he finally ceased
doubling and for the last fifty yards walked on a long rein to get his
breath back.

At a quarter before seven o'clock he reached the doors of the
United Service, his face glowing, the blood coursing through his
veins, feeling as if he were being scrubbed by a *tellak* in a Mogul
steam bath. The invigoration was complete, the demon gone. In its
place there was resolution, clear-sightedness, energy. He took the
stairs at a bound, flung open the door of his room, threw off his
clothes, put on his robe, gathered up his razor, brush and soap bowl,
and took possession of one of the bathrooms, to emerge in half an
hour clean-shaved and cleansed. He put on the frogged coat he had
not worn in months and then assailed the room in which his good
friend was still sleeping.

'In God's name!' protested Fairbrother at the intrusion of daylight as the curtains were pulled roughly back.

'"Sick Call" at Hounslow was half an hour ago,' said Hervey
breezily.

'I told you last night I would sleep long and then see a barber.'

'I don't recollect,' replied Hervey, picking up his friend's coat
from the floor.

'That's because you were paying no heed. It was like supping with
a waxwork.'

'I am sorry for it, but I am all attention now. Let me draw your
bath while you shave. Then we shall eat a hearty breakfast and go
to Hounslow.'

They took a hackney, although the cabman drove a hard price;
Hounslow was a deal further than he ranged as a rule, and Hervey

could only persuade him by agreeing the fare back, even if in the end they might not take it – for the cabman must return by dusk, he insisted, or else he would not get home to Southwark before his licence required. Nor did he prove inclined to go at more than a half-hearted trot: the ways, though not exactly deep, were, to his mind, treacherous, and 'I've me hosses' wind to consider', so that it was late morning by the time they arrived at the barrack gates.

The picket turned out even before Hervey had paid the fare and agreed what hour they should journey back. His heart warmed at the sight of his own uniform again. His troop at the Cape were as 'regimental' (as the sweats called it) as any – for first Armstrong and then Collins had made sure of it – but there was something about detached duty which was never quite . . . entire: it was the absence of the regiment's god-head, the commanding officer, its high-priest, the adjutant – and, not least of the trinity, the serjeant-major, the apotheosis of the rank and file. It was they who set the tone, regulated the routine, and chose the NCOs, the apostles of the regiment's creed. A detached troop was a fine command, but not sufficient unto itself. And, in truth, he could not see how a regiment *en cadre* could be so either.

'Guard, pres-e-e-ent arms!'

It was sharply done: seven dragoons and the picket commander fallen-in at 'Attention', carbines at the 'Shoulder', a drill which, uniquely, the Sixth had adopted in the Peninsula so that in one movement they could pay compliments to either field or regimental rank – 'present' for the former, butt-salute for the latter. Hervey touched the peak of his forage cap in return as he and Fairbrother came through the gates.

And unlike in many another, in the Sixth the picket commander did not wait to be spoken to. 'Good morning, Colonel Hervey, sir!'

Hervey recognized the man as one of the dwindling number of dragoons who wore the Waterloo medal, an NCO who knew the regimental form as well as any. He wondered if he would ever hear, simply, 'Good morning, Colonel' – the acknowledgement of the all-important detail, that he *commanded* the Sixth rather than merely possessed the same rank as the commanding officer. 'Good morning, Corporal Adcock. There's a good fire in the guard-house, I trust?'

'There is, sir!'

'Is the colonel at orderly room?'

'No, sir.'

'The adjutant?'

'He is, sir.'

It was one of the proprieties, unwritten, learned only in the school of regimental soldiering, that the picket answered to none but the commanding officer – and in his place the adjutant and, in silent hours, the picket officer; and so although a sentry paid compliments, and the whole picket turned out for a visitor of rank, it was never inspected, reproved, commended, assigned or dismissed by any other but the commanding officer or his deputy. It was therefore with neither arrogance nor negligence that Hervey walked on without ado, leaving Adcock to fall-out the attendant dragoons by his own authority.

'Quite a show,' said Fairbrother good-humouredly. 'Had they word of our coming, do you suppose?'

Hervey was undeniably pleased by the 'show'; it spoke of good order and military discipline, as well as of his recognition (he had, after all, been on detached duty for eighteen months, even if during that time he had been home on marriage leave). 'I fancy it was part chance. I rather suspect that Adcock's expecting Lord Hol'ness at any minute.'

He looked across the square to the flagpole, but the pennant was not fixed for hoisting: the commanding officer was 'not at orderly room', as the saying went, nor his arrival imminent, it would seem. 'There again, Adcock's a seasoned NCO. And the sar'nt-major's wrath's not worth risking. I should beg his pardon for doubting his address. Come, let's see how things are within.'

Fairbrother was not strange to Hounslow. He had dined triumphantly with the officers six months before. He had admired the barracks' generous proportions and the solidity of its buildings, and the more so on closer inspection, for the brickwork and all the furniture was of quality. He recalled, too, that the slate roofs were good and solid (though this morning they were white-clad), and the workmanship inside and out very neat – all bespeaking a high regard for the common soldier. Or so it might seem, but in truth the date '1793' above the gate arch told the fuller story, as it did on many of the barracks about the capital. On the first day of February that year, Britain had declared war on France: the soldier could no longer be despised and billeted on reluctant innkeepers if he were to be the safeguard of the nation when the French came (or else be a bulwark against Jacobin ambitions within); he needed the constant drill and regulation of men in barracks. And so Mr Pitt would beggar the Treasury and build them their martial homes (and make an income tax to continue his war).

But this morning the barracks were not the bustle as before. There were no signs of actual dilapidation, yet the absence of dragoons was all too plain – no band, no foot drill, no skill-at-arms, no sound of the blacksmith's forge. And Hervey could not but admit to himself that this was how it would be every day with the regiment *en cadre*. The adjutant was at orderly room, however (and had been for many hours), for the work of the lieutenant-colonel's executive officer was scarcely diminished when the squadrons were out of barracks; here, at least, they would find, so to speak, the regular pulse of the 6th Light Dragoons.

For some years the Sixth had employed 'regimental' officers as adjutant rather than those commissioned from the ranks, the more usual practice, and in Lieutenant Thomas Malet, though he had but a fraction of the service normally accrued by a former serjeant-major, they considered themselves possessed of a most diligent executive.

'Good morning, Colonel Hervey. I knew you would be come, though I only lately saw your name gazetted,' he said, rising, and smiling with evident pleasure at seeing the man soon to take the place of Lord Holderness. 'And you, Captain Fairbrother: it is good to see you again.' He called one of the orderlies to bring coffee. 'Or Madeira, perhaps?'

'Coffee,' replied Hervey.

'Captain Fairbrother?'

'Coffee, thank you. Or should I withdraw?' Hervey had said neither one thing nor the other, but Fairbrother had no wish to intrude on regimental business.

Malet looked at Hervey, who shook his head, and the three of them sat down.

'Your groom is safely arrived, by the way, sir. He is making himself useful to the sar'nt-major, it seems.'

'I am glad to hear it,' said Hervey, returning the now distinctly ironic smile. 'But I shall reclaim him presently, the sar'nt-major will be pleased to learn.'

The orderly returned with a silver tray and the regimental Spode.

Once he had dismissed, Malet turned to the serious business of the orderly room. 'Let me own at once that I fear you will find things rather ... straitened. Every troop but Vanneck's is called away. First has gone to Bristol, no less.'

'The price of light cavalry,' replied Hervey, with a gesture of resignation. Dispersal in penny-packets, the commanding officer left with no more to command than clerks and bottle-washers – such was the cross to be borne. 'Where *is* the colonel?'

'York. A court martial.'

He raised an eyebrow. That, too, was the price of light cavalry –

the commanding officer at first call for the administration of military law, for others were thought more indispensible to their corps.

'A deuced tricky court martial, it would appear,' explained Malet. 'The adjutant-general particularly requested his lordship as a member.'

'Indeed?' Hervey took a sip of his coffee. 'What have you heard of the measure to place the regiment *en cadre*?'

Malet looked surprised. 'I had not imagined the news was abroad. Lord Hol'ness was told only when he called on the Horse Guards before proceeding north.'

'I was at the Horse Guards yesterday. I am glad the news is not yet abroad. It could do untold harm.'

Malet nodded. 'May I enquire what are your prospects, therefore, sir?'

'They are not yet clear,' replied Hervey, truthfully (he saw no occasion to add to the untold harm by saying that he had been offered the Fifty-third). 'I have first the commander-in-chief's assignment with the Russians. You knew of that?'

'I did.'

In any case, Hervey had other concerns before his own at this moment. 'How is Sar'nt-Major Armstrong?'

Fairbrother had wondered how long it would be before he enquired: Hervey had brooded on the matter during the passage home, but had said nothing since coming to London. He knew that Armstrong stood as strong in his friend's particular regard – affection, indeed – as any. And Malet's face, lifted by the mention of the name, was testimony too to the high opinion generally in which the sar'nt-major was held. Here, if he had ever needed it, was clinching evidence that the Sixth held themselves in peculiar mutual affinity. There were the rogues, the villains, the 'bad hats', to be sure, but he had never had the sense that officers and men stood in constitutional antipathy to one another, as sometimes they did else-where. In his own former corps, the Royal Africans, the officers had had a sense of ownership – though with little enough *pride* of ownership – the other ranks merely serving out some wretched indenture. Yes, a good many of those were 'options men' – prison or the King's shilling (and often enough without even the option) – with little good character to which a decent officer might appeal, but, even so, the discipline of the Royal Africans and that of the Sixth were as the proverbial chalk to cheese. Would it be so with the Fifty-third? From what he had seen and heard of Lord Hill, their colonel, he could not suppose that it would be exactly so, but he perfectly understood his friend's desire to command these dragoons. The only question was at what point the Sixth ceased to be the regiment of his understanding.

But meanwhile there was good news of Armstrong to buoy the spirits. When last Hervey and Malet had spoken of him it was in connection with Caithlin's funeral. Hervey had himself made the arrangements, for Mrs Armstrong was a Catholic, and there was no one else to deal with the unfamiliar obsequies; and then, on return to the Cape, he had broken the news to his old NCO-friend, seeing him afterwards, brave but bowed, onto a steam packet home. 'He is married and very well.'

Hervey was all astonishment. 'Married? To whom?'

'Serjeant Ellis's widow.'

'I didn't know Ellis was dead.'

'An aneurysm, while on revenue duty.'

Hervey did not know Ellis well, and his wife even less. But if Armstrong had found a mother for his children then he exulted for him. 'Where is he – Armstrong, I mean?'

'With Worsley's troop in Bristol, doing duty for Cox who's gone to St John's Wood for three months.'

Hervey looked quizzical.

'I have a mind to put Cox in charge of rough-riders. If, that is, the regiment has an RM when it's reduced.'

Fairbrother was as silently thankful for Armstrong's good fortune as any man might be who knew him only very partially but with infinite admiration. He wished he could intrude on this easy regimental conference, but was wary of breaking the spell. What was St John's Wood?

By some intuition, his friend turned to him. 'St John's Wood is the new Riding Establishment. I say "new", but it was first at Pimlico. They've built a fine school there, roofed-over for winter.'

Fairbrother nodded appreciatively; he had no idea where was St John's Wood, but that could wait.

'Well, I am excessively glad that Armstrong is back at muster,' declared Hervey, warming once more to the news.

'So are we all,' said Malet, but with a note of caution in his voice. 'Though he is not rightly himself, I fear.'

'It will take time,' said Hervey, sounding unsurprised. He had his own experience, after all.

'I hope profoundly that that is all it will take. He appeared to me to be quite worn out. I am no doctor, of course, and the surgeon made no remark on it, but I have read of these things.'

'I am no doctor either, Malet, but I should say that he was in the best of health when he went aboard his ship – for a man who had been eviscerated almost as cruelly as if by a Zulu spear. I think that time and regimental duty will work a cure. And Mrs Ellis, of course – Mrs Armstrong, I mean.'

Malet nodded, more dutifully and in hope than with conviction. 'Did you want him with you in the East?'

Hervey smiled. 'Any man would be a fool not to want Armstrong with him when there was the prospect of action. But I must concede there are prior calls on his service – and not least *Mrs* Armstrong. I shall need a coverman, though. Wainwright's not yet back to condition; he was cut up a good deal in that stand of Armstrong's against the Xhosa – else I should have brought him back with me. There are others who would serve, but the Cape troop's in need of its best NCOs, which is why I'm applying for a serjeant – or a corporal – from the home troops.'

Malet thought for a moment. 'I would ask the sar'nt-major were he here, but he's with the RM, in Yorkshire, buying remounts.'

Hervey hoped fervently that the regiment would have need of remounts, rather than the need to cast them, but more immediately he wondered if Mr Rennie, brought in last year, would know which NCO was the best sabre and possessed the best *coup d'oeil*. He would not venture his misgivings on that account, however; and the serjeant-major would anyway consult the troop serjeant-majors. He simply nodded.

'Do you recollect Acton, D Troop?' tried Malet. 'He was made corporal a year ago, won "Sabre and Carbine" and did sar'nt-major's orderly corporal for the annual inspection.'

Hervey did recollect: a fine-looking man who might pass for an officer of sorts in plain clothes. And if he had won 'Sabre and Carbine' – even in the absence of the competition of his own troop at the Cape – then he was a good prospect for coverman. 'Where are D?'

'Guildford. I can send for him today if you wish it.'

Although the adjutant had the authority to act on the commanding officer's behalf in all matters, Hervey would have preferred the courtesy of asking Lord Holderness. Time was pressing, however; a letter would have to suffice. 'If you would. Now, to return to the reduction in the regiment: is Lord Hol'ness intending to issue any orders?'

Malet shook his head. 'He scarce had time to tell me what the Horse Guards were thinking. He understood there would be nothing decided presently, and in any case he thought it rightly a business first for the colonel.'

'Indeed so. Has there been any communication with Lord George?'

'By the Horse Guards? I cannot say. Lord Hol'ness has not yet written – or rather, he gave me no letter before leaving. As I said, he was told somewhat irregularly, just before leaving for the north. You do know that Lord George is at this time in Canada?'

'I did not know. How so? For how long?'

'He's gone to inspect the defences at Fort York on behalf of the Ordnance. I can't say when he'll return, only that in September he's to hold a levee for the colonel-in-chief.'

Hervey groaned inwardly: the absences seemed to be conspiring against him. And he knew he had stretched Malet's loyalty as far as he ought: these were properly matters for the commanding officer, even if their consequences would – might – be his. 'Then I must write to Lord Hol'ness and trust that we shall be able to meet over the business before I embark for the East. Meanwhile, might we speak, you and I, about the sar'nt-major?'

Fairbrother rose. 'With your leave, gentlemen, I will take a turn around the barracks.'

Malet stood and made to open the door for him.

'No, permit me,' said Fairbrother, a shade abashed. 'I will look over the stables if that is in order.'

Malet bowed. 'By all means, Captain Fairbrother. And you are at liberty, of course, to take your ease in the officers' house.' He turned to Hervey: 'You will lunch here, sir?'

Hervey nodded.

Fairbrother had no special desire to look over the stables. He had seen the Sixth's troop horses in the summer and he did not suppose they were in any way changed in the six months since then – what few remained here (except that he had a passing interest in how the Sixth shaved their troopers). His reason for leaving the adjutant's

62

office was simply to spare both men the discomfort of speaking of a matter of regimental delicacy within his hearing. Besides, he knew exactly what was Hervey's opinion. Instead of the stables, therefore, he went at once to the officers' house.

It was empty, although it had the signs of occupancy. There was a good fire, and a copy of that day's *Times* on the writing table, in which he was happy to engross himself for an hour or so until his friend was satisfied with what arrangements he could make, or influence. He had no need of refreshment, so did not seek out the servants. He would read the news in every detail.

But almost as soon as he had taken up the paper he laid it down again. He was not given greatly to introspection – at least, not recently – but he began wondering about his welcome at Hounslow. He had been most civilly received at dinner, paid compliments by the commanding officer, no less, and every captain and subaltern had shaken his hand. And this morning, too, the adjutant had received him with the greatest courtesy. Was all this not, however, an exaggerated politeness, a way of asserting superiority through a sort of patrician graciousness? Had he truly been admitted an equal, would the greeting have been so courtly? At least at the Cape, where the late governor had repeatedly cut him, he could believe himself a man; whereas here he might be no more than an object of exotic interest, of amusement even, tolerated because he was the friend of another and rather senior officer, and because there was scarcely any ill consequence in it. He liked the Sixth – not least for what he had seen of their capability in the field – and he liked London and Hounslow and Horningsham and everything he saw (almost) of England. But what if Hervey were to take command, especially of a reduced Sixth; what then would be his welcome – a too-frequent visitor, a hanger-on, a resented confidant of the colonel? In embracing the offer, did he not merely succumb to the worst of his self-indulgent side (of which he was all too aware, whatever appearances suggested otherwise)? Wasn't it, albeit in a pretty minor way, a *folie de grandeur*? Ought he to have quit the sphere, even if temporarily, in which he had been raised and in which he had found a comfortable niche at the Cape – not truly in trade, connected just enough with the product of his father's plantation to give his enterprise respectability (he was concerned with selling, crucially, not buying)? *Mislike me not for my complexion, the shadow'd livery of the burnish'd sun* – ha! Here it seemed they all *liked* him for his complexion. But it could not last. And, indeed – should it ever come to this – what would some English Portia say to his advances? He had once been crushed (he knew he bore the marks still) by such a one in Spanish Town.

Sighing, he took up the *Times* again. His life had been that of the outsider, from the earliest days of his consciousness. Would it not be better that he sought a place where he did not mind that status, rather than here where he wished most fervently to be wholly a part of things?

V

THE VOLUNTEER

Later

Luncheon was a quiet affair; there were but nine at mess. Even Myles Vanneck, captain of the one troop still in barracks, was out, hunting stag at Windsor. To Hervey it was another foretaste of the hollow life of a depot troop, as the regiment *en cadre* would become and the more disagreeable for its being manifestly unwarranted. Why the Sixth? After the war with France it had made sense that so many of the regiments hurriedly raised to fight Bonaparte should be equally hurriedly disbanded, but then had followed corps which had served for sixty years and more – the 18th, 19th, 20th and 21st Light Dragoons, regiments not much younger than his own, but which by some quirk of seniority (itself a somewhat precarious attribution) found themselves laying up their guidons. And now even seniority appeared to be no guarantee of preservation.

But were there not grounds for hope? It was one thing to disband a regiment, as those had been, and another to reduce it in strength, with the implicit prospect of raising in strength at a later (he hoped not much later) date. Did he not dismay himself without cause therefore? He just wished he could be certain of it, for once a

65

regiment were reduced to a 'representative' troop, it would be easier to remove it subsequently from the Army List: it would raise no great tumult in parliament to dismiss, say, a hundred or so half-forgotten dragoons. Indeed it appeared to be a process not unlike the hunting of Vanneck's runnable stag – harboured, tufted, set at bay, despatched. It looked, at this moment, very much as if the Sixth were being harboured. If they were, could they outrun the tufters before fresh hounds were brought up? He began wondering if Bulgaria were not the very last place he should be; for with Lord George Irvine in Canada, and Lord Hol'ness in the north (and anyway soon to receive his promotion), who would see that the stag was allowed a free run?

In one respect, however, he was pleased to see that there was yet no sign of a falling off: the Sixth kept a good table – a righteous dish of mutton, a stew of green vegetables in a rich cream sauce, potatoes roast in the mutton fat, with a very passable claret, and then an orange dessert simply done with baked sugar, delicious. Fairbrother found himself answering to questions on the boiling of sugarcane, which he did with easy authority.

'May I ask,' tried one of the new cornets, 'what are the prospects for the plantations now that sugar is being extracted from beet?' The Royal Navy's late blockade of the Continent had meant that sugar-beet had supplanted cane in France and Prussia. 'I had occasion last year to visit a factory in Silesia which made syrup from it.'

'Thank you Mr Townshend,' said Malet, with mock solemnity. 'Your people in Norfolk will no doubt soon be essaying the same with the turnip?'

There was good-natured laughter, and Fairbrother was content to let his earlier misgivings subside. 'My understanding is that it takes a very great deal of beet to make a very little sugar. Does not Adam Smith write that the real price of a thing is the toil and trouble of acquiring it? I suppose in the end it will therefore be but a simple matter of whether there is a greater return on a beet crop than another. And of that I confess I know nothing.'

Hervey too was content to enjoy the banter – and his friend's erudition – but at the suitable remove of contemplating the Romney portrait of 'Queen' Caroline, now restored to its rightful place in the dining room. It was perhaps one of his few Whiggish inclinations, and he always smiled at the thought of it. Although the regiment had not for a dozen years borne the honorific 'Princess Caroline's Own', he had never seen reason to put her portrait away privily. She had been dead these eight years, and if the King chose to dine with the regiment ever, then it was an easy enough affair to have the painting removed. And while the common view was that Caroline's appearance was not exactly . . . striking, it was by no means displeasing – certainly not in Romney's portrait of regal girlishness (he had more than a suspicion that Hayter's great conversation piece, of her trial before the House of Lords, which made her fat and coarse, was painted thus for a purpose). In the Romney, her eyes were agreeably large, though her mouth was, he had to concede, simply too small to tempt. Henrietta's mouth had been generous, while Kezia's was perhaps the most perfect, her lips slightly thinner than Kat's. An image of marble came to mind, for Kezia was the perfect subject for the sculptor's art . . .

'Colonel Hervey?'

He woke. 'I'm sorry . . . ?'

'We were speaking of Trimalchio,' said Malet. 'Mr Agar says the Sybil of whose acquaintance he boasted was of Cumae, and Mr Jenkinson disputes it.'

As the senior officer present, Hervey assumed his position of adjudicator. It had always been the way in the Sixth: one minute the conversation might be of the most advantageous degree of curve in a sabre, and the next upon some point of antiquity or philosophy –

or equally on the relative ratting prowess of officers' terriers. Conversation was never dull for long, and often as not ended in the wagers book. 'What brought the talk to Trimalchio? He was rather a low fellow, was he not?'

'Captain Fairbrother said that Trimalchio could not have served better mutton than he had just enjoyed.' Malet wore just the suspicion of a complicit smile; he knew the cornets well, and intended letting them have a little rein.

Hervey was tempted to be grave, but he too could not entirely keep a smile from his face. 'Why say you otherwise than Mr Agar, Mr Jenkinson?'

Cornet Jenkinson, new joined from Oxford in the year just gone, had the air of a questioning, even puzzled curate. 'I recall, sir, that Plato spoke of but one Sybil, and she at Delphi. And since the Delphian oracle was the best known to all, why should Trimalchio boast of another?'

Hervey inclined his head in a way that acknowledged the proposition. 'Mr Agar?'

Cornet Agar, new joined in the same month as Jenkinson, and also from Christ Church, had an altogether acuter air, though not lacking in warmth. He and Jenkinson had lived cordially on the same staircase for several terms despite the difference of their families' politics (the Jenkinsons were Tories of a most unbending sort – Lord Liverpool, the prime minister, had opposed Catholic relief to the last day of his administration; while Agar's family stood prominently among the Whigs). 'There is no doubt of it, sir. Petronius writes of the Sibyl of *Cumae*, who because of her great age was suspended in a pot – *ampulla* – for eternity. And since Trimalchio's estate was at Cumae, why indeed would the Sybil be the Delphian?'

Hervey raised an eyebrow, and turned to Cornet Jenkinson for his response.

'I cannot dispute it further, sir. Agar's memory serves him better than does mine.'

'You are well that it did not come to the wagers book,' concluded Malet, signalling that the conversation could resume its former dimensions.

Hervey turned a little in his chair to where Fairbrother sat with a fathoming look. 'It's as if I were a cornet again and Laming were here, sporting. I'm quite transported. You would have found his company most engaging. A considerable scholar ... Something troubles you?'

Fairbrother shook his head. 'Not *troubles* me, no. But I had thought that a *Sybil* spoke her own prophecies, not those of an oracle.'

'A very apt observation. You should put it to Jenkinson.'

Instead he put it to Agar, quietly, as they rose from the table.

Agar nodded confidentially. 'Just so. It was the *Pythia* who spoke for Apollo at Delphi. The Delphian *Sybil* spoke for herself. But it wasn't necessary to make a show of that too. Jenkinson's an excellent fellow.'

Hervey heard the exchange, and he warmed to Agar for it.

In the ante-room, to which they returned to take more coffee, Jenkinson took his leave for picket duties, while Malet engaged Fairbrother in an examination of the wagers book (always a diverting pastime). Hervey chatted dutifully to the new paymaster, but after a few minutes that officer excused himself, for the imprest account was due its monthly reconciliation.

Agar saw, and detached himself from the little knot of other regimental staff hugging the fire. 'Colonel Hervey, sir, I understand you are to observe the war in the East.'

'That is so.'

'Sir, I should like very much to accompany you.'

Hervey, slightly taken aback – not so much by the desire as the directness of the request – made an expression that suggested the notion was impractical.

But for a new cornet, Agar was singularly undaunted. 'Sir, if I might add, I have travelled throughout Greece and a good part of Macedonia and those places close to the seat of the war, and I speak a little Persian.'

Hervey nodded appreciatively, though he feared Agar misjudged the nature of the business. 'It is not a *dragoman* I need but a coverman.'

Agar looked earnest. 'I should be honoured to serve as your coverman, sir.'

Hervey suppressed an instinct to smile (for pluck was not to be derided); but a greenhorn cornet was no substitute for a winner of 'Sabre and Carbine'. He shook his head. 'The place is taken, though I take note of your zeal.'

Agar stood his ground, however. 'Sir, there is no pressing need of me here – and I might add, no useful work – and since there is so little action to be seen other than scattering riotous assemblers, I must seek it out.'

Hervey frowned. 'I wonder you did not choose an India regiment then,' he said, suddenly inclined to be a little severe.

'My mother's people – cousins – served with the regiment, sir. That was my reason for wishing to join, rather than an India one.'

'Indeed? Their name?'

Agar cleared his throat. 'Lankester, sir.'

Hervey was too practised to betray emotion, but no mention of the name Lankester could be without effect. Both brothers had died at the head of the regiment; and, not least, Kezia had briefly borne the name – of which Agar must be aware. 'Your mother's people, you say?'

'Cousins, sir.'

It guaranteed nothing, of course – only that his reason for joining was copper-bottomed – and yet here was a man of evident learning and eagerness, and there was no reason why he should not come with him to the war. Hervey supposed that the Horse Guards would have no objection (Agar could surely pay his own way), and nor in the circumstances could Lord Holderness. Malet would anyway be able to say how needful they were of a cornet not long passed-out of riding school and skill-at-arms – which, he imagined, was not at all.

He nodded several times, thoughtful. 'Very well. I shall have Malet speak with Lord Hol'ness.'

'Thank you, Colonel Hervey.' Agar bowed, and made to withdraw.

'One more thing.'

Agar looked wary, as if Hervey might have second thoughts. 'Sir?'

He wanted to be absolutely sure that this 'cornet of letters' was no chancer. 'You were very decided in your opinion on the Sybil. *Ampulla* ... You are certain it was the word? Or is it what you suppose it would have been, were you correct?'

Agar seemed genuinely perplexed. '*Nam Sibyllam quidem, Cumis ego ipse oculis meis vidi, in ampulla pendere.** Petronius, sir.'

Hervey was reassured. He was also doubly impressed, and not a little intrigued. 'I don't know of these things, yet I don't suppose Petronius was a standard text at Oxford?'

Agar smiled (he had never dared tell his tutor what he was reading). 'No, indeed not. But in truth, the prescribed texts were lofty in their subject and language; I wanted to learn also how and of what the *un*heroic Roman spoke.'

Hervey raised an eyebrow. 'That is singular, Mr Agar. My compliments to you.' But he wondered if this cornet took interest

---

* For with my own eyes I saw the Sibyl at Cumae hanging in a bottle.

in the world other than from a scholarly perspective; he would not be at all surprised if his enthusiasm waned with the miles from Oxford.

Agar bowed and took his leave, and Malet and Fairbrother rejoined him.

'What amusement your wagers book affords,' said Fairbrother, smiling as if about to reveal a confidence. 'Mr So-and-so wagers Mr So-and-so that the latter's first charger cannot beat his first charger over a quarter of a mile on the flat. Mr Someone-else wagers Mr Likewise that the first issue of Caleb's concubine Ephah was called Haran. Mr Black wagers Captain White that the Duke of Wellington will not be prime minister beyond Lady Day.'

Hervey returned the smile. 'The hours can sometimes pass excessively slowly.'

'I'm not sure the latter wager should have been allowed,' said Malet, suddenly looking stern.

'Probably not,' agreed Hervey. 'In any case, I think "White" is safe. There was talk at the United Service last night: even Peel's now an emancipator. The duke will have his majority.'

'And what a conversion that was,' said Malet, in a tone not altogether approving (which was why 'politics' was a subject disallowed at mess): '"Orange Peel" himself prepared to sit next to a Catholic in parliament!'

Hervey nodded, equally diverted by the notion.

'You know,' continued Malet, his brow furrowing in a sign of more sincere wonder, 'since Mrs Armstrong's funeral, several dragoons have been taking instruction of the priest here.'

'The *Catholic* priest?'

'Ye-es. You don't have objection, do you, sir?'

'No objection, no. Merely am I taken aback by my own astonishment – if such it is. The funeral was a very singular occasion.'

'And there's an officer, too. Takes his instruction quite openly.'

That, perhaps, was of rather less note, if greater consequence, for there had been Catholic officers in the regiment since Hervey had been cornet (if only a couple) – and Strickland had been a most exemplary officer, too. His death had gone hard with the mess. 'Who is he?'

'Rennell.'

Hervey looked surprised. 'That will go hard with his people. His father's dean of Winchester.'

'What a compendious knowledge you possess,' said Fairbrother, in as much astonishment.

'My father and he received their ordination at the same time. They visit together, in London, still.'

'I meant of cornets not clergy.'

Hervey was momentarily abashed, but the clock on the chimney piece began chiming the half-hour. He put down his cup. 'We must go.'

Fairbrother slept during the journey back. Hervey, for once, would have preferred to think aloud, but he could hardly chide his friend for assuming otherwise. He made himself think with system, therefore, rather than allow thoughts to come as they pleased.

Above all, there was the good news that Armstrong was set on the road to restoration. Command without his old NCO-friend would be wanting indeed; and the thought of Armstrong and his children in some orphan household would have been truly dispiriting. But the prospect was blighted by, as it were, the farrier's axe. How could the Horse Guards – he could not bear to think that Lord Hill was himself responsible (in truth was it not the Secretary at War?) – contemplate the reduction of a regiment such as the Sixth, a regiment whose officers wagered on the prowess of their horses and discoursed on classical texts? They had stood in the order of battle since 1759; the experience of the French wars and lately of India (and his own troop at the Cape), hard won, made of them a regiment that knew its business second to none. Not one in ten of those dragoons 'listed now had heard a French cannon, he supposed, but the understanding of all who had gone before them, whether to the grave or discharge, was in some way communicated to the newest recruit, so that in but a few months a man believed himself to be not just a member of a body of veterans but a veteran himself. It did not matter if he had been but a boy at the time of Waterloo; he somehow thought of himself as truly having been there. The quill-drivers in the Treasury might scoff at it, but how otherwise to explain whence came a regiment's élan?

Waterloo was of diminishing memory, however, Bengal and the Cape a long way away. Hervey sighed. England, he must conclude, was overgrown with peace. Had he the stomach for such a place?

VI

TOUCHES OF SWEET HARMONY

Hertfordshire, the next day

The sound of Kezia's distant piano commanded silence as Hervey entered the panelled hall of Walden Park. The servant holding open the door bowed mutely and, taking his coat, made no enquiry after his post-horses and boy (they were, however, being attended to efficiently, he saw with a backward glance); there was no eruption of butler, housekeeper, or of any one of the family, in welcome. It was as if the morning hour – hours – of practice at the keyboard required the Great Silence of a monastery.

Hervey could not call himself a music lover. He loved the sound a band made, he enjoyed a song, and he could be entertained by an opera if its absurdity did not overcome the melody. He had never learned the fortepiano, as his sister had (and as Georgiana was learning). He would admit he knew very little; but he had recognized that Kezia's talent both with hands and voice was of an unusual order – much greater than that of Elizabeth; much much greater. Whether or not it compared to those who earned their living thus, he could not know; but he did not suppose that Signora Colbran, whom he had heard sing in Rome, or Herr Moscheles, who played one evening at Apsley House when he dined there, could practise more.

He stood listening, not sure what to do. The music sounded not so . . . *severe* as it sometimes did. Indeed, he listened with increasing pleasure, for poor ear though some might say he had (his sister, for one), his taste was not confined, as Elizabeth teased, to marches. What Kezia played this morning was not music to dance to – or rather, he could not imagine her lowering herself to play jigs – but dance was exactly what the music invited. And it was strange, for as a rule Kezia would spend an age in scales, chords, arpeggios and all the other exercises of the keyboard which he knew of from his sister's practice, but rarely anything to which the exercises were a prelude. It was almost as if her music were to be kept, so to speak, in a vault, to be taken out only on some special occasion, and under strict guard. He was fully conscious of the need for drill, of course – for constant practice was the foundation of execution, whether before an audience or the enemy. But to practise to exhaustion, as frequently it seemed to him was Kezia's intent – to subdue, as it were, the keyboard, like a rough-rider with an unbroken colt – these things he could not understand. Not that their time together had been long – not at all; but it had been long enough for him to perceive that for a part of every day that they lived together they did so in what might be, to all intents and purposes, separate worlds.

He was at first reluctant to disturb her; she had ill disguised her annoyance once when he had interrupted her playing, so that she mis-keyed and had to begin again the sequence of scales, but he thought it poor form for a husband returned from months away to have to wait on a perfect cadence. He went into the music room as quietly as he might, though when Kezia looked up from the Broadwood which had been his wedding present to her, she smiled as she continued with the lively tune. It was not the smile of a Henrietta, or a Kat, but it registered a certain happiness, perhaps even pleasure.

When the music was finished – or it seemed to him that it was finished (there was a rather fine descending passage which ended with a final-sounding chord) – she smiled even broader. 'There, Matthew, is it not the most charming piece?'

'Charming indeed.'

'In point of fact it is quite astonishing,' she declared, and then frowning ever so slightly, added: 'I had your letter last evening, but did not expect you until tomorrow.'

Hervey raised his hands as if a supplicant, but self-mocking. 'What is the music? I shall not guess who is the composer. You would only despair of me.'

'*Rondo à la Krakowiak*,' replied Kezia, soberly, closing the sheet music with something of a flourish. 'You can have no idea how difficult it is to play – *rubato* and strict rhythm at one and the same time.'

Hervey had little idea of what she spoke, but would readily concede that it sounded difficult. 'The composer – Russian, evidently?'

'Polish. A prodigy of but eighteen called Chopin. They say his left hand plays as a metronome while his right is all liberty. I confess I am far from mastering it myself; the syncopation is extraordinary.'

Hervey still had only the faintest comprehension, but the music plainly enlivened her – as it had him. 'Chopin. Polish.' He had had cause to fear the Polish lancers at Waterloo – *le Régiment de Chevaux-Légers Polonais de la Garde Impériale* . . . He would not mention it.

'Yes, Polish,' said Kezia, as if she was herself intrigued by the fact. 'The *Krakowiak* is a peasant dance.'

'Well, I liked it very much indeed,' said Hervey, advancing to the piano to kiss her, which she allowed rather than welcomed, rising and gathering up the music in the same motion as the touch of lips.

'And do you know why you like it so?' she asked, with a sort of frown that was both playful and yet somehow disapproving.

Hervey, not allowing himself to be put off, feeling that the smile could not be wholly unconnected with his homecoming, returned it with a look of bemusement. 'I fancy it's rather happy music, contented peasants making merry in the fields' (he almost said making 'hay').

She arched an eyebrow. 'It is because, Colonel Hervey, the *Krakowiak* imitates the movement of the horse.'

'Ah,' he said, sounding deliberately deflated. 'You think me minded only of horses, ma'am?'

'Horses with dragoons astride,' she replied, quite determined to drive home the jest – if jest it was.

But Hervey was not inclined to take offence, even mock. 'The dragoon dismounts to do his work. The horse is merely his servant.'

'Come now, Colonel Hervey; you think me ignorant of soldiery.' She went to the chimney piece and gave the bell-pull a tug. 'I am most reliably informed that nowadays a dragoon thinks himself no less a cavalryman than does a hussar. And a light dragoon was dressed as a jockey from the beginning, was he not?'

Hervey had to concede (with a polite bow) – and in some admiration, for she had taken her instruction (somewhere) well. Did it portend a zeal for becoming the colonel's lady? He thought it improbable. Whatever the reason, however, his spirits were much lifted: here was nothing like the *froideur* of the days before he had left for the Cape.

But then, he was no longer contemplating a command in Canada, so disagreeable a prospect to her: his letter just before embarking for home had told of his good news, that he was after all to have command of the Sixth. There would now have to be some qualification of that news, of course, although he knew it would scarcely be of moment to her what the precise establishment of the

Sixth would be: Kezia would be content if they could take a house at Hounslow in which the six-octave Broadwood might be played to advantage. Need he mention anything, now, of that dim possibility, Gibraltar?

A footman came. 'Charles, would you bring coffee?'

She remained at the chimney piece with a hand just touching the mantel, and Hervey was as taken by her poise as he was the first time he saw her. Her self-possession was every bit as alluring as when he had observed it at Lady George (Irvine)'s dinner, when poor Strickland had been there, not so very long before the mortal smash. And in appearance she was, if anything, even more tempting. She wore a dark-green velvet dress with high, close neckline, cut generously at the shoulders but otherwise following very faithfully the curve of her breast and waist. It was irony indeed that such was called 'undress' with covered arms and neck while 'full dress' meant scarcely any covering at all. And yet perhaps there was method in it, since what was not shown but otherwise so expertly intimated might drive the imagination more vividly. He smiled to himself at the artifice of female fashion.

The footman left, and Hervey resumed his engagement with Kezia's music, since it was quite evidently a happy medium for intercourse where otherwise there might be some awkwardness. 'Are you practising for a particular occasion?'

A look of both satisfaction and keen anticipation overcame her. 'I am to play before Herr Mendelssohn when he comes to London.'

Hervey felt suddenly and peculiarly estranged. He had heard of Mendelssohn (another young man; he had heard his music at the theatre), and if Kezia was to play before such a person then her accomplishment must be great indeed. He had not the acquaintance of a single other who could thus lay claim to talent of (he supposed) the first rank; and it gave him much cause for thought. 'I, I am all admiration. I had not . . . Forgive me; it had not occurred to me that you were so well . . . received in your art. My ear would never be able to tell me.' He smiled rather hopelessly.

'It might have, my dear Matthew, had you enquired of those with an ear that could.'

'I stand rebuked, ma'am.'

And there he did indeed stand, cuttingly rebuked and wholly at a loss for words with which to banter further, not knowing how to move the conversation to the next level, or even what that next level was, yet seeing how grotesque was the predicament in a new-wed couple.

Charles saved him prolonged anguish, however. The coffee was very fast brought, as if the servants were waiting, ready, for the end of the exercises. Hervey took his up and stood by the fireplace, wondering if he might put on another log – and troubling himself the more at his want of self-assurance. 'Your people are well?'

'They are very well,' replied Kezia, stepping aside to allow the footman to attend to the fire, and taking up a thick silk shawl.

Hervey moved to help her with it, but too late, so that he had to withdraw again awkwardly. 'They are at home?' (The house was large enough for all to be secreted in comfort.)

'They are in London – unseasonably so, it must be said, but my father has business in connection with the Catholic Act.'

'Indeed?'

He was not expecting any explanation of what that business was, but Kezia took him more exactly. 'Yes. He has written to the government to enquire how it may be that Catholics, who refuse to submit to our laws and who deny parliament's authority over their church, might yet be admitted to parliament to make laws for the Church of England.'

Sometimes Hervey found it trying to be a Tory (even if he knew the alternative to be insupportable), and wondered how it was that the squire of Walden, albeit with the parliamentary borough in his pocket, might claim the attention of the government on this or any other matter. He fancied he knew how the Duke of Wellington would receive him, Tory or no – if he would receive him at all. 'I recall that that was the very question which the Duke of York himself put when the bill was last before parliament.'

Kezia looked surprised. 'You are well informed,' she replied, more with curiosity than approval.

'Well informed, but, I confess, scarcely by my own efforts. Captain Fairbrother told me of it. He takes a keen interest in affairs of state. He's been to see Wilberforce on abolition matters.'

'And you would support the Relief bill?'

'If the Duke of Wellington does, I could scarcely gainsay him. Even Peel is now for it.'

Kezia smiled ironically. '*Oh! Member for Oxford, you shuffle and wheel! You have altered your name from R. Peel to Repeal!*'

Hervey smiled too. 'That is very droll.'

'He's said by one and all to have ratted on his oath of allegiance.'

'And do you yourself believe it? I've always taken you to possess a broad and enquiring mind.'

Kezia put her coffee cup down on a side table and pulled her shawl closer about her shoulders. 'I confess I have never to my knowledge met a Catholic, and so I have no prejudice in their favour or otherwise, but my father is of firm conviction in the matter.'

That seemed to be that. The conversation had taken a decidedly darker turn, and Hervey was relieved when Kezia then enquired almost breezily after his friend. 'Where *is* Captain Fairbrother, by the way? Does he return with you from the Cape?'

'He does indeed. I left him to savour the delights of London – at his own request, that is, for he had little chance before to see the sights. He's to come with me to the East, and I hope very much to . . . to the regiment when I take command.'

The hesitation was not lost on her, and she looked at him quizzically enough to throw him from his stride. He had wished to choose his moment; but there could be no dissembling now.

'I very much fear we are facing the same situation as before. Hol'ness is relinquishing command, and I am to have it, but it will likely be a hollow one, for the Horse Guards – or, rather, the War Office – is intent on reducing the regiment to a troop. Such is the parlous state of the army estimates. Lord Hill wants me to have command of his own regiment, the Fifty-third.'

Kezia looked at him with a degree of suspicion. 'And where are the Fifty-third?'

Hervey tried hard to make his reply sound as if here were not the rub. 'Gibraltar. Lord Hill says that it is a coming station.'

There was no immediate reply.

'The climate is most agreeable.'

Kezia pulled her shawl closer about her shoulders again, which Hervey thought might induce her to think of the benefits of balmier weather – but not for long. 'I should not wish to quit this country, Matthew. I . . . I have no desire to live a solitary life. India, though but a short time, was enough to persuade me that content-ment is not to be had elsewhere.'

Hervey had more than half-expected this opinion of Gibraltar, but he was nevertheless disconcerted by Kezia's reasoning. 'It would hardly be solitary, my love. Gibraltar is a considerable garrison, and my duties would not take me more than a mile or so from you. Indeed, in many respects it is the most confined of postings.'

But as he said the word 'confined' he knew he was lost.

Next morning, before he had taken his bath, an express arrived. Kezia had risen before dawn, saying she must speak with the nursery maid (Hervey had woken with her, but she bid him stay abed), and had drawn the bolts of the doors herself to admit the letter. A footman who had come scurrying was put to looking after the expressman while she took the letter upstairs to see if it needed reply.

Hervey was shaving by very moderate candlelight as she came into the dressing room, and it was all he could do to read it without scorching the paper. Fortunately its contents were brief:

> *The United Service Club,*
> *Thursday, 15th*

My dear Hervey,

Word has just come from the Horse Guards that there is passage in a frigate for St-Petersburg five days hence, on the twentieth instant, and Lord Hill wishes you to take it. Passeports and letters of introduction I am to take possession of tomorrow, also for Agar. Pray let me know by return what is to be done.

Ever yours,

Edward Fairbrother

Hervey swallowed hard. This was ill news. 'Lord Hill wishes . . .' A request from a superior officer must be taken as a command. There was no escaping it. Five days hence – five days from yesterday, indeed; there was no opportunity now of seeing his people, above all Georgiana; nor Peto, nor . . . And his renewed honeymoon (if that it could be called) would now be curtailed, as before. Was it so very important that he take passage in this frigate? Once before, not long after Waterloo, he had been sent with rude despatch from the Horse Guards to take passage east in a frigate. No, he would not dwell on that mission (the train of events which led to the snows of Canada was too hard a memory). This was very different. Oh, indeed, it was different! For Kezia would not follow

83

him, as Henrietta had done. The news would be to her no cause for dismay.

'What is it, Matthew? Nothing unwelcome, I trust?'

Hervey sighed (an express with good news was a rare thing, to be sure). 'It is not what I would have wished. I am to leave for Russia on the twentieth.'

'Oh,' replied Kezia, rather flatly. 'That is vexing for you. Why to Russia? I thought you said it was to Bulgaria?'

He shook his head absently (was 'vexing for you' merely an unselfish response?). 'Since I am to join the Tsar's forces, it follows I suppose that it is most expedient to do so via their own lines of communication.' He quickened. 'I must first send word to Fairbrother, and then . . . I must needs leave you, my love,' he added, as if an after-thought, consoling himself just a little with the knowledge that he left at least for less chilly climes. 'Is there pen and ink?'

'There,' she said, pointing to the writing table in the bedroom beyond. 'I will bring coffee.'

But his instructions to Fairbrother – brief, terse almost – were complete before she returned:

My dear Fairbrother,

Pray make all arrangements that you see fit, but in any event have Johnson stand ready, and send word if you will to Hounslow for Cpl Acton to join. And then go to Durham's off the Strand and order upon my account at the Agent's, Messrs Greenwood, Cox & Hammersley of Craigs-court, all that is requisite in camp furniture. I shall myself be returned by evening, but it is better that matters be placed in hand at once. And anything else that in yr judgement is seen fit.

Ever Yrs,
Hervey.

Kezia returned with a tray. She poured a cup as the footman withdrew. 'Milk?'

Hervey shook his head (milk was a fashion he could not fathom). 'Thank you, no,' he said, dripping sealing wax less than artfully onto the fold of the letter.

'At what hour will you leave?'

He stood up, the return-express at last sealed. 'I . . . I think as soon as may be. I must write to Wiltshire, though perhaps that is better done from London.' He hesitated, and then asked uncertainly, 'Shall you come with me?'

Kezia said she could not: there were all manner of things to detain her at Walden. And in truth Hervey could not resent it, for he had come – if not unannounced – with little notice. Walden was a considerable estate, and her people were away . . . But, then, was there not a steward, and a housekeeper? He, Hervey, would be much occupied in the next few days, it was true, but if she were to come to London they would have time together . . . But he would not press the matter; not now, at least.

'It is doubly a pity, your early leaving, for you shall not hear me play for Herr Mendelssohn, nor meet him.'

Hervey checked himself; she meant it kindly, no doubt. 'I must bear the deprivation,' he replied, trying hard to avoid any note of indifference, resentment – or any other of the sentiments welling up within.

Kezia noticed no dissent, however. 'I shall ring for breakfast and have them get your horses ready. And the express-return,' she added, tugging at the bell-pull.

'I had hoped to see Allegra. Does she speak yet?'

Kezia looked at him plainly astonished. 'She is rising three years, Matthew.'

'Ah . . .' But he was no wiser, not knowing whether her astonishment proceeded from his imagining Kezia's daughter to be either precocious or retarded. He realized with considerable discomfort that he could not calibrate the child's progress with his knowledge of Georgiana's, for in truth he had scarcely observed the latter.

And that gave him no satisfaction either in the present state of affairs. It had been his profound wish that Georgiana might have a mother, that she need no longer rely on her aunt to take that place. In fact it had been this consideration perhaps as great as any that had determined him on his course to marry again. And yet Georgiana was with Elizabeth still.

Kezia took the letter from his hand. 'I will go and make the arrangements. Come down as soon as you will.'

He was still fretting over the cost of the express (perhaps because it distracted him from worse thoughts) many miles after Walden. Why had he thought to send instructions to Fairbrother post-haste, which could only reach him mere hours before he himself was come? Had he thought he would tarry at Walden, even for an hour or so? Kezia had given him no encouragement. He had taken his bath quickly, dressed sharp and had come down before it was full light, but Kezia had absented herself soon after he began his break-fast – there were matters to be arranged, she told him – and when she returned it was with every appearance of wishing to help him in his declared haste to be away. He had a momentary doubt once again: it was his own expectations that were unreasonable; he had arrived, presented unpalatable news of a foreign posting, retired to bed as if it were an everyday occurrence, and next morning was summoned by the trumpet to quit with all despatch for a distant place whence he might very well not return; how agreeable was this to a wife of any sensibility? And yet, had this not been implicit in their vows – and in the knowledge of marrying (not for the first time) into a cavalry regiment of the line? Could she not have embraced him, even?

86

The semi-silent running in the snow – hoofs dull-thudding, and only the sound of the axles turning instead of iron tyres on metalled road – somehow gave space to his thoughts, so that one thing led perilously to another, his grievance mounting, until at last and inevitably came the comparisons with the past. For once, when he was just married, he had had the offer of a comfortable billet – command of a regiment of yeomanry. An *exceptionally* good billet, indeed, with a fine house and even the advowson of a well-tithed parish. If he had accepted it he would now have been lieutenant-colonel these dozen years – and perhaps much greater rank, for it was not unknown for officers of the lieutenancies (the lord-lieutenants of the counties conferred the commissions in the militia and the yeomanry) to be taken back by the King. His father and mother might have had a comfortable rectory roof over their heads, rather than the hand to mouth parish at Horningsham; his sister might have had the pleasure of greater society than that into which she had entered in Wiltshire (though he knew he ought to forget all reservations about her intended bridegroom); Armstrong might now have been quartermaster. Caithlin Armstrong might still have been his wife. And – he could not stop himself – Henrietta would be with him now (and Georgiana with them both).

As the frozen miles passed, he wondered how the warmth of those years had turned to such unremitting cold. He felt suddenly so sick that he reached for the window strap.

VII

DIPLOMATIC RELATIONS

That evening

Hervey reached the United Service Club just after six. It was no distance from Walden – not thirty miles – but for most of the way the roads were deep with snow, and he and the postboy had to change a wheel when the chaise skidded hard against the bank on Watling Street out of St Albans (though the exercise had helped restore his spirits).

Fairbrother was writing yet another letter with great speed and fluency in the empty library. 'A cold and *arduous* coming of it, it would seem you had,' he said, looking up from the desk to see a coat which bore the signs. 'I trust you had an agreeable morning before your forced march?'

Hervey was not inclined to rise to the fly. 'I left just after first light. We had to change a wheel, and it was the devil's job to get the pin out. I was minded to take one of the post horses instead, but the boy would never have managed on his own.'

'*Noblesse oblige.*'

'You may say so; though had there been a saddle I might have *disobliged*.'

The welcome at Walden had evidently not been rapturous, Fairbrother concluded, just as he had predicted, if to himself. There was no denying it; he did not like Kezia. He did not like her strange indifference towards his friend. He did not like her *hauteur*. He did not much like her fortepiano playing (though what did he know about it?). But he did concede that she was a strikingly good-looking woman, though he, unlike Shakespeare's African prince, was not in thrall to fairest creatures northward born – *Where Phoebus' fire scarce thaws the icicles*. For that was the point exactly: she was a creature of cold climes.

'I spent the midday buying camp furniture. It will be delivered to Craig's Court by the close of business tomorrow. I went thence to Leicester Street to take delivery of the pair of travelling pistols duly modified, and, too, a single Deringer pistol which Forsyth's had found – though at a premium. I have sent expresses this way and that, obtained gold coin, had Johnson hasten the boot-makers to effect the repairs to our hessians, collected our passeports and the letters of diplomatic authority – all in fact that is requisite to proceed on His Majesty's service. Your friend Colonel Youell showed me every consideration. Really, we might set out tomorrow evening,' he declared, with some satisfaction.

'I am all gratitude,' Hervey assured him. 'I'm only sorry to have occasioned you so much effort, while I was . . . at my ease in Hertfordshire.'

Fairbrother smiled wistfully. 'It was by no means all effort. After I had sent the express last evening, and made what dispositions I thought apt, I supped in Covent Garden.'

'Indeed?' replied Hervey, almost absently, as he perused Durham's invoice for the furniture. 'You were not at too much of a loss for company?'

'Not at all. I met with the flower seller. We had a most agreeable time.'

Hervey eyed his friend cautiously. 'Indeed?'

'Indeed. And you have to call on an under secretary at the Foreign Office.'

'Why?'

'Youell said he looked after the Secret Vote.'

'And you will tell me you have no idea what is the Secret Vote, I imagine.'

'Just so.'

Hervey cleared his throat. 'Well, doubtless I shall discover it. I . . . I thank you again for everything so expeditiously arranged. I have myself been writing letters. I must have the porter send them on for me.'

'And I sent an express to Wiltshire. It was the only point on which I was uncertain how to act, but it seemed to me you would wish your people to know at once, in case they were able to come to London. I hope I did right.' Fairbrother seemed not anxious but genuinely uncertain.

'Ah, well . . . that is very good indeed of you. Yes, indeed it is. They will not be able to come up, I feel sure, but they will be glad I have shown sufficient forethought.'

'Your sister might, might she not?'

'Oh . . . yes; she might. That would be . . . most welcome.' It occurred to him only then that she might even be in London at this time, at Major Heinrici's townhouse. He thought he ought to call. 'I'm only sorry that we shan't be able to travel down there before we leave.'

Fairbrother raised his hands in a gesture of 'no matter'.

'No, I was looking forward to it keenly.' Hervey smiled at the thought. 'I'd promised you we could shoot bustard.'

'There'll be another time. When we're returned.'

Hervey inclined his head, doubtfully. 'There may not be. Bustard are very few on the Plain these days.'

'Then we must trust there'll be a brace that survive until your homecoming.' Fairbrother suddenly remembered: 'Oh, and there's this,' he said, holding up a sheet of writing paper with finger and thumb to reveal the embossed coronet at the head. 'You are summoned this evening by Princess Lieven.'

'Princess Lieven?'

'The Russian ambassadress.'

'I know who is Princess Lieven,' said Hervey, and rather more sharply than he wished he had. 'What business have I with her – or she with me?'

'I rather fancy it must be something to do with your going to the Russian war,' replied Fairbrother, sufficiently drolly as to exact a penalty for his friend's brusqueness.

'At what hour am I expected?'

'Nine. Johnson is laying out your court dress.'

'I suppose I'd better go. She's by all accounts an arch-intriguer. I fancy she'll have some scheme she would have me embroiled in. But if she can give me an introduction to a decent horse-coper in Petersburg I shall count the evening worthwhile.'

Fairbrother smiled knowingly. 'Her reputation *is* formidable, is it not? "An ambassadress is an honest woman sent to lie abroad for her country"?' (Princess Lieven had kept an influential drawing room when the Congress of Vienna had removed to Verona in later years – and, it was said, an even more influential bedroom.)

Hervey frowned, taking the letter from him at last. 'You are very clever. But I sometimes think that before we met you did nothing other than acquire gossip.'

'That is precisely what I did!'

'Well, I fancy that that said of Princess Lieven is no more than what is invariably peddled of a woman with a mind of her own.'

'That is very *liberal-minded* of you.'

Hervey shook his head. 'It exasperates me that a woman must be so particular to guard her reputation – no benefit of the doubt, none of the . . . *latitude* that a man is permitted.'

'My dear fellow, what has come over you?'

Hervey sighed and sat down in a leather tub beside the writing table. 'Nothing has come over me. I had wanted a little time to . . . pay a call this evening. That is all.'

'May I make the call in your stead? I had intended supping in Covent Garden, but I am at your disposal.'

Hervey smiled indulgently, extending a hand to the bell-pull next to his chair (the club's system of springs and wires made for more agreeably effortless communication with the servants' hall than in the former premises). 'No, you have done enough. In any case, at this hour it's perhaps better to be calling on the garden than the convent. I had intended speaking with the nun I told you of, at Hammersmith.' In the chaise down he had conceived the notion that the convent might be the source of advice he knew he needed; on the last occasion, the counsel had been incomplete, interrupted by the call to the Cape.

'That, I own, I should find beyond my powers.'

'You mistake the matter. You would find it easy to speak with Sister Maria.'

Fairbrother leaned back in his chair. Though they had spent the greater part of their time in each other's company these past eighteen months, there were yet matters marked 'out of bounds'. It puzzled him, troubled him in fact, for it was alien to the freer and easier world that had been his youth. 'I have not said it before, Hervey, but you intrigue me by your partiality for popery. You'll forgive the word.'

Hervey was certain he would forgive his friend anything. Nevertheless he looked askance at the proposition. 'I have no partiality for popery, as you call it, only that I have found its adherents to be uncommonly attractive. Not, I mean, the superstitious creatures I observed in Spain, although their religion did them no great harm, I suppose. Nor even, for that matter, the wretched people in Ireland. I confess, however . . . *yes*, there is something reassuring in the skirts of a nun, or indeed of a priest.'

'A party at Princess Lieven's or a tryst in a cold convent: can there truly be any choice? I doubt there's an officer in the Sixth, or the rest of the cavalry, for that matter, who'd deem it worth a moment's consideration.'

Hervey frowned again, sensing his own absurdity.

A waiter came, allowing him to change the subject.

'Shall you take a little wine? Or spirit?'

'I thank you, no,' replied Fairbrother.

'You are unwell?'

'I am excessively well. But I should like to finish these drafts before repairing to the theatre, and I should not care to fuddle my head any more than it is presently.'

'Well, I have no intention of fuddling mine either, but unless I take some restorative I fear I shall be of no use to Princess Lieven. Brandy and seltzer, please, Warley.'

'I wonder if Metternich fortified himself thus.'

'Metternich? I don't follow.'

'You are slow this evening. The *Congress* System.'

Fairbrother said it gravely; and then, with the suggestion of a smile and the arching of an eyebrow, signalled the pun.

Hervey began laughing. 'Infamous,' he protested; 'but really very funny.'

Before leaving for Dover Street, the residence of the ambassador of His Imperial Majesty, Autocrat of all the Russias, to the Court of St James's, Hervey spent a profitable half hour in the United Service's library. His Serene Highness Prince Khristofor Andreyevich Lieven, or Count Lieven as then he was, had been first a soldier: some seventeen years Hervey's senior, he had been with Tsar Alexander at Austerlitz and promoted lieutenant-general but two years later – not yet his thirty-third birthday (Hervey had shaken his head in some despair). Two years later, in December 1809, he had been sent to represent the Tsar at the Prussian court, and then when Bonaparte prepared to march on Moscow, and Britain and Russia became allies once more rather than enemies (if half-hearted enemies), he was appointed to London. And there he had remained ambassador, receiving the title Prince three years ago when his mother was created the first Princess of Lieven.

And yet it was the ambassadress who possessed the greater distinction among London society. Hervey knew a little of her reputation, especially as an unbending patroness of Almack's assembly rooms (which had once turned away the Duke of Wellington himself for wearing trousers rather than breeches), but he had not before required to know more. Again the United Service's library supplied him with notable detail: Dorothea (Darja) Christorovna Benckendorff was born on 17 December 1785, at Riga, where her father, a general of infantry, was military commandant (a branch of the family of the Markgrafschaft of Brandenburg had settled in Esthonia and entered the Russian service). General Benckendorff had taken a German wife, nevertheless, Baroness Charlotte Schilling of Cannstadt, confidante of the Princess Maria of Wirtemberg, who afterwards became the wife of Tsar Paul I. On Charlotte Benckendorff's death in 1797 she had commended her four children to the Tsarina's care, whence Dorothea's bounty then flowed. Hervey had to count the years twice when he calculated that she had married at fourteen, and that her husband, though even then a major-general, was but eleven years her senior.

A few minutes after nine o'clock, therefore, he presented himself at Number 30, Dover Street, feeling himself possessed of enough information by which to judge any proposal that came his way (he considered himself to be already embarking on the commander-in-chief's service – or even that of His Majesty himself). Prince Lieven was not at home, however, both to Hervey's disappointment and surprise. Princess Lieven's had been the invitation, but he had assumed this to be merely the customary form. Now he realized that it was she herself who gave the soiree, and for a moment he contemplated turning on his heel, for if the evening were to be an imitation of Almack's, he felt insufficiently in sorts to stay. But there were already a dozen couples gathered, with more carriages queuing without, and he imagined therefore that it would be easy enough to make his introductions, take a turn about the room and then leave without offence.

He was announced in a high, almost singing voice to (as it were) the room rather than simply his hostess   'Colonel Hervey' – though mispronounced, Bristol fashion, and he noticed several men in uniform, and others, glance his way, so that he did not know whether it was on account of his own reputation (the newspapers had made free with his exploits among the Zulu) or the presumption that here was a representative of that talented but tainted family.

Princess Lieven bid him welcome with a smile. And self-conscious though he had been in making his entrance, he observed that she had not done so with those immediately ahead of him. Indeed, her manner with them had appeared rather formal, as if aware of her husband's status and her own rank. Fairbrother's parting words, so absurdly arch, came to him: 'Princes of such new creation are not to be excessively reverenced'. Hervey had no intention of showing excessive reverence: he would bow in the military rather than the court fashion. But the Princess's smile threw his stride somewhat, so that he found himself returning it perhaps too appreciatively. He realized at once, and bowed quickly.

Once he was safely joined to the party in the drawing room, taking a glass of champagne, he turned to appraise her from the cover of a flank. Her manner he had already had opportunity to observe; it entirely became her reputation, and more. She was known also as a woman of striking attraction, if not of conventional beauty; and indeed he found her so, despite – perhaps even because of – her proud air. Her height and slender figure were certainly to her advantage (she might fill a dragoon's tunic without any betrayal of her sex, her breast was so fashionably flat), and the angles of her face were made for the portraitist. She was about Kat's age, yet appeared to him at once to be both older and younger, depending on whether he observed the mien of the ambassadress or the ringlets which fell about her swan-neck and bare shoulders, and the fringe of girlish curls. Her eyes were large and undoubtedly intelligent, and her mouth undeniably tempting. Yes, he could see that the combination of her talents and position were a priceless asset to the Tsar.

'Colonel Hervey, good evening.'

He turned to find his recent acquaintance of the Horse Guards, Colonel Youell, in 'the drawing room dress' – crimson sash, white breeches and stockings – of the First Foot Guards. He returned the bow gladly. 'I am pleased to have the opportunity to thank you for your assistance today. Captain Fairbrother told me that you showed him every consideration.'

'It was my pleasure, Hervey, I assure you.' He then drew him to one side. 'You will receive your orders in writing, but we had word this evening that the Russians are to begin their new offensive sooner than we had been given to understand, and Wellington is to send a *note verbale* to Petersburg. That is why the frigate is stood by.'

'Am I to have sight of the *note*?'

Youell seemed surprised by the question. 'I don't think even Lord Hill shall have sight of it.'

'Then how am I supposed to know how to proceed?'

'My dear Hervey, your mission is to observe the conduct of operations. It is not necessary that you are acquainted with every affair of state. It is merely the coincidence of sailing instructions that places you within a mile of the matter.'

Hervey smiled, ruefully. 'My dear Youell, I can assure you, from considerable experience, that the moment one begins to act in such circumstances is the moment one finds one's written orders do not extend to the actual situation that presents itself!'

Youell nodded. 'You are right, I don't doubt. It could surely do no harm, and quite possibly some good. Forgive me. I shall ask of the Foreign Office tomorrow – you are going there yourself, are you not?'

'I am.'

'But I believe they may say that it might be more expedient that you are told by the ambassador in Petersburg.'

'Very well. I presume I am to convey this *note verbale* to him?'

'No; that is the business of a King's Messenger. Your berth on the frigate is but a chance consequence of its carrying him.'

'I may enjoy the passage to Petersburg without undue anxiety, then?'

The smile which accompanied this did not entirely convince Youell that Hervey was sporting. 'I fancy you are not one given to undue anxiety, Colonel. You forget, perhaps, that I have read at first hand your despatches from the Cape.'

Hervey nodded to acknowledge the compliment. 'Did you, by the way, arrange this invitation?' he asked, gesturing to the room with his glass.

'No, I did not,' said Youell, and with a note of curiosity. 'I had imagined that you yourself had.'

'Then I wonder who did. Do you know the Princess?'

'Not well. She is inclined to be generous with her invitations: she is wont to send them to the Guards marked "three officers", or whatever number she requires, without elaboration.'

Hervey could not resist it: 'Perhaps she considers that you are all of a piece?'

Youell smiled. 'Perhaps, indeed. She has been known to refer to such guests as her picket officers.'

'You are not acquainted with her, then, from Almack's?'

Youell smiled even broader. 'My dear Hervey, there are not half a dozen officers in the Guards who have a voucher for Almack's. I had one a few years ago, but no longer.'

'How so? I can't suppose you wore trousers rather than breeches.'

'Because I am really not excessively fond of dancing!'

'Ah.' The explanation was unconvincing, but evidently all that he would receive.

'And you?'

For an instant Hervey was caught by a memory, for Henrietta had loved Almack's, and it had been her resolve to take him there. 'I was once fond of dancing.'

Youell, every inch the officer of Foot Guards, caught the change of voice nevertheless, and made no reply, save to suggest they repair to the supper.

In the dining room there were tables arranged informally around the walls, and in the middle a long, dressed board with a dozen silver dishes and warmers, to which the two proceeded without ceremony. Hervey filled his plate with a veal frigize, and took a seat in a corner with his new friend, though after not many minutes they were joined in turn by three couples, the last of which – and to Hervey's mind the most attractive – claimed a connection. 'Our hostess suggested we might present ourselves to advantage, Colonel Hervey. Agar-Ellis,' (he bowed) 'and my wife, Lady Georgiana.'

'Member for somewhere in Wiltshire,' whispered Youell as the Agar-Ellises made their introductions to the rest of the table.

'Whig, though descended from Marlborough on his mother's side. Lady Georgiana's father is the Earl of Carlisle, who broke with Wellington last year over Reform.'

Hervey nodded admiringly; it was one thing to possess such information, but quite another to render it so privately and concisely. Youell most assuredly knew his job.

The table made room for the new arrivals to sit next to Hervey, the object of their interest.

'I am at a loss to know what advantage I can be to you, sir,' he said, as a footman began pouring claret. 'But I am at your service, if that may be.'

The Honourable George Agar-Ellis smiled warmly and disarmingly. The MP for Ludgershall (on the closer side of the Plain than lived Hervey's people), was half a dozen years his junior. He possessed to Hervey's mind a most pleasant, even sensitive face. Here was no martial man, but agreeable company nevertheless – of that he had no doubt. And if he were a Whig, then he did not have the air of a radical one.

'You would do me inestimable service, Colonel, if you would take care of my young brother. He is to accompany you to the Russias.'

Hervey smiled with the realization. 'Indeed; of course. I met your brother but two days ago. But one half of his name only was given me, which is why I did not make the connection. He was fearful eager to join my party.'

'I know it. He dined with us last evening.'

'He would not have known last night that we're to leave almost at once.'

'That will be no discomfort to him. Is the assignment especially hazardous, Colonel?'

Hervey stopped to think. It was not something he had considered. All assignments in the presence of the enemy entailed hazard – even if, in this case, he wished the 'enemy' (the Turk) no harm. Indeed, there *was* no enemy as such. 'I think your brother will not be disappointed. He expressed a desire to see action, and he will be gratified; though he will see it at a remove.'

Lady Georgiana inclined her head, her countenance still fixed in the smile of their greeting. 'Please do not think my husband importunate for the safety of his brother, Colonel Hervey; we are well aware that his profession is a perilous one. It is more that – if I may speak for my husband – we wish young Agar to be tutored wisely in military matters. He has none in the family with the qualification to do so.'

In its evident sweetness, Hervey was inclined to think the entreaty entirely proper, however awkwardly put. 'I shall do my best, ma'am.'

Colonel Youell's expression was of suppressed amusement. He decided it was time to come to his colleague's aid. 'How stands the House on the Irish bill today?'

Treating the enquiry as more than mere table talk, Agar-Ellis laid down his knife and fork and turned to his questioner. 'The Act for the Relief of His Majesty's Catholic Subjects?'

Ears pricked up about the table.

To Agar-Ellis's mind it was a most reasonably worded title, one that seemed calculated to appeal to the Englishman's sense of justice and patriotism, and which his own enunciation had made full play of. 'I think that the duke will succeed in the house of Peers; he already has it in the Commons. His standing among his fellows is too great, and they would not in any case risk bringing him down, for which of them could say what would then follow?'

The answer to this latter was, according to the smoking room of the United Service, a Whig government and then wholesale parliamentary reform; and which Tory peer wished to see the constituency in his pocket thus taken away? Hervey had no settled opinion on the matter of Reform. In some measure he was persuaded by his sister's advocacy (which was indeed radical, including like suffrage for her own sex), but he had not spent half his life in uniform to throw over the ways of this land for any extreme, Jacobin notions. 'Let us hope, therefore, that their lordships know their duty,' he said, with just enough of a smile to make known his own loyalties with good grace.

'If every man does his duty, Colonel Hervey, then the country will have nothing to fear.'

'I am tempted to propose a toast to duty,' said Youell equably.

To which all at the table were able to nod in happy agreement (leaving Hervey in no little admiration of his new friend's facility with felicitous phrases – a talent which he himself regretted he did not possess).

There then followed some more general conversation, while duty to the other guests claimed the attention of the member for Ludgershall and his lady. Hervey found himself watching fascinated, as if he were observing the behaviour of some exotic species of the natural world. Principally was he engaged by the delight that the couple took in each other's company – a true match of temperament and mind, and an evident intimacy that was by no means common (he supposed). It was not long before he found himself in envy of it, so that he had to force himself to break off from his observation and instead listen attentively to the wife of the Bavarian minister resident, whose husband was not present and who was being escorted by a younger man in a uniform that he could only recognize as vaguely Rhenish. Both of them spoke English, but with a strong accent, so that Hervey wished they would speak German instead.

Die Bayerin's conversation was anyway inconsequential, and Hervey was relieved when they rose again for the board, though chiding himself that Youell would probably have been able to make more of it. He accompanied her particularly attentively therefore.

'*Kasha russkaya pod nazvaniem Gur'evskaya!*'

She said it with such delight, her expression transformed, that for the moment he wondered that he had been so dull. And she pronounced the Russian with what sounded a true accent, and he would have asked her of it were she not intent on explaining that it was a dish that had become her favourite at the Lievens'. 'Count Dimitri Gur'ev, one of Tsar Alexander's ministers, confected it to celebrate the victory over Napoleon Bonaparte.'

He noted the strictly neutral style with which she chose to refer to the Great Disturber (Bavaria had been a late-come member of the Coalition), but again he chose simply to listen as she listed the ingredients and the laborious process by which it was made, though to her frustration she could not for the moment recall the English for *mannaya krupa*.

'In German?' he suggested, helpfully.

She looked at him a little surprised. '*Grieß.*'

He smiled. 'Semolina.'

'Semolina,' she repeated warily. '*Wo haben Sie Deutsch gelernt, Herr Oberst?*'

He told her of his Alsatian governess. And there was more inconsequential chat, in German, as they returned to the table.

But Agar-Ellis soon reclaimed him (Lady Georgiana diverted *die Bayerin*). 'Bavaria is a country I should wish to see,' he began, in a manner that suggested a higher purpose than to walk in the Pfälzerwald. 'I think their king admirable, a considerable patron of the arts, and of pronounced liberal disposition.'

'I confess I know nothing of the country,' replied Hervey a little flatly. He was minded to say that his sister was on the verge of marrying into Hanover, and that he might at some time have opportunity to see the south of the German *Bund*, but his inclination, even with one he found as agreeable as Agar-Ellis, was yet to keep silence.

'Not, perhaps, productive of great art, though certainly believing in the common worth of it. Did you know the Wittelsbachs opened their collection to the people a dozen years before the Louvre? We have several studies by Altdorfer in our own collection, but nothing more.'

Hervey perceived there was something missing in his understanding. 'You speak of your own collection?'

Agar-Ellis smiled modestly. 'I was speaking of the new *national* collection.'

'I confess I am in ignorance of it.'

'It is very modest by comparison with those abroad, but then we began with but a modest sum of money.'

Fairbrother had spoken to him of a collection he had visited in Pall Mall, which he said was a public gallery, but in truth he had taken little notice, preoccupied as he had been.

'Perhaps you will let me show you the collection, Colonel Hervey – when you are returned from the East?'

It was no hollow invitation – Hervey saw full well – and in truth at that moment he would rather have delayed his sailing to be able to take it up. There was something so effortlessly attractive in this man – in both of them. 'Thank you. I shall look forward to it.'

'It is a pity you are to leave so soon. Might you be able to dine with us before you go?'

Hervey bowed appreciatively. 'That is very civil, but I fear that every hour between now and the twentieth is already filled with more than I can hope to acquit.'

'Then we must suspend the pleasure. You are not married, I presume, Colonel? Only my brother did not speak of it. Forgive me.'

'As a matter of fact, I am married, but only lately.' He was perhaps a little surprised that Cornet Agar had not told him of the greater connection – that he was married to the widow of a Lankester. But equally he was glad that the warmth of his brother's manner could not be thought consequent on it.

'Then I am discomfited, Colonel. The invitations are extended to your lady, of course.'

'Thank you. She would be delighted, though I fancy she will have seen the collection, for she has a very lively acquaintance with the arts.'

'Well then, Colonel, we may look forward with pleasure to receiving you both on your return. And I must say that I am considerably reassured that our brother will be under your protection in the East.'

'Under his protection' was not as Hervey would have put it, although he would see it as his duty to preserve Cornet Agar from unnecessary peril – as any man under his command; but he understood perfectly what lay behind the sentiment. 'I am glad you think so.'

The conversation now became general again until the minister resident's wife, who had assumed seniority, at last led them to the drawing room. Here, Hervey talked with two or three prettyish wives of the Almack's stamp, and then at some length with a French *vicomtesse* lately returned from Algiers, yet who had nothing to say of the place, only that it might become so much more agreeable when more of her fellow-countrymen settled there, so that, after a polite ten minutes, he felt able to excuse himself to find his hostess and make his exit.

But it was the Princess who found him, and, it seemed, very deliberately. 'Colonel Hervey, I regret that we have not had opportunity to converse before now,' she began, staying him by a touch to the shoulder with her fan. '*Per cortesia*, I would speak with you about my people.'

Before he could make any sort of reply she was guiding him to one side with the very lightest of touches, the consummate hostess. He noted too (or so it seemed to him) that others within earshot moved away a little, accommodatingly, as she did so.

For one so slender, if not lacking in height, her presence was commanding; indeed, Hervey found the presence fascinating, not least for knowing that such others as the Tsar and Count Metternich had done so too. She stood closer to him than he would himself have presumed to, if by the smallest measure (perhaps, indeed, by no measure at all), and her eyes, no longer engaged in surveillance of the whole company, fixed him in a sure and steady gaze. He took his guard, though hoping he made no show of it.

'Do you have any Russian, Colonel Hervey?'

'I regret I do not, ma'am,' he replied, puzzled that she should think he had, or that it might be useful – unless she referred to his coming mission, about which he must presume she knew.

'Then your French will serve.'

She had evidently heard his exchanges with the *vicomtesse*; it made him warier still. 'I trust so.'

'And your German?'

He was not sure how to answer, his instinct being to reveal as little as possible to someone who might relay any and all to St Petersburg. 'Does the Russian army use the language?'

'There are officers whose first language is German, Colonel' (as soon as she said it he recalled her own birth). 'The Bavarian minister resident's wife tells me you speak excellent German.'

He began wondering if his chance conversations with *die Bayerin* and the *vicomtesse* had been quite so by chance as he'd supposed. 'I cannot deny it,' he said, with a smile.

'Then I think it may interest you to hear of what we ourselves have lately learned, that a Prussian officer has arrived in Constantinople – one Moltke, a lieutenant who though but a junior officer is especially well connected in Berlin.'

Hervey was largely indifferent to the intelligence itself (a Prussian observer with the Turk army, especially a lieutenant, seemed hardly more significant than an English officer with the

Russians), but the vouchsafing of intelligence was always intriguing. For notwithstanding the action at Navarino, when squadrons from both countries had engaged the Turks side-by-side, Britain was neither an ally nor a co-belligerent with Russia in this war with the Ottomans (Lord Hill himself had made the position very plain). He was therefore at once both cautious and keen to understand the princess more. 'Indeed, ma'am?'

But she, likewise, was intent yet on drawing him out. 'We are most anxious to discover what this portends. It may well be, in the course of your duties, that you have opportunity to meet with this Moltke; indeed we would urge you to seek such an opportunity, and to report as you find as soon as may be.'

Hervey frowned just enough to convey that there was some misunderstanding. 'Your Highness will know that it is on His Majesty's service that I proceed, and no other.'

'But of course, Colonel. That is perfectly understood, but our two countries share, do they not, the same endeavour in respect of the Turk? You know full well, I am sure, what passed at Navarino?'

Navarino – how the guns evidently echoed still. He must redouble his guard. She spoke English with such precision, and with so indeterminate an accent – not obviously Russian, a little German perhaps, and possibly some French (the experience of so many courts) – it would have been so easy to join her scheme. He took refuge in the Duke of Wellington's turn of phrase: 'Indeed, ma'am: the "untoward event".'

He thought he detected the merest signal of distaste in the movement of her lips, but she was too practised to allow anything more definite. 'Admiral Codrington did most noble service that day, Colonel.'

Even had she known that as a consequence of the action that day, his old friend Laughton Peto lay *invalide* in Norfolk this very moment, she could not have played him better. He knew it, and he struggled hard. 'I understand the King sent him the ribbon of the Bath.'

'But do not you yourself believe our cause to be just, Colonel Hervey? You would not, I think, favour the Turk over Christian people?'

He smiled again to attempt to disarm her. 'I am but a soldier, ma'am. I cannot choose sides.'

'But even as a "mere" soldier you may recognize . . . *comment dit*? – dispassionately, which has the nobler cause. Surely that is so?'

'Without possession of all the facts, ma'am, which a soldier is unlikely to have, all he may do is conduct himself honourably, in accordance with the articles of war. And to observe how others conduct themselves.'

The princess nodded. 'I perceive you will be fastidious in this, Colonel. I have no doubt that you will find our army bears itself with courage and honour in equal measure. Your Lord Bingham found it so.'

'You have spoken with Lord Bingham?'

'Yes, indeed – both before he went to the war and again when he came back. He was greatly impressed by all that he saw.'

This much seemed singular, for Hervey knew that not even Lord Hill had spoken with him, and his despatches, which he had lately read, were non-committal. 'I am sure Lord Bingham spoke as he found,' he replied graciously, wishing only to ask by what experience of these things did Bingham judge?

'And that is all that I beg of you, Colonel Hervey, upon your return . . . though if there is anything that might be thought pressing, I hope you will not hesitate to write it to me.'

He thought he had the advantage. 'What might be pressing?'

She realized that she had been, as it were, flushed from covert. There was the merest flicker of awkwardness (but Hervey saw) before she proceeded boldly. 'What this Moltke does, and what might be thereby the Prussians' intentions at Constantinople.' And then, before he could make reply, her countenance regained its steel. 'But I forget myself, Colonel: I did not say that I dined with Lady Katherine Greville last month, before she went to Ireland.'

He reeled, if not visibly (he hoped), then in his mind's composure. Rats began scrambling in his stomach, and he had to summon every ounce of self-possession to keep the 'mask' in place.

'You are acquainted, are you not?'

'I am.' It was all he could find to say, and the effort was prodigious. He awaited the *coup*.

'General Greville – you served together, no?'

He felt sure his expression had betrayed him, yet this mention of Kat's husband was an unexpected deflection. If she 'knew' they had served together, she surely knew they had *not*. Was she toying with him? Was she offering a line of withdrawal? He took a breath to fortify himself. 'How was Lady Katherine? I have not seen her in the better part of a year.'

'She was very well, though I thought it improvident that she should travel in her condition. And I told her so, for we are very close; we have known each other these many years.'

Hervey checked his instinct to say that Kat had never mentioned it. 'She . . . That is, does General Greville accompany her?'

'Oh, indeed, yes. For he is all excitement at the prospect of an heir. And so late come! Really it is very remarkable, is it not, Colonel?'

He hesitated for as long as he dared (certain now of her ruse). 'A blessing indeed.' And he cursed himself for the blasphemy.

The princess touched his shoulder again, ever so lightly. 'Colonel, I lost my brother Constantin but a few months ago in the Dobrudscha. This war is very grievous to me. Your intelligence of it would greatly favour me. I should be ever in your debt.'

PART TWO

'A VERY OBSCURE PORTION OF EUROPE'

The Spectator, for the week ending 5 July 1828

THE THEATRE OF WAR IN TURKEY

The ignorance which prevails respecting the situation of the Russian army has been displayed in many of the speculations on its progress ... The truth is, that the Danube debouches in a very obscure portion of Europe, and, except in the case of a contest, like the one commencing, there is very little reason why we should trouble our heads with its geography. Between 1805 and 1812, however, a most sanguinary struggle was maintained between these two ancient enemies on the same ground, so that it might have been supposed that some recollections had remained on men's minds. The slowness of the progress of the Russian army, for instance, and that the Lower Moldavia, by which the Russians approach the Danube, is a perfect swamp. In 1736, Count Munich required no fewer than 90,000 waggons to conduct the supplies of an army that never exceeded 80,000 men – and the features of nature are not changed. It is now supposed that, because the Russians have passed the Danube, they have nothing to do but march to Constantinople. Russian armies, however, as vigorous and as resolute as this under the Emperor Nicholas, have done the same thing frequently enough, and been compelled to return. We will endeavour, in a brief compass, to explain the geographical position of the parties.

The Danube flowing to the east separates Bulgaria from the provinces of Wallachia and Moldavia – dependencies only of the Porte. Between the Danube and Constantinople lie this Bulgaria and a principal part of Roumelia. Bulgaria is an agricultural district, rich in soil, but thinly inhabited. The part of Roumelia, towards

Constantinople, chiefly consists of downs: between these two provinces exists the great obstacle to the progress of the Russians. Roumelia is cut off from Bulgaria by the chain of mountains called the Balkan, which runs from the Black Sea to the Adriatic: over the lofty and precipitous ridges there are five passes – by either one of the two lying to the east the Russians will, in all probability, attempt to pass: these precipitous passes are, in length, about twenty-seven or thirty miles across, though, as the mountains push outworks, and form ridges a considerable distance before the most elevated points are arrived at, the roads difficult to pass, may be said to be ninety-six or a hundred miles across. The passes are such as a few troops could defend against any greater number: wretched bridges over ravines must constantly be passed; the paths are slippery, and it would be almost impracticable to convey artillery along the ledges of the precipitous sides of the mountains. Among the ridges which strike out from the main chain, lies the fortified town of Shumla, whence the two paths across the Balkan just mentioned, diverge. This town contains about sixty thousand inhabitants: its fortifications would be weak and contemptible in the eyes and in the hands of European troops, but are a very efficient defence when manned by Turks. They consist of earthen ramparts and brick walls. It is here that the Turks form their entrenched camps in their contests with Russia; and the Russians have always found it impregnable.

VIII

THE BLACK SEA HOST

Siseboli, on the Black Sea, 3 April 1829

'Bastard!'

Private Johnson lay sprawled in a stinking pool, half-stunned and pride wounded.

The others rushed to his aid, Hervey leading.

'Are you hit? There's no blood.'

'Ah don't think so,' Johnson gasped as they pulled him up. 'Bastard thing. What wor it, sir?'

'A rifle,' said Hervey. 'And a Turk with a damn fine eye – or the Devil's luck. See, the ball struck your knapsack' (the corner was holed). 'Keep your head low. I want to find yonder marksman.'

He turned to clamber over fallen masonry to a half-demolished wall, pulling out his telescope from the holster slung over a shoulder. Fairbrother, Cornet Agar and Corporal Acton scrambled after him.

There was a billow of white smoke, a report – louder in the warm, still air – and a flutter, bat-like, as the ball passed close and then struck the wall of the house behind. And it had been less than a minute: a Turk adept with powder and ramrod – or were there *two* rifles?

'Mark the time, Mr Agar. What would you say it was, Fairbrother
– three furlongs?'

His friend was observing with naked eye. 'At least. Deuced fine
shooting.'

'I wish *I'd* a rifle!' snarled Johnson as he struggled out of his
soiled tunic below the wall. 'I'd knock *'im* over all right!'

Hervey kept the glass to his eye as he addressed the aspirations of
his long-time companion: 'To begin with, Johnson, His Majesty
would not approve of your firing on our friend the Turk. Recollect
that he *is* our friend, every bit as much as the Russian is. Or rather,
the Turk is no more our enemy than is the Russian. Our situation
here is as strict neutrals. And, even more to the point, yon fellow
must be using double the charge. Your shoulder would be bruised a
good deal more than it is now were you to try the same.'

Johnson chose to ignore the challenge of a double-charged rifle,
offended even more by the notion of being fired on by a friend. ''Is
Majesty ought to 'ave a word wi''is friend t'Sultan. I thought we was
just supposed to be 'ere watching?'

'Observing. Observing the conduct of the belligerents with
complete impartiality.'

'Well, either way it's not right to shoot an' us not meant to shoot
back!'

'I dare say so. But at this range, ethics are anyway otiose.' He
knew pretty well how to silence Johnson in his canteen-advocate's
hat.

Another loud report, more smoke, then the fluttering ball – and
this time the breaking of tile.

'Forty seconds, sir,' declared Agar.

'Mm. Indeterminate. Certainly it might be the same rifle. Do you
think he sees us, or having first seen us does he fire speculatively?
What's his game, eh, Fairbrother?'

'One of *us*, if we're not careful,' replied his friend ruefully, unable to resist the pun. 'Wily devils, I fancy. If there's a pair of them, the other will be waiting his chance.'

Wily for sure, but this was indeed a very ... sedentary way of making war. He could not get the measure of it. The Russians had landed at this place almost two whole months ago, a full dozen leagues south of the Balkan, the mountains beyond which no Russian general had marched for a thousand years, and still the Turk made no substantial move against them. Just this *franc tireur*. Perhaps he – they – were not even Turk? Tatar, maybe, for that people were hunters, and might have facility with such a weapon; or else one of the Albanians who fled the place without much of a fight when the Russians landed.

The Seraskier (commander-in-chief), so the spies said, was at Aidos, only three days' march north-west, with ten thousand men. Why did he tarry when every day the Russian fleet brought more men – three thousand, now – and stores enough for the whole army? Perhaps he thought it not worth the trouble, that the stores would never see the mouths or the guns they were meant to feed. It would be a brilliant thing indeed for the Russians to bring off: the army marching south from the Danube, gaining the passes of the Balkan, debouching on the plains of Thrace – and at once their lines of communication shortened to a fifth by this bold seizing of Siseboli. He was full of admiration for this new Russian general-in-chief's art (though it was one thing to make a plan, and quite another to execute it).

Yet he would concede that the Russians had wasted no time here at Siseboli. It was an ancient place, with ancient walls that might once have withstood a powderless siege, and now the garrison had dug entrenchments, thrown up breastworks, hauled forward guns and made it into a decent fort. But they scattered their waste around as bad as anything he'd seen in India. The place stank; the air was foul with incipient disease (and the sun was not yet half its

115

summer strength). Admire this *coup de main* as he did, he could not wait for their passage out – north to Varna, the Russians' principal base, or, better still, to join General Diebitsch himself before Silistria. If this new man was to lead the army over the Danube and then the Balkan, he wanted to witness it.

'I think I must go and see General Wachten,' he said at length, replacing his telescope in its holster.

'To what purpose?' asked Fairbrother, likewise giving up his surveillance of the distant hawk-eye.

'To propose that we take a ride towards Aidos to see why the Turk does not come to evict us.'

Fairbrother was inclined to be wry. 'I suppose the Russians have spare horses and no objection to lending them to impartial observers.'

'I trust so.'

'Or perhaps I should say "the Germans have spare horses": shall we meet *any* Russian generals, do you think? Wachten, Roth, Diebitsch – does the Tsar trust only those with German names?'

Hervey smiled. 'The Tsar himself had a German mother, and his wife is Prussian. That must count for something, though I can't say what with any certainty.'

Corporal Acton asked leave to speak. 'Sir, might I try and borrow a rifle and return the Turk's fire, sir? Not to 'urt 'im – just to try an' bustle 'im out. As an aid to observation, sir.' His expression was made the more ironic by the accent of Bow.

Hervey thought for a moment. 'Admirable idea, Corporal Acton – ordinarily. But in truth I'd rather not have our Russian friends here think the Turk's our enemy. It wouldn't do for them to think we considered him a friend either, mind, but there's no cause for raising doubts.'

Acton looked disappointed. If there were no enemy, what use was a covering corporal? 'Sir.'

*

General von Wachten was a compact, solid-looking artillery officer of about fifty years, friendly enough if not exactly warm, active but not energetic. Hervey and his party had travelled in his company by frigate from Bessarabia, where the greater part of the army had wintered after the campaign of the previous year. He spoke German with the accent of Silesia – in which he preferred to curse, seemingly, rather than in his workmanlike Russian – as well as passable French. Hervey supposed he had been appointed for solidity rather than dash: his mission was to *hold* Siseboli, no more. That much might be entrusted to an artillery officer.

Wachten was at his headquarters, the residence of the customs official, eating cheese and drinking coffee, as was his habit in the middle of the morning.

'How is your Latin, Colonel Hervey?' he asked, nodding to acknowledge the salute as Hervey was ushered in, and indicating two books on his otherwise empty desk.

Hervey supposed it to be an attempt at affability, and thought to chance a little in his reply. 'It has been out to grass for some years, General.'

'And Greek?'

'Even longer. But if you have need of translation, the cornet accompanying me has ample of both.'

Wachten smiled ever so slightly. 'The priest here brought me those. Pliny and Herodotus. They both write of these parts, he says, and he wanted to give me something in gratitude for the repairs my engineers have made to his church.'

Hervey nodded. As soon as the Russians had landed they had begun rebuilding the church of the Virgin. It had been ruined in the Ottoman depredations, they told him (though he thought it perhaps more in ignorance than with malign intent). They taught him a word even – *two* words: *lúkovichnaya glava*, onion-dome. It had been broken in half. The engineers made it whole. And then they gilded it. Where the gold came from they would not say, but they were fiercely proud of what they did. He had remarked on the will with which they went about it, and Wachten had said that it was relief from the labour at the defence works, and good also for the spirit of his troops to see their religion restored ('They will have many more to gild in Constantinople!').

'I can have Mr Agar read them, General, and apprise you of anything worthwhile.'

Wachten nodded. 'This place was called Apollonia in ancient times, a colony of Miletus. Did you know that, Colonel Hervey?'

'I did, General.'

'There was a temple of Apollo, from which Lucullus carried off to Rome a statue of the god, whose height was thirty cubits, which he afterwards erected in the Capitol.'

'I did not know that.'

'Well, perhaps your cornet would be so good as to read these books to see if there is anything to learn from General Lucullus. It would amuse me to find, say, that there was some secret passage that my engineers have not discovered. Or where the statue stood, in case Lucullus left behind any treasure.'

Wachten laughed, so that Hervey was unsure how serious were his expectations. He was obliged to humour him, however; he did, after all, rely on his good offices for both bread and horses. 'Of course, General. But may I be permitted also to know your intention in reconnoitring – now that, it appears to me, the defences of the town have been placed on so sound a footing?'

The general looked suddenly grave. 'Colonel Hervey, I have been remiss. Coffee – and cheese?'

'The general is very kind. Coffee, please.'

The orderly standing at attention by the door evidently understood German well enough, and began pouring him a cup.

'Be seated, Colonel,' said Wachten, looking – to Hervey's mind – just a little pleased with himself. 'I am aware that you are a cavalryman, and therefore restless to be about the business of searching out the enemy. You will have wondered daily, no doubt, why I do not send out my Cossacks on such a mission.' He leaned forward and lowered his voice slightly. 'I tell you a secret. There is a most excellent system of spies here in Roumelia, and I intend keeping my few and precious horsemen for some more definite purpose than riding all about the country.' He sat back and pulled a disapproving face. 'Besides, they would doubtless carry off more than they could pay for, and I have no wish to make enemies of the people hereabouts.'

Hervey nodded appreciatively: such an enlightened attitude was worthy of the Duke of Wellington himself. But reliance on spies? It had nearly been the duke's undoing before Waterloo. How, though, might he make his point without giving offence? Indeed, was it right that he should do so – for he was not an adviser but an observer?

But before he could scruple too painfully, Wachten took him aback. 'I have learned, for example, that this morning, at dawn, the Seraskier marched out of Aidos at the head of five thousand foot and cavalry. And I have ordered the Cossacks out at dawn tomorrow to make contact with them.'

Hervey tried to hide his surprise, anxious not to suggest he had doubted Wachten's efficiency. 'May I accompany them, General?' he asked, in a tone of purposeful admiration.

'I have ordered horses to be made ready for you and your party.'

Hervey made appreciative gestures, then rose to request leave to dismiss, adding inadvertently, 'And if there is any service I can be . . .'

Wachten shook his head. 'I have every confidence in the men under my command, thank you, Colonel. But if there is occasion for service to His Imperial Majesty, I trust I shall be able to call upon you.'

Hervey braced, a useful mechanism for covering mistakes (as well as being the customary courtesy). 'I trust I shall know where my duty lies, General. Thank you, again, for your kindness.'

He put on his forage cap, gathered up his sword, saluted and took his leave.

Outside, a battalion of the Pavlovsk Grenadiers, the general's quarter guard, was forming up for inspection. The garrison mustered at dawn each day for roll-call and stood down afterwards to breakfast before being detailed for the fatigues of the day, which for the Line battalions principally consisted in digging trenches and bringing up defence stores from the harbour. But the Pavlovsk Grenadiers, besides the guard duty and escorts, were at the provost-marshal's call, and therefore did not take turns on the defence works.

He stopped to watch the parade. The Pavlovsk were an undoubted cut above the Line – five hundred chosen men in close order. Recruits to all the grenadier battalions, not just to the Pavlovsk, were handpicked from the Line regiments for their bearing, good conduct and courage. They wore the same close-fitting white linen trousers as those of the Line battalions, but the workaday dress of the Line was baggy overalls tied at the ankle, invariably filthy from fatigues. They wore much the same tunic too – green, long-tailed (with red facings in the Pavlovsk) – but they wore it better. It was the mitre cap, however, that truly set them off. At first it had looked to him strangely old-fashioned: grenadiers in English regiments had long since given it up (before he had joined, indeed). But its singular appearance worked its effect, for, claimed the Pavlovsk, it was a mark of their special bravery at Friedland. They alone had been allowed to keep it.

He had not seen Russian troops since Paris, after Bonaparte's final exile. These little moments of unlooked-for display were therefore instructive, for there was much that a seasoned soldier could tell from how a regiment mustered – how observant were the officers, how the NCOs cut about, the economy in the words of command, the sharpness of the drill. And by these measures he judged that the Pavlovsk would stand immovable during an attack, and would in their turn go to it with the bayonet in determined fashion. But then, from what he had seen of the Azov Regiment – a very legionary unit – at their fatigues, he did not doubt that they too would be obedient and stalwart. The Pavlovsk were the pick of the Line, but their grenadiers were conscripts too: both regiments were from the same peasant stock, hardened to adversity by the time they drew their first *kopek*. He found himself musing that if he were to command a regiment of infantry when he returned, he would wish it to be as well ordered as these grenadiers.

As he left them to the rest of the muster parade, he resolved to write his first despatch to the Horse Guards that evening. Though there was little to report by way of true intelligence, he would render in writing how and by what means he had come to the seat of war without His Britannic Majesty's ambassador (for it was in the ambassador's suite that he had been accredited). It did not matter to the mission on which he was engaged, he supposed, but if anything were to go wrong in the course of it, it were better that he did not first have to explain how he had come to be travelling other than in diplomatic company. If Lord Heytesbury chose to remain in St Petersburg with the Tsar, who had returned to his capital at the close of the former campaigning season, then what business could it be of the Horse Guards?

As he side-stepped yet another filthy pool, Hervey began forming in his mind the impressions of which he would write to Lord Hill. First, however, he must present his compliments to the Cossacks.

*

He watched with the others from the edge of the *maidan* on the old causeway which (said Cornet Agar) linked what had once been an island, where Apollo's statue had stood, to the mainland, although it now had all the appearance of a natural peninsula. Siseboli was not without charm. Some of its houses were substantial, even elegant by provincial standards, and the rest were well found, although to the landward end of the peninsula they became rather meaner, and some were little more than shanties. The people, those that had stayed when the Russians landed – Bulgars, in the main – were swarthy but upright, and for the most part they looked to the sea for their fortunes rather than to the land. They had been ruled by Constantinople for so many years that they no longer thought of any other condition but servitude – or so Wachten had told him. They were not (yet) as the Greeks, clamouring for their liberty.

About the Cossacks' exercise ground – 'parade' ground seemed wholly inappropriate for so irregular a band of troops – lounged the bearded horsemen on whose legendary exploits so much of the Tsar's military reputation rested. No two of them were dressed the same, as far as Hervey could see. Most wore dark blue overalls with a broad red stripe, but some wore looser bags; many were bare-headed, some wore a sort of forage cap, but others had on a fleece shako pulled to one side *alla Turca*. Some were in the short, blue summer shell jacket, some wore the winter *cherkesska* smock still, with its rows of cartridge loops, while others had on just shirts, and of several different colours. There was but one common item of 'uniform': as it was the hour of repose after the midday dinner of mutton and the issue of *kvas*, every man had his pipe lit. When Hervey had first learned what was the strength of the garrison, he asked the *esaul*, the Cossacks' captain, why there was only a squadron (*sotnia*) of them, two hundred lances, to which the reply had been that they were Chernomorski – Cossacks of the

Black Sea Host – and that one Black Sea Cossack was equal to three from the Don.

Seeing now the approach of the *Anglichanye*, the *esaul* rose from his camp stool, and, with his *sotnik* (lieutenant), bid them welcome. He was a burly, dark-skinned man of indeterminate age (Hervey knew little of him other than that he had been at Borodino, and then Paris) who spoke the worst Russian, so Wachten's chief of staff told him, of any officer in Siseboli. He certainly spoke no other language Hervey knew, though Cornet Agar, by a combination of Persian, Greek and bazaar Turkish, was able to communicate with his *sotnik*.

They had looked over the Cossack horses soon after landing, and Hervey had made admiring noises to the *esaul*, for they were hardy animals, fifteen hands or so, and evidently good-doers. They were bred (if Agar's understanding was correct) out of Kabardin mares from the Caucasus, put-to by Turcomans and Arabs, so that they were equally at home on the wide steppe or tricky mountain paths.

While Hervey and the *esaul* saluted, embraced, shook hands, exchanged mutually incomprehensible greetings and generally made like officers of rank, Agar and the *sotnik* spoke in tongues.

'The *sotnik* says that all the arrangements are made for us, sir,' said Agar, after some explanatory gesturing. 'They will bring our horses as soon as it is light.'

'You are sure not before?' asked Hervey. 'The general said they were to leave before dawn. I don't wish to find myself late on parade.'

There followed another exchange with the *sotnik*, who then spoke to the *esaul*, bringing broad smiles from both.

'The *esaul* says he wants the whole place to see them march out.'

Hervey smiled too. He perfectly understood – not least that General Wachten's command was not absolute when it came to Cossacks.

The *esaul* spoke again: Hervey heard the word '*kvas*' and braced himself to the challenge. He would not be picking up his pen for an hour and more. And he wondered how prudent it would be to do so when he did.

IX

THE *ESAUL*

Next day

At a quarter past five the signal guns on the old walls called in the pickets for the morning stand-to-arms – three shots, five seconds between. Hervey was standing ready for parade outside the house where his party was billeted, taking in the pure air of the pre-dawn, looking forward keenly to his ride in the country, away from the rankness of the camp and its confining defences. Beyond the out-works it would be spring, whereas within there were only the few signs of it. Bugles began sounding reveille. In twenty minutes the sun would be rising, the pickets would be in and the guards stood to. In twenty more, the rest of the troops would muster by com-panies and battalions, and another day of garrison routine would begin. Now came the sound of hoofs – the *sotnik* and a dozen men bringing horses. His heart beat faster; he would soon be in his element again.

Pack-saddling the camp stores did not take long, thanks to Johnson's practice of twenty years and the deft hands of the Cossacks (expecting to be on patrol but two days and nights they rode with only light scales). Just after full light the rest of the *sotnia* came up in noisy good spirits – horseshoes ringing on the cobbles, *chaghanas* jingle-jangling, and hearty Cossack babble. But for the forest of lances, they might have been a band of gypsies breaking camp. Hervey smiled to himself at the thought: these were the men whom Bonaparte's veterans had feared.

He would stay his opinion, however. In appearance the Cossacks had much in common with the irregular cavalry he had fought alongside in India – Skinner's regiment especially, which he counted second to none in ranging and raiding. With English troops it was generally the rule that good appearance was a sure indication of capability, but it was not invariably so with native troops – and not, he suspected, with Cossacks. He smiled to himself again, for the *esaul* was having his way: men from every regiment were turning out to watch them leave.

'Very well, let us join our host,' he said to his little party, with a look of amused curiosity. The *sotnik* had brought him a compact, almost jet-black mare. He checked the girth, gathered the reins and sprang into the saddle (he would not risk his weight in the stirrup with an unknown horse).

'It is too early an hour for puns, Hervey – even pert ones,' groaned Fairbrother, as he took an obliging Cossack's hand to mount. 'Deuced early for anything, indeed.'

The *sotnia*'s exuberance was infectious, however. 'I have always considered "reveille" to be an order to wake, not a mere notice of the hour of day,' Hervey replied, relieved that, knowing he'd had a despatch to write, he had not stayed long drinking *kvas* – and supposing his friend to wish he had had the same pretext to quit.

He glanced at the others – Agar, Corporal Acton and the two dragoons who had volunteered as servants – and felt a curious sort of 'cornet's lease', as if conscious of the sober mask of command (blue *or* red) that awaited him. In any case he liked pressing Fairbrother on points of military correctness, not least because they brought wit by return, and occasionally a counter that was worthy of serious consideration, and even approval. He had learned much from this most contradictory of men – at one moment the image of apathy, of indolence even; and at another, of the most astonishing address. He owed his life and reputation to him on more than one occasion (and one occasion alone was sufficient to forge a bond between fighting men).

They were at once into a jogging trot – not the way the Sixth would have begun a march – and his little Kabardin mare was anxious to be with the others. But Hervey knew he would just have to content himself with sitting to it and enjoying the jingling of the *chaghanas* (might the Sixth's band have use for one?) and the admiration of the infantry. Only after the best part of a mile, with the well-wishing behind them, did they slow from the trot. There were no audible words of command; it seemed that the *esaul* transmitted his intention by some instinctive means, so that the *sotnia* simply rippled to a walk. It was unmilitary, but it was not without a certain style; and without doubt it was done with economy.

Hervey and his party marched parallel and to the off-flank, the going either side of the road flat, on good spring grass, ungrazed. In the far distance the rolling, wooded hills   mountains even – lay as a barrier the like of which he had not seen in twenty years, when the duke's army had at last crossed the Pyrenees into France. The Balkan range, the Haemus Mons of antiquity and his schoolroom – he had never dreamed he would one day behold them. *Tunc etiam aërei divulsis sedibus Haemi* – 'the summit even of lofty Haemus shall have crumbled'; the words he had declaimed an age ago at Shrewsbury. They were famous days, simpler days, infinite in their promise, with books innumerable, war, heroes . . . He envied Agar his Oxford learning and his footing, now, at the threshold of soldiery. And *such* a threshold – Haemus Mons, which no Tsar's general had crossed since ancient times. How strange it felt to be at their southern side when still the Turk held them, as if they had come into a house basely.

'Hervey?'

He woke. 'I beg pardon. You were saying?'

Fairbrother smiled indulgently. 'Only that I am excessively grateful for your asking me to accompany you. This is the first I have ridden on the soil of Europe. And deuced fine too. Yonder sea – as blue as at the Cape.'

Hervey nodded. England was, strictly, a part of Europe too, but he could only think of her so when he was in another continent altogether. It was strange, moreover, that they had waited so long to ride, that their journey hither had been so little by land. They had come to St Petersburg by frigate, thence almost at once to Riga by coaster, thereafter along the Dvina by steam to Vitebsk, then a day and a half's post to Smolensk, and from there on down the Dnieper by sail and steam to Kherson, a mean city in which to wait for onward passage by warship, first to Varna, and finally to Siseboli. He did not complain, for they had seen much, and he had made sketches of what he thought to be of interest to the Horse Guards; they had read much, talked much and written much; except that Fairbrother had written not at all, for he saw no cause for a journal – to whom would it be of interest in the event of his death? he asked – nor occasion for letters, his father being content with but an annual report. He was, he said, and with an admixture of seriousness to the archness, content to pass without note, 'A youth to Fortune and to Fame unknown'.

Hervey had remonstrated with him, lest his friend think him in thrall to either fortune *or* fame: he did not seek either, merely the command to which he was by temperament and long years of service suited. And Fairbrother, while protesting that he had never intended to suggest anything base, had pressed him nevertheless to answer 'to what end?' To which Hervey had replied that there *was* no end: the judicious exercise of command was of itself sufficient. He had no ambition then, Fairbrother had asked. Indeed he had, Hervey had answered – the perfection of his command, so that it accomplished whatever the Horse Guards ordained, and with the greatest economy of life, effort and treasure. And Fairbrother had smiled, for he knew that he himself could never give his life to such a thing (or so he said), while acknowledging – exalting, even – the ideal itself; and he had even quoted the *Iliad*, when the Trojan prince Sarpedon urges his comrade Glaucus to fight with him in the front rank of the coming battle: ' 'Tis ours, the dignity they give to grace/ The first in valour, as the first in place.' And Hervey had pondered a good deal on it.

He woke again. A night heron flapped unperturbed across their line of march, and in the distance, along the shore and around the great lake behind Bourgas, there were grebe and ibises, and more geese than he thought he had ever seen. It was a fine place; it seemed a fine country; and for the briefest moment he thought that they intruded, that they had no cause to be here. Whose was this land that these Cossacks – men every bit as fine as the country, and whose company he was relishing – came to fight over? Would the Tsar wade through more slaughter to a greater throne, and trample the country and the poor souls living here? He shrugged; it was not his business – only to observe the methods by which they made war. It was difficult, anyway, not to side with a former ally, especially one that had in great measure helped bring down the tyrant Bonaparte. And although he did not bear the Turks ill will for the crippling of his old friend Peto (these things were the 'exigencies of the service', and to be borne without bitterness), he could not think of the Sultan without the epithet 'cruel'. He had no romantic attachment to Athens; he was no philhellene of the Byron mould. He supposed it was unnatural that the Turk should be master of the land of the Greeks – and of almost the whole of the country between the Black

Sea and the Adriatic – but that was the way of history, was it not? And the Turks were, as the word ran in London, 'an ancient ally'. Yet all this was of no import when riding in the company of Cossacks (though he *had* explained his situation to the *esaul*, who had replied that he did not understand neutrality but nevertheless understood what were its practical constraints). And so now he and his party rode just a little apart from the *sotnia*, as if by this he somehow made his situation plainer.

But the *esaul* . . . Hervey liked him, liked him very much, thought him the sort of man to rely on in battle. In any other circumstances he would gladly have ridden with him stirrup to stirrup.

They marched all day – with the briefest of halts as the sun reached its highest (though it had as yet no great heat) – at the jog-trot, which the Kabardin seemed to prefer to walking collected or even on a long rein. Perhaps the *kvas* last evening had magnified the Kabardin's quality in Hervey's mind. They would climb mountains, cross torrents, fight with wolves, the *esaul* boasted; the Kabardin mare foaled onto frost-bitten earth – little wonder her progeny would carry her rider for hours on end without so much as a blade of grass. Hervey had expressed his admiration, if perhaps (he was not sure he remembered) guardedly, but would readily admit, now, that his was the most tractable mare he had ridden in some time. What, he marvelled, might come out of her by an English Thoroughbred!

They saw few people, nor even animals, wild or pastoral. It was as if the word 'Cossack' had gone before them, emptying every dwelling, fold and byre. But not once had the *sotnia* fallen out to loot – not even to raise water from a well – so that Hervey began wondering if it were not they from whom the populace had fled but the Turks who were marching hither. The people of Roumelia – Bulgars for the most part, hereabouts at least – had no love of

Ottoman rule, and, no doubt, a healthy fear of marching armies of any flag. Empty country he always found dispiriting to cross, as he had the rolling plains of Natal and the Cape Colony, but he would own that this was indeed deuced fine country, wholly belying its reputation as a wild and brutish place where brigandage stalked.

An hour before sunset they fell out to bivouac in an abandoned vineyard. Hervey was surprised they had not made camp in the deserted village they had passed through half an hour before; it had been a mean sort of place, and godless, the little church ruined, but, as the soldier's saying went, a half-decent billet was better than a good bivouac.

He asked the *esaul* why, and was met with a smile: 'My Cossacks would not enter the home of simple people without invitation.'

It was impossible to tell if it were the truth, or even a part of the truth. The *esaul* smiled enigmatically, and at almost everything. But every time he smiled, Hervey liked him the more.

They were not off-saddled long before a fire was sending up a cloud of thick white smoke, fed by a Cossack sprinkling gunpowder on the flames.

'To whom do they signal, sir?' asked Agar.

Hervey had unshipped his carbine, nodding for Johnson to take the saddle from him. He looked across to the plume of smoke again. 'At what distance did the scouts ride today, Mr Agar?'

'I . . . I did not see that any scouts were posted, sir.'

'Nor did I. But we rode as if there were, which means that either the *esaul* is foolhardy, or the scouts left Siseboli before light. I'd lay my money on the latter.'

'So they are now signalled in?'

'They'll be ranging too far to hear the trumpet, and besides, so I observe, the *sotnia* has no trumpeters.'

Fairbrother now joined the inquisition. 'But why signal your presence to the Turk, if he's about?'

'I don't know,' said Hervey, genuinely puzzled. 'There'll be method in it, no doubt. Go and ask the *sotnik*, Mr Agar.'

'Sir.'

He returned after ten minutes (during which time Johnson and the two dragoons had laid out the bedding rolls and got the pots simmering) with the answer that indeed the *esaul* wanted the Turks to know they were hereabout. Hervey could only shake his head, puzzled; it was contrary to all the practice of reconnaissance by light cavalry.

Fairbrother had an idea. 'Perhaps he would fire them thence like foxes?'

Hervey looked at him, puzzled.

'*Lear*: "He that parts us shall bring a brand from heaven and fire us hence like foxes". The *esaul* intends bolting the Turk with smoke and fire.'

Hervey looked thoughtful. 'I had not thought the meaning to be thus. I had always thought it a reference to burning the Philistine corn.'

Now Fairbrother looked puzzled. 'I have a dim recollection, but I confess it eludes me.'

Hervey smiled. 'Then at last my memory surpasses yours. It was the foxes that did the burning out. Samson caught three hundred of them and tied them in pairs, then set their brushes alight and loosed them into the Philistine corn.'

'Of course; now I remember. Deuced clever of him. I wonder if the *esaul* knows the story.'

'I *suppose* there are foxes in Roumelia . . .' replied Hervey, pensively. Then he smiled again, fondly, at the remembrance of a Horningsham sermon many years past. 'I recall my father one day, in his pulpit when the lesson had been read, and it had been that chapter of Judges, and Lord Bath and a good many farmers were in the congregation, and he said something along the lines of "Now here you might lament the ill keepering, and the docility of the hunts in Philistia at that time, that there should be three hundred foxes at liberty . . .".'

'I am all eagerness to hear your father in his pulpit, as I told you in England,' said Fairbrother agreeably.

'And what say you on the subject, Mr Agar?'

Agar cleared his throat apologetically. 'I believe, sir, that Shakespeare had read *Orlando Furioso*, for there is a notable passage therein concerning the fox bolted by smoke and fire into the terrier's mouth. I think it more probable that Lear alludes to foxes *being* bolted by fire than to their spreading of it.'

Fairbrother's face was a picture of mild triumph.

Hervey nodded, conceding. 'I'm run to earth.'

When the scouts came in – three of them, towards last light – Hervey took Agar with him to find out what they had learned. But Agar found the *sotnik* now more difficult to understand, the subject less conducive to gestures of the hand. Eventually he was able to establish with some confidence that the Turks were marching in the general direction of Siseboli, though at no great pace, and had begun to make camp for the night at Sagora, three leagues to the west – an eccentric route perhaps, but evidently the Seraskier wished to give Bourgas a wide berth, for he could not know for certain that the Russians had not landed there as well as at Siseboli. The *sotnik* said that the scouts were to return to their posts, to be ready to resume contact with the Turks at first light. And as for their own camp, there would be an in-lying picket, but no greater precaution.

'A gamble,' said Hervey, as he walked back with Agar. 'But probably a safe bet.'

They slept under the stars – slept well. There was no stand-to at first light, except that Hervey's party turned out and watched, carbines in hand, as the sun rose over where the horses were tethered, along a low wall at the south-east corner of the vineyard.

The *esaul*'s disregard for field discipline made him uneasy once again. He did not doubt that the chance of one Turk, let alone a sufficient force, traversing the country undetected during the night and assaulting the camp at dawn was practically nothing, but it remained a possibility, and to ignore it therefore reckless. But, then, Cossacks – irregulars in all but name – were not circumscribed by standing orders; they *lived* by gambling.

No Turk attacked the camp, and the *esaul*, had he seen them, would have smiled at Hervey and his men. So the morning routine was that of the camp at Siseboli – a leisurely breakfast, no muster. When an hour had passed, without ceremony or words of command the *esaul* simply climbed into the saddle and put his mare into a jog-trot, and the rest of the *sotnia* vaulted astride behind him and formed twos in apparently random fashion. Even Fairbrother, no advocate of drill, shrugged his shoulders and smiled as Hervey looked at him quizzically. And yet, they conceded, it seemed to work – and, again, with no little economy of effort.

Hervey and the others mounted and took post as before, this time on the near, landward flank (for that towards the sea was broken by numerous dry channels), but they were not long marching before a single rider came over the rise at a canter. He made straight for the *esaul*, reined about and made his report while circling. The *esaul* heard him without remark, nodded, and turned to the *khorunzhiy* (cornet) at his side. A few words followed, and then the *khorunzhiy* and his coverman were into a hand gallop back whence they had come before Hervey could make up his mind whether to sit and wait or close to learn what he might.

The *sotnik* rode over to them.

'The Turks broke camp at first light and their cavalry now lead.' Agar was able to translate quickly and with confidence.

'Cavalry leading: you're sure that's what he said?' pressed Hervey.

'Yes, sir.'

He was intrigued. He knew that Turk practice was for the cavalry to march at the rear and to the flanks so as not to disturb the ground for the infantry. Placing them in advance meant the Seraskier expected opposition or wanted to quicken the pace. Perhaps the fox had indeed been fired from his hole. In either case it was ripe news; little wonder the *khorunzhiy* had been sent speeding back to General Wachten.

'The *esaul* believes they might be before the walls of Siseboli by evening. We shall therefore close with the Turk at once. The bat-horses are to go back to the vineyard.'

'Very well. They can go with the Cossack servants.'

Hervey did not doubt the *esaul*'s appreciation of the situation. It was possible that if the cavalry hastened and the infantry made a forced march, their fires tonight would be seen from the walls of Siseboli; but after so many weeks' delay, what should now compel the Seraskier to hurry?

'What is the *esaul*'s intention on closing with the Turk?'

Agar asked the *sotnik*. He heard '*khameereh*' – Persian – in reply, and had to press for explanation.

'Well?' said Hervey, becoming impatient.

Agar turned, looking unsure. 'He says, I believe, the *esaul* wants to test the *mettle* of the Turk.'

'How?'

Agar asked the *sotnik* again.

'*Napadat!*'

It was one of the handful of Russian words that Hervey had acquired. He looked at Fairbrother, disbelieving. '*Attack?* Two hundred against – how many?'

Fairbrother shrugged. 'If one Black Sea Cossack is equal to three from the Don, perhaps he's equal to ten Turks?'

It had occurred to Hervey more than once that the object of the Horse Guards' interest ought perhaps to be the Ottoman army rather than the Russian, for a good deal was known of the Tsar's troops, but very little of the Sultan's new army, the 'Mansure' – *Muallem Asakir-i Mansure-yi Muhammadiye* ('the Trained Victorious Troops of Muhammad'). The Mansure had been formed three years before, after the mutiny of the Janissaries gave the Sultan his chance to disband that corrupt corps. For a century the Janissaries, non-Turkmen, had held the Porte to ransom, while the empire fell apart. The Sultan had brought in foreign officers to advise him, or so it was believed; the artillery and transport had been reorganized, and there were new regiments of infantry, though the cavalry – the *sipahis* – remained as before, since unlike the Janissaries they were all Turkmen. In Hervey's estimation, London could not remain indifferent to a new and efficient army astride a road to India.

In an hour there came the first sighting, at about three-quarters of a mile – a cohort of Turk lancers, two hundred strong at least, ambling in column along the road due east. The country was rolling, unbroken, coverless, with short springy turf, not too hard underfoot; it was very apt, thought Hervey, that they should make their first contact on ground so good – 'cavalry country'.

'Odd that they come on in column still,' he said, reining to a halt and taking out his telescope.

Fairbrother and Agar were already following suit.

'I must say, the time and course couldn't be more favourable, with the sun low and in their eyes.'

Fairbrother glanced at him questioningly. 'Is "favourable" entirely apt? Should we have a preference for the way the sun shines?'

'Apt for observation,' replied Hervey, blithely but perfectly aware that his friend had detected the slip. 'Lances and green dolmans, would you say?'

He threw out the question generally, to any who had answer. Corporal Acton was first to speak (even with the disadvantage of a poorer glass). 'Green, sir, ay – and a gun, half a dozen files rear.'

Hervey found it. 'Bronze, too – you have a hawk-eye, Corporal Acton.'

Johnson, relishing not being sent back with the bat-horses, did not have a telescope, but he had an opinion nevertheless. 'Dressed for paradise, then, sir, like some of 'em'll be seein when them Cossacks gets at 'em.'

Hervey continued observing. 'Not the time for riddles, Johnson, thank you.'

'Weren't a riddle, sir. That's what them Turks believes in, that they wears green pee-jams when they goes to 'eaven.'

Hervey frowned. 'Where on earth did you hear such a thing?'

'One o' them Bulgars in camp, sir. Mr Agar'll know.'

'Mr Agar, what can you tell us of this?' asked Hervey, content to play along while still surveying the field.

'Of the Turk's beliefs, sir, or their appearance now?'

'If there be anything at all, pray speak.'

'The Koran promises that a believer will wear green silk in paradise.'

Hervey lowered his telescope momentarily and glanced at his groom. 'Then I stand corrected. I beg pardon, Johnson.'

'That's all right, sir. Mrs 'Ervey told me that ages ago.'

By 'Mrs 'Ervey' he meant Henrietta. Johnson never could grasp, or never would, that on marriage to plain Captain Hervey, Lady Henrietta Lindsay became Lady Henrietta Hervey; just as he could not or would not that on marrying Lieutenant-Colonel Hervey, Lady Lankester became plain Mrs Hervey – for these things, he was convinced, were a conspiracy to confuse simple folk. Hervey smiled to himself: it was typical that Johnson remembered something Henrietta had told him an age ago. 'Admirable recall,' he replied, amiably.

'Strange, I see no scouts,' said Fairbrother, bringing the conversation to earth; 'nor flankers either. A cool customer, our Turk, it would seem.'

Hervey had been searching for the same, certain they must be selecting their lines of advance with uncommon craft.

Suddenly the column came alive.

'Ah, they deploy. We are discovered.'

The Turks looked well drilled, too. They halted in column of route, turned left and right by alternate troops and then wheeled into line. In less than two minutes they were formed in close order in three ranks, the cannon unlimbered front and centre.

'Prettily done,' said Hervey. 'A support and a reserve line, too.' He looked across to where the *sotnia* had come to an unruly halt.

Not for long. The *esaul* yelped a single word of command, dug his heels into his mare's flanks and galloped for the Turks full tilt.

Hervey struggled to keep his own mare still as the *sotnia* took off like hounds on a running stag. 'What in heaven's name . . .'

He watched in some amazement as the *esaul* pulled up after a furlong as abruptly as he'd taken off and the *sotnia* extended in a single line either side of him.

'Extraordinary!' he declared, stowing his telescope and taking the reins in both hands.

Fairbrother was equally impressed. 'I wonder how it looked to the Turks.'

'No pivot, no words of command . . . I don't believe a troop of ours could have done it with fewer than ten.' (Hervey had long held that the Dundas drill book was a thing of aptness no more, but 'It beat the French!' was the usual retort to any suggestion of a better way.)

Not that he wished to substitute any old swarming tactics for good regulation. The Cossack line overlapped the Turks' by a furlong on either flank, but it was a single line only: cavalry could not fight through without supports – nor extricate itself if the tide turned.

'Do they intend attacking – or receiving a charge?' asked Fairbrother, equally incredulous.

But before Hervey could answer, the line billowed into a fast trot.

'They attack – and with that crest yonder! There's no knowing what's beyond it.' He took up his telescope again.

Fairbrother was not so measured. 'Madness!'

'Intrepid, certainly. Mark, Mr Agar: to advance with dead ground to the rear of an objective, in which might be concealed more cavalry, is perilous in the extreme.'

'When the scouts came in just now, might they have reported that the Turks were without supports?'

Hervey shook his head. 'It's a possibility, but in half an hour there's no saying what might have come forward. Except that yonder *esaul*'s had uncanny fortune so far.'

The *sotnia* had picked up speed – a hand gallop – and with half a mile to run.

The Turks started to show a flank left and right, but did so hastily. Their support line buckled rear and some of them began turning, making the reserve line give way. In a moment the cohort had lost its solidity.

'He's checking the pace a fraction,' said Hervey, shielding his eyes although the sun was on his back. 'I wonder if . . .'

Down came the Cossack lance points, and the flanks began extending.

'I do believe he intends enveloping them! By God, he has nerve!'

'*Look*,' called Fairbrother, standing in the stirrups; 'the reserve line's high-tailing!'

They had turned about as one, then galloped for the crest. It was so uniformly done that Hervey wondered if it was by design, except that the support line now disintegrated, half of them following the reserve and the other taking shelter with the front rank in what had become a misshapen and hollow square.

'I can scarce credit it,' he said. 'What a reputation these Cossacks must have.'

'You would have charged just the same in India, I think,' suggested Fairbrother, his telescope out again.

'Perhaps it's easier to execute than to watch,' said Hervey drily, scarcely able to credit, too, that his sabre was yet undrawn. And what silent battle this was, with not a shot yet fired. 'Your first taste of action, Mr Agar, and quiet as the grave.'

'Sir.'

Hervey assumed the gun had canister loaded, waiting the moment – fifty yards. The Turks lowered their lances. Without artillery to make holes in the great steel-tipped hedge, the Cossacks would find it a deadly fence to take. What had induced the reserves to turn tail?

Fifty yards . . . forty . . . and still no fire. Hervey tried in vain to make out what the gunners did, his line of sight obscured.

But the Cossacks had no intention of taking the fence of steel. Just short of lance-contact they inclined left and right, tilting as they galloped the length of the line, taking advantage of their extra reach (the Turk lances three feet shorter) and the oblique attack. *Sipahis* fell here and there, but not a single Cossack.

'And thus they test their mettle, it seems,' said Hervey, not sure what to make of the Cossacks' aversion to charging home, or the Turks' to counter-charging.

Round to the rear they galloped, deftly picking off any *sipahi* who stood a foot proud of the man to left or right. 'Tent-pegging,' muttered Hervey to himself; 'pure sport.'

But the game suddenly changed.

Fairbrother saw it first. 'My God – look yonder!'

The crest was now topped by a line of red, as if a curtain had gone up – two hundred *sipahis*, perhaps more.

'They don't see them!' gasped Hervey.

The tent-pegging continued.

'No – they *do*. They're breaking off. But they'll never get away in time. Damned impetuous Cossacks! Come on!'

He put his mare into a gallop.

Fairbrother dug in his spurs after him. 'What in God's name are you doing? This ain't your fight. Let 'em break off and run for it!'

But he would not. Hervey galloped for another hundred yards, pulled up hard by a dry stream bed a furlong in front of the skirmish, and looped his reins. He had not once looked behind to see who was with him; theirs was to be there. 'Unship carbines and make ready!'

They did as they were told – seven men in extended line.

Fairbrother closed to his side and spoke quietly. 'It's not our affair, Hervey. Don't hazard all in an unworthy scrap.'

'If we stand by and the Cossacks are worsted, we'll never be received by a single Russian again.'

Fairbrother said nothing. He would himself have taken that risk, but he did not have his friend's obligations. For now, he was prepared to take a spear in the chest, but only because his friend was prepared to. He smiled at the contrariness of his own logic, and at what meagre price (to those who did not understand) he held his life.

They loaded afresh, having drawn the charges after stand-down. Corporal Acton's hands were as nimble as a card-sharp's, tamping the wadding before the other two dragoons had yet dropped in the ball. 'Bite harder when you reload,' he told them, sharp but encouragingly. 'And don't fret about spilling at the pan. It's always a business loading astride: the best of 'orses never stand stock still.'

Even Johnson, sweat that he was, found Acton's words welcome. As a rule he disliked NCOs, but it was strange how when there was trouble . . .

'Volley or aimed shots?' asked Fairbrother archly, seating the butt of his carbine on his off-foreleg.

Hervey took no notice, clipping back the swivel ramrod while trying hard to fathom what they could do to help.

Down the slope at a slow trot came the line of red, lances up.

Why not just charge? he wondered.

'Do they suspect a trap, sir?' asked Agar. Even to his novice eye the Turk advance looked feeble.

'Perhaps they've felt a Cossack lance too often. That or they're wary of what might be concealed behind *our* hill. But rarely have I seen such passivity.'

But the Cossacks too were leisured, peeling away from the fight as if it were a *gen-khana*.

He shook his head. 'It won't serve.'

But his dismay grew as he saw the *esaul* slip from the melee, like Reynard from the back of covert, and trot unheeded towards the cannon which the gunners had abandoned.

'Great Gods, do you see, Fairbrother?'

'I do. His folly knows no bounds.'

The *esaul*, with two others now, cast lassos around the barrel to begin hauling it away.

'Madness!' gasped Hervey. 'What the deuce does he mean?'

'Booty: it's in the blood!' sighed Fairbrother.

'And blood's what they'll pay for it if those fellows charge.'

Yet still the mass of Turks was all confusion, and the line of red seemed content to let its steady advance drive off the Cossacks without clash of steel. None looked to save the cannon.

But to Hervey it was plain as day: the line of red, unchecked, would overtake the *esaul* and his lassoers. Couldn't they see that – *any* of them? He could only marvel at the Cossacks' sang froid – and despair equally of the *sipahis'* lifelessness. This was not war.

And then abruptly, as if they woke from torpor, the flanks of the red line quickened pace, wheeling inwards in an envelopment that would catch the *esaul* and half the *sotnia* if they didn't gallop clear at once.

'Leave the damned gun and retire!' spat Hervey. 'What in the name of God . . .'

But there was nothing he could do except rage: if the rest of the Turks recovered and advanced too, the whole *sotnia* would be overwhelmed.

Still the *esaul* made slow way with the cannon (if only he had lassoed the trail instead of the barrel . . .).

'Martyrs to their own folly, Hervey, but we can't sit idly by,' said Fairbrother, fretfully (and only too aware of his change of tune).

'Yes, but I can't see what—'

In the strangely quiet battle of the *arme blanche* – for not even a pistol had been fired – the cannon's sudden discharge came as a monstrous thunderclap.

Hervey drove in his spurs instinctively. The others followed hard on his heels for the cannon. He jumped from the saddle. One Cossack lay dead, a bloody pulp; another writhed moaning, his knee smashed. The *esaul* staggered blindly, blood streaming down his face. His horse was dead; the others had bolted. Johnson reined his mount to a halt beside Hervey. Fairbrother jumped down to help get the *esaul* across Johnson's saddle. Acton and the two dragoons covered them, Johnson holding the horses, leaving Agar alone to try to rescue the other Cossack. But he hadn't the strength with one arm while holding the reins with the other. He leapt down. Acton saw and turned, leaning far out of the saddle to get a hand under the man's shoulder. They just managed to haul him atop Agar's prancing mare, and then Acton pulled Agar himself up.

'Kick on back, sir. Fast!'

Hervey and Fairbrother were back astride, the *esaul* across the pommel of Johnson's saddle, turning to get him away.

Acton swung round to see *sipahis* coming at them from every angle – and Cossacks.

'You two,' he roared to the dragoons: 'to your front, ready, *fire!*'

A volley of three: 'farting against thunder', he rasped. He could scarce believe they did it.

At fifty yards it was a wonder even one ball struck, let alone all three. But strike they did, and toppled three Turks.

There was a collective groan from the rest, as if at the parting of a great spirit: one of the three was the *miralay*, the commander.

'Reload!' barked Acton.

The Cossacks had rallied and formed a lance shield. But Hervey knew it wouldn't be enough. He drew his sabre and spurred to the middle of the line, waving it left and right – the signal to extend. He checked only for an instant, just enough to see they were with him, then plunged towards the wall of *sipahis*.

Down came the Turk lances – the instinct to protect – but the charge was unnerving. The Turks bumped to a halt and the Cossacks fell on them with all the advantage of momentum.

Hervey lofted his sabre and brought it down in a slicing blow to the nearest lance – Cut Two – striking it aside and driving the point into the *sipahi's* chest (the lance was a fearsome thing, but useless in a melee). Stirrup clashed with stirrup as he forged past, recovering his sabre in time for a second – Cut One – at the bridle arm of the *sipahi* to his left.

Acton, exactly placed as if at a field day, followed him through at two lengths and finished the Turk with the point.

Hervey, clear through the line, glanced back. *Sipahis* were reining round desperately to escape – and on either flank disordered ranks of red stood mesmerized.

Fairbrother all but grabbed his reins. 'Hervey! Enough! See the breach there' (a gap in the middle of the Turk line): 'Let's get through and back before they rally!'

There was nothing ordered or martial about their flight. All Hervey knew was that his own men were ahead as he galloped clear, and that he would drive his little Kabardin until she dropped. They rallied – stumbled exhausted – at the top of the rise whence they'd first seen the Turks (he could see none now), and the Cossacks were cheering – cheering *him*.

X

REDOUBTS

Siseboli, 8 April (three days later)

Hervey turned up his collar. Smuts from the smokestack flecked his cheeks as the tender ploughed through the swell back to harbour. He had passed a good hour aboard the hospital ship with the *esaul*, whose face had not once betrayed the pain of wounds from which, Hervey knew, laudanum gave but partial relief. Such pride, such spirit – he was all admiration, if still doubtful of the soldierly judge-ment which had occasioned the wounds. But the *esaul* had said he wanted to test the Turk's mettle, and so he had – to extreme, per-haps to excess (who could say?). The Turk cavalry had been inactive in the face of every inducement, and that was intelligence worth having. Even as the little band of Cossacks had fallen back on Siseboli, no *sipahi* had chanced within carbine range.

Hervey had estimated their number in all to be fifteen hundred; it was a mystery why they had not used their advantage. But as for infantry, he had seen none. Had the *esaul* not been so anxious to be at the *sipahis'* throats, he might have been able to observe the marching regiments at a distance from a flank; but after the debacle, the Turk cavalry had pulled themselves together, extended

146

their front and thrown out flankers, so that it had been a vain hope to get round them.

He shrugged; there was no use comparing Cossacks with a squadron of English light dragoons. In any case, they had achieved the object of the patrol, to discover if the Turks were coming – and had given General Wachten twenty-four hours' warning of the approach of the investing force. They might have learned even more, but with their captain *hors de combat* and surprise lost, there was little more Hervey could have done. He had taken command, by general acclamation, and had tried to handle them as if they had been a squadron of the Sixth . . . At least he had brought them all back without harm.

And how they had all cheered him for it when they rode in through the gates of Siseboli. He had thanked them and told them what a privilege it was to lead them, but that it had been his duty to his own party alone that had compelled him to act, for his status was that of a neutral. Between Cornet Agar and the *sotnik* the meaning of that qualification had probably been lost, however; the *sotnia* cheered him even more.

It was a strange sight before him now – a town under siege, observed from water. Howitzer and mortar shells arched high before plunging to their mark, and it was as if he watched a display of fireworks, for their effect on the ground was hidden from him. 'Mark', anyway, was scarcely apt, for the Turk gunners aimed blind, with no sight of the fall of shot – nuisance stuff, meant to demoralize. It was the big siege guns, the 24-pounders, which *aimed* for their mark – the walls of a fortress – and saw the result. Yet, although the Turks had begun the investment the evening before, they had yet to bring up their siege train. When they did, they would find the town a tougher nut to crack than perhaps they supposed, for the Russians had been daily strengthening the defences. Hervey wondered if he would still be here when the guns came up, for the time was surely close when General Diebitsch's great offensive on the Danube would begin, and it was this above all that he wanted to see.

Not that he had done other than help himself in that ambition by his conduct with the Cossacks. General Wachten now treated him as one of his own officers. Indeed, he had asked him to continue in command of the *sotnia* (though cavalry in a siege were little use except in the sally), which Hervey had been able to decline without too great an affront. For before transferring to the Danube, he explained, he wanted to see the infantry at their work (at this Fairbrother had ribbed him that it was in anticipation of defending the Rock of Gibraltar), and he had begged a *laissez-passer* for the defence-works.

As the tender came up to the quay he leapt out purposefully. There was just time, before visiting the outworks again, to hear the day's intelligence. He had to all intents and purposes now a *laissez-passer* for the headquarters too.

Here, Wachten received him as before, but, observing the prize at his belt, he did so with even greater assurance. 'So now you wear the insignia of the Cossack!'

Hervey glanced at the *sashka*, the guardless sabre which the Cossacks alone carried. 'The *esaul* gave it to me. You have no objection? I think it handsome, though in truth I would think it more use on foot than in the saddle.'

Wachten smiled. 'Colonel Hervey, I should be glad if you put on the *cherkesska* too. Be that as it may, the Cossacks brought in another prisoner this morning, and if he's to be believed, there are now five thousand laying siege to our fortress. I consider it an additional feat to have drawn the Seraskier and so many of the Turk's best troops on to my own, and yet not excess of them.'

'Did you not suppose they would come in that strength, General?' asked Hervey.

'In several times that strength, or not at all. My orders were not to hazard a defeat if the numbers were overwhelming, and to withdraw whence we'd come. But these odds are not overwhelming – merely formidable.'

Formidable though not overwhelming – it would have been the conclusion of any who had attended sieges in the Peninsula, except that Siseboli was not Badajoz: the defences were earthworks, and the walls of the town were those that the Greeks had first built – well-made, but hardly bastions. 'Did the Turk prisoner say anything of guns, General?'

'He said, apparently, that he has seen none – no siege guns, that is. But by all accounts Hussein Pasha commands in person, and so I conclude that he does not intend merely investing the garrison and waiting for us to sail away. There'll be siege guns coming up, all right; and in their wake an assault.'

'What is your assessment of our situation therefore?'

'It is on this point I would engage your assistance, Colonel Hervey. I am already greatly in your debt, and I appreciate your orders forbid you to take up arms, but I'd deem it the greatest favour if you were to make an inspection of the defences and report your findings to me. My officers will make their dispositions according to the regulations – of that I am confident – but your eyes are not so regulated, and it may be that you observe some weakness that the enemy, being also not drilled in our regulations, sees also.'

Hervey hesitated. He might be able to persuade Lord Hill that his actions in the reconnaissance had been dictated by necessity, but what Wachten asked was for calculated assistance.

'General, my mission requires that I observe what I can of your methods of war,' he said slowly. 'It would be greatly to the advantage of my mission, therefore, if I were to inspect the defences, and it is only gentlemanlike that I tell you what I write to the commander-in-chief.'

Wachten smiled. It was a bold as well as subtle line of reasoning. 'Colonel Hervey, your conduct as a gentleman has never been in doubt.'

Whoever had chosen Siseboli for the *coup de main* had chosen well. Bourgas, with its stronger garrison, would have been a harder place to capture in the first instance, and although it offered a better anchorage, it was closer to the Balkan forts and would almost certainly have brought swifter and stronger retribution (though why the Seraskier had delayed for so long before marching on Siseboli was everyone's question). Siseboli also had the advantage of being on a promontory, a peninsula, which could be covered by the fire of Russian warships from either side. Even were the Turks to overcome the defensive outworks to the landward end, the isthmus was too narrow a defile for them to exploit their strength. Unless Turk warships could drive off those of the Russians, the town itself ought to be able to withstand attack. Cornet Agar began speaking of Spartans and Thermopylae as, half an hour later in their billet, Hervey readied himself for his survey of the defence-works.

The isthmus was two furlongs at most in length, and one and a half wide – rocky ground, short, scrubby grass. When he had first seen it, he had been surprised that with so many orchards, market gardens and shanties at its landward end there had been no encroachment. Guarding the approaches to the isthmus, at a distance of seven hundred yards (easy cannon range) from the walls of the town itself, were two redoubts which Wachten's engineers had built. Covering these, as well as the isthmus, were two gunboats moored either side of the peninsula. It was an admirable disposition, he reckoned; by night or in fog the Turks *might* be able to slip past the redoubts, and even across the isthmus, but it would take prodigious skill (the like of which he had not so far witnessed). And as soon as the alarm were raised the gunboats could fire blind and the isthmus would be barely tenable. Even if a sufficient number of Turks were able to cross, they would have to force the gates or storm the walls – almost certainly without artillery, which they could scarce bring up under fire from the gunboats – and even if they succeeded in *that*, the buildings within the walls were solid affairs and would make formidable strongpoints. Fire would be a danger, of course; though the lower floors were stone-built, the houses were half-timbered; but setting the town alight would be perilous for the Turks, too. Except that, Hervey supposed, they might have no compunction in razing Siseboli if it fired out the invader.

But what if the Seraskier did not intend attacking, only laying siege? He would know, probably, that the Russians were not landed in strength enough to drive his force off. Would it matter if they were penned in here? But the Russians' purpose in taking Siseboli was to use it as the point of entry for supplies once General Diebitsch had marched south through the Balkan; the Turks could scarcely maintain a siege with a Russian army approaching from the rear. Since the garrison could always be reinforced by sea, the fate of Siseboli lay therefore in action to the north, in the Balkan. Hervey recognized that meanwhile, all that Wachten had to do was avoid defeat rather than take the offensive. Fairbrother might have been sporting with him when he compared Siseboli with Gibraltar, but Hervey was of a mind that the two had indeed much in common.

'Sir?'

He had been too deep in thought, even while readying himself. 'Yes?'

'I have finished the Pliny and Herodotus,' said Agar, as one who was not about to impart good news.

'And?'

'Herodotus has nothing to reveal, as I expected. He frequently conflates myth and truth. Pliny's more agreeable to read, but not instructive. Indeed, I was at times uncertain which Apollonia he was writing of; there are so many places of that name between Sicily and Palestine.'

Hervey checked his stride as he made for the door: 'Mr Agar, I am content to take your scholarship as read, else I should not have troubled the general with expectations. Pray tell me what you have learned, or nothing at all.'

Agar looked rather abashed; he was all too aware he could sometimes detach himself from the here and now. 'He speaks of bitumen in the water hereabout, that it is injurious to horses.'

Hervey nodded. 'But that much we may suppose the people of the town know after so many years drinking it. I shall inform the general nevertheless.' He smiled. 'It will show him that we have not been idle. Thank you, Agar.' In truth, he supposed that Wachten had only given him the books as a test of his resource rather than in serious expectation of discovering anything of use.

Agar was warmed by the thanks, nevertheless. He had received high praise for the rescue of the fallen Cossack and did not wish to lose the smallest part of his future commanding officer's esteem.

The sudden *whoosh* of a mortar bomb overhead and then the crash of tiles in the street behind recalled them both to the present. There was no explosion, though. Was it solid shot, or a fuse not ignited on firing? Deuced tricky things, fuses; like the Turkish cannon – the slightest fanning of an all-but dead ember, and . . . 'A mistake, of course, to allow the enemy's mortars to come up so close,' said Hervey, lengthening step.

'*Enemy* mortars, Hervey?' said Fairbrother.

'I was speaking from the point of view of the Russians, no more.'

'I'm glad to hear it. We might otherwise feel obliged to do something to *distance* the mortars.'

Hervey smiled, knowingly. 'I might yet be persuaded – for our own safety.'

There was a huge explosion from the direction of the gates.

He checked for an instant, feeling instinctively for the pistol at his belt, though he knew what must be the cause (he'd heard powder kegs go heavenwards in his time). 'Pray it's not brought down the walls,' he said grimly as they began doubling.

It had not, but it had brought down every horse of the ammunition train, and a good many men. As they came round the corner they saw the gate garrison (a company of the Pavlovsk) already tending the wounded.

But not the horses. 'Pall Mall drill,' he called, running to the wreckage.

Fairbrother cursed; Agar retched. It was one thing to draw blood with sabre or pistol in the heat of battle, and another to come cold upon a slaughterhouse.

The explosion, like all explosions, had worked its own peculiar destruction. The superstructure of the leading caisson-waggon had been blown high and scattered wide, doing little damage, except that the driver, headless but still holding the reins, lay between his team, which had crumpled as if felled by a poleaxe, bloodless save for a trickle at the nose. The four horses of the caisson following were down also, but thrown apart so that they lay on their side as if sleeping. The driver had been hurled backwards from his seat and lay gorily impaled on the tarpaulin spike, while the serjeant in command of the train had been blown from the saddle with such force that his uniform was stripped from his back. He lay by the gatehouse, unrecognizable but for the remains of a sleeve with its broad white chevrons of rank, his horse lying grunting nearby – butchered meat like its rider. The corporal lay dead but unmarked beside his horse at the rear of the second caisson.

To the flank of the lead waggon was the worst destruction: every man of the two-dozen escort had been cut down by shards from the copper hoops of the powder barrels, as if they had marched into a discharge of grape. Those not dead or close to death sat with expressions of bewilderment. Chaplains were already making the sign of the cross.

Hervey went first to the leading waggon team. All were dead, though he could not believe it at first since they lay with their legs under them as in a close stall. He doubled back to the second team. Three were dead but a wheeler was breathing, though ill, like broken bellows. He ran a hand along the near foreleg: the cannon-bone was shattered. 'Mr Agar, your pistol to this animal, please.' It would have been the work of seconds for him to use his own, but some good might at least be had from the business (it was well that Agar practised his drill now rather than for the first time in front of the enemy). He nodded to Corporal Acton to keep an eye on him.

Next he found the corporal's horse a case for the veterinary surgeon, not the pistol – no bones of the legs broken, although there were splinters in the near shoulder. 'Let's get him up.'

A pistol shot told him that Agar had done his duty (cleanly, was all he could hope).

Fairbrother took the reins, slipped them over the gelding's head and coaxed him up with clicking noises and soft words, while his friend ran a hand along the backbone to feel for displacement. There were men dead and dying yards away; Hervey was not immune to their cries, but it did not absolve him of dominion over the horse. For lead was too free a medicine on the battlefield – he himself had dosed it too often – and if one steadfast creature could be saved with a little attention, then the effort was worth it.

The other two had rejoined.

'Take him, if you will, Corporal Acton. Mr Agar, do you suppose you can communicate with yonder officer?' (indicating one of the staff near the gates). 'Find the veterinarian.'

'Sir.'

He looked about and saw there was no more to be done. 'Captain Fairbrother and I shall carry on to "B" Redoubt. Come after us when you've seen to things.'

'Sir.'

Hervey was becoming accustomed to Agar's usefulness: for all his inhabitation of the ancient world, he was by no means unpractical. If he himself were to have command of the Sixth, even – perhaps especially – if it were reduced to squadron strength, he would want him with him.

They quit the bloody work of the explosion, and left the partial shelter of the walls for the gabion bailey, to survey the isthmus before crossing to the defence-works.

Fairbrother looked troubled. 'How do you suppose it happened?' he asked, as if there might be some mystery attached. 'The explosion – evidently not a shell that struck.'

Hervey shrugged. 'Powder's a deuced hazardous thing.'

'Quite. So why do they wait until the town's invested before taking it to the trenches?'

But Hervey was not inclined to see anything untoward. 'Well, I don't claim knowledge of how the Ordnance works – in any army, let alone the Tsar's – but in my experience waggons are always scuttling about. Like ants. Perhaps it's the best way of making sure the powder keeps dry.'

'I confess I'd never seen a caisson, strange as it may sound. I think of powder in cartridges. I suppose I've never been obliged to think of it otherwise.'

'There's no knowing that it wasn't a fragment of mortar, glowing red still. Deuced ill luck, that's all.'

Fairbrother could only admire his friend's phlegm. His own fighting had been in what the French called 'la petite guerre'. Of organization and method when it came to large armies in the field

155

he was wholly ignorant save from his reading – which did not extend to supply. That, indeed, was one of the attractions of this singular mission – to see what the old Peninsular hands had seen – for a start, this exchange of artillery (although his friend said it was nothing yet). The Turk field pieces had been keeping up (to his mind) a brisk fire against the redoubts since this morning, and the Russian guns, brought ashore from one of the warships and manned by bluejackets, had been answering with equal vigour. He had watched it from atop the walls while Hervey was seeing the *esaul*. The earth would tremble when the siege guns came up, they all said, but the distant roar of a 6-pounder and the fountains of earth thrown up were infernal enough. He was not afraid to admit that it made him tremble.

But the mortars' haphazard destruction was behind them in the town, and the field artillery too far away to trouble them; between the walls and the redoubts, the isthmus was empty haven. And Hervey now studied it from beside a wicker gabion which, he observed, had been woven with the skill of the seamstress.

Wachten had chosen neither to occupy the isthmus nor to construct any obstacle to movement across it, for it was here that he intended forming up his reserve to counter-attack if the redoubts fell. And since the Turks would face a murderous fire from the gun-boats if they themselves tried to cross, it made no sense to offer them shelter by throwing up earthworks. Hervey understood precisely. What Wachten had asked him, however, was to look with an 'unregulated' eye; and it was only from the approaches, the vantage of the attacker, that he could do so. He put away his telescope and looked at his friend. 'Let us take a walk,' he said, cheerily.

To Fairbrother it felt like stepping from the wings onto a stage – and a very empty one at that – as they slipped from the bailey. And it seemed the strangest thing to be walking alone between two points of danger and yet quite safe from molestation by the enemy (or rather, the Turk). On the other hand, his friend appeared wholly unaware of anything exceptional, and he wondered, as he had done more than once, if it were the quality of every true soldier (as opposed to those like himself whom he thought dilettante) that in the face of the enemy he was not conscious of his own presence. For it seemed to him that Hervey possessed the most remarkable facility in this regard; and yet he knew him to be a not-unthinking man. On the contrary, his friend was capable of (to his mind) ruinous contemplation. Not that he counted himself as possessing excessive caution, only that in Colonel Matthew Hervey caution appeared to be but a consideration rather than an instinct.

Such as now, as they tramped across this empty space, and all he could speak of was his surprise at the ease with which they had quit the walls and the bailey: not a sentry had required them even to halt, let alone show their *laissez-passers*. And he, Fairbrother, had replied that he supposed it was taken for granted that anyone passing out of the town was friend not foe, and that this did not seem unreasonable – especially since neither of them looked Turk. Yet Hervey had countered by saying that that was how many a ruse had worked. 'Perhaps you are recognized as a Cossack, then,' he had tried, and only half-ironically

The sun was due west, or he was sure he would have seen him earlier – a galloper speeding towards them from the redoubts. He shielded his eyes for a better view, but Hervey remained oblivious to the intruder on the empty boards, more absorbed in crouching to discover the extent of what he called 'dead ground' (Fairbrother supposed that a galloper must have been an everyday of the Peninsula).

At a hundred yards he could make him out clearer. 'An uhlan, Hervey.'

The only uhlans were the general's aides-de-camp.

He galloped past with a touch to the peak of his *czapka*.

'A pretty sight. The best uniform I ever saw on a post-boy,' tried Fairbrother, hoping it might bring his friend back to the present.

Hervey frowned. 'Don't decry gallopers; a general can't be everywhere himself. But he *was* rather splendidly arrayed. How many cavalry d'ye suppose could cross the isthmus at a gallop while being enfiladed by the gunboats?'

Once again Fairbrother could only wonder at his friend's unswerving application. He was minded of the precepts of Marcus Aurelius, of whose wisdom he had long made a study: *A man's true delight consists in doing what he was made for.* 'With you at their head?' he asked, archly.

Getting into the trenches at the postern in the earthwork curtain of the south-west (B) redoubt was considerably more difficult than getting out of the bailey. Indeed, for all that they were but a few furlongs from the walls of the town, they might have been in a different world. Here was all alertness and edge. The *laissez-passers* meant nothing to the musketeer of the Azov Regiment who stood sentry at the postern (for he could not read), nor even to the corporal; and the lieutenant was uncertain (and anxious). Only the captain would admit them.

'*Qu'est-ce qui se passe? Que font les Turcs?*' (the cannonade was increasing).

Hervey put the questions so abruptly that Fairbrother expected some coolness in reply, but the captain merely smiled. He had fought as an ensign at Borodino, he explained, and lately against the Persians, and in the years between he had battled with the tribes of the marches; he did not think very highly of Turks. 'They make a great deal of noise, Colonel; that is all.'

An old soldier – an *efreytor* (lance-corporal) – was boiling potatoes in a corner of the trench. He had perhaps seen even more service than the captain, and was watching the exchange – in a tongue he could hardly have recognized, let alone understood – merely as a diversion from routine. Fairbrother thought he looked curiously indifferent to any fate. It was not unlike being back with the Royal Africans.

Yet Hervey was clearly exhilarated by the experience. And when he had finished interrogating the captain he explained why: it was the first time he had been in the trenches with infantry under cannonade. Yes, he had gone forward at Badajoz, and he had joined the assault at Bhurtpore, but those were siege-works, temporary means to an end. Here, on the other hand, the infantryman had chosen his ground and intended holding it. Here the earth beneath his feet and above his head was bosom friend, whereas to Hervey as a rule it was a mere acquaintance, to be avoided by adhesion to the saddle. And the sweat of men rather than horses – it was, indeed, exhilarating.

A roundshot ricocheted from the glacis, arched over the blue-jackets in the battery and crashed into the postern gabions not a dozen paces from where they stood. Fairbrother stared at the hissing ball half-buried in the sand. What if it were fused?

The captain said the Turks had fired nothing but solid shot so far. 'We presume they intend to pound first before frightening us with shell,' he added, and then with a wry smile, 'But we shall not know for certain until it does not explode.'

Fairbrother frowned. 'I confess I should not be content to sit and let them pound, nor even just to answer with artillery,' he replied in French as impeccable as Hervey's.

'Ah, but we do not,' said the captain. 'The *strelki* are even at this moment making ready to attack.'

Hervey quickened. 'Then we must see them.'

Fairbrother was wary. He had no objection to watching an attack by skirmishers, only to his friend's propensity for action rather than observation.

But the captain looked gratified. 'By all means, Colonel.'

The redoubt proper, in which sat the battery, was a natural, elongated mound the size of a frigate, fortified by gabions and stonework, the embrasures revetted with logs, but the surrounding trenches were dug only three feet down, with breastworks of four feet built up from trench spoil and that from the dry moat which encircled the whole redoubt. Besides the gunners, there were, said the captain, two and a half companies in the trenches – three hundred men – who would be relieved before last light by the battalion's reserve companies from the town. Five hundred yards to the east was the slightly smaller 'A' Redoubt, guarding the approaches from the south and south-west and able to support 'B', just as 'B' could support 'A'.

The trenches were wide by the usual standards, and progress was easy. Nearer the far side, closest the Turks, they were narrower, and tighter packed with *strelki*, who pressed their backs up against the side of the trench to let them pass, silently knuckling their foreheads, economical salutes.

'Our best men, Colonel,' explained the captain as they picked their way forward. 'From the grenadier battalion.'

Fairbrother had read somewhere that Russians were not good at skirmishing, seeing no point to it when there was a mass of bayonets at hand and an unquestioning willingness to advance. But he had heard much, too, of the new Tsar's reforms; he supposed that skirmishing must be one of them.

In an angle of the trench forming a salient they found the commanding officer, Vedeniapine, a tall, athletic-looking man about forty, in forage hat and *kolet* (the short tunic), chatting easily with his men and carrying the same rifle. They had met before, at Wachten's headquarters. Fairbrother was intrigued by his manner of greeting them – an undeniable satisfaction in receiving visitors of distinction, and at the same time an air of confidence which suggested that the honour was his visitors' as much as his own.

'Colonel Hervey, Captain Fairbrother, we are honoured that you visit,' he said in effortless French, albeit punctuated by cannon fire. 'But I fear we are about to take our leave. The Turk is being impertinent, and we mean to chastise him. You may watch from here; you should have a fine view.'

'You are going yourself, Colonel?' asked Hervey.

'Certainly.'

'Then I should be privileged to accompany you.'

Fairbrother groaned, but to himself. As a rule he did not concern himself in the slightest with what others thought (indeed, it often seemed that he took perverse pride in it), but he was conscious that he acted for his friend, and had no wish to do or say anything which impaired his mission. And yet he could not for the life of him see how clambering out of this trench to 'pepperpot' (as the Cape Riflemen called it) in front of the Turks would be of service to the Horse Guards.

'A word, if you please, Colonel,' he tried, hoping the Azov's commanding officer had no English.

Taking Hervey aside, he made his objections sound as matter-of-fact as possible so as not to betray any dissent within hearing of their host, but to no avail; his friend was clearly intent on playing the infantryman (doubtless in some effort to conclude what should be the colour of his jacket in future), and so he too must revert to his old colours.

When it was done, Hervey turned back to the Azov's colonel and asked what exactly was his design. Vedeniapine replied that his design was straightforward: they would '*faire une démonstration*' – make the Turks believe they were about to be attacked by a larger force, obliging them to withdraw their guns.

Fairbrother kept his counsel, though he had every suspicion that this manly colonel would not be content until he had captured at least one eagle – or whatever it was these heathen Turks paraded about with. He and Hervey would get on famously. Then he chided himself for thinking thus, for he knew that Hervey was wholly without vainglory. Nor, too, ought he to suppose that the Azov's colonel was made of any less stern stuff; it was just that he feared his friend was no longer thinking quite as acutely as was his custom.

'*Eh bien; à cheval!*' Vedeniapine nodded to the captain along the trench who would command the *strelki*.

The captain saluted, signalled left and right with his hand, and sprang from the banquette onto the parapet like a gymnast.

Riflemen scrambled over the top eagerly, extending into skirmishing order without a word from an NCO, kneeling while the line formed, dressing in silence; and then on a single note of the whistle stood up and advanced with rifles at the trail. The apostles at Shorncliffe could not have found fault, said Fairbrother as they watched from the banquette, but with a note of 'however . . .' that made Hervey frown back at him.

Undaunted, Fairbrother suggested the watching Turks, six or seven hundred yards distant, could not but be impressed too. 'How long do you suppose it will take them to begin loading canister instead of shot?'

Hervey shrugged. 'If the Turks are still at their guns as we close to canister range we'll simply have to withdraw in good order, as now.'

Fairbrother sighed and resolved to say no more. It was time to become a skirmisher.

'*Allons*,' said Vedeniapine, determined to be the same, and with a hand from an orderly, as if mounting a horse, climbed onto the parapet.

Hervey likewise took Fairbrother's hand, and in turn pulled him up.

The sixty riflemen presented a front of a hundred and fifty yards, with the captain and half a dozen junior officers and serjeants to the rear to direct them. Hervey and Fairbrother were hastening to take post either side of the colonel when Agar and Corporal Acton rejoined them.

'Colonel Hervey, sir,' (Agar saluting) 'the veterinary surgeon is sick. A farrier does duty in his place. Leave to fall in, sir, please.'

Fairbrother was amused by the sudden formality – 'leave to fall in, sir'. He supposed it must be some infantry contagion.

Hervey made the introductions (quite the strangest circumstances for presentation that Fairbrother could recall).

Colonel Vedeniapine bowed to both men (a courtesy that did not go unnoticed) before resuming his watch on the *strelki*.

'What do they do?' asked Agar as he fell in beside Fairbrother.

'The general idea seems to be that they make a demonstration against the Turk batteries and force them to withdraw.'

'These men alone?'

To Fairbrother's mind, Agar's was a commendable tone of disbelief. 'The rest of the battalion will form line in front of the trenches so that there's the appearance of a general attack. I think they count on the Turk being laggardly,' he replied, sounding not wholly convinced.

The Russian battery opened up again, shot angrily tearing the air above them. Agar looked mildly startled.

Fairbrother shook his head. 'Don't trouble yourself. If you hear the shot it has passed.' That much, *petite guerriste* or not, he could say with assurance, having been shot over by the Cape artillery.

But Hervey came to his cornet's aid. 'It is, however, deuced queer to be advancing on the Turks with a pair of pistols and a sabre, and no horse.'

'You have your Deringer, I hope?' said Fairbrother with mock earnest.

'I have,' replied Hervey, unabashed.

Colonel Vedeniapine looked rear to signal the waiting battalion. Out from the trenches clambered three companies of muskets.

The *strelki* marched on, rifles still at the trail, dressing perfectly from the centre.

A minute passed silently, then another, and then another.

There was a flash and a roar. Six roundshot sped from the Turk battery. The first graze was a hundred yards ahead of the skirmish line, throwing up dust and stones. The rounds lofted ten feet (the ground like iron) and passed harmlessly over the line before their second impact two hundred yards behind. By the time they reached the battalion companies, bowling along the ground like balls in a skittle alley, they had lost pace and the men could sidestep them.

'They've time for one more of shot, I think, and then it'll have to be canister – or else limber up,' said Hervey, glancing back to watch for the Russian battery's reply.

'Or else the entire camp stands to arms,' suggested Fairbrother.

The problem was that the entire camp lay in dead ground: it could be observed neither from the redoubts nor from the walls of the town – nor even from the tops of the frigate west of the peninsula. There was a Cossack vidette on the shore, a furlong or so from the battery, but it had been held at a distance by the Turk pickets (Fairbrother had seen the position: there was so much scrub that any patrol was bound to get itself into trouble). The Turks might even now be forming up in column of attack. Had they been French or Prussian – or so his reading told him – they would have counter-attacked at once, and with more than mere artillery fire. So what did their caution – timidity – portend? Was it a sign, perhaps, that the Turks knew they could take their time here? Did they know something that Wachten did not? Had the offensive in the north faltered? Could they, so to speak, sit around the tree here at Siseboli and wait for the fruit to fall?

A whistle blast brought the *strelki* to a halt. As one man they knelt down and brought their rifles to the aim.

Fairbrother couldn't understand the order which followed, but at three hundred yards there could be no doubting the target.

'Fire!'

The line was at once shrouded in white smoke – a perfect volley. He tried to make out its effect, but the smoke hung stubbornly in the still air. At three hundred yards a bullet could be two feet wide of the mark, even with the rifle in good hands. And the Turk gunners were firing from behind gabions. It was all too possible that not a single round had struck home.

The *strelki* were back on their feet, reloaded and resuming the advance – in line, yet, not pairs, for there was no counter-fire.

Another minute, another whistle blast – another perfect volley. But even more smoke.

Fairbrother thought it strange not to cover more ground before a second volley – or perhaps the effect of the first had been prodigious?

They hastened through as the smoke of the second volley thinned and drifted.

'Damnation!' he said, quietly but insistently as they saw what had brought the rifles to the aim again.

'Very tricky,' agreed Hervey, stroking his chin with the air of a connoisseur appraising a work of art.

Fairbrother needed no schooling in *la grande guerre* to appreciate the danger. Two, possibly three squadrons of Turk cavalry were drawing up on the left flank of the battery. They placed the *strelki* on the proverbial horns of the dilemma: did they choose to stay in skirmishing order, less vulnerable to both musketry and artillery, or did they risk bunching in 'close order' to fend off the lancers?

He looked back towards the Azov's muskets. They were shouldering arms.

Hervey saw too. 'I trust they'll stand their ground.'

Fairbrother said nothing; he thought that rather too much had been left to trust already.

Seconds later they had their answer: the line of muskets advanced.

'Admirable initiative,' said Hervey.

'Do you know, sir, that there's no word in Russian for "initiative"?'

'Thank you, Mr Agar. Later, if you will.'

Fairbrother smiled. There seemed little else to do.

The Russian battery spoke – four rounds, in sequence rather than volley. And explosive shell instead of solid shot.

Two burst in the air, the other two – by Fairbrother's estimation – a little long. He saw several lancers tumble. If the gunners corrected well they'd draw much blood. 'What now, Hervey?'

The captain of the *strelki* turned to ask the same of Vedeniapine. The colonel raised his right arm and made a leisurely circling movement.

Three short whistle blasts. Half the line rose by alternate men and began doubling rear while the other half remained kneeling, rifle butts to the ground.

'Here they come, sir,' said Corporal Acton, first to detect the Turk movement. 'At the trot.'

The captain of *strelki* had seen them, too. Up went the rifles into the aim, and the line volleyed as one.

Three short whistle blasts again. The line rose without reloading and began doubling back to where the other half-company had formed.

Another volley as they cleared the line of fire tumbled several more Turks – at three hundred yards. Very passable shooting, reckoned Fairbrother.

But even if every round of the next volley found its mark it could scarcely be enough to halt the *sipahis*.

The captain knew it too. Rapid whistle blasts transformed the extended line into a daisy-chain of riflemen in tight bunches, four or five standing back to back, bayonets ('swords') fixed.

Colonel Vedeniapine beckoned Hervey and the others to the nearest. The riflemen greeted them with much saluting and grinning.

They drew sabres.

'Like a square at Waterloo?' suggested Fairbrother, wryly. It looked as if they would have a fight of it again.

Hervey would not rise to the fly. 'Smart work to be sure. Exactly from the book. They evidently have trust in the supports.'

The battalion companies were indeed still advancing.

'Have you space to parry, Corporal Acton?' he asked blithely, turning to his coverman.

'Sir, I 'aven't space to salute if the Sultan 'imself rides up, let alone parry.'

Hervey smiled. 'If the Sultan himself rides up then Mr Agar shall explain to him we are here to observe and not to fight.'

'Knew there was nought to worry about, sir,' replied Acton, happy enough to share the joke.

Fairbrother said nothing – though if ever he were minded to write a memoir of his association with his friend, this exchange would have its place.

The battalion companies, two hundred yards rear, halted and began throwing out flanks. Whatever else happened, it was plain to him that the Turk cavalry would not be able to shift these, covered by the battery in the redoubt. The *strelki* could therefore chance a dash to safety behind them.

'Couldn't they have advanced another hundred yards though?'

Hervey agreed with the sentiment, but as his friend must know, the evolutions of a line of infantrymen in close order were not to be compared with those of a troop of dragoons, he said. Even a troop could take an inordinate time at the beginning of the drill season.

And as if to prove his point, only now, with the Turks getting into a gallop, did the Azov's major give the order to the companies, 'Front rank, kneel!'

Hervey took one of the pistols from his belt and ported it defiantly. Fairbrother and the others followed.

The Turk line was already losing cohesion, however, confused by the *strelki*'s dispersion. By some instinct, the Turk horses, or perhaps their riders, made not for the huddled riflemen but the gaps in between, as if in a race to the more distant line, and the *strelki* merely obstacles on the way.

Riflemen fired exuberantly as *sipahis* galloped past, like guns with driven game. Men and horses tumbled. Those that galloped on did so with no attempt to close up or rally, so that what should have been a charge by a wall of lancers became instead an affair of dis-united spearmen. Whistles blew, and the daisy-chain lay prone.

And now the battalion companies proved their mettle – rolling musketry by platoons, an almost continuous show of flame and noise, and no little lead.

Losing all cohesion, the *sipahis* faltered, circled, turned and then spurred for home, barging back through the risen line of *strelki* with scarce an idea of the bullets now taking them in the flank once more. Here and there a bolder Turk took a rifleman on his lance, and one cluster was scattered by riderless horses that were too hemmed in to evade, but the daisy-chain held, turning check into rout by their fire, and the battery hastening them with shell.

But the Turks were not completely done. Their guns, the field of fire at last clear again, now answered – and this time with shell too.

They had the range at once: air-burst over the *strelki* line – a murdering hail of iron balls. A dozen men fell dead, and as many wounded.

'That should not have happened,' said Hervey, turning to look for the others in the melee of riflemen. 'Agar, you are hit?'

Agar stood dazed-looking, as if a prize-fighter had struck him. Blood covered his left shoulder.

Corporal Acton saw, and put an arm round his waist. 'Sit down, sir, please.'

Agar hardly needed the invitation, his legs giving way.

'Deep breaths, sir. Just keep taking deep breaths.' He took off Agar's crossbelt and unfastened his tunic to examine the wound. It looked savage, but the blood was oozing not spurting. 'No artery severed, sir.'

He took a lint dressing from his pocket and then a bandage to hold it in place – once round the chest and twice over the shoulder. Then he refastened the tunic, tight. And finally the crossbelt.

'I'll carry 'im rear, sir,' he said, helping Agar up and then crouching to take him over his shoulder. 'Wouldn't want to wait for another o' them charges.'

'Good man,' said Hervey, taking up Agar's sabre and pistols.

'They're rallying!' called Fairbrother, who had kept an eye on them throughout, not able to believe they could be quite as supine as in the affair of the Cossacks.

The whistle signalled retreat.

The Russian battery fired again, and moments later the Turk. Hervey felt shell-splinter nick his right ear. Fairbrother swore as a splinter struck his cartridge case and broke the fastening, so that his crossbelt fell apart. Another stung Acton's elbow. He swore too but he wouldn't quicken pace – not with a wounded cornet on his back.

'Here they come,' said Fairbrother.

'Double time, Corp' Acton!' barked Hervey, seeing they could just make it rear. 'Your life on it!'

XI

MAN OF LETTERS

Later

Hervey lay back in a wicker chair and closed his eyes, the exertions of the previous hours at last claiming their due. If they had been English cavalry, or French, he would not have lived to take his ease. He was certain of it. What had become of the wild Turk of legend? Three companies of muskets had driven the same number of cavalry from the field without even forming square. And the regiment, moral masters of the ground as much as by weight of fire, had been able to recover their dead and wounded.

But what had they gained for the price of half a company? Respite, certainly: the Turk guns had been silent since. Perhaps they had even thrown over a general attack; who knew? Colonel Vedeniapine was defiant. He had staked his claim on the ground before his regiment's redoubt, and seen off the first challenge. He had fought the Turk in 1810, and he had no higher opinion of them now than he had had then; he was sure they would not chance against the Azov again.

Acton had been stalwart. He'd spared neither wind nor muscle bringing Agar in; only the greatest pride had been able to keep him on his feet when they'd gained the line of muskets.

'That were a good surgeon, that Russian,' said Johnson as he put down a tray of glasses. ''E knew 'ow to use them pincers all right. 'E 'ad that piece o' shell out like lightning.' Johnson had observed the work of surgeons often enough to know good practice when he saw it.

'He was indeed,' said Hervey, his eyes still closed. 'They say he studied in Paris. Mr Agar is fortunate.'

''E'll be right as rain in a week.'

'I'm sure of it.'

'An 'e wants t'bit o' shell as a keepsake – to give 'is brother.'

'Mm. I met his brother just before we sailed. Not, I fancy, a collector of warlike relics.' Hervey did not suppose that George Agar-Ellis would hold him personally responsible for injury to his younger brother – and a fragment of shell was far removed from the condoling letter *post mortem* – but all the same he disliked mementoes of brushes with death. 'Is Captain Fairbrother returned yet?'

'No, sir.'

Fairbrother had gone to ask the Cossacks for the loan of horses the following morning, for Hervey wanted to see the videttes.

Johnson continued laying the table.

'I have come to a decision, Johnson, but I would know your opinion of it.'

'About what, sir?'

'I intend taking command of Lord Hill's regiment, the Fifty-third.'

Johnson had finished arranging the glass and china which the previous occupants of the billet had obligingly (or perhaps unwillingly) left. He picked up a fork and began polishing it. 'Them as is in Gibraltar?'

Hervey's eyes remained closed. 'Just so.'

'So all that wi' them Azovs pleased thee, then, sir? Cap'n Fairbrother said it were like being a skittle at a fair.'

'If it were, then the balls were singularly ill-aimed. The fact is, it would be an empty command at Hounslow, and I cannot be inactive – not when there is the prospect of activity elsewhere.'

'And you'd allus be able to go back t' regiment if they gets bigger.'

Hervey shook his head. 'No. It would not serve. The die would be cast.'

Johnson polished a little more. 'And Gibraltar's in Spain?'

'At the southern tip. Almost Africa. But ours, not Spanish.'

'Will Lady 'Ervey like that, sir?'

Hervey opened one eye to check the expression on Johnson's face (which was as before). '*Mrs* Hervey, confound it!' He sighed. 'No woman can be entirely content to leave her native shore, but I have every hope that Mrs Hervey will be content enough. See, can we return to the question?'

'Tha didn't ask me a question, sir.'

Hervey opened both eyes and sat up. 'Perhaps I didn't. My question is would you be content to come with me to Gibraltar?'

Johnson made a little 'ha!' of astonishment. 'What choice do I 'ave, sir? I'm thy groom, an' if tha goes to Gibraltar ah'll 'ave to come wi' thee.'

'Charmingly put, Johnson, but in point of fact I cannot compel you to change regiments. It is against the terms of your enlistment.'

'I didn't know I '*ad* any terms.'

'Not many, it's true,' replied Hervey, with a smile. 'But that's one of them, since you enlisted before "General Service".'

'Why can't I stay wi' t'regiment *and* come to Gibraltar?'

'It doesn't work like that.'

'I'd rather I didn't 'ave a say then.'

'Does that mean you are content?'

Johnson put down the fork. 'Ay, sir. Gibraltar sounds all right.'

'It would mean you would have to be corporal. It would not do for the commanding officer to be served by a private-man.'

Johnson screwed his face up. 'Just as long as ah'd not 'ave to do duties.'

'You would not. The RSM would not dare touch a hair of your head.'

'Right then.'

Hervey lay back and closed his eyes again. 'It will give me the greatest satisfaction to know that, when I write the letter.'

'An' Captain Fairbrother'll be coming?'

'He will.'

'An' Sar'nt-Major Armstrong?'

'That I can't say. Or anyone else, for that matter.'

'Well, as long as tha's 'appy, sir, everyone else'll be.'

'I saw it all, Colonel Hervey, from the sloop. A gallant affair by the Azov, if ultimately to no advantage.' General Wachten was just returned from the redoubts, and had bidden Hervey to the headquarters.

'Not without moral effect, however, I should say, General.'

'True. The Turk cavalry were lacking in all dash. I never witnessed anything so feeble. That must in no small part be on account of their rough handling by the Cossacks.'

The wild Turkish charge, the fear of centuries, seemed just that – a thing of the past. Hervey wondered if the whole army had become a slave to 'progress'. Why did the *sipahis* now carry the lance when from time immemorial the scimitar had been the natural extension of the Turk hand? Why had they let the foreign officers of instruction make them ride long instead of with the traditional shovel stirrup? The descendants of Saladin might well bump along the parade ground prettily enough, but they appeared to have lost all quickness in the saddle. Was it the belief of the Mansure that observing the outward forms and details of European practice was the magic charm that ensured victory? Hervey was quite decided in his opinion if the experience of the past days was a faithful guide.

'It is well that the Tsar has chosen to strike now,' continued Wachten, 'before the Sultan is able to make his army in our image – if such a thing is possible.' He drained his glass of wine, which a servant at once replenished (and then Hervey's), and unbuttoned his collar. 'Your cornet is receiving all the assistance and comforts we can afford him, I am assured. I rely on you, Colonel, to tell me personally if there is any deficiency.'

'You may rely on it, thank you, General; but the sisters have him excessively well disposed. Admirable women.' Hervey took a sip of his claret, as if to indicate that he intended changing the subject. 'You asked for my opinion of the defences, General. I have but two observations.'

'Proceed.'

Hervey put down his glass and took out a notebook, though he had no need to consult it. 'Both gunboats are well placed to sweep the approaches to the walls of the town, but neither of them could support the redoubts this afternoon, as I understood they were meant to be able to do.'

Wachten held up a hand. 'I saw for myself. I have given orders for a second sloop to be moored to the east, broadside to them. It will take but a day or so.'

Hervey nodded. 'My other is, I think, only fully observable from those very approaches – which occurred to me as we were making our way back to the redoubt this afternoon. If the western – 'B' – redoubt were under assault, it would be possible to assail the Turk in the flank from landwards with such surprise as I think might have decisive result. Nor need the attack be in great strength – the *strelki*'s effect was out of all proportion to their number. They could be embarked at the old battery here in the town and hauled by steam round the promontory without discovery and disembark south of the eastern redoubt. I think, from what I have observed so far, the sudden fire from so unexpected a quarter could only shock the Turk greatly, and at very little peril to the attacker since he would have the redoubt on which to fall back if events went ill for him.'

A smile crept across Wachten's face. 'A capital idea, Colonel Hervey – and one that has the merit of not requiring me to weaken the town's defences at the outset. I shall instruct the colonels of the Pavlovsk and the Azov to make the arrangements forthwith. I chide myself at not having seen the possibility before.'

Hervey raised a hand. 'With respect, General, when the enemy is at your heels, as he was today, possibilities suggest themselves!'

Wachten laughed. 'You will dine with me, Colonel?'

Hervey shook his head. 'The general is very kind, but if he will excuse me, I had intended dining with my captain so that we may speak of arrangements for the morning – and seeing my cornet again.'

'Then you shall join me tomorrow night, and your captain. Colonel Vedeniapine will join us too. We shall make merry.'

'I am honoured. I have a request meanwhile, General. I have letters for London, and I understand a frigate leaves for Kherson in the morning.'

Wachten nodded. 'By all means. The letters may go with the Ordnance courier for St Petersburg.'

At their billet, Johnson was just beginning to grow anxious. He had acquired a goose, and roasted it a good while, with onions and rice. Fairbrother had been sitting for an hour with a bottle of burgundy sent by the Cossacks, eating cheese and reading Hazlitt's *Notes of a Journey through France and Italy*.

Hervey returned looking preoccupied. 'Forgive me, Fairbrother; Wachten was most insistent on every detail. He was just back from the trenches. And afterwards I went to the infirmary to see how was Agar.'

Before Fairbrother could make reply, Johnson exercised his right of regimental seniority. 'Sir, yon goose'll be like old boots, it's been roasting so long. Sit down, sir, please – an' Cap'n Fairbrother an' all, sir. I'm bringin' it now.'

Fairbrother would have said that it was not by his choice that he was not seated already, but thought better of it. Hervey simply took his place as bidden.

Johnson returned at once with a silver tray on which sat the deep-bronzed goose.

'It has the appearance of perfection, Johnson. You excel yourself,' said Hervey, keen to make amends.

'Well, it would've been even more perfect 'alf an 'our ago. Anyway, there's enough fat run off to keep us a month.'

'And rice, it would appear,' said Fairbrother, eyeing the white mountain which the Bulgar youth they had engaged was placing on the sideboard.

'That's because it all fell out o' t'sack into t'copper, sir, an' it were too 'ot to fish out.'

'I did not mean to complain,' replied Fairbrother, gravely. 'I am excessively attached to rice – as much as I am excessively disobliged by potatoes.'

Johnson had started carving. 'Just as well we're off to Gibraltar, then, sir, an' not I'land,' he chuntered.

Fairbrother looked at Hervey. 'Is this news?'

Hervey nodded. 'I have reached a decision.' But then he turned back to Johnson. 'I don't believe I have ever seen you carve goose before,' he said, amiably. 'You do it most deftly.'

'When I were a bairn, one Christmas,' (Johnson never needed much encouragement to revisit his origins, real or imagined), 'I were let out t'union to 'elp at a big 'ouse in Sheffield – it were t'Master Cutler's – an' they 'ad a goose for all t'servants, an' I watched 'em carve it, see. An' I never forgot. We 'ad goose once or twice in Spain.'

'I suppose we must have,' said Hervey, a little ashamed at his vagueness in the matter. 'Did you have some of the goose at the Master Cutler's?'

'I did. An' it were t'last proper meat I 'ad for a month when I went back t'union next day. But that's all done wi' now. It were a long time ago.' He finished carving and laid down the irons. 'There y'are, sir. It's not so dried up after all. And there's them onions, an' a bowl o' gravy, and then jelly 'n' oranges.' He nodded to the sideboard.

'And is there a second goose below stairs?'

Johnson smiled. 'Corp'l Acton an' me's 'avin a puddin.'

'Then if the pudding is not too much for you, take the legs.'

'Oh, thank you very much, sir. Corp'l Acton were only just sayin' 'e'd never 'ad goose afore.'

'Remove the legs and leave us then, and take your ease. I'll snuff the candles myself. Reveille the same time as this morning.'

'Right, sir.' He beckoned to the houseboy to come away. 'I'll send up some coffee a bit later.'

Hervey nodded, and Johnson closed the door.

'You know, I really do believe he's indispensable,' said Hervey, and with no semblance of exaggeration. 'I asked would he come with me to Gibraltar, and I could not say for certain what I should do if his answer had been "no".'

Fairbrother was already helping himself at the sideboard. 'I know what I would have counselled.'

Hervey joined him. 'Indeed?'

'That you withdraw your application for Gibraltar.'

Hervey said nothing at first, taking a spoon to the meat and rice, then sitting down and contemplating his friend. 'What would your reason have been?'

'Very simply that if Johnson judged that Gibraltar – or, more exactly, command of a battalion of infantry there – were inimical to your wellbeing, then every instinct of mine would tell me that it were so.'

Hervey smiled. ' "He that troubleth his own house shall inherit the wind: and the fool shall be servant to the wise of heart".'

Fairbrother took a large measure of wine to wash down his first taste of goose. 'I say "Amen" to that. And also that this bird renders fine service too.'

'It does indeed.'

'A pity, therefore, that Agar shan't taste it.'

Hervey hesitated a moment. 'The exigencies of the service. He would not have had it otherwise.'

Fairbrother sat back. 'You're not inclined to see today's action as beyond the call of duty then ... beyond the requirements of neutrality indeed?'

Hervey looked thoughtful. 'I concede it's a moot point. But I don't consider that any harm comes of it.'

Fairbrother held up his hands. 'Nor am I your keeper.'

'I did not believe for a moment you acted as one.'

'Have you written to Princess Lieven?'

'As a matter of fact I have decided to write this evening.'

Fairbrother raised an eyebrow. 'May I ask why?'

'Courtesy, in part.'

'Mm.' He leaned back. 'If you asked my counsel it would be that first you should sleep on the matter. It has been a hot-blooded sort of day.'

'I can't sleep on it: a courier leaves for St Petersburg in the morning.'

'There'll be others.'

'I judge it best not to delay.'

Fairbrother kept silence a while. 'So deuced difficult to tell if a ball's fused or not, sometimes.'

Hervey perfectly understood his meaning. But there was nothing to say.

Fairbrother let him off the hook by changing the subject, ostensibly. 'By the by, what would you have decided had I said that *I* could not accompany you to Gibraltar?'

Hervey sat up. 'In truth I don't know, for I had not then made up my mind – as I had with Johnson.'

'Well, I make my acceptance now conditional,' said Fairbrother gravely.

'Oh?'

He smiled. 'I have found Hazlitt's account of his time in Rome so intriguing that I am intent on seeing the city as soon as may be, and since you are fully acquainted with it, and Gibraltar is so near, I would claim you as guide.'

Hervey returned the smile. 'You know, Fairbrother, I do believe I should find that the most agreeable thing – quite the most agreeable thing indeed.' It was only the strictest self-mastery that would not let him admit his friend as indispensable too.

After dinner, Hervey took candles to his room, resolved to have his letters ready for the Ordnance courier. The first was easily done – a single sheet to Colonel Youell, telling him of his decision to accept the lieutenant-colonelcy of the Fifty-third. As soon as he had sealed it he felt a weight rise from his shoulders; all else now was but a consequence of that decision. He wrote equally briefly to his agents, Messrs Greenwood, Cox and Hammersley of Craig's Court, instructing them to take the necessary action in the disposal of his regimental majority. He wrote at greater, more respectful length to Lord George Irvine, a most difficult letter expressing his regret in not being able to take command of his regiment. He toyed with the idea of explaining himself more fully (for what of the regiment was there left to command?), but in the end he could not find words of the appropriate substance, and he closed the letter in the confidence that his erstwhile commanding officer would understand his reasons – or that no acceptable reasons could in any case be advanced. Next he wrote to Elizabeth with the briefest summary of his movements to date, an equally brief announcement of his decision, and an enclosure for Georgiana telling her that soon she would be able to join him in Gibraltar, which she would surely like a good deal. He then began a letter to Kezia. He wrote the salutation easily enough, but then his pen froze in his hand. No words would come to him. He even thought to unseal the letter to Elizabeth to copy its lines, but he could not do so, for it scarcely seemed meet, and the recipients were so unalike that the same words could hardly be apt. In the end he decided he would rise early and write with the courier's posthorn to hasten him.

It was now late; he felt drowsy. But with the mere act of taking a fresh sheet and writing 'Dear Princess Lieven' it was as if he had been touched by an electric arc. So great in fact that he stopped momentarily to ponder the cause. None that came to mind was wholesome, however, and he shut them out very determinedly in order to write on. But at the end – seven whole sides in his compact hand – he shuddered with distaste at the thought that he had not been able to manage a single page for his wife. And try as he might, he could not shake off the sense of perfidy. He found it infinitely easier to scruple less about corresponding with the ambassadress of a foreign power, for he would tell the Horse Guards of what he wrote, and Princess Lieven was a woman of experience and discretion in diplomatic affairs, and besides he told her nothing that was detrimental to His Majesty's interests (or so he very much trusted).

It was, after all, a very tame account – a summary of their itinerary with not a mention of St Petersburg, the briefest explanation of the purpose of the landing at Siseboli, the defence-works about the town, the bearing of the Pavlovsk Grenadiers, his patrol with the Black Sea Cossacks, the action by the *strelki* of the Azov

Regiment, and the admirable arrangements for the sick (such as he had had occasion to observe). He did not write of the deficiencies or derelictions, only that 'there are some instances where, in my judgement, the practice could be amended to advantage' – and his intention to join the main army when it was ready to renew the offensive. There was not the remotest possibility of its falling into unfriendly (or even suspicious) hands, but even so, there was nothing, individually or severally, that could be construed as bearing allegiance to any but the King.

He signed it quickly – *I remain, yours faithfully, Matthew Hervey* – and sealed it before he could have any more troubling second thoughts, and placed it with the other letters inside an oilskin envelope addressed to his agents, which he left unsealed to await the morning letter to Kezia. By now he was feeling the hour keenly (it was past two o'clock and the candles were beginning to gutter). He rose from the table at which he had sat for two hours, and without even recourse to the nightstand lay down on his bed and closed his eyes.

There was no easy repose, however. At once Kat appeared – so vividly as to make him open his eyes and sit up. He shook his head, willing her away. She had visited him daily before they reached St Petersburg, then less frequently during the journey south, and hardly at all since coming to Siseboli. He had hoped that time and distance would work its usual cure. But such confusion as were the circumstances with Kat could not be resolved by the mere passing of hours and the accumulation of miles. He cursed himself for the weakness of will that had brought those circumstances about, and shivered with the shame of it. It pained him to think how Fairbrother and Johnson (and Agar and all the others) looked to him for his assured command, for his certainty in what to do, and yet he was so in error in his private affairs as to render himself unfit to exercise any authority. Or so it would be thought were his affairs to cease being private. Not that there was immediate danger of that; not if he kept his head. And therefore he would exercise his authority in pretence, deceit – the 'mask of command' writ large.

Would it matter? He didn't know. There was in the Prayer Book, in the 'Articles of Religion', an affirmation concerning the unworthiness of some ministers of religion that might equally apply to the exercise of military command: 'Neither is the effect of Christ's ordinance taken away by their wickedness'. He had always found it curiously fortifying, upheld, as it had been, by his father, who would always quote it in adversity, when some wickedness of the diocese oppressed him. But for all that the article gave comfort, it contained a rider: 'Nevertheless it appertaineth to the discipline of the Church that inquiry be made of evil ministers, and that they be accused by those that have knowledge of their offences; and finally, being found guilty by just judgement, be deposed.' There was no assured refuge from reckoning, therefore. He could go to Gibraltar, wear the badges of rank, exercise the power of command – but ruin lurked, perhaps even stalked.

He lay down again, sick in his stomach, and closed his eyes. He gave desperate thanks for the fellowship of his good friend and his much older one; what a barren office would any command be without their company.

XII

THE BOOT AND THE BAYONET

Early next morning

The signal gun in 'B' Redoubt – unshotted, twice as loud – woke Siseboli an hour before its expected reveille. Hervey sat bolt upright, full awake, the instinct of twenty years' campaigning, which many a time had saved his skin. The nightlight by his bed was still burning. He reached for his hunter – ten minutes before two o'clock. Bugles sounded 'Alarm' above the distant rattle of musketry. He was up, buckling on his sword, reaching for his pistols, grabbing telescope, spurs, crossbelt, cap, and making for the door. The first thing that mattered was speed.

Corporal Acton was at the foot of the stairs. 'Signal rockets from the redoubts, sir – red 'ns. The Turks are attacking.'

'You saw the rockets?'

'I did, sir. I were gone to the groyne for a see if they'd caught any fish, when the gun went off.'

Fairbrother came hurrying downstairs, booted and spurred (Hervey was always intrigued how his friend could rise with alacrity when the occasion required, yet otherwise remain abed all morning). 'It might be a false alarm,' he said, as if to excuse his promptitude, 'but I take no chance. I'd wager your Colonel Vedeniapine knows his business.'

Johnson now appeared, barelegged but in his greatcoat, shielding a candle. 'Sir?'

'Captain Fairbrother and I are going to see what's the alarm. Stay here and make ready. Have Brayshaw and Green help.'

'There's water on t'boil, sir. I could mash some tea, quick.'

'No,' said Hervey, pushing his spurs into a pocket, and telescope into his tunic bib. 'If the Turks are attacking we must see it at once.' He remembered: 'On my desk – a letter for London. See it gets to the headquarters for the courier if I'm not back in the hour.'

They went into the street. There was the faintest notice of coming dawn in the moonless sky, but the torches everywhere made it seem midnight still. An infantry detail doubled past, two *efreytors* barking time. The distant musketry swelled and then slackened like fireworks at a fête.

'If the Turks have got in the trenches they've duped us,' said Fairbrother, pulling his cap down. 'They must've been toying with us yesterday; that musketry doesn't sound like a picket skirmish.'

'It does not,' agreed Hervey, striding out after the grenadiers. 'We must pray if they *have* got into the trenches it was more by good fortune.'

Both men had given up any pretence at disinterest: the Turk was an intruder; he must be seen off.

In the square behind the main gates the guard company was already drawn up in two ranks, standing easy, while others of the Pavlovsk were getting on parade. Officers of the reserve battalion of the Kozlov Regiment were gathering for orders while the men mustered outside their billets at the further end of town. A party of Cossacks – twenty or so – came clattering along the cobbles at the trot, and then General Wachten arrived with his staff and escort of grenadiers.

Hervey kept a respectful distance. In any case, he would not be able to understand the orders, and could hardly expect Wachten to translate for him while disposing his troops. It would soon be perfectly apparent what the orders were.

A rocket shot up from the castellation above the main gates, bursting in a bright green shower at a hundred feet. Seconds later the gunships moored either side of the isthmus opened a sweeping fire on the approaches.

Fairbrother frowned. 'What in God's name do they shoot at?'

'Wachten told me they'd fire blind on signal.'

'It goes hard, then, with any messenger.'

'The order is that messengers light a torch.'

Fairbrother merely raised an eyebrow.

The cannonading and musketry continued. The troops in the square stood fast.

In a quarter of an hour the sky was lightening distinctly.

'Come,' said Hervey, no longer content to wait now that imminent daylight promised them a view. 'Let's get up on the walls.'

As they crossed the square one of General Wachten's staff officers hurried up to them. 'Colonel Hervey, we did not know where you were,' he began, in French. 'The general would see you. Please, this way.'

He took them to the door of the staircase of the gate tower, and then up to the battlements.

Here they found the general standing tall on the parapet. 'Colonel Hervey, I feared you had gone over to the other side!' he declared boisterously, rolling his German with evident relish.

'Had I the inclination, General, it would surely be a most perilous venture with those gunboats raking the ground so.'

'I shall signal for them to cease firing as soon as I am able to see the ground. It cannot be but a false alarm. But it serves nonetheless: a little practice with powder – always good for the circulation!'

'The picket, I imagine, is long called in, General, but are the Cossacks?' Hervey was uncertain if they maintained the watch by night.

'They retired after last light.'

'May I ask your design, General?'

'There is no yellow rocket; Vedeniapine has not signalled the redoubts cannot stand, so as soon as it is light enough to know where to direct the counter-assault, I shall do so. If the Turks are in the trenches they shall find us falling on them, and if they are not they shall have to fight us in the open.'

He turned to one of his aides-de-camp and rattled off an order. The officer saluted and hastened away.

'The Pavlovsk and Kozlov regiments will advance in ten minutes,' he explained. 'It should be light enough to form ranks, yet not be seen distantly.'

He turned to a second aide-de-camp and gave the order to cease fire.

Seconds later there was a noise like the hiss of steam from a boiler, and another of the signal rockets raced high over the isthmus, bursting red. The fire from the gunships ceased.

Hervey took out his telescope to peer into the lightening darkness, trying to avoid the glare of the burning pitch barrels which the redoubts had lit. He could make out shadowy movement on the extreme right of 'B', the western redoubt (from which they had made yesterday's sortie). It was rapid – darting, even – but without form. Yet what could it be but Turks, for all the Azov's men must surely be standing to in the trenches? The flashes of musketry, besides playing the devil with his night eyes, revealed a fight of some sort, but whether it was Turk or Russian musketry, or both, he could not know.

'What do you make of it all?' he asked Fairbrother.

'Quite evidently an affair of some heat, but what's beyond it? For all we know the whole Turk force might be drawn up waiting for the storming party to take the forward trenches. Or equally possible that it's a raid in strength, and no more.'

'Just so,' replied Hervey, lowering his glass and closing his eyes to recover from the sudden flaring of another tar barrel. 'Yet they must know that daylight's at hand. If it's merely a raid they'd want to be away before it's full light.'

'I see 'orses, sir,' said Corporal Acton, who had borrowed Cornet Agar's telescope.

Hervey took up his glass again. 'You have better eyes than I, Corp' Acton. Where?'

Acton closed to his side, and pointed. 'Go right, sir – furthest end of the Plough 'andle, and then below to where all that smoke's drifted.'

Hervey searched. Even half a mile, perhaps more, from the trenches the white smoke was reflecting the flaring light of the pitch barrels and occasional bursting shell – but he could see no horses. 'You're sure of it?'

'Sure of it, sir. Just a dekh, and then you smoke must've drifted again.'

It was good enough. Hervey turned to his host. 'My corporal had a glimpse of horsemen, General.' He reckoned he did not need to say that it might mean artillery.

'The devil! Clearly an attack of some weight then. Well, I am going down to accompany the regiments. You may accompany too.'

'With pleasure, General.'

Fairbrother took hold of Hervey's arm. It was one thing to wish the Turks their congé, but quite another to become embroiled in delivering it. Had they not had scrapes enough? 'Are you quite sure it's the place from which best to observe?'

'We can hardly stand here as if it were a race meeting,' Hervey replied.

187

'But we ain't declared, either. What will it serve if you're shot?'

'The odds are agin it.'

Fairbrother turned to follow his friend. 'Who would live for ever?' he said wearily, bracing himself to more action.

The gates swung open and the regiments began marching out in column to the taps of the company time-beaters. It was now light enough for Hervey to make out the colour of the facings, and for the NCOs to see an errant man and bark at him to keep step – but still too dark to see with any certainty what was happening at the trenches. Not feeling bound to hang on the general's coat tails (who was, in any case, mounted), he, Fairbrother and Corporal Acton slipped through the gates and scrambled atop the rubbled wall near which Johnson had been bowled over by the *franc tireur* not a week ago.

The Pavlovsk, leading, began forming at the halt, two companies abreast, two in support, with all the regularity of the parade ground – sharp but unhurried. And then the Kozlov, with less majesty, but with no less efficiency, forming double-company front, abreast and left of the Pavlovsk. Hervey was impressed.

Into the interval of a dozen yards between the two regiments rode General Wachten and his staff.

Hervey sighed. 'I suppose we'll see no less for being on foot, though it makes it deuced awkward having any conversation with Wachten.'

'Shall you need to converse with him?' asked Fairbrother guardedly. 'I really do counsel caution.'

'You are always judicious.' Hervey understood perfectly his friend's reluctance, but also that Fairbrother could never run from a just fight; he was, as the saying in India went, a man to go tiger shooting with.

There was the sound of hoofs, and then the unmistakeable jingling of Cossack bridles.

'Perhaps they bring your seat at the general's right hand,' said Fairbrother archly as the *sotnia* came through the gates at a jog-trot.

'I doubt it.' But he was still inclined to excitement. It was the only way he could dismiss his friend's caution (for he could not fault his reasoning). 'I would see the battle as does the infantryman. I have quite a taste for it now.'

'Leave to speak, sir?'

'Wear away, Corporal Acton.'

'I've just seen 'orses again, sir,' he said, still peering through his telescope.

The light was increasing rapidly. Hervey thought he too could see what might be horsemen. 'Well, we shan't have long to wait,' he said, putting away his glass as if to say they were now committed to the fight.

Five minutes later, the sun broached the horizon and its first horizontal rays began searching the plain.

And then it was revealed – infantry, a brigade and more, standing waiting a mile hence, a mass of cavalry on either flank, artillery drawn up forward. 'I believe the Seraskier has stolen a march,' said Fairbrother decidedly. 'Vedeniapine's chaplains had better be on their knees.'

'I'd never discourage prayer,' said Hervey thoughtfully, 'but Vedeniapine's situation may by no means be as perilous as you surmise. The Seraskier can't have wanted his position revealed by daylight thus. The storming parties should have broken into the trenches while it was yet dark so the rest could close with the redoubts as daylight came – rather than standing yonder in review order.'

General Wachten's *coup d'oeil* evidently accorded with Hervey's. Pointing with his telescope in the direction of the massing Turks, he gave the order for the regiments to load.

'See,' said Hervey, nodding to the suddenly animated lines of infantrymen; 'we might be with Marlborough for all that the drill's changed.' He supposed that Peter the Great himself would have approved (certainly the Duke of Marlborough would have found the drill entirely familiar). He could not understand the Russian, but he soon saw what it meant.

'*Prime and load.*' Each man made a quarter turn to the right, brought his musket to the hip and opened the pan.

'*Handle cartridge.*' Back snapped the frizzen, out came cartridge from cartouche bag, and a thousand well-drilled soldiers of the Tsar bit off the bullets and spat out the paper.

'*Prime.*' Hammer to half-cock, pinch of powder in priming pan, frizzen snapped closed again.

'*About.*' Musket butt to the ground, rest of powder into barrel, spit in the ball and push in the cartridge paper to wad the charge.

'*Draw ramrods.*' Pull the ramrod half-way from the barrel hoops, seize backhanded in the middle, draw out and turn it simultaneously to the front, place one inch into barrel.

'*Ram down the cartridge.*' Drive wadding, bullet and powder to bottom of barrel, tamp down with two quick strokes, return ramrod to its hoops.

Half a minute.

The brigade shouldered arms, and waited.

General Wachten rode forward five lengths. 'Troops will advance!'

Battalion commanders repeated the cautionary.

'By the left – *March!*'

Out stepped the line to the beat of drum in the left flank company, taken up in turn by the time-beaters the length of the brigade. The Cossacks followed at a hundred yards.

'Come on,' said Hervey, scrambling down the pile of masonry.

Fairbrother was past remonstrating. In any case, he had never marched to the beat of drum in a parade like this. He fancied he would enjoy it.

They fell in between the Grenadiers and the Kozlov Regiment.

'A fine prospect, then. Don't you agree, Corporal Acton?'

'Can't understand why I didn't take the Fusilier serjeant's shilling and not Serjeant Deakin's, sir.'

Droll; Hervey smiled. And since there was little else to do in the advance but march in step, he might as well pass the time of day: 'You were 'listed by Serjeant Deakin, were you? C Troop man – the image of a dragoon. No question that you preferred his shilling. How much was the bounty?'

'Nine guineas, sir.'

'I hope there were not too many off-reckonings.'

'I was able to buy a small interest in a public house, sir.'

Hervey laughed. 'Ale for all who drank your farewell! I've never heard it thus expressed.'

'No, sir. I means it proper. My uncle's landlord o' the Marquis o' Granby in Bromley.'

Hervey was a shade discomfited. 'I beg your pardon, Corporal Acton. My compliments to you. An admirably named place.'

Fairbrother had detached himself from the marching repartee, and was first to notice the activity off-shore. 'Look yonder.' He pointed to the gunships off the west side of the isthmus.

They had lowered small-boats, and the crews were pulling hard. It was not yet full light but the towing ropes were clearly visible. It wouldn't take long to swing the ships on their moorings so the guns could bear.

'Smart work,' said Hervey. 'As we observed yesterday, they'll have targets aplenty if the Turk obliges and stands fast in the open much longer . . . What do you estimate their number?'

'I confess I've never seen the like,' said Fairbrother. 'Who knows how many stand to the rear. Our perspective on foot is very limited. Thousands?'

'What say you, Corporal Acton?'

Even though observation was the dragoon's business, and the tricks of the trade practised every field day, it was still a tall order. Yet Acton was undaunted. He shielded his eyes (the sun was now gathering strength) and calmly surveyed the distant 'enemy'.

'There appears to be three distinct musters of infantry, sir. If that's three battalions, suppose upwards, say, of two thousand? The cavalry I can't make out at all well, but there must be half that number at least. And where else would all them we saw with the Cossacks have gone?'

'So your report would be?'

'Estimate two thousand infantry in brigade, with cavalry supports at least one thousand, and artillery troop.'

'Excellent summation. There must also be a battalion in the trenches, else the fighting would not be so active. We must count on there being four thousand in all.'

'And we are, what, fifteen hundred?' asked Fairbrother ('we' seemed natural enough, marching in line with a Russian brigade – and he was certain the Turks would make no distinction).

'And a thousand in the redoubts,' replied Hervey.

'The odds are not oppressive, then, as long as yonder general knows his business?'

'My sentiments entirely. We shall just have to see whether Wachten is as capable of manoeuvring as he is of organizing.'

They tramped on to the growing rattle of musketry and, now that it was light enough to lay, the Turk guns which had opened fire with solid shot at the redoubt. Hervey was relishing the novelty – except for the stench. The smell of horses was sweet; that of the *rekrut* was not. The stale sweat of a winter unwashed, the pungent exhilaration and fear of coming battle, the sulphurous flatulence, the belching onion breath laced with *kvas* – he had thought his nose inured to rankness until now.

'Infantry,' he said, sighing. 'If the Turks would only oblige, I'd wheel the entire line to the right and march them into that sea. I never smelled anything so foul in so fair a place.'

Fairbrother shook his head. 'A maroon's cabin wouldn't stink as bad.'

'The powder-smoke will be a fumigatory. I'd welcome some musketry for medicinal purposes alone.'

Hervey could hardly suppose, though, that an English brigade would smell much sweeter in the circumstances – not, obviously, of *kvas*, and possibly not of onions, but there would be something just as rank. In other respects he imagined things would be much the same; these Russians advanced at a slower pace – about eighty to the minute, and a shorter step – but infantry were infantry.

He began calculating: the step was a foot and a half, he reckoned (red-coats managed two); eighty to the minute meant a hundred and twenty feet – forty yards – in the minute; there was half a mile till volleying range – so twenty minutes, say. He took out his watch and marked the time. Strange the things that were possible on foot.

The regiments began singing, the Pavlovsk first – *Preobrazhensky*, at once recognizable. Then the Kozlov, full-throated, a swaggering tune he didn't know but that made them all step out and quicken pace, so that the Pavlovsk's fifers and time-beaters had to speed theirs to keep the dressing. General Wachten turned in the saddle, smiling broadly and encouraging the beat with clenched fist. One of the Kozlov *rekruty*, short-legged, short-backed, skipped out of the front rank and began a capering *Hopak* along the line, urged on by the officers.

'Not for the Horse Guards, I'd wager,' said Fairbrother, bemused. 'But what a joyous way to go to your death.'

'Perhaps I shall instruct the Fifty-third to sing on the march.'

'Did the army sing at Waterloo?'

'The French did, when Bonaparte reviewed them. I don't recall any on our side of the field.'

They were across the isthmus now, with a breeze bringing a taste of the sea sparkling blue behind them, the sun full up. And then the gunships began their cannonade – thunderous unison and clouds of smoke. The left flank of the Kozlov were now skirting the breastworks of 'B' Redoubt, singing louder against the roar of the battery and the broadsides. Flankers fell to fragments of Turk shell which exploded long; the singing faltered momentarily but picked up with renewed determination.

Turk and Russian were now in full view of each other, a furlong and a half at most. Wachten halted the advance and trotted over to where the Kozlov's commanding officer stood with his adjutant and drummer.

Hervey watched as the general's hand indicated a change of direction. 'I believe he intends they enter the trenches,' he said, with a sufficient note of surprise to alert Corporal Acton.

'Going with 'em, sir?'

'I trust not,' said Fairbrother, before Hervey could reply.

'No. There'd be nothing to see except at close quarter. I want to observe what the general does. I don't see his purpose in entering the trenches.'

But that was not what Wachten had instructed them to do – only to present a flank while the rest of the line advanced.

The singing stopped abruptly as the battalion officers began the complicated evolution of forming left at the halt.

'Would not wheeling be quicker?' asked Fairbrother.

'You were the infantryman, not I – but I've watched a line take an age to dress when it had wheeled too tightly.'

It was five minutes nevertheless before Wachten was satisfied that his flank was properly protected, and he could give the order 'Forward!' to the Pavlovsk.

Hervey now found himself on the left of the line. Shot hissed this way and that at fifty yards. The Turk gunners had not yet changed their lay from the redoubt; it would be an easy switch when they did.

'I'd say Wachten's been deuced adroit. If he can fright off yonder Turks, as Vedeniapine did yesterday, likely as not he'll bolt the ones in the trenches without a fight. I wonder what he'll have our Cossack friends do?'

He glanced back to where the Cossacks stood with what he imagined must be uncommon patience, waiting for the infantry to gain ground. Had Wachten given them licence to act as they saw fit?

The Pavlovsk were now at volleying range – two hundred yards – but there was no sign of the Turk muskets presenting, or the guns switching and changing to case-shot. They simply stood their ground as if on parade.

'They don't seem to be frighted this time,' said Fairbrother coolly, like a spectator at a field day.

Indeed, the Turks had begun moving forward not back, and inclining left so as (it appeared) to meet the Pavlovsk squarely.

'You see what it's to be, then?' said Hervey.

'A volleying contest. I do dislike the thing; so bludgeonly.'

Hervey had no desire to stand in a rain of lead either; all his cavalryman's instinct was for movement. 'At least I'll be able to look the Fifty-third in the eye,' he managed, sounding resigned.

'If you haven't first lost your head,' replied Fairbrother, with some asperity. 'And I hope there's to be no *"tirez les premiers"*.' (At Fontenoy the officers had lifted their hats in greeting, and, so legend had it, invited the French to fire first, to which they had replied: '*Messieurs, nous ne tirons jamais les premiers; tirez vous-mêmes.*')

Hervey agreed. He had once thought the Fontenoy drill the essence of gentlemanlike conduct in the face of fire – but had long since considered it the action of the amateur.

But Wachten's instinct was also for movement (what chance of it there was). Out went the *strelki*.

A roundshot struck the ground in front of the Pavlovsk's left-flank company, ricocheting low and bloodily, cutting a grenadier in two, taking off the head of the man behind, spattering half a dozen others in gory debris. Several threw up, and some fouled themselves – men who had not seen action before, or perhaps who had and knew there was more to come. The singing seemed an age ago.

Another roundshot flew high, close to the general and his staff, and then dropped harmlessly to the rear. Yet another struck the ground in front of the left-flank company but lofted just as harmlessly.

'Deuced odd,' said Hervey coolly. 'They must have left their canister in the limbers.' Shot was never very destructive unless the ranks were deep or in enfilade.

'Small mercies. *Deo gratias*,' replied Fairbrother.

'I'll say "Amen" to that.'

The *strelki* opened up a galling fire, and with no Turk skirmishers to counter.

'Mightn't our own guns show a little address?'

'*Our own?*' Hervey half-smiled. At least they were now on the same side. 'I'll warrant that Wachten would give half the Pavlovsk for a horse troop.'

In any case, they would count themselves lucky that only three Turk guns bore – and the gunners damnably slow at their work; it was a full minute before another roundshot ploughed its bloody furrow through the ranks.

On marched the line, leaving the wounded to the drummer boys.

Hervey and Fairbrother fell into silence, the noise too great and the roundshot too grisly. Only the barking of NCOs could be heard, to make a man fear his fate more at their hands than at the cannon's – or here and there the softer word of an officer to pluck at a man's faint heart.

Two more minutes and then (thank God) 'Halt! Make ready!'

The officers took post to flank and rear, clearing the line of fire.

'Present!'

Up went the four hundred muskets of the front rank.

'*Fire!*'

Smoke billowed the length of the line. The second rank advanced five paces, waited for it to drift rear, and then presented.

'*Fire!*'

It mattered not what the Turk guns did now: the Pavlovsk had eyes only for their cartridges and ramrods – work they could warm to. The clatter was like power looms in a mill.

It was impossible to see the effect, the smoke was so thick, but men now began falling to the answering fire. NCOs cursed and officers waved their swords, the Pavlovsk firing now by platoons, the old Marlborough drill, giving the Turks no respite. Unless the rounds were wide or high in the fog of powder-smoke, Hervey could not believe the Turks could stand it long.

But the Pavlovsk too were receiving withering musketry. How long could *they* bear it?

A musket ball knocked off his forage cap, and was lodged in the band when Acton picked it up. Another glanced off his boot, with the pain of a mule kick.

And then the Pavlovsk were fixing bayonets.

And now they were advancing . . . breaking into double time.

And Hervey was running with his sword at his shoulder, pistol in hand.

Fairbrother cursed as he stumbled and almost fell.

'Have a care, sir,' chirped Acton, a sword in each hand.

And into the smoke of the last volley the line charged – yelling, screaming, baying like hounds on to the quarry.

No man waited on a bayonet charge scarce ever: they fired, counter-charged – or fled. The Turks fired – some wild, some well – but the Pavlovsk charged on, unstoppable.

The Turks turned tail, but the press of men was too great. Into their backs ran the bayonets, a melee of blade, butt and boot – anything to stun and then kill.

Hervey plunged into the frenzy like a wild man, sword flailing. Fairbrother likewise – booting and stabbing with all the savagery of his ancestors. Acton, desperately at Hervey's hand to catch a blade, used every cut in the drill book.

Long minutes of muscle-tearing, lung-bursting execution, of bloody hacking, thrusting and slicing – and then, as suddenly as they'd charged, it was over, the fighting ceased, the noise ended. Piles of dead, of heaving, writhing, wounded, dying men, others on their knees, and a few running for all they were worth, unencumbered by weapons – all that was left of the Turk brigade.

And now came the sobbing and groaning, the cries of pain and the rattle of death. The Pavlovsk Grenadiers surveyed their work with exhaustion and elation in heady mix. The officers would now begin their work of mercy.

Hervey stood half-bent, sword at his side, unbelieving, panting. Fairbrother put a hand on his shoulder, as if to support himself. Corporal Acton wiped his sabre on a Turk cloak and sheathed it, drawing his pistol to take up guard next to them.

With his breath back, Hervey straightened up. His eyes smarted with the smoke, and the ringing in his ears was infernal; but he could hear faint cheering from the far side of the redoubt – the Azov Regiment, come from nowhere, charging with the bayonet into the flank of the Turk reserve; and far over on the right the Cossacks slipping the leash and going at the Turk cavalry like fire racing through stubble. The Seraskier's corps was finished. By God, Wachten had judged it well!

Hervey saw him approaching – the general hailing him, indeed, as if he were surprised to find him safe in the midst of so much slaughter.

How should he form the German? – 'A very perfect victory, sir'?

But Wachten was already forming his own words of appreciation.

It was indeed a very perfect victory – the best part of two brigades overthrown, destroyed; many prisoners and many guns captured. The Cossacks might even have seized the Seraskier himself had he not quit the field so hastily. Siseboli – it was as plain as day – could not be taken by a force less than five times the number that had tried this morning. And where would the Seraskier find such a force, unless by drawing off those facing the Russians to the north? Wachten had cause indeed to be pleased.

XIII

HONOURS OF WAR

Before Silistria, 4 June 1829

Hervey stood waiting in the marbled hall of the villa over which flew the flag of the Tsar's new general-in-chief, resplendent in best undress which Johnson had spent half the night primping and polishing, the gold wire of his crossbelt looking new-drawn after the lengthy attention of toothbrush and shaving soap.

They had left Siseboli three weeks ago. Since the battle for the redoubt, all there had been quiet; the Seraskier had withdrawn to Bourgas leaving only a force of observation. So Hervey had taken leave of General Wachten, and travelled by frigate to Constanta, and then, to the great delight of Cornet Agar (returned to hale condition), the party had made their way along the remains of Trajan's Wall (an earth *vallum* which Agar insisted was very doubt-fully Roman, and more likely Byzantine), which ran forty miles or so to the Danube. They had journeyed thence upriver to Silistria (where Hervey was surprised to find the Turks still resisting the most determined siege), arriving two days before. The general-in-chief had returned from Varna only the latter evening.

Hervey carried with him a further letter of introduction from

General Wachten (who had left Siseboli too, but for Varna, whence he was to take charge of the garrison at Pravadi). But unknown to him, Wachten had also sent a despatch to Silistria relating in detail the Turkish attack and its prelude, and Hervey's part in them.

The doors of the general-in-chief's office were suddenly opened, and out marched an officer of Cossacks, his face aglow with satisfaction.

An aide-de-camp made the introductions. 'Captain Pugachev is promoted major in recognition of his riding from Pravadi with despatches.'

Major Pugachev had no French, so Hervey was obliged to make his congratulations by smiles and handshakes. 'In what way was the ride singular?'

The aide-de-camp tilted his head, as if to express surprise at the question. 'The distance from Pravadi, via the necessary outposts, is almost a hundred miles, and the enemy is at large still. Pugachev took but twelve hours, and on the same horse.'

Hervey nodded in recognition of the feat. 'And the horse?'

The aide-de-camp frowned. 'I cannot say, sir. You wish me to enquire?'

Before Hervey could respond (he would have liked, at least, to know the animal's breeding), the doors opened again, and a second aide-de-camp appeared.

'General Diebitsch will see you now, Colonel.'

Hervey acknowledged, and turned once more to the Cossack. 'I trust the despatches contained favourable news. My compliments to General Wachten when you return.'

The French was turned into Russian by the first aide-de-camp. The reply, short, exuberant, needed no translation.

Hervey marched confidently into the general-in-chief's office, spurs ringing on the polished stone. He halted, saluted, and announced himself in French.

General Diebitsch was already standing, with half a dozen staff officers in a semi-circle behind him. All wore plumes, the appearance more of ceremony than of orderly room. The general returned the salute, greeting him not in French but German.

Count Ivan Ivanovich Diebitsch – or, in the language he now spoke, Graf Karl Friedrich Anton von Diebitsch und Narden – was a boyish-looking man with black hair combed forward in the classical manner, and an easy smile. Hervey had acquired all the knowledge he could of his former service to supplement the picture that Princess Lieven had painted of him. Like Wachten, Diebitsch had been born in Silesia, and been a cadet in Berlin, but had followed his father, one of Frederick the Great's aides-de-camp, into the service of the Tsar. He had been wounded at Austerlitz, had fought at Eylau and Friedland, and in 1812, after distinguishing himself at Polotsk, was made major-general. He was thereafter at Lutzen, Dresden and Leipzig, was promoted lieutenant-general, and entered Paris in 1814. Then he had joined the glittering congress at Vienna, and was afterwards made adjutant-general and later chief of the general staff. Tsar Nicholas had made him baron and then count, and in 1825 he had been active in putting down the Decembrist revolt. The Tsar, despairing of the ailing Field Marshal Wittgenstein in the campaign of 1828, had then appointed Diebitsch to command of the army in the field. And he was but six years Hervey's senior (a fact which Hervey tried hard to put from his mind, for the slowness of his own promotion – if in considerable part his own making – stood sometimes as a rebuke).

Another aide-de-camp stepped forward with a blue velvet cushion.

General Diebitsch took from it a medal suspended from a long, yellow-edged, red ribbon. 'Colonel Hervey, by the power devolved upon me by His Imperial Majesty the Emperor and Autocrat of All the Russias, I invest you with the Order of Saint Anna, Second Class, With Swords.'

Hervey, astonished as he was, managed nevertheless to keep his countenance, and bowed to permit the ribbon to be placed about his neck.

Diebitsch then shook his hand. 'Colonel Hervey, your action in taking command of the Cossack patrol was worthy of the highest praise, and the advice tendered to General Wachten at Siseboli, on which he acted during the Turkish attack, materially affected the course of the battle and saved the lives of many of His Imperial Majesty's soldiers thereby.'

Hervey cleared his throat. 'It was my privilege to be among so many brave men, General.' (It had only been evening, when they returned within the walls, that he had learned that Wachten had sent the reserve company of the Azov Regiment by boat to make the surprise attack on the Turk flank.)

'Please take a seat, Colonel, and a glass of champagne.'

An *efreytor* in a white shell jacket appeared from behind a screen with a tray and glasses.

Hervey breathed a sigh of relief that they were not to drink 'without heeltaps', for he wanted the clearest of heads. He made a few more complimentary remarks about the resolution of the Pavlovsk Grenadiers and the élan of the Cossacks.

'Your German is admirable, I may say – exactly as Wachten informed me. You had a German governess, I understand?'

'From Alsace. It was she who taught me French too.'

'I imagine therefore that it would take little time for you to acquire Russian?' He beckoned the staff officers to leave.

'I have acquired a very little, General.' Hervey smiled ruefully. 'Though perhaps I should acquire more if your officers were not so fluent in French.'

Diebitsch smiled too. 'Colonel Hervey, it is in my power to offer you command of a brigade forthwith, in the rank of major-general. A division would follow soon thereafter.'

Hervey was taken aback, both by the notion itself and by the directness of the proposal. He struggled hard to compose his reply so as not to give offence (it was, after all, a most handsome offer; and changing flag need not be treason). 'The general is most gracious, but he will understand that I serve His Majesty the King.'

Diebitsch was well rehearsed. 'I understand perfectly, Colonel, but also that you are an officer whose considerable experience of war is not matched by his rank. The Princess Lieven writes that it is well known that the army of England is diminishing in size, and that what promotions there are to general rank are reserved for the closest acquaintances of His Majesty.'

There was some mischief in the latter suggestion, but enough of truth for Hervey to be less than affronted – not least because of Diebitsch's entirely benign expression. Indeed, it was all he could do not to reflect the sympathetic smile. The shock, if it could be described as such, was in learning that Princess Lieven was in communication with the general-in-chief, though it was by no means clear if this were direct and recent, or included reference to him personally. And he did not suppose he would be able to discover more. 'It is true that there are reductions in the establishment,' he conceded, a trifle reluctantly. 'As to the appointment of general officers, I am not privy to what passes between His Majesty and the commander-in-chief.'

'Prettily put, Colonel, but it does not alter the material point. I am able to offer you a command fitting to your abilities – a command, indeed, decidedly shy of your abilities, which with a year or so's service and acquisition of the tongue of our Russias would be superseded by greater rank. I am made general-in-chief of the army; I shall have need of an officer of your particular resources in my headquarters in St Petersburg, as well as on active operations.

At twenty-seven, Colonel Hervey, I was made lieutenant-general, and baron not long after. Princess Lieven writes that your own regiment is to be disbanded.'

Hervey was now in no doubt what had transpired – nor of the power of the general's patronage. If he were able to confer honours and rank in the field, his influence in St Petersburg must indeed be entire. Russia was no enemy of England's, after all – nor even great rival. What reason was there, then, for him, a professional soldier, to decline such an offer of advancement? At the very least it demanded some deliberation.

'General, you press me on a matter of the profoundest consequence which I beg leave to think over.'

Diebitsch nodded. 'I would have been offended had you turned it down at once, and suspicious had you accepted likewise.'

Hervey was at least diverted by the knowledge that he had passed the first test of Russian generalship. He bowed.

Diebitsch rose. Hervey followed, expecting to be dismissed, but was beckoned instead to a map table. 'Let me apprise you of the situation facing the army of His Imperial Majesty in the seat of war before Constantinople.'

Hervey, trying hard to put the momentous promise of generalship and military honours from his mind, was flattered to a high degree by this admittance to the realm of strategy. He felt certain, now, that all that had recently gone before – Princess Lieven, the Cossack patrol, the affair of the redoubts – was justified: Lord Hill could not have wished him to be in any other position but this – to have gained the confidence of the Tsar's general-in-chief.

Diebitsch's air of assurance was arresting, even as he pointed on the map to the trials that must lie ahead. Between his army and the Sultan's capital lay first the Danube, deep and wide, with the formidable defences of Silistria still in Turk hands. A hundred miles distant, the Balkan mountains lay square across his path, impassable but in a handful of places. And guardian of those crossing places, standing like Cerberus at the gates of Hades, was the fortress of Shumla, greater perhaps than Silistria. Yet even with the passes forced, there still lay ahead a march of two hundred and fifty miles, open plain for the most part (Hervey had ridden a corner of it with the Cossacks) that could scarcely go uncontested by the Turks. Hervey vaguely recalled that the Balkan was called Mons Haemus because the Greek word for blood was αἷμα (haema); and he could not but think, seeing on the map what the Tsar's soldiers would be put to accomplish, that the name was prophetic.

His unease was evident. 'I will not sport with you, Colonel Hervey; the previous season did not go well – to which I owe my present advancement, as doubtless every camp tattler would tell you. And then many men were carried off by the frosts and the plague. I have spent the latter part of the winter garnering the army's strength, which is why I have opened offensive operations later in the season than I should have liked – that and the infernal bad weather of late, which has swelled the Danube and washed away the roads.'

Hervey nodded gravely; here was uncommon candour. 'Is it true – may I ask – that the loss of horses was even more grievous?'

'It is true. And I have had to bring remounts from the furthest pastures of Russia. And camels from the desert regions – two thousand Turcomans – as well as draught oxen, whose meat we shall take when their work is done. I have, now, a hundred and forty thousand cavalry and infantry, and five hundred artillery pieces in addition to those with the Cossacks. I have two months' rations and warlike stores in the depots at Varna and here before Silistria. The navy is at my command, as you have seen, and I am confident that not a ship shall venture from the Golden Horn and do us harm.'

Hervey did not doubt it. Perhaps the Sultan feared repeat of the losses he had suffered at Navarino (not for the first time did he think it singular that he should become engaged in the same theatre of war as his old friend Peto). But whatever the reason, in more than two months he had not seen a single Turkish ship.

'Shall you make any further landing than at Siseboli?' he asked.

'No. I shall not dissipate our strength. My intention is to bring the main force to battle in the field, then reduce Silistria and Shumla before what remains of the field army and their garrison is able to withdraw into the Balkan passes. Then I shall march hard on Adrianople. Siseboli shall be my base of supply once we have forced the Balkan. Despite what has gone before, I do not consider the task a difficult one. The Turkish soldier, although he has fought bravely and endured much, is become . . . *bedrükt.*'

Bedrükt – despondent, downhearted. There was without doubt something amiss in the fighting spirit of the Sultan's army. Would the Janissaries have let Siseboli stand as a rebuke to them? Not the Janissaries of old. And yet here they stood, reviewing the coming campaign, not *within* the walls of Silistria but without. Hervey nodded, but cautiously, 'There was nothing of élan in their action at Siseboli, or before.'

Diebitsch nodded. 'It is, they say, in the Turk nature – a tendency to *fatalismus*. And it is my intention to persuade them of their inevitable fate, and quickly.'

'General – you will forgive me if I appear impudent – but are there more solid grounds for believing the Turks will not fight as once they did? Especially once we – you – cross the Danube.'

Diebitsch nodded thoughtfully (and smiled to himself, for he ought to have expected as much from a man he wished to make major-general). 'My spies report that there have not been the reinforcements from the west on which the Sultan was counting. The Servians and Arnauts have sent but few, and the Bosnians, the best of their auxiliaries, none at all.'

Hervey nodded too. 'That would indeed bear on their fighting spirit.'

'And I believe they have lately made a grave mistake, which I am now about to take advantage of.' Diebitsch pointed to Shumla on the map. 'Here the main Turk force has been assembling since the snows were past, and Reschid Pasha, the new Vizier, arrived at the end of March to take personal command. You are aware of his aptitude?'

'Yes,' said Hervey: the reputation of General Reschid was well known to London from his campaign against the Greeks in Morea.

'But I perceive in this a measure of alarm,' continued Diebitsch. 'You may not know it, but Reschid is the son of an Orthodox priest, a Greek. He was made captive as a child, then rose by sheer capability – the Sultan's first minister, a remarkable transformation. Yet I wonder if the Sultan or any other can have complete trust in his loyalty. That is something on which it is futile to speculate, but it *may* from time to time impel him to action in order to prove it. In any case, he has miscalculated. General Roth, a capable man despite the reverses of last season, of his own initiative has placed a force of two corps before Shumla – they wintered in Roumelia – and a line of defensible posts between there and Rustchuk, which is the westernmost Turk garrison of any importance. And I have now a line of Cossack patrols between Pravadi and Turtokai here on the Danube,' (he pointed to the latter fortress, almost equidistant between Silistria and Rustchuk) 'so that, in truth, the country of the Dobrudscha, though it is not yet ours, is denied to the Turks. The Dobrudscha is good farmland, valuable to the army. And to there,' (pointing to Rasgrad, half-way between Rustchuk and Shumla) 'my headquarters are being transferred as we speak.'

'*Before* Silistria falls?'

'Silistria is now surely invested. Its garrison is made prisoner. And – here is the point – the more so for Reschid's miscalculation:

he attempted to recover Pravadi two weeks ago, but his letter to the Pasha at Rustchuk, to send troops to his assistance, was intercepted by my Cossacks, and so Reschid was thrown back. But because he has a reputation to maintain – and perhaps that need to reassure the Sultan – he now marches thither again with the whole garrison of Shumla.'

Hervey could see the opportunity in this, but it would be to no avail if the Turks were simply to entrench themselves at Pravadi instead of Shumla. 'Can Pravadi stand in the face of such numbers?'

'It has been most carefully fortified since we captured it.' Diebitsch took an engineer sketch from beneath the map. 'An inundation here,' he went on, pointing, 'covered by a battery, protects the northern side of the town. There is a hornwork constructed on the commanding ground to the west, here, while the town itself is surrounded by a wall flanked with *tenailles*, so that although it rests in a deepish sort of valley, it is perfectly defensible.'

'How strong is the garrison, General?'

Diebitsch paused only momentarily before disclosing the number. 'Eight thousand. With some of my best engineers.'

'So I take it you intend besieging Reschid as he himself besieges?' Hervey smiled. 'Like the Gauls laying siege to Caesar as he laid siege to Alesia?'

Diebitsch looked at him warily.

'I did not mean to suggest that yours would be the fate of the Gauls, General,' added Hervey quickly. 'Only that the ground and the situation seem greatly to your favour.'

Diebitsch shook his head. 'I have done with sieges. I shall force Reschid to withdraw once more to Shumla, and in that withdrawal I shall destroy him in the open. Upon that battle the key to the Balkan lock shall turn.'

Hervey could make no reply. The design was inspiring. All that was necessary to bring it off was that the Tsar's officers had the requisite acuity. And of that he could not yet be certain.

When an hour later Hervey returned to their quarters, he found Fairbrother lying back in a chair, his face being vigorously lathered by a wiry Bessarabian barber.

'I have ripe news . . . but it must wait a little longer.'

Fairbrother could not reply until the barber began stropping his razor. 'For what?'

Hervey nodded and raised an eyebrow.

'Have no fear on that account. I've had the devil of a job to explain I wanted my upper lip shaving.'

'I take no chances.'

Fairbrother decided that his own news could be aired instead. 'Well, I tell you the strangest thing. While you were away I borrowed a horse from the commissaries and took a ride upriver, and behold – I saw camels drinking in the Danube.'

Hervey looked puzzled. 'Why strange? They'll need *some* water, I dare say; and the river seems to have excess of it. They're Turcomans, to make up the losses in pack horses.'

'Yes, I learned that. But is it not extraordinary: the prophecy is come true, eh?'

Hervey took off his forage cap and sat down, already sensing that his friend had a meal to make. 'I have not the pleasure of knowing what prophecy.'

Fairbrother wiped soap from his mouth. 'Hervey, you astound me. "*Dans le Danube et du Rhin viendra boire le Grand Chameau*"?'

Hervey shook his head. 'Thou speakest in riddles.'

'But of course; I quote Nostradamus. You've heard of Nostradamus, have you not?'

'Of course I've heard of Nostradamus. And the three witches on the heath.'

Fairbrother chose to ignore the comparison. 'Did he not prophesy the Mussulman would drive all before him in his march westward?'

'I've never read his work. In any case, General Diebitsch intends driving his camels in the other direction, to Constantinople.'

The barber now began with his razor, and conversation ceased until he had scraped off the last of the soap.

As he took to the brush and the strop for the second, close shave, Fairbrother could contain himself no longer. 'I must tell you of a considerable piece of intelligence I acquired during my ride. I watched the engineers blow up a *fougasse*. Not, however, by quick-match but with electricity. Is such a means known to English engineers?'

'I think not,' replied Hervey, at once engaged by the notion. 'But why were you so close to the siege works? Were the Turks making a sortie?'

'No. I came upon the engineers at their practice ground. They fired the mine from six hundred yards off, with a Voltaic pile.'

'I am no electrician.'

'Nor I, though I've read enough to comprehend what they told me – which they were content enough to do until their superior arrived. He was greatly perturbed by my presence, so I feigned ignorance. I have, however, made extensive notes.'

'Excellent. I fancy the Board of Ordnance will be pleased to read them. But I wonder why we haven't used electricity, and yet the Russians have?'

'I suppose it's that their army has been active these late years. Others, dare I say it, have become decidedly cobwebby.'

The barber began lathering again, and conversation ceased until he was done with his razor and had left the room for the wash-house where he was boiling up towels.

Hervey took the opportunity to explain his own news, the

general-in-chief's intentions. Without being able to point out the various places on a map, however, he imagined he would have to reprise them once his friend had left the chair.

The barber returned with his hot towels, and soon Fairbrother's head was swaddled like a mummy, but for his mouth.

'What distance is it from Pravadi to Shumla – a dozen leagues or thereabouts?'

Hervey took out the map from his sabretache and consulted it. 'It is.'

'Do you not think it perilous to try to manoeuvre against such an accomplished general as Reschid, especially with such support as he has at close hand in Shumla, for he cannot have left the place empty? And if Hussein Pasha at Rustchuk is summoned to his aid, it is but fifty miles from there to Shumla – two days' forced march at most.'

Hervey was now less impressed with the possibility that the barber was a Turkish spy and more with the ability of his friend to picture the country in his mind. Nevertheless he proceeded with caution. 'The intelligence is that there are but . . . *quattuor cohortes* remaining there. But . . . *our friends, with whom we rode*, their patrols tie up very neatly the force at the other place. The venture is risky, of course, but the . . . *imperator* is rightly impatient for success.'

He sat back to observe the barber applying one last towel, wondering again at his friend's contrary disposition. It was extraordinary that – and in so chance a fashion – Fairbrother could one minute display an indolence that was proverbial of the race to which he partially belonged, and yet in another demonstrate the most remarkable percipience. That in its way, perhaps, was part not just of his charm but of his worth: there was something in his friend's haphazardness that made him look at things differently, not taking them quite at face value, for Fairbrother seemed at times capable of divination (whereas he himself proceeded entirely from – he believed – a proper soldierly impulse or from the application of dispassionate logic). The haphazardness no doubt derived from, among other things, his eclectic reading (which apparently, now, even took in scientific papers), which, though never of the depth that would make him a scholar, gave him nevertheless a passing acquaintance with almost everything of the moment. Of the two of them, Hervey was sure that Dr Johnson would have judged Fairbrother the more 'clubbable'. Yet with Fairbrother's intuition added to his own more measured approach, he would count himself almost unassailable. He was certainly resolved to have it so in Gibraltar – or even (he smiled to himself – preposterous notion!) St Petersburg.

'When do we begin?' asked the diviner, emerging from the towels.

'*Crastinum*. They are providing us with horses.'

Fairbrother stood up, fished out silver from a pocket and dismissed the barber with a smile and a handshake.

'I thought to try him by telling him to come back *crastinum* – but I suppose we shall be leaving at too early an hour?'

Hervey sighed. 'I have spent too long in India to underestimate the possibilities of spies. But, yes, I believe we shall leave early.'

Fairbrother began brushing his hair back vigorously. 'What else did you learn? Diebitsch – is he as his reputation?'

'I would judge him a very considerable general. He has a very . . . *complete* view of strategy. I'll tell you more when we dine, but this I must first tell you: I was made a member of the Order of Saint Anna, Second Class – With Swords.'

Fairbrother put down his hair brushes and turned to his friend, his face shining with the polishing of soap and an admiring smile. 'And most deservedly so. Congratulations!'

'And – here's the ripest news of all – Diebitsch wants to make me a major-general and give me a brigade.'

Fairbrother's expression turned to one of curiosity. 'Does he, indeed? Not empty honours, then: he sees your true worth. What reply did you give him?'

'That I esteemed his offer greatly, but that I required time to consider it.'

'You did not reject it forthwith? I am heartened. How much time was agreed?'

'It was not specified. He gave me to understand that he wished my services to be with him principally in St Petersburg. I don't believe my leading a brigade to Constantinople is an essential element in his design.'

Fairbrother frowned. 'We must trust not. There is no greater admirer of your talents than I, but even you might find the taking of Constantinople with but a brigade an uncertain venture.'

Hervey frowned back. 'There was no suggestion of a forlorn hope in brigade strength, I assure you. I confess I am excessively attracted by the offer, however.'

'Of course you are. But are you serious in thinking you could accept? Would not the language be a trial, for one thing?'

'Have we met a Russian general yet who is Russian?'

'We have not. And, of course, Mrs Hervey would find St Petersburg congenial to her music.'

Hervey started. Somehow they never spoke of Kezia. 'Just so. But' (he almost added 'more importantly') 'what would be your answer? Would the clime be to your liking?'

Fairbrother laughed. 'It might be said that I have had a surfeit of sun. I suppose they have good fires in winter? But what should be my part there? It's one thing to make me an honorary member of your mess, but another to co-opt me into service of the Tsar.'

Hervey was silent.

Fairbrother buttoned the collar of his tunic in a way that said he was to impart something of substance. 'Hervey, I may tell you that

I am resolved to give up my interest at the Cape. Such business as is there can hardly be thought sufficient to provide worthy occupation. In the long run I shall transfer my interest to London, but in the shorter term I am at your disposal. Should you choose Gibraltar or St Petersburg I am indifferent, as indeed I am to Hounslow. You may make your decision entirely as you see it best befits your condition. I shall bear with it happily.'

Hervey rose, held out his hand, and with a catch in his voice said, 'I am truly very fortunate in your friendship.'

XIV

THE VIZIER

Yeni Bazar, 8 June

Fairbrother had been disappointed to leave the luxuries of the Danube so quickly. And in truth he had been intrigued, for he had never witnessed a siege before. He thought it scientific to an impressive degree, what little he had been able to observe, and the sheer magnitude of the supply – the vast organization of stores and transport – he found fascinating. But he understood the imperative to seize the opportunity, and indeed he expressed himself in admiration of the general-in-chief's evident determination to strike a felling blow rather than merely a series of safe ones. And so he had packed his camp comforts once again and readied himself for the saddle once more. Here at least, though, they had been extraordinarily well favoured, for Hervey had been given the pick of the remount lines for his party; and all seven of them were mounted well.

The country they were now coming to was different. The hills, a northerly spur of the Balkan which might, at a pinch, answer to 'mountains', were steep-sided and abundantly wooded, with deep, narrow ravines in which streams ran with sometimes uncommon force. Such country, reckoned Hervey, from his vantage of the plain, would hide an army and devour scouts; the Russians would need the most active patrols unless they were to fall foul of Turk trickery. Any encounter beyond an affair of pickets would be difficult in the extreme, the ground unsuited to manoeuvre. A few men and guns might hold up a considerable force; and a force might lose many men in the process of driving in a defended position. But it was, of course, the same country for the Turks: the forest had no partiality for one side or the other. The 'Varian disaster' in the Teutoburgerwald, which had held him spellbound on first reading in the remove at Shrewsbury, and which exercised still a potent influence on the minds of officers who studied their profession, was not a victory for the *Wald* but for the German tribes who out-thought and outfought the legions of Quintilius Varus.

They had left Silistria on the 5th and made good distance at first on the plain of the Lower Dobrudscha, but for most of the third day they had ridden in thick fog, with little idea of their progress except by a very rough dead reckoning. And tedious going it had been too: they tramped for hours on end, leading the horses amid a vast press of men and animals, for by some miscalculation the baggage of the reserve division had come onto the road in advance of the main body. And then in the middle of the afternoon the sun had managed at last to burn through and they were able to see the distant hills. But while the mist had slowed them, certainly, it had also masked their advance. There was no sign of Turk patrols. They had continued marching until after dark, reaching Yeni Bazar at about nine o'clock, when the army made camp.

Such as he could make out, it seemed a prosperous sort of place by the standards of the country. Yeni Bazar – 'new market' – was a town of about fifty families, Bulgar, Turk and Wallachian, most of which alike had fled on hearing of the approaching army. There was a church, which appeared whole, and a mosque, and some substantial-looking houses, many of stone, and the streets were wide – and clean (though not for long). Hervey went to find Diebitsch's headquarters while the others sought a bivouac, and the general had just invited him into a chamber of the *madrasah* on which he had planted his pennant when Count Pahlen, commanding the forward detachment, came in to report.

With no other officers but a single aide-de-camp present, Pahlen spoke in German. 'At four o'clock my Cossacks made contact with Turk cavalry on the road to Shumla, ten miles hence. The Cossacks drove them back a mile, but came then on formed infantry – a force in all, I estimate, of two thousand. I brought up my leading regiment and dislodged them, and as darkness approached gave orders to occupy a blocking position astride the road at Madara strong enough to stand against a counter-attack at dawn.'

Diebitsch nodded approvingly – admirable action, exemplary reporting.

Pahlen continued: 'I at first imagined it to be a sortie in connection with our own advance, but the prisoners reveal that their orders, from the Vizier himself, were to march towards Pravadi to threaten the rear of Roth's force.'

Diebitsch had explained to Hervey before they marched that Roth's force of two corps, which had made camp before Shumla, would detach a small number to maintain watch on that place and then march east towards Pravadi and occupy blocking positions in the hilly, wooded defiles. This would prevent the Vizier from bolting back to Shumla from before the walls of Pravadi when he learned of Diebitsch's approach – to fix him, as it were, so that Diebitsch could close up and then defeat him in open battle.

Hervey reckoned that on learning Pahlen's news, therefore, Diebitsch had a right to look gratified. But the general was doubly pleased, for the report seemed also to confirm that surprise was still his. 'Do I take it that they believed you to be a part of Roth's force, and that they had no suspicion of our advance?'

'That is exactly as I read it,' replied Pahlen. 'Indeed, I have let the most senior of the prisoners, a colonel of artillery, escape towards Shumla with the intelligence that I was commander of Roth's own rearguard.'

'*Vollendet!*'

Consummate indeed; Hervey, too, was all admiration.

Pahlen asked what further orders there were before leave to rejoin his corps.

Diebitsch surprised them both. 'Since our march went un-molested – indeed, unobserved – at first light this morning I sent orders to Roth to leave two regiments only in the defiles, but to make a great show that they remained there in strength, and to slip away with the rest of his corps and rally here at Yeni Bazar.'

It was Pahlen's turn to look impressed. His general-in-chief was stealing march after march on the Vizier.

Diebitsch called for wine.

Other officers came, and soon the talk turned Russian. Hervey occupied himself with his map, until after an hour – and just when he was wondering if it were not better to withdraw for the night – a galloper arrived from Roth.

As Diebitsch's chief of staff read the despatch aloud, the smiles and general agitation indicated that it was more good news.

One of the aides-de-camp translated. 'General Roth intends coming away under cover of darkness. There is no sign that the Turks have detected his intentions. He expects to be able to effect a junction here towards midday, or at the latest by last light.'

Hervey acknowledged, but not without concern. If the Vizier did withdraw, and overpower the token rearguards, then Roth's move-ment would turn out to be a flank march to that of the Turks, and his situation would be perilous in the extreme. 'What are the general-in-chief's intentions then?'

'To await the junction with General Roth's corps,' replied the aide-de-camp simply.

Hervey had learned all that he needed. It was time to take his leave.

He had some difficulty finding their billet – a confusion with one of the provost-marshal's staff – but at half past one he stumbled blinking into what had been a sort of drapery. Fairbrother, Agar and Corporal Acton were fast asleep on the bare floor. Johnson was crouching in a corner lit by an oil lamp, blowing on the fire under a simmering camp kettle, smoke leaving more or less obligingly through a broken window.

'I was getting a bit worried, sir,' he said in a loud whisper, sounding decidedly relieved. 'Them sentries are right jumpy. 'As tha 'ad anything to eat?'

Hervey shook his head. 'Not hungry. Is that coffee?'

'No – 'ot water, sir. I could mash-up some tea. It'd be quicker.'

'And better for my constitution at this time, no doubt.'

'Ah've got some eggs an' all – 'ard-boiled, and some for breakfast.'

Hervey recognized that finding eggs was a considerable feat. The one disappointment that General Diebitsch could have admitted was that the country they had come through was more derelict than he'd expected, the villages deserted, with barely a sign for mile upon mile that the land had ever been cultivated. But he would wait until morning to enquire of the eggs' provenance. 'Just the one, then. Thank you. I'm obliged you've remained on watch.'

'Ah told Brayshaw and Green to bed down. Corp'l Acton'll relieve me in an hour.'

There was no reason to mount watch within their own quarters, except against 'proggers' (as Johnson had it), but Hervey supposed that at least it meant the fire would be lit at reveille. 'There's no early move tomorrow. It's make and mend till the middle of the morning. Where are the horses?'

'In wi' them from t'headquarters, yonder.' His thumb indicated somewhere close by. 'Them Rousskis 're good. They put a new shoe on Mr Agar's in five minutes.'

Presently he handed him a canteen of sweetened tea.

Hervey took a good sip. 'Where did you find milk?'

'T'Rousskis killed a nanny-goat, an' there were a bit, still, in 'er udder.'

'Posthumous milk – I do believe it's the first I've had.'

It wasn't, but Johnson would not gainsay him, instead picking off a last bit of eggshell before handing over the meagre supper.

'Thank you,' said Hervey, suddenly feeling too tired to ask if by any chance there was a little salt. 'Is that my bed?' he asked, hopefully, nodding to a blanket the other side of the stone floor.

'Ay, sir. There's a bit o' straw underneath, an' a nice piece o' silk I twisted into a pillow. This place were full o' stuff when we came in, but t'Rousskis said they wanted it, an' Cap'n Fairbrother said as not to stop them.'

'Eminently sensible,' replied Hervey, picturing with some dismay Johnson trying to defy a looting party.

It was colder than the night before, which they had passed in a tent at the roadside amid cherry and walnut trees (the dew had fallen like rain); but the single blanket would do. He would sleep again dressed – but tonight with the comfort of his boots off.

Johnson did not wake him until after seven (reveille was a quiet affair, no trumpets). An orderly had come soon after six and, with General Diebitsch's compliments, asked that Hervey come to the headquarters at nine. Agar, just returned from stables, answered for him.

As ever, Johnson woke him with tea, sweetened and with milk

judged to have another day's life, just, and with the additional information that he was expected at headquarters and that there was a bowl of hot water ready for him to shave. 'And there's bacon 'n' eggs.'

'Where did you find bacon?' asked Hervey, rising stiffly on an elbow to sip the tea, wondering how much sleep he had had, for it felt like very little.

'It were 'idden in t'chimney. It's all right though.'

'I don't doubt it. A good-sized flitch, was it?'

'It'll last us a few days.'

'Then perhaps you might make up some sort of forage bag. I intend taking a ride.'

'Right, sir. I'll make some more 'avercakes an' all.'

Hervey shaved quickly and then breakfasted at a table, which somehow had been spared the looting party, Fairbrother and Agar joining him for more coffee. He told them the headquarters news.

Fairbrother looked uncertain. 'A good deal seems to rest on the word of the prisoners. What if they had indeed discovered our march and were making a sortie to test our strength?'

'It's not impossible. But Pahlen's position at Madara serves as an impediment to movement from east *or* west.'

Fairbrother seemed content.

'Might I go to Madara, sir?' asked Agar. 'There is a carving there of great antiquity I should like to see.'

'A carving?'

'Of a horseman spearing a lion.'

'What is its significance, beyond the appeal of art?'

Agar looked puzzled. 'Well ... it is thought to be Thracian-Greek, some three centuries before Christ.'

'And there are not many of these?'

Agar realized he had not described its singular dimensions and situation. 'It is about twenty feet in height, carved high up in the side of a cliff.'

'I see. I had imagined it to be yet another statue.' (There had been many during their wanderings.) 'By all means you may go. Corporal Acton shall accompany. Only return in good time – before last light.'

'Thank you, sir. If I may I will start out at once.'

When he was gone, Fairbrother lit a cheroot and stretched out his legs, until his chair creaked ominously. 'How many men did you say the Vizier has in all?'

'The estimate is thirty thousand, and upwards of fifty guns.'

'Mm. A very even match, then . . . except in guns. Diebitsch has, what, three times that number?'

Hervey nodded. 'But in country so trappy it's not perhaps so decisive. I think he'll have the devil of a job bringing the Vizier to battle.' He drained his coffee cup and rose. 'See, I want to take a ride into yonder foothills. There's nothing to occupy us here until Roth comes in. Will you ride with me?'

'Of course. It's a deuced tedious business riding with an army; I'd relish a gallop. But first, while you attend on the headquarters, I shall take a bath.'

Hervey looked at him doubtfully.

'There's a Turkish bath here.'

'Truly?'

'*Tellaks* and all. The provost-marshal put it under guard, reserved it for the staff, but I fancy I'll be able to get a ticket.'

The summons to headquarters proved something of a misunderstanding, merely an invitation to breakfast with the officers. Hervey took coffee with them and left as soon as he was decently able, but not before the courtesy of seeking leave of the general-in-chief (or rather, his chief of staff) to ride out from the lines. He turned down the offer of an escort of Cossacks, explaining that he intended merely to see the country rather than the enemy. Besides, a pair of horsemen ought to present no alarm to Turkish scouts.

They set off at eleven and headed due south. It was not yet hot, although the flies were troubling, and it was a relief to get into the fresher air beyond the outposts.

'How was your bath?'

'Quite excellent, thank you. There were only two others admitted. You should have come. But here's the strange thing: the *tellaks* were Bulgar – and very good, too; very adroit with tired muscles – but no lover of the Turk, certainly. Not at all. There was much thanksgiving for the arrival of the Russians – all this was through the Russians of course, who obliged me with their French, but I believe it to have been honest – and they said there'd been many deserters of late, all complaining that the Vizier demanded of them unreasonable, impossible things.'

Hervey nodded, as if unsurprised. 'Then why had the rest of Yeni Bazar fled?'

'Erring on the safe side to protect their women? Half the inhabitants were Turk anyway, it seems.'

Hervey pondered. 'Deserters – it certainly augurs well. But I've been thinking: if the Vizier doesn't break off his siege at Pravadi, Diebitsch will have to force him to – and that would not be a battle in which he would have the advantage.'

Fairbrother was doubtful the Vizier could stay put. 'He *must* break it off when he learns Diebitsch might get between him and Shumla.'

'I think you must be right.' Hervey cleared his throat. 'Then might we not ride towards Pravadi and see what's afoot?'

'I do believe it was your intention from the outset.'

'Truly it wasn't. I regret to say the significance of the timing of the Vizier's withdrawal occurs to me only now. I confess I was deucedly tired last night.'

Fairbrother pulled up suddenly. 'There, yonder!'

Hervey reached for his pistol.

But his friend was pointing at the sky. 'Is it an eagle?' He took out his telescope. 'I believe it is. But Golden or Imperial?'

'I fear I'm unable to help. I've no knowledge how to tell between them,' replied Hervey, and with some regret, since he had once prided himself on his eye for raptors.

Fairbrother, in the way of his sudden interests, had become a student of ornithology during their journey out. He had bought Temminck's *Manuel d'ornithologie* in London for his 'campaign library', as he called it, and had been annotating it almost daily with his sightings. 'The species is only lately defined. The Imperial's slightly smaller than the Golden, but how can one compare at such a distance? It might be a Bonelli's, but that's smaller still, and much lighter on its underside.'

'Bonelli?'

'Italian. A considerable naturalist.'

'Do you recall the skirmishing line of vultures at the Cape, how grateful we were of their timely intelligence of the Zulu?'

'Vividly.' Fairbrother lowered his telescope and shook his head; he would not be able to make a definitive entry at this range. 'You know, I wonder that no one has yet devised a practicable use for the balloon in such work.'

'Quite so. To observe an eagle in its *milieu* would be a fine thing indeed.'

'No – I *meant* to use the eagle's vantage of the plain. Napoleon – I beg pardon; *Bonaparte* – used balloons, did he not?'

Hervey smiled. It was not often his friend turned his thoughts to soldiery when there were other distractions. 'Forgive me. Indeed he did – *aéronautiers*, they called them. I think they saw service against the Austrians, but nothing of consequence. I have a notion they had some in Egypt too, and Sir John Moore destroyed all their apparatus. Strange, really, Moore being so innovatory a man. A pretty sort of toy, I suppose they all thought. I remember Peto saying he'd considered raising one from his quarterdeck to see beyond the horizon, but that he was always afeard the rigging would foul its cable – or the other way round. You know, I myself nearly made an ascent in Paris.'

'I suppose *nearly* making an ascent has some distinction,' said Fairbrother drily.

'There was a longer waiting list than for the United Service, and when my turn came the wind was too strong.'

They rode on for two hours thus, talking of balloons, the feathered world, ships and books, and all manner of tangential affairs, seeing a good many birds, but no Turks – nor even sign of Turks. Indeed, but for a goatherd, with whom they could make no communication at all, they did not see a soul, for the half-dozen settlements that passed for villages were as deserted as those on the road to Yeni Bazar. Whether the inhabitants had fled on the appearance of the Vizier's men or General Roth's, there was no way of telling.

They began to climb – a gentle, even slope, ungrazed meadow with many violets; peaceful. When they reached the tree-line, however, they heard distant cannon. It was barely perceptible at first, but continual, and it increased as they gained height. And then it ceased abruptly, so that they found themselves once more in a still world, serene, the sunlight filtered by the green canopy; and then into a broad glade, with a slow-running stream. It was a fine place to make a halt.

'How far do you say we've come?' asked Hervey as he pulled out his map.

They had trotted for no more than half an hour in the three. 'A dozen miles . . . fifteen perhaps?'

'Which must place us nearer to Pravadi than the sound of the cannon suggests. It's a devil of a business being certain with maps like this.'

'Pravadi's in a deepish sort of valley, is it not? If the guns are at the foot of the cliffs surrounding it, there's little wonder they make no great noise.'

Hervey nodded; it made sense. 'I wonder why they stop?'

Fairbrother shrugged. 'Perhaps to face Mecca. Who knows?'

Hervey smiled. There was always cause, but it did not always follow that the cause was reasonable. 'I fancy we might take our ease here a while. Do you note the flies are gone?'

'I do.'

'Let's have our feast by the stream yonder, let these two drink and then picket them in the shade for an hour.'

They dismounted, loosened the surcingles and girth straps and led the horses to the pool. The geldings drank long but steadily, for they had been watered in Yeni Bazar. Nevertheless, Hervey was again taken by the docility of these big Dons. He had no idea of their turn of speed, but they looked as if they could cover ground; and yet they were not so long-backed as to lack handiness.

When the geldings had drunk their fill, Hervey and Fairbrother drove picket pegs into the ground under a spread of mountain oaks, and tethered them not too short. It was as peaceful as the great park at Windsor of a summer's afternoon, or the hills above Longleat, but the discipline of years would never let Hervey indulge such a thought too long. 'Better not off-saddle,' he said.

They unshipped their pistols and took the haversacks to a sunny bank of the stream. The Ordnance's black bread, the hard-boiled eggs of unknown provenance, the bacon from a draper's chimney, Johnson's oatcakes, strawberries from the draper's garden, and a flask of red wine of the country – a rough and ready picnic, but nonetheless agreeable.

It was now beyond warm. Hervey's brow had been wet beneath

the band of his forage cap. It was good to be inactive at this hour, with shade and running water. The flies were no longer troublesome; only the occasional buzz of a mosquito intruded.

When they had eaten, Hervey lay back with his hands clasped behind his head, looking at the clear blue sky beyond the leafy canopy, trying to fathom if it were different in any way from that he would have observed at the Cape, or India, or Spain, or even Wiltshire, on such an afternoon as this. He closed his eyes, conjuring with the thought of home in distant, simpler days.

'Good heavens, see there,' said Fairbrother suddenly, his voice all pleasant surprise.

Hervey opened his eyes. 'See what?'

Fairbrother was peering with his telescope upstream towards a clump of willow. 'There – hanging from the lower branches yonder, where they reach over to the middle stream.'

Hervey took the telescope. 'I see them. Like plumped pears hanging from cords. What are they?'

'Unless I'm very much mistaken, nests of the penduline titmouse. I'd rather come to think they were never to be found. According to Temminck the eggs are quite exquisite.'

'Perhaps we should gather some,' suggested Hervey, studying the hanging colony of a bird he'd hitherto never heard of. 'Do they make the nests themselves, or is it just such a thing as they take up?'

'They weave them from whatever's to hand – grass, spiders' webs, hair. Do you see a bird?'

He had not yet, though even with a telescope he sensed it would be difficult to spy a titmouse of any species in such cover. 'Perhaps the apertures are on the other side, and the birds approach unseen. Would that not be Nature's way?'

'Let's take a closer look,' said Fairbrother, getting to his knees. 'There must be eggs, or a brood.'

Hervey was happy to indulge his friend. The horses were quiet, it would not take too long to stalk a hundred yards, and in any case he thought it a fine thing to be able to tell Georgiana. '*Allons.*'

The friends stalked the diminutive bird with the stealth of the hunting cat. A full quarter of an hour – more – crouching, crawling, making like statues. But they discovered that Hervey was right: the entry to the nest was on the other side. Like good scouting dragoons, the birds approached from cover.

As they drew within whispering distance, the titmice became visible – all activity, to-ing and fro-ing, endlessly purposeful.

They lay watching, silent.

A breeze got up from the south-east. The leafy branches of the willow trembled, the nests swayed slightly, the birds remained active.

Then Hervey braced. 'Voices,' he breathed, gesturing.

At once the birds flew from Fairbrother's mind. He was back in the wild country of the Zulu.

The voices were indistinct, but raised. No knowing how far off.

Hervey looked back at the horses – quiet, and pretty well concealed in the shadow of the oaks. 'Let's get to the top of this hill and see where they're coming from.'

Fairbrother nodded.

They rose to a crouch and waded cautiously across the stream, keeping close to the willows for concealment. They climbed the hill easily – the earth was firm, with roots and branches enough to get a hand to – and made the lee of the crest noiselessly and with breath to spare.

The voices were now clear – and present.

They crept on hands and knees, and broached the crest crawling leopard-like to observe beyond.

Tents, pennants, caparisons – all the panoply of rank. A hundred yards away, no more.

The Vizier sat in an ivory chair (there was no mistaking him), officers attending – anxiously, it seemed to Hervey. A horseman was dismounting. He wore a red cloak despite the heat of the day. He took off his *kalpak* – the high-crowned hat of the country – and advanced with it in both hands held close to his chest as if in supplication.

The Vizier spoke. His words were indistinct, but it seemed he was giving leave to approach the throne.

The horseman now addressed him boldly. Hervey could catch none of it (how he wished Agar were with them). Except for three words, repeated by both men – the horseman with certainty, the Vizier with incredulity: '*Bir schei yok.*'

In vain Hervey looked at Fairbrother for enlightenment.

The Vizier flew into a rage, springing from his chair, gesturing at the horseman violently and shouting abuse.

The horseman stood his ground, protesting.

The Vizier raged on.

The horseman angrily flung off his cloak. The Vizier's officers stepped forward to examine it.

'What do they do? What is it?' whispered Hervey.

Fairbrother took up his telescope. 'It looks as if he's showing that it's shot through.'

Hervey's brow furrowed; what did it signify?

Fairbrother had no idea either.

Only remember '*Bir schei yok*'. They would know what it meant at Yeni Bazar. But for the moment they could only watch and wait – if only they could dare.

And then as suddenly as he had become enraged, the Vizier sank back into his chair, head lowered. His officers looked at him, as if waiting on his decision. He rose again and gestured that he was finished with the matter. He laid a hand on the man's shoulder and dismissed him with equability, then turned; and both Hervey and Fairbrother heard the word quite distinctly – 'Shumla.'

Officers began hurrying in all directions, horses were brought, tents were taken down. Had it not been for the rage and despondency, they might have thought the Vizier was about to lead his army through the breaches. But the air was of defeat, not victory – and the word 'Shumla' could mean only a retrograde movement?

'The siege is abandoned,' whispered Hervey. 'What else?'

It must have been the message the horseman brought – news, perhaps, of the approach of the Russians. Or that the walls withstood the fire? What did it matter; the Turks were beginning the movement that Diebitsch wished.

Hervey inclined his head to signal that they themselves should withdraw.

Fairbrother nodded thankfully.

They scrambled back down the hill, scarcely believing the Vizier's camp could be so careless of intruders. But then, why should there have been cause to think otherwise? What trespassers could there be here in the wooded fore-hills of the Balkan, the distant rampart of Constantinople?

At the bottom they froze. Before them were Turks, looking over the horses.

How many?

Hervey could see three. He looked at Fairbrother, and mouthed silently, 'Attack?'

What was the alternative? Fairbrother nodded.

Hervey motioned to him to cross the stream and cover him from a flank while he crossed closer to the horses. That way they might confuse the Turks and make them think they were more. It ought to be done with the sword – they didn't need the Vizier's camp alerting, even while it was being struck – but would they oblige?

No time to waste. Hervey drew his sabre silently, took a pistol from his belt (Fairbrother held one in each hand) and began edging

231

along the bank while his friend slipped into the stream, the sudden surge of birdsong welcome ally.

There were three Turks, and a fourth holding their horses fifty yards downstream. Would he take off at the sound of a fight and alert the camp?

Three Turks. He would have surprise for an instant, but *three* of them . . . It was risking too much, was it not? Pistols and be done with it. He had his Deringer too . . .

The Turks were now laughing. No time to find out why – attack now! But which of them first – middle, risking both flanks, or left, leaving two together? Take the most brutish-looking – middle.

Three plashy strides, up onto the bank and into them.

They turn as one, but too late.

'Give point' to the chest.

The middle man falls.

'Cut five' to the left.

The Turk screams, his face slashed through.

The third slices with his scimitar.

Hervey guards, but no time to lock his arm. His sabre breaks.

The Turk, off-balance, cuts upwards, late.

Hervey swings his left arm round, fires.

Nothing.

Fairbrother's pistol goes off like a cannon.

The Turk falls as his scimitar touches Hervey's tunic.

A momentary glance of gratitude, and Fairbrother's relief in return.

But the fourth Turk is already astride and away.

They tighten girths, spring to the saddle and ride for Yeni Bazar scarcely drawing bit.

XV

AN OFFICER'S WORD

Later

General Diebitsch had not returned from Madara when they reached Yeni Bazar. Hervey related what had happened to the chief of staff.

General Toll listened without a word, and then turned to one of the interpreters. '*Bir schei yok?*'

'"It was as it was",' came the reply, in Russian.

'*Es war wie es war*,' repeated the general helpfully.

Hervey was disappointed – and puzzled. 'It seemed more portentous. I can't think what it meant. Except that the Vizier may have doubted what the horseman said, and he in turn insisted it was so – that the Turks could make no impression on the walls, perhaps?'

'Well, there's no profit in speculating, Colonel. You are sure it was the Vizier, and that he broke camp?'

'No, General, I can't be certain it was the Vizier, only that it was a man of highest rank. But he broke camp – no doubt of it – and he was in angry spirits.'

Toll – Karl Wilhelm von Toll – had been a colonel on Kutusov's staff at Borodino when Hervey was but a cornet. As the character of the Baltic Germans tended, he was not to be hastened to any decision. He thought for what seemed an age, and then nodded determinedly. 'Very well, it will be dark in three hours; I shall give the order to be ready to move by stand-to-arms. By then we ought to have heard from the Cossacks, and Roth. You saw nothing at all of him?'

'Not a sign. There again, we followed a path in the forest for a good deal of the way.'

But it was the news he needed to hear, that the Vizier was making his move back to Shumla. Now they could bring him to a battle of manoeuvre. Toll looked grateful at last. 'Very well. And thank you, Colonel Hervey. You may indeed have gained us time.'

Hervey gathered up his leather and took his leave.

He made straight for his quarters where he found Fairbrother studying a map, and Johnson making a stew of bacon and lentils.

Johnson greeted him cheerily. He put the makeshift lid on the camp kettle and wiped his hands on his overalls. 'There's some coffee in that degsy, sir,' he said, nodding to the stove.

'Thank you, yes. It was rank stuff they had at the headquarters.'

Johnson poured the thick black brew into a china cup.

'Cap'n Fairbrother says tha were in a bit of a *tamash*, sir.'

Hervey nodded. It amused him sometimes to contemplate con-founding the code-breaker's art by combining Johnson's enunciation and his Hindoostani and rendering it into Greek script. 'We lived to tell the tale, as you see. Is Mr Agar returned?'

''E's just off-saddling now, sir.'

'My damned sabre broke. And my pistol misfired.'

Johnson looked anxious suddenly.

'I carried that sabre all the time we were in India.'

'I'm sure I can find thee another, sir. Them Cossacks 're very obliging.'

Hervey had his Mameluke still, but he'd never thought to use it. It was lighter than the service sabre, and the curve was shallower, so it handled differently. It was a thing of court dress, no more. 'I'd be very obliged if they *were* obliging. By all means see if they'll spare me one. Thank you.' He sipped his coffee. It was very bitter. He screwed up his face. 'Have we sugar, or honey?'

'I'll ask t'Cossacks for some an' all.'

Hervey smiled; Johnson's simple cheer could be restorative. It was quite like old times. 'Where *is* Mr Agar?'

As if answering the summons, Agar came. He looked decidedly happy.

Hervey nodded in acknowledgement of the salute. 'A report, if you please, Agar.'

'Well, sir, I believe I may say with certainty that the carvings are not of Thracian antiquity. The—'

'Mr Agar, in the circumstances – our being on active operations in the proximity of an enemy – I consider the military details to have priority over the antiquarian, absorbing though the latter doubtless are.'

Agar looked rather abashed. 'Oh, I'm sorry, I . . . That is,' (he braced himself) 'we saw no sign of Turk activity on the way to or returning from Madara – only, about a league east of that place, a good number of bodies, Turk, on which a pack of wild dogs was scavenging. We dispersed these, but I fear that they will return. At Madara, General Pahlen has erected gabions and mounted several guns to command the principal road, which is wide enough to admit the passing of waggons side by side, and has dug many rifle pits. There is very little opportunity to outflank the position, and not in any strength, save debouching either north or south of the entire ridge, a considerable diversion which would in turn expose a flank to the general's cavalry and, in the north, too, to troops in Yeni Bazar.'

'Thank you. Admirably clear. Quite exemplary. And the carving?'

Agar's expression turned to delight. 'Ah, it is most intriguingly done, though much of what must once have been carving in high relief is eroded. It is nearer to Kaspichan than Madara in point of fact, some hundred feet above the level of the river, which is also called Madara, in a vertical cliff standing about three hundred feet. The horseman, a prince, I would hazard, is thrusting a spear into a lion which is lying at his horse's feet, and an eagle flies in front and a dog runs after him.'

'Why was it carved?'

'Scenes such as this elsewhere are symbolical of a military triumph.'

'But not Thracian.'

'No, I am sure not.'

Hervey listened, almost spellbound, as Agar then expounded at length on the crucial dissimilarities with extant Thracian symbols, and on how the inscriptions, though indecipherable, indicated a much later date, perhaps even medieval. What good fortune was his: Fairbrother, Agar, Johnson – such capable and diverting company. It fell to few men, he supposed, to know three fellows of such infinite jest and excellent fancy.

But time was pressing and he adjourned the discourse.

Corporal Acton now appeared, his jaw set.

'Sir, may I speak, sir, please?' he asked, holding the salute.

'By all means, Corporal Acton. Stand easy.'

Acton cleared his throat. 'Confidentially, sir.'

Fairbrother rose to leave.

Hervey stayed him. 'I will come outside.'

Acton took a step back, turned about smartly and marched a dozen paces, until they were out of earshot.

'What is the trouble, Corporal Acton?'

'Sir, you was in a scrape with Turks, and your sabre broke and pistol misfired.'

'It was nothing. Captain Fairbrother put a ball in the man before I knew it.'

'That's not the point sir, with respect. It's my job to put balls in Turks. What would've 'appened 'ad the captain's pistol misfired too?'

Hervey frowned. It seemed futile, pedantic even, to point out that it was the business of none of them to put balls in Turks. 'Captain Fairbrother is an officer of too great experience to . . .' As he said the words he realized the retort they invited. 'What I mean is that it would be highly improbable that my and Captain Fairbrother's pistols would both misfire.'

'Sir, with respect again, Captain Fairbrother isn't regiment – more's the pity, if I may say so – and *I* am your coverman.'

'With respect' was not a locution to be ignored. Acton was right. 'Very well, I concede the matter entirely,' said Hervey, with a sigh.

'Thank you, sir.'

'Your attachment to duty is most commendable.'

Acton smiled, just a shade wryly (the Sixth took its duty seriously, but not piously). 'Thing is, sir, my promotion would be all behind me if I was to go back to 'Ounslow deficient a colonel.'

An hour later General Diebitsch returned, and soon after, gallopers from Pravadi. Hervey made at once for the headquarters. An aide-de-camp told him the news: the siege had been lifted at three o'clock, and the Vizier's army was in retreat. Hervey was gratified to hear the confirmation of his own assessment.

But by which route would the Turks march? Whatever the answer, there was scarce a moon to speak of, and so it could not be at speed if they marched through the night. 'Forbear waste of time' had been Cromwell's maxim, and Hervey had always found it apt; but in this instance, time was on Diebitsch's side. It would be no waste of it to rest his army here at Yeni Bazar and then move at first light when the Vizier's intentions were clearer.

He slipped into the general's office as the intentions were being discussed, but he could only stand uncomprehending. At length the confab ceased and Diebitsch appeared to issue a series of orders. Toll added words of his own and then the assembly broke up, with staff officers striding out purposefully.

Seeing Hervey, Diebitsch beckoned him. 'Your ride proved opportune.'

'It did, General. May I ask what are your orders?'

'You may. The army is ready to move as we speak, which is in no small part thanks to your address. Roth has had trouble extricating himself, getting his guns and waggons down the hillsides, and will not join before morning, so we shall sleep here and march in the morning to intercept the Vizier – as soon as I know by which route he comes. Or, of course, in the event he reveals himself this night, we shall march at once.'

Hervey felt keenly the satisfaction of one whose address had bought advantage, which was ever the wish of the cavalryman. 'Then I will take your leave, General.'

Diebitsch took off his sword belt and sat on the edge of the desk. 'One more thing, Colonel Hervey. You saw something of the country; which route would *you* choose?'

'As a Turk, General?'

'As you will.'

Hervey had, in fact, seen only something of the northern route, and a very little of the middle, but he knew the Cossacks had ranged throughout of late and reported that the roads on the southern route through the numerous tributary valleys of the Kamtchik were so bad that it would be nigh impossible to take artillery that way. The northern route might oblige the Vizier to battle in the open – close to Yeni Bazar – with Roth's corps, for he must assume Roth was withdrawing by this route (once he had discovered the ruse of the campfires and that Roth *was* withdrawing).

The northern route – faster because of the open country – might well represent the best option, however, for to take the centre route would be to traverse country not greatly more favourable than that to the south, and with the risk of both his flanks being assailed.

'I suppose he must soon learn of our presence here, and of General Pahlen at Madara?'

'Yes, though perhaps not as quickly as he would need to. Roth's corps will act as a screen of sorts. But the Vizier will certainly have word of Pahlen – though, we hope, thinking them but a part of Roth's old force before Shumla. But Pahlen has learned of re-inforcements at Shumla: five thousand Arnauts have lately come in. So it may be that the Vizier believes the Arnauts will clear his line of withdrawal.'

'Ah,' said Hervey. 'That would indeed favour him towards the middle course. But for myself I would still regard the northern route as the most expedient. I should rather battle with an enemy in the open, especially having raw troops, as the Vizier's are, than have trees to cower behind. But I would hazard that the man I saw today will take the middle route.'

Diebitsch nodded. 'I cannot of course hazard all, Colonel Hervey, which is why I am determined to wait on the dawn reports.'

'Indeed, General.'

'But one way or another we shall bring Reschid Pasha to battle tomorrow or the next day. He shall not enter Shumla.'

Hervey believed him.

As he was leaving, an aide-de-camp called him to General Toll's office. The chief of staff was dictating instructions for the order of march. He broke off and asked the officers to leave them for the moment.

When the door had closed, his expression turned to something approaching a smile. He had, indeed, a naturally benign face – large eyes, red cheeks – but the reverses of the previous season had weighed with him, whereas with Diebitsch they were but stimulant. 'Colonel, I don't believe I expressed adequately my esteem earlier. The army will be in immeasurably better condition tomorrow for your intelligence of the Vizier. It will stand down this evening in all respects ready to move. The general-in-chief knows this, too.'

Hervey bowed. 'No further expressions are required, General, though I am honoured to receive them.'

Toll continued to study him, without a word but with approval, until at length he was ready to speak his mind. 'Colonel, I am aware of the offer which the general-in-chief has made to you, for an active command and the prospect of a senior post. I hope you will consider very carefully the offer. It is the duty of generals-in-chief to bring on new blood, and in the service of the Tsar there are many who were not born to it. I myself was not born to it, nor indeed the general-in-chief, as you know. New blood, Colonel – not excess of it, but enough to refresh that which is shed for one reason or another.'

'I could not but consider such an offer very carefully, General, I assure you.'

Toll nodded very deliberately. 'I myself hope to have time to plant cabbages on my little estate on the Dvina.'

An hour before dawn they were up, shaved, and breakfasting, lit by a 'windfall' of candles, as Johnson put it, and watered from the copper boiler in the rear of the building, whose removal and onward portage he was in the course of planning. The otherwise unappealing black bread made very passable toast on the charcoal stove, with olive oil from the Cossacks in the same barter as a new sabre, as well as a bag of sugar and a doll in Cossack dress for Georgiana. Another flitch of bacon had 'been found' (Johnson was particular in using the passive voice), and, truly remarkably, more eggs, now hard-boiled, as their field rations of the day. So far they had not had to resort to the issue biscuit.

At stand-to Agar had the dragoons bring the horses to the door.

'I'll wager the Turks come this way,' said Fairbrother as they swung into the saddle.

'You've changed your opinion?' replied Hervey, unsure whether in fact Fairbrother had expressed one before.

'I was thinking as I lay last night. The Vizier was an angry general yesterday, and he's a proud one – he took Messolonghi did he not? – and if he's been humiliated before Pravadi a second time and learns that an army's advanced as far as here he may well throw himself in his rage at us. He may be the Sultan's chief minister, but he's got Greek blood.'

Hervey rehearsed again his reasons for believing the Vizier would take the middle route, but an hour later it looked as if Fairbrother would be proved right. Just after the order to stand down, a party of Turk horse appeared at the edge of the forest, on the nearer ridge about a mile distant. Hervey saw them clearly, and so, he observed, did General Diebitsch, sitting in the saddle nearby amid a clump of cherry trees. But no alarm was sounded, the pickets remained out and the battalions went about the routine of breakfast and first parade.

'I think we may conclude that Diebitsch is not a general to be bustled. He means to dictate the terms of this battle. The duke would heartily approve.'

Fairbrother smiled to himself. He supposed that divining what the duke would do would be the practice of the army for years.

But half an hour passed, and the Turks made no move. Perhaps they were transfixed by the smoke of the hundreds – thousands – of impromptu fires? It would mask the assembly of a fair-size army. Hervey agreed, yet was still amazed they were not on the move, for Diebitsch had seemed sure the first-light reports would reveal the

Vizier's intentions. But General Roth had not appeared, nor had there been any word – not that he had heard of. There had been distant cannon fire, muffled by the forest, but it was desultory, and there was little to glean from the pattern. He decided he should ride over to the cherry trees and enquire.

A train of mules with pannier baskets came plodding along the line, staying Hervey's plan; he did not want to intrude on the general's breakfast.

Instead they dismounted.

Five minutes later the aide-de-camp of the night before rode over to thém with one of the mules. He had no news of Roth, save that his corps was in a running fight. 'The general-in-chief is resolved to remain here until the situation is known. Meanwhile General Toll sends you these for your favour.'

An orderly unhitched a basket.

'Please thank General Toll,' said Hervey, conscious of the consideration of so senior an officer towards a junior. 'Will you join us?'

The aide-de-camp shook his head. 'No, Colonel, thank you; I must attend on General Diebitsch.' He saluted and returned to the cherry trees.

'Well, I call that uncommon civil,' said Fairbrother, devilling into the basket. 'After all the haste of last night . . . and here we have a regular *déjeuner à la fourchette*.'

Johnson's feast of the pre-dawn was not long past, but the sight of sheep's cheese, sausage, rice cakes and preserved figs was a strong stimulant to appetite, as well as chocolate hot from the stove, and wine. 'Corporal Acton, take your fill,' said Hervey. 'And then, if we decently can, we must stow what's left. I don't count our chances of a regular dinner too high this night.'

'Oh, thank you very much, sir,' said Acton cheerily, driving a picket peg into the ground to tether his mare.

'This is what you would call in the ranks "hurrying up to wait".'

'Sir.'

'Well, I confess that the last time I breakfasted in sight of the enemy – if we may call the Turk that, for the purposes of argument – was at Waterloo. And Bonaparte sat watching us a deal too long. What think you, Fairbrother; are those Turks yonder the Vizier's advance guard, d'you suppose?'

'How shall we know until they move?' replied Fairbrother, making a thorough mash of cheese and sausage and figs. 'Recall that it was you who told me that the way to identify a bird was to observe what it does.'

'Just so.' Hervey turned to his cornet. 'Mr Agar, you are in command of the advance guard of the Vizier's army. Your axis of advance is the defile of Yeni Bazar and Kaspichan and thence directly on Shumla. Tell me your course of action.'

Agar appeared already to have contemplated the question, for his answer came at once. 'From the vantage point of yonder cavalry I can survey the whole of the line which the enemy – the Russians – here has taken up. I cannot see what reserves are concealed to the rear of Yeni Bazar, but I must assume there to be a force of cavalry and guns. I cannot therefore throw out a defensive flank and march through the defile here; I must attack directly and force the enemy to withdraw beyond Yeni Bazar, which place I must garrison in order to allow the main part of the force to pass through.'

Hervey nodded appreciatively. It required not the mind of a Marlborough or a Wellington to conclude thus, but it was well expressed. 'And how strong is the enemy – the Russians – here?'

'I cannot be certain, for my communications with Silistria are severed – the Cossacks intercept all my gallopers – but I must assume that a prudent general would not advance so far without being able to match my forty thousand, of which I have thirty-five thousand in the field and the remainder in Shumla. I know that the corps which has watched Shumla this past month is about ten thousand strong, and that I am pressing them hither from Pravadi, and also that there are strong forces – say five thousand – at Madara, as well as perhaps three thousand in the garrison at Pravadi.' He paused to calculate. 'It may be, therefore, that the main force of the enemy at Yeni Bazar is in excess of twenty-five thousand.'

'Admirable. But ponder on those, gentlemen: this will be a battle of numbers the like that I myself have not seen since that day in 1815. So, Mr Agar, your course now is to . . . ?'

Agar was only momentarily distracted by the thought of Waterloo. 'The Vizier has placed a quarter of his force in my advance guard – of which those yonder are the scouts – and therefore I shall attack here with seven or eight thousand to test the enemy's strength and intention.'

'To where would you direct the attack?'

'The right – west – flank, sir.'

'Why?'

'Because the enemy could not weaken his left flank since it could then be assailed by the main body. But I too have my apprehension in that respect, for General Roth's corps might fall upon *my* right flank.'

'What say you, Fairbrother?'

Fairbrother, breaking from his feast, looked approving. 'I say that Mr Agar's appreciation is worthy of the senior class at Addiscombe. But that which is unknowable is the extent to which Roth is engaged.'

There was no gainsaying it, and Hervey was beginning to wonder why Diebitsch did not send patrols out of his own rather than waiting on Roth's gallopers. 'If, however, the Vizier marches by the central route, what do yonder Turk do?'

Again, Agar did not hesitate. 'Vantage over the defile here, sir, to guard the right flank.'

'Just so,' said Hervey decidedly – and thought what an admirable aide-de-camp would Agar make him.

Towards eleven o'clock, the heat now becoming uncomfortable, and the distant Turks still making no move, a galloper from General Roth at last arrived – a lieutenant of the Narva Hussars whose proud uniform was caked in dust and dried mud.

Hervey could no longer contain himself. He rode over to the cherry trees to gain what he might, but the obliging aide-de-camp had been sent elsewhere, and so all he could do was stand at a respectful distance and observe.

The general-in-chief, his countenance sternly fixed, was personally interrogating the hussar. From time to time there was pointing on the map, and the chief-of-staff would ask, evidently, a supplementary question.

Ten minutes passed, fifteen perhaps – the officer of hussars, who even with his face begrimed looked scarcely older than Agar, spoke with confidence and certainty, not in the least daunted by either the braid before him or the consequence of his report.

At length Diebitsch turned to his assembled staff with a look of grim satisfaction. General Toll smiled admiringly. And then all was staccato orders and staff officers hurrying this way and that. And when every Mercury had flown, and the clump of cherry trees was empty but for a handful of his closest staff and the officer of the Narva Hussars (with, at last, a flask of wine in his hand), Diebitsch saw Hervey and beckoned to him.

'Colonel Hervey, the situation is developing to our advantage. General Roth has broken clean. He is seven miles hence but in good order. The Vizier is marching by the middle route. We march at once therefore for Madara to join Count Pahlen, leaving a detachment here to guard our lines of communication. You may accompany or wait on Roth as you please.'

An orderly brought coffee on a silver tray. Diebitsch offered him the first cup.

Hervey took it and bowed. 'I'm obliged, as ever, General, for your giving me such licence; I will of course ride with you to Madara.'

Diebitsch said he was glad of it.

'May I presume that Count Pahlen's cavalry will screen the army as it deploys?'

'You may. And you may presume you have leave to ride with them too. It will be a bruising battle tomorrow. There will be no easy victory over a general of Reschid's reputation, or over troops desperate to gain the safety of Shumla. I should want you to see it all – and tell London of it.'

XVI

THE BLOODY BUSINESS
OF THE DAY

Next morning

A hand on his shoulder woke him as the army began rousing for the dawn stand-to.

'Tea, sir.'

Hervey propped himself up on a forearm. Any tea at such an hour and place was welcome, but this was good tea, and sweet (he had come to prefer it so of late) – and he savoured the remembrance of many such times in their service together. How Johnson had found their bivouac before dark last night was still a wonder.

'Where did you come upon the cow, or was it a goat?'

'It's almond milk, sir. I swapped it from a Tartar.'

He smiled to himself. Almond milk – what luxury there could be in fighting in these parts . . . or India, or the Cape; anywhere the sun shone bright – Gibraltar? What appeal had the 'hoary-headed frosts' and 'contagious fogs' of Hounslow (and he shivered at the thought of St Petersburg in snow)?

He peered left and right at the shadowy reveille. He could make out nothing beyond his companions, except the noise of an army

247

waking. He had not slept amid so great a number since that day on the ridge of Mont St Jean, when Johnson had brought him tea despite the night's downpour. What a fight of it they had had the day before, in rain all the way back from Quatre Bras, and then to make a sodden bivouac in the corn, knowing they would fight the battle of their lives in the morning. The rain had stopped with the daylight, and they had got themselves up and into line, and the French had pounded all day, and they had beaten them. A close run thing, the duke had said. No doubt it had been, but victory was victory. And afterwards they had marched sharp on Paris.

And soon they would be standing to here, and within but seven days of that date in 1815, the infantry to their muskets, the cavalry to their horses. Not as many as at Waterloo, nothing like as many, certainly not guns, but if General Diebitsch had his way it would be as capital a battle. And then it would be onwards to Constantinople. From Yeni Bazar to Madara was about eight miles, the same, just about, as from Quatre Bras to Waterloo. But yesterday there had been no rain to dowse them or cavalry to harry them. They had marched beneath an unkind sun, but along a fair road in flat country and perfect peace, and then a mile or so on to the place where Count Pahlen had planted his pennant, a ruined church on prominent ground half-way to the little village of Kulewtscha. It was an admirable post from which to command, protected by a river that looped the promontory – at this season more a muddy stream, but an obstacle of sorts nevertheless.

And here they had rested while Diebitsch and Pahlen conferred, and staff officers came and went. Before them, on the forward slope, posted as guard were five battalions of the Bugskiy Mushketerskiy Polk, the Regiment of the River Bug, men of Ukraine and the descendants of Moldavians, Wallachians and Bulgars who had thrown in with the Tsar in earlier wars against the Turk (though not one battalion numbered more than three hundred, for such had been the sickness before crossing the Danube). A brigade of uhlans were covering, and two troops of artillery. Hervey recalled how the line at Waterloo had been posted thus, but that the duke had pulled them back behind the crest when he saw the massed French batteries. He did not suppose the Turks could muster anything so compelling.

But would he see, when the sun came up, the Russians in their place, as the duke's men had been? That night before Waterloo they had stumbled, wet and weary, onto the ridge at Mont St Jean, not knowing how many others were there or would come before morning, and then at dawn as they rose from their moist mud beds they had seen in amazement the great assemblage of regiments the length of the ridge as far as the eye could behold – and beyond. The duke's work, certainly, but his staff's above all – and they very hastily called together (not least their chief, poor de Lancey, whose bride of but a few weeks nursed him in vain in the days that followed). Diebitsch's staff were practised, for sure, and had had the marker fires burning as darkness fell.

He smiled as he recalled Agar's bewilderment of the afternoon: 'Can the Second Corps be *so* long in coming up, sir? The road is good. It cannot have been a march of more than three hours. Can they have taken a false turn?'

'Tell him, Corporal Acton,' Hervey had said, turning to his coverman, for here was a case of prodigy needing practice.

'Sir!'

And Acton had turned to the cornet with the relish of an NCO given a class of instruction.

'It's like this, Mr Agar, sir. The march takes three hours, say, so the leading rank arrives 'ere three 'ours after setting off. But a corps's ten thousand men, see – maybe more – so the rear of the column ranks past the finish 'owever long it takes for the 'ole corps to rank past. It's called the pass time, sir. And for ten thousand infantry it would˙be at least an hour, not counting the baggage.'

Cornet Agar had looked suitably mortified. 'Thank you, Corporal; I had not considered it thus. A very elementary point, clearly.'

'And they'll need to rest, sir,' Acton insisted, still relishing his commission. And the rests are added to the pass time, he explained; but in such heat and dust as they'd marched in yesterday there was no alternative, nor to spacing between battalion columns; and then they would have to form up at the end of the march so as to be able to deploy in the right way. There was little prospect, he judged, of more than a division's worth reaching the field before dusk. The only consolation was that the Turks would not be managing any faster pace, for they had the worst of the going.

And Hervey had praised the exposition.

But when the 2nd Corps *had* begun arriving, with what spirit it had been! Even he, Hervey, had stood and watched as they marched with a spring in their step, smiling and singing to their appointed musters. These were not the exhausted men of a forced march, as he in his imperfect knowledge of such things might have ordered, nor even, it appeared, the worn-out remnants of last year's bloody campaign and sickly season; these were men who looked possessed of the 'first courage'. Perhaps a good many of them *were* – new recruits and reinforcements who had not yet been shot over. And down they had settled to their dry rations – peas boiled up with whatever scraps of pork were saved from morning – and thought it a feast.

And now, shaved and breakfasted, he climbed a statue atop one of the more substantial graves beside the ruined church as the sun broached the hilly horizon to spy out the field.

There was no sign of Turks. The only movement was that of the pickets making ready to come in. But neither was there sign of the 6th and 7th Corps, Roth's. And with the 2nd Corps posted well to their right, he realized that he, and Diebitsch and his staff, with just the Regiment of the Bug and a brigade of uhlans, had stood as Roth's advance guard during the night. It defied all the normal usages, but it had evidently paid off. Diebitsch was a cautious man, not committing himself to a course of action until it was certain what it should be – yet in that caution was there not considerable daring, for to wait was also to risk? Herein, evidently, lay the general-in-chief's shrewdness; and Hervey marked it well.

In half an hour he was in Diebitsch's headquarters tent, a thing of some size bedecked with flags, pennants, and coloured bunting, all of which must have risen by the light of torches. Here he found the general in perfect spirits and readying himself for the saddle, surrounded by staff officers looking as keen as he for the off.

The reason was soon apparent. 'Colonel Hervey, I have just received word that Roth is but a short hour's march away. Pahlen's corps will therefore deploy forward to the ground we rode over last night, with an advance guard under General Ostroschenko in Kulewtscha and Tschirkowna.'

Hervey hoped the wretched inhabitants of those two places – what few remained – had taken to some place of safety after seeing the party reconnoitring the villages last evening.

Diebitsch's voice then changed slightly, to one of speculation. 'I am also sending General Buturlin in a reconnaissance along the road to Marasch to see if the Vizier makes any attempt to march by that place. Cavalry were observed last night on the heights above Kulewtscha – or so the village elders report. I consider it most unlikely they would come by other than the direct road from Pravadi, but it is as well to be certain. You may accompany if you wish.'

Hervey thanked him. 'With your leave, General, I should rather remain here where the Turk is expected.'

Diebitsch smiled and said simply, 'I should consider it a favour if you rode with Buturlin.'

Hervey hoped he did not hesitate; as ever, the invitation of a senior officer, even if not properly his superior, was best taken as an order. Surely Diebitsch did not imply any lack of confidence in Buturlin? Perhaps it was that he wished him to meet this general (was there to be more extolling of life in the service of the Tsar?). 'I am, of course, happy to oblige, General.'

Diebitsch made light of it by a wave of the hand. 'And you may of course thereafter ride where you please.'

'Thank you, General. And, if I may, my compliments to the soldiers of the Tsar in manoeuvring the Vizier thus.' It was not given for a junior officer to praise a senior, even if the senior were not properly a superior, so praise of his troops was the artful alternative. Artful and heartfelt.

General Diebitsch smiled knowingly. 'What was it that your Lord Nelson said before the Nile: "Tomorrow it will be a peerage or Westminster Abbey"?'

Major-General Dmitry Buturlin was a year older than Hervey, wore the ribbon of the Pour le Mérite (though he spoke no German, and so Hervey supposed it to be a mutual honour in the defeat of Bonaparte), and had seen a good deal of the Continent, including Spain, all of which he related in excellent French. He was well versed, almost bookish, and gave his opinions freely. Hervey found him an engaging companion. Several times he spoke of St Petersburg in a way that suggested he knew what the general-in-chief had offered his riding companion. An attractive prospect, the city, by his account.

They chatted inconsequentially for an hour and more (Fairbrother and the others had fallen back respectfully). It was good to ride at the head of a brigade of hussars – a brigade, not merely a regiment. For when might his own army ever brigade its cavalry again, except for a field day? He was content, with sadness, to have sent word that he would have the Fifty-third.

They found no Turks, however, nor any sign of them. It was not difficult country to reconnoitre – flat and open, for much of it. Hervey was soon of the opinion that a standing patrol of cavalry was all that was needed: they would see soon enough if the Turks did for some reason try to come by this way – soon enough, to be sure, for the general-in-chief to adjust his plans, to throw out a flank and muster some artillery to prevent their debouching into the valley where General Ostroschenko's advance guard were posted.

Buturlin shared that opinion. Presently he detached a squadron of hussars to watch the road, and turned for home with the rest. He was in no hurry, though. They had come out at the trot, a full two leagues, and they would return at a walk: he wanted wind in reserve for when they charged, which he was certain they would do, and for pursuit when the Turks broke, of which he was equally confident.

The walk gave them time to range widely, over all manner of affairs, not least of the wars to come. Buturlin was convinced that tumult in Europe was at hand. He himself had been with the French in the suppression of the revolt in Spain six years ago; he predicted similar uprisings in Belgium, in Italy, in the Austrian marches, and – he shook his head – in Poland. In all of these the Tsar had his interests – well, perhaps not so directly in Belgium – and the army would be much occupied.

Hervey was now certain that Diebitsch's only purpose in asking him to ride with Buturlin was to entice him with the promise of abundant action. He smiled; he had never before heard of a major-general recruiting officer.

By the time they regained the ridge west of Kulewtscha, the scene before them was transformed.

'See, Mr Agar – you may never do so again: three *corps d'armée* drawn up for battle.'

Agar at once hitched up his sabretache, took out paper and char-coal and began sketching rapidly.

'The frontage is somewhat greater than at Waterloo, and not so many men by half, but it has the same appearance of . . . majesty.'

'I imagine your vantage point was not the same that day,' said Fairbrother playfully.

Hervey smiled as he recalled it. 'The briefest look as we galloped back after a charge.'

Fairbrother knew of the charge from what the Sixth had told him. He felt suddenly chastened. 'The ground is not so regular here?'

'No indeed,' replied Hervey, studying it carefully once more.

At Waterloo the long, low ridge had faced one of equal height and length, which the French had occupied during the night (there was still no sign of Turks here) and from which they had descended in one forlorn attack after another, seen off by the strongpoints on the forward slope – the château of Hougoumont, La Haye Saint farm, the hamlet of Papelotte – or by the regimental musketry atop it, or else by counter-charges from the cavalry. Here, on the other hand, the field was not one of parallel lines but a partially inverted triangle, the base of which was the Russian line, which ran north-east to south-west, about five miles long; and the apex, some five miles from the base, would be the entry point for the Turks. The ridge at Waterloo – Mont St Jean – on which the duke had disposed his army, had been continuous, but here the high ground on which the Russians intended to bar the advance of the Turks was cleaved in two by the valley of the Bulanik, with Pahlen's 2nd Corps to the west of the stream – the left of the base of the triangle as the Turks would see it – and the 6th and 7th Corps to the east. And whereas the French had watched the dawn from their ridge, and could choose their point of attack anywhere along the line, here the Turk would enter the field with little room to manoeuvre, through a green defile made narrower by crags to north and south. All the Vizier would be able to do would be to expand his front as the ground opened up – as the sides of the triangle diverged – but since General Ostroschenko's advance guard stood in the middle of the triangle, the Turks would have a fight on their hands even to deploy. If the Vizier did not make use of the road from Marasch to try to turn Ostroschenko's flank (and why would he – for he could not have known of Diebitsch's intention to stand here?), his only course would be a frontal attack; and Diebitsch had both the numbers and the ground to defeat him. The duke had said after Waterloo that Bonaparte 'came on in the old way, and we saw him off in the old way'; Hervey had a dreadful notion that it would be the same today, for the victory of Waterloo was one thing, remembrance of the field that evening quite another.

'One of Diebitsch's aides-de-camp reckoned thirty thousand,' said Fairbrother, now with his telescope to an eye.

Hervey nodded, searching with his own. 'I think that was the very number of English and the King's Germans. The rest were a hotchpotch. Some of them fought deuced well, mind. What strange echoes. Can you make out Ostroschenko's men?'

Red coats would have been conspicuous enough among the verdure of Tschirkowna, a ruin of a village – the blues and greens of the Russians much less so. Once the eye became accustomed, however, the lines were discernible enough. And they appeared to be on the move still.

'I think we'll go and see what they do,' said Hervey, pushing his glass back into its sleeve.

A quarter of an hour later, picking their way through feral orchards and untended vineyards, they saw the Irkutzk Hussars – unmistakeable in their raspberry *chakchiry* breeches though a mile away and more – forming line on the far right. It boded action of some sort. Hervey put his gelding into a canter to close with them.

The ground was much broken; it took them ten minutes to cross the valley.

He approached the Irkutzk from the rear, the greater courtesy. And handier, too, for he was met by the *rotmistr* (captain) of the right-rear squadron, who spoke French. '*Ce qui se passe?*'

The *rotmistr* explained that Turk infantry – the advance guard? – were halted where the road from Pravadi debouched from the forest, a league distant, that they were bringing up guns and forming square, and that General Ostroschenko was ordered to probe them to discover their intention.

Hervey was dismayed that he'd not seen them from the ridge, or even as they descended towards Tschirkowna, but there were so many folds in the ground . . . Did the colonel speak French, he asked.

'No,' said the *rotmistr*.

But if he were to ride with the Irkutzk he must observe the proprieties: he persuaded the *rotmistr* to come with him as interpreter.

As they rode forward, Hervey pulled out the new ribbon at his collar a little way in the hope that it would be his *laissez-monter*.

He need not have worried. Colonel Voinov, a man of impressive height and bearing, seemed to recognize him, inviting him and the rest of his party to ride with the regiment – sabres drawn – in the front rank.

Hervey thanked him and was just able to beckon forward the others and tell them what was happening when the trumpeter sounded 'walk-march'.

'Trot' soon followed. The lines billowed on the uneven ground, the NCOs cursed the troopers' dressing (though he didn't understand a word, Hervey smiled to himself: he could have been in the ranks of the Sixth), and the right-flank squadrons began bunching.

In a hundred yards they came back to a walk. More cursing. But what was the hurry? As well let the infantry keep up. The horse artillery looked happier too.

'No sign of the Turks,' said Fairbrother when they had gone half a mile, sounding uneasy as he looked left and right at the wooded heights.

Hervey was perfectly able to read his friend's mind as well as the ground. 'Yonder crags would be the devil for us to climb,' he said, nodding to the closer right flank, half a mile perhaps. 'I imagine Pahlen has them picketed. A few Cossacks would flush out any game.' Whether there were any Cossacks on the heights he did not know; but why would there *not* be?

'Like being in a piss-pot,' muttered Corporal Acton.

A quarter of an hour later, when they had gone a mile and a half, crossing two streams and half a dozen dry courses at right angles to the line of advance, they came at last on the objective, halting along the top of an incline in full view of the Turks three-quarters of a mile ahead.

Corporal Acton whistled beneath his breath.

It was difficult to estimate the number, not least because the sun was in their eyes. Hervey swept the line with his telescope. It was a good mile, square after square, and cavalry beyond. To be disposed thus he reckoned they must be the spearhead of a complete corps, ten thousand. How many guns would that mean? A corps would have, what, sixty, seventy? He could see twenty, perhaps, the lighter pieces.

'A cork in the bottle. Can it be drawn out, or does it have to be driven in?'

'Does it have to be removed at all?' asked Fairbrother.

'Diebitsch won't just let them sit there.'

'"O, how shall summer's honey breath hold out/ Against the wrackful siege of battering days . . ."'

'Very apt,' said Hervey, searching the slopes on either flank of the Turk line. 'Shakespeare?'

'Who else?'

'Uncommon apt, indeed. The Turk has no time, but Diebitsch disdains taking advantage of *his*.'

'Just so.'

'Well, we must see. That's our business, after all.'

Fairbrother made a muted 'Hah!', and frowned. 'We are resuming our status of indifference, then?'

Hervey ignored the jibe. 'I suppose Ostroschenko will now try to drive them in to force the Vizier's hand, but there's scarcely space for artful tactics. Mr Agar?'

Agar edged his mare forward. 'Sir?'

'How might you discern the Vizier's intention here? Without excess of time.'

He had already been considering it. 'I was wondering, does he tempt us to attack him, and in turn to counter-attack us? My preference would be to scout rather than fight. If we got into the cover of the trees on this flank, we'd be able to work around the advance guard and see what troops stood ready in reserve.'

'And what if tempting us *were* his scheme?'

'Then I do not see what alternative there would be to waiting on *his* move. Unless the whole of the Russian force were to be brought forward to attack first. And that would be a perilous affair for both sides in so confined a space.'

Hervey shook his head. 'I think it the best rule never to let the enemy alone.'

The trumpet sounded 'walk-march' again.

Hervey raised his eyebrows. 'But I see there is yet another course of action.'

What it might be, though, was not yet apparent. They surely did not intend charging? He couldn't conceive of any outcome but ruin.

Even at a walk it was a continuous effort to maintain the dressing, and a dry channel two feet deep was soon disordering the front rank, bringing yet another blistering torrent of 'advice' from the NCOs.

On they struggled.

And then a great thunderclap of artillery far over on the left flank stunned all. Even Hervey started.

All eyes turned left: heavy case-shot at four hundred yards, from a battery hitherto concealed, rocked the advancing columns of Ostroschenko's infantry – a mile away and more, but still the screams carried. And then the Turks sprang their terrible ambush – *sipahis* hurtling down the crags, men and horses tumbling headlong, but crashing like a great wave into the exposed flank of Ostroschenko's columns desperately trying to form square.

'Poor devils,' groaned Hervey, looking right to see what danger faced *them*.

Seconds later it was the same: down a near-vertical cliff plunged the Turk horse.

Colonel Voinov's instinct was to haul away and re-form. 'Columns!'

Too late.

Voinov changed his mind. 'Charge!'

It was a desperate rush at a great host of lances. But surprise counted. The Turks scattered like chaff in a sudden gust of wind. Not a point touched a single hussar; some of the *sipahis* even took cuts from the faster sabres.

Hervey had not even lofted his when they pulled up. 'That was fortune smiling,' he rasped, shaking his head in disbelief. 'We'd better retire and re-form, or else if they ever see we're unsupported they'll roll us up like a damned carpet!'

Fairbrother had already seen – horse and infantry threatening to lap round their other flank. 'Quickly, Hervey!'

The squadrons turned as best they could – no trumpets, only shouting – trying to regain order as they bustled rear. It was no field-day drill, to be sure.

They began galloping, hastened now by the re-emboldened Turks.

Hervey despaired. They must rally soon, or else it would be rout.

Another two hundred yards – a dry course on which to form: 'Hold hard!' he growled, as if any would heed, let alone hear.

Besides, Voinov knew his job. The Irkutzk turned about, rough but ready.

'Look, sir!' called Agar.

Five hundred yards left, a phalanx of Turk infantry had detached the Murom Regiment from the rest of the line. They were frantically forming square, surrounded on three sides already, and losing order. Muskets from another phalanx swarmed on them like angry wasps. It would be a pure killing match.

'My God, where did they come from? Brace yourself, Agar. They're lost.'

Where were the supports? But all of Ostroschenko's cavalry were fighting to break clean or else retiring apace. The Irkutzk couldn't wheel and charge or they'd open a flank to the *sipahis*.

He shook his head. This was not well-handled. Turk numbers were beginning to tell. Some of the gunners were bravely serving their pieces, but they too couldn't stand without supports. Where *was* Ostroschenko?

'There's the general, sir,' called Acton, pointing to the middle of the field.

Hervey saw: he, too, was in a perilous place. 'He makes a stand! Does Voinov not see him?'

'Look, sir, they're breaking away!' shouted Agar excitedly.

Hervey looked again. Men were streaming from the crumbling Murom square. Unchecked and they would throw away their muskets and be cut down.

'We've got to rally them, Fairbrother. No one else will.'

He didn't wait for opinion. He took off at a gallop, calling as he

260

went. 'Mr Agar, when I pull up, remain in the saddle with the others to bar the way. Fairbrother, we shall dismount. They'll never rally otherwise.'

Fairbrother was past protest. Death by Turk lance or Russian bayonet – what did it matter?

'Flats of the sword, no pistols.'

The noise was great, and the smoke increasing. A hundred yards, a dry channel to break their flight: that's where he'd rally them.

'Here!' He drew hard to the halt and sprang down, Acton taking the reins.

Cornet Agar motioned Brayshaw and Green to stand left as Acton turned in on the right.

The fugitives from the Murom Regiment came on like hounds in full cry. Hervey raised his sabre and began hallooing.

The first of them took the dry course in their stride. Acton ran in obliquely, leading Hervey's gelding, blocking. Several gave up, fell exhausted, though some got past. Agar sent two sprawling with the flat of his sabre. They looked up at him strangely grateful. Another jabbed with his bayonet. Acton sprang from the saddle cursing but still holding both sets of reins and felled him deftly with a swipe in the small of the back. He grabbed the man's tunic straps and hauled him to his feet, shouting the while, turning him round and pushing him back towards the dry course, where Hervey and Fairbrother were manhandling and cajoling. He shouted to Brayshaw and Green to take the reins, then ran to their side.

Exhaustion helped. There was soon a line of twenty Muromskiye standing in the course. Stragglers now began making for them of their own accord – safety in standing numbers. An NCO had recovered himself and was barking reassuringly. A drummer boy struggled manfully with his drum.

Hervey saw him, half aghast: he looked no older than Georgiana. 'Drum! Drum!' he shouted.

The boy looked terrified.

Acton ran and showed him, and he began a plucky roll.

Hervey wished he had a dozen more.

They were soon fifty, and most with muskets still. A horse battery galloped up and began unlimbering – six gleaming brass cannon. Hervey cheered them. The Murom fugitives cheered with him.

The Irkutzk Hussars had been pushed back a furlong. If only they would come up and support . . .

The sun beat down, their ears were filled with the infernal noise of slaughter, but Hervey and his fugitive company watched in silence the death of the Regiment of Murom – a monstrous firing squad. No, *worse* – for they were shot down with all the sport of netted rabbits. He was sickened. Not even at Waterloo had there been such execution.

But, curiously, it seemed to steady the fugitives. In ten more minutes they were a hundred, and a mix of regiments, like a life-raft in a sea of drowning men.

The battery was in action now – deafening, yet fortifying.

But there was none that could speak a language other than their own.

Acton, however, by some Babel-process given to NCOs, now had them volleying – and sharp about it too, even if their targets were a hundred yards too far for any appreciable effect. That didn't matter; the drill was galvanizing. In four rounds of ball cartridge – two minutes of biting, ramming, presenting and firing – the flotsam of the field had regained a semblance of soldierly purpose, and Hervey began thinking they might hold.

'Sir, look behind,' called Agar, still astride.

Thank God – the Irkutzk coming up at the trot. Hervey nodded; he was *sure* they would now hold.

'And I think it's General Ostroschenko as well.'

It was indeed, and making straight for them. Hervey checked

that his buttons were fastened – the instinct of twenty years.

The general rode up to the guns and embraced the captain warmly, and then along the line of 12-pounders with encouraging words for the gunners.

Then he turned to the improvised company of infantry. The senior of the NCOs called the line to attention, and then arms to 'Present'.

Hervey saluted with his sword. '*Bonjour, monsieur le général.*'

Ostroschenko touched the peak of his cap to acknowledge.

Hervey tried to explain who they were, but the general nodded and stayed him.

'*Je l'ai vue, monsieur le colonel anglais. Tout.*'

Hervey was glad of it; it spared him the discomfort of speaking of 'stragglers'.

'*Et je n'en oublierai pas!*'

Hervey returned his sword, and bowed.

Ostroschenko pointed right and rear to the ridge. '*Et voilà Pahlen!*'

Hervey turned; and sighed with relief. Count Pahlen's corps, two divisions and another of cavalry, were coming down the slopes in column. Did Diebitsch sense victory, or fear defeat of his advance guard? For now, it hardly mattered: in half an hour Pahlen's men would be close enough to support them, and his cavalry in no time at all. He saluted in acknowledgement.

This was the battle they had sought, said Ostroschenko. They would see it through where they stood. Then he smiled and nodded reassuringly: '*Tenez ferme, mes braves!*'

Agar had out his telescope. 'A great number of guns, too, sir,' he said when Ostroschenko had galloped back for his vantage point.

Pahlen's batteries were moving by the valley of the Bulanik to keep clear of the columns. Hervey saw, yet he could not make out what it tokened, though only too aware of his worm's-eye view of the battle. 'Can Diebitsch believe the Turks have shot their bolt?'

Fairbrother had been too busy on the right of the volleying line to take much note of what was happening elsewhere. 'The Vizier must have a deal more arrows in his quiver than that,' he replied, doubtfully. 'I'll warrant we'll have the fight of our lives within the hour. Might we try to find a Russian officer to take command here?'

It was a reasonable request, but Hervey could see no very practical way of addressing it. Corporal Acton, meanwhile, was strolling along the front of the line like a regimental serjeant-major. They were now a hundred and fifty, and at Hervey's bidding Acton had somehow got them into two ranks – and then to stand easy. There was now laughter and the smell of pipe smoke. At that moment Hervey was unsure he would *welcome* a relief.

The sun was no longer in their eyes but beat down unsparingly, and canteens were running dry. Had there been a stream nearby he might have risked sending half a dozen men to fill them, but there was none. There was nothing for it therefore but to ask the hussars. He pulled the medal ribbon out from his tunic once more and strode back the hundred yards to where the Irkutzk stood.

Colonel Voinov sent for the *rotmistr*. When he came, Hervey explained the predicament. Yet Voinov was unmoved: the Muromskiye must live with the consequences of their indiscipline, he said.

Hervey persisted: the men had stood long in the sun, they had rallied bravely, and their mouths were parched biting off the cartridges.

Still Voinov was unmoved: they were fortunate to escape the lash and the firing squad for running away (and then a remark which the *rotmistr* did not translate, but which seemed to imply some contempt for the Muromskiye, as opposed to the manly Sibirskiye).

'They are soldiers of the Tsar, Colonel. They will bear their condition without complaint – or else they will answer for it.'

There was no animus in Voinov's remarks, only a gulf between their notions of authority. Hervey knew he had no experience of conscripts, and took his leave courteously, but with a look that spoke his mind.

'They are soldiers of the Tsar,' he told Fairbrother simply.

Fairbrother raised an eyebrow. 'At this moment they look pretty much like soldiers of anybody's. And putting them against a wall tomorrow doesn't help now.'

Hervey smiled, grimly. He had at least the comfort of knowing that Voinov's sabres would make bloody work of any who ran – and that the Muromskiye knew it too.

The attack began a little before half past three with a storm of roundshot on the jangled orchards and groves of Tschirkowna, pounding General Ostroschenko's brigade of chasseurs which had stood throughout with impressive resolution. Pahlen's artillery answered with shell, and soon the field was a blanket of smoke, so thick in places that none could see beyond a dozen yards. The gunners close-on Hervey's men hastily began hand-spiking the 12-pounders back to their original lay and reloading with canister; if the Turks came on in this fog of battle there'd be no time for other than case-shot.

The smoke drifted, thinning, then rolled in again thicker. Hervey became anxious: this was the time the faint-hearted – and the straight cowards – would slip away. 'Get them to fix bayonets, Corporal Acton.' There was no point in giving the order in English; best let Acton do it by demonstration.

'Sir!'

Acton marched to the front, seized the bayonet from the belt of a startled *rekrut* and held it aloft. 'Rousskis will fix bayonets,' he bellowed (he had once seen the Militia do it). He waited a few seconds to let the cautionary sink in, and then roared the executive: 'Fix bayonets!'

A hundred and fifty bayonets – those the *rekruty* had not lost or thrown away – were somehow fixed. Now, at least, if the Turks appeared out of the smoke they would have to stand a volley and then run on to steel. In truth, though, Hervey was confident of neither volley nor bayonet.

A commotion to the rear made all eyes turn.

He could scarce believe it: out from the 'fog' came the sutler of the erstwhile Regiment of Murom leading a train of donkeys.

There was cheering, and all order vanished as the *rekruty* flocked to him.

Hervey looked anxiously beyond in case it excited the Irkutzk to draw sabres.

For the time being they stood impassive. Perhaps the smoke worked to his advantage?

'Corporal Acton, get these men under discipline!' he barked as he doubled after them.

Acton was momentarily at a loss. Then he did what he would in the Sixth – except that a dozen dragoons the worse for wear of a pay night scarce compared to these.

Yet the raised voice, the jabbing finger, the confident assertion of authority somehow brought silence of a sort, and then a respectful (or fearful) edging back.

'Now what is all this?' demanded Hervey, tapping the panniers. 'Water? Aqua?'

If the sutler understood, he didn't answer. Instead he got out a ledger from his satchel and held it towards him balefully: his fortune in credit extended to the Murom was no more.

Hervey had scant sympathy. His prices – like any sutler's – would have out-jewed Shylock. And yet, who but he brought comforts to the regiment in the middle of battle – even at such a price?

'Rum, sir,' said Corporal Acton, sniffing one of the flasks. 'Good rum,' he added, tasting it. 'And nice water as well.'

Hervey thought of commandeering the entire train, but that would have been just one more thing to guard. Instead, he took a handful of gold from his cartouche box – sovereigns and five-rouble pieces – and by the universal process of bargaining (to the continual accompaniment of the cannonade) bought the entire stock.

He beckoned the NCOs closest and motioned them to distribute the water, appointing Acton quartermaster.

'A measure of rum to each man. A gill, no more – perhaps half a gill. Is there enough?'

'Ay, sir, if I go easy – two dozen bottles, I reckon,' replied Acton, taking down the precious keg.

'Thank God it's no more,' said Hervey to himself. The worst of the heat was past, but to men who were parched, the drink would be double-strength. 'And quick about it, please!'

A gill for each man – it was asking for trouble. How in God's name would he get them back into ranks – other than calling on the Irkutzk?

The 12-pounders came to his aid – a thunderous volley. Speeded by every curse that Acton possessed, and reinvigorated with rum, the provisional company rushed back to the dry course and formed line as before, the NCOs suddenly regaining a notion of duty and hastening the laggards with the butt of the musket.

They stood, if less steady than before, with a new look of defiance. They could see no Turks in the billows of smoke, but the guns wouldn't be firing at phantoms: they were there somewhere. Soon it would be retribution.

The smoke was drifting, thinning – and now clearing.

The company began jeering.

Musketry answered them – skirmishers.

Two or three *rekruty* fell.

Hervey knew he must give an order; rum or no rum, they were trained to fire only on the word of command.

Acton seized the musket from a flanker and ran to the centre of the line. 'Give the word, sir!'

Hervey raised his sabre. 'Make ready!'

Up to his side went Acton's musket, the hammer cocked. He looked left and right, gesturing for the line to follow.

Up went the muskets, and the cocking of the hammers.

'Present!'

Up to the aim went Acton's musket.

The front rank followed.

Hervey waited for him to step back in line. '*Ognya!*'

Not a perfect volley, but good enough – though with so much smoke he couldn't see if a single ball had struck.

The rear rank stepped forward.

'Make ready . . . Present . . . Fire!'

More smoke. Nothing for it but to keep volleying.

The rear rank was reloading fast.

'Front rank retire!'

The words meant nothing, but the hours of drill did. The rear rank now fronted again.

'Front rank . . . Present . . . Fire!'

Smoke drifted rear and left. They could see a hundred yards clear, now, and hazily beyond – a good harvest of the lead, an even line of fallen Turks at fifty yards, and at a hundred a tight-packed battalion in column of companies, halted.

The 12-pounders thundered again, cutting a swathe through the right-flank column and felling the leading ranks in the other four. Now was the moment for the Irkutzk to charge, but he couldn't catch sight of them in the smoke behind.

He daren't risk another minute, though. He ran to the centre of the line and waved his sabre. 'Charge! Charge! Charge!'

He didn't look to see who was with him, only Fairbrother at his right.

He ran faster than he ever thought he could.

His lungs were set to burst; his ears rang with cannonading and musketry – and the cries of the men behind him.

He didn't need to look how many; the Turks told him – a whole *brigade* of Russians – no? – charging out of the smoke? They turned tail and ran without a parting shot.

Hervey stopped as they reached the fallen skirmishers, and hastened the departure of the rest with a ragged volley.

Yet the Turks had come on bravely in the first fight. Breathing deep to recover himself as his own men fell out to loot, Hervey shook his head, hardly able to believe his – their – luck. There was just no knowing the collective mind of infantry at the culminating point; that much he had understood a long time, but never so perfectly as now.

'Still, sir!' shouted Acton.

Half deafened as he was, the pounding hoofs had taken him by surprise. Hervey froze as horses galloped left and right – the Irkutzk, late but not too late to turn the reverse into rout.

And then Count Pahlen, indeed – and General Diebitsch.

He stood straight, and saluted.

'Colonel Hervey, you try me sorely,' Diebitsch declared, touching the peak of his cap in reply. 'What do you do exposing yourself thus?'

'General, I didn't think you—'

'You thought the smoke would conceal it, did you?'

Hervey held out his sword as if to admit his guilt.

'It wasn't enough to rally stragglers, then – Ostroschenko has told me all. Colonel Hervey, how would it look to your Duke of Wellington if you were killed at the head of a company of infantry? Retire at once, sir. You have done enough!'

'With respect, General, I should not care to leave these men until "Retreat" is sounded. They have fought bravely.'

'It is a soldier's duty to fight bravely.' But his countenance softened. 'I grant you your request. Leave the field at once, and take these men with you. The provost-marshal shall muster them afresh.'

'I am obliged, General.'

Diebitsch nodded, and with something approaching a smile. 'Have a care, Colonel Hervey. You would be much mourned.'

PART THREE

THE PURSUIT OF VICTORY

The Times

The Paris papers of Sunday, containing an account of the fall of Silistria, extracted from the *Allgemeine Zeitung*, arrived yesterday. The German paper was brought to Strasburg by express, and the Prefect of that town transmitted the news to Paris by the telegraph. He had, however, previously received this important intelligence through the *Prussian State Gazette*, the official character of which renders the confirmation given by the despatch of the French Prefect superfluous. It is stated that immediately after the battle of the 11th of June, the Emperor NICHOLAS transmitted to each of the Allied Courts a copy of the bulletin announcing General DIEBITSCH'S victory, accompanied by a note, in which he renewed the assurance of his wish to avoid further effusion of blood by concluding a peace with the Porte. It remains to be seen whether the loss of Silistria will induce the SULTAN to listen to the propositions of Russia. After the surrender of Silistria General DIEBITSCH closely invested Shumla; but it is not yet ascertained whether he means to undertake a regular siege of that fortress. It is not improbable that he may leave a corps to observe it, and advance with the main body of his army into the plains of Adrianople . . .

273

XVII

WORDS OF APPRECIATION

Thrace, two months later

> *In Camp before Adrianople,*
> *17th August 1829.*

Dear Princess Lieven,
You will have heard, and possibly seen account, of General
Diebitsch's victory at Kulewtscha on 11th June over the principal
force of the Grand Vizier, and of his march thereafter through the
Balkan, which had hitherto barred the way of all armies. I may tell
you that I myself was witness to the battle and thought it a very
great clash of arms, the greatest I have seen since Waterloo. The
Turk did not fight with any great skill, or even great courage, I
might say, but he was present in so great a number that there was
the utmost danger to the Emperor's troops, which the excellence of
the General-in-chief and of Count Pahlen in particular was able to
mitigate, and the steadiness of the troops themselves. But the
victory was not achieved without grievous loss, and I myself
witnessed the destruction of the Murom regiment, which was a
most terrible sight to behold but yet which did not deter the rest of

274

the Army who witnessed it from standing their ground and in turn attacking the Turk with the utmost resolution. There was very heavy fighting throughout the afternoon in which General Diebitsch was gradually able to gain the upper hand by bringing those troops of General Roth's corps and of General Rudiger's, which had principally arrived on the field in the morning, into the centre where the Turk made his effort, and at about five o'clock his artillery was able to do very great destruction to the Turk artillery and to his reserves, so that several caissons exploded and wrought confusion among the Turk ranks and much hastened their retreat. Towards evening, indeed, despite the Vizier's bringing up his reserve of regular regiments, the Turk army was in flight and in no little state of dissolution, losing almost every one of their guns and leaving at least three thousand dead and dying on the field, being one tenth of the force with which he had tried to relieve Pravadi and which, had he been successful in so doing, would then have laid siege to Varna. General Diebitsch's losses were not very less numerous, for such was the nature of the fighting, including a great many officers. The nature of the country did not permit of the pursuit and surrender of the Turk, however, and in lesser numbers and without the necessaries of war, and wholly disordered, he was able to reach Shumla in the weeks that followed, although many of them starved for want of any food whatever in the forest, and I myself came upon the remains of those who had succumbed beneath that want.

The day after the battle, General Diebitsch endeavoured to open a negotiation with the Turk, but he was referred by the Vizier to the Sultan on this point, and so he resolved instead on making a pretence of investing Shumla while restoring the Army's strength and awaiting the reduction of Silistria, which was accomplished on the 19th June. About nine thousand Turks laid down their arms in that place, (Silistria), and perhaps half as many had been killed, and with them more than two hundred and fifty guns were surrendered, some of great size.

Agreeably to the original plan of campaign, the siege of Rustchuk was to have followed that of Silistria, and the line of the Danube was to have been maintained till the spring. But the battle at Kulewtscha caused a change, by preparing the way for more decided operations. General Diebitsch was aware of the moral effect produced on the Turk by the loss of this battle, and he knew also of the dissatisfaction which prevails at Constantinople on account of the Sultan's reforms (I mean principally in consequence of the innovation of regular troops instead of the Janissaries), and, encouraged by these and certain other circumstances, he determined on a course of the greatest daring, which was the passing of the Balkan in preference to undertaking a further siege (of Shumla) to secure more effectually his lines of communication. Once he was joined by the troops hitherto employed in reducing Silistria, he made therefore a more formidable demonstration against Shumla. The Vizier, in the expectation of immediate assault, recalled a portion of his troops from the mountain passes to aid in the defence of a position on which, by the evidence of all of history hereto, everything depended. The defenders of the Balkan passes being thereby seriously diminished, it only remained to attempt the passage before the Vizier had time to discover and remedy his error.

In order, however, to complete the deception which was required to pass troops through this formidable barrier without further great loss, the General-in-chief instructed General Krassowski, with ten thousand men, to press closely upon Shumla, whilst the main force of about thirty thousand feigned a retreat towards Silistria. On reaching Yeni Bazar, a distance of about six leagues, General Diebitsch at once turned right and moved on Devna and Kupriquoi. Each soldier was issued with four days'

276

rations, and ten more were carried in light waggons attached to the regiments. The bridge over the Kamtchik was taken with élan, and from that point it was not possible for the Vizier, who even now had detected his error and managed to detach ten thousand to intercept the Army at the pass of Kamtchik – but too late – to interfere with the passage south, for by now the Army had passed the most difficult part of the country and were far on the road towards Eski Bashli. I must hasten to add, however, that the road leading to Aidos is the most difficult of all the eastern routes, crossing the same stream forty times in the Delidah Valley, and traversing a defile barely sixty yards wide, all of which I myself saw in company with General Rudiger's corps.

In the meantime, General Roth advanced along the coast to Misivri, which capitulated on his approach, and he was thence enabled to march on Bourgas and open a communication with the fleet. It was at this point that the alarm occasioned by the Bulgars worked its greatest favour, for they had, it is reported, likened the numbers of the Army to 'the leaves of the forest', and Aidos, with all its stores, was abandoned by the retreating Turks even before the arrival of General Rudiger.

There was but one moment of supposed peril, when the posts occupied covered about eight hundred miles of country, which might be cut off, and this latter consideration, together with the reported junction of Hussein Pasha, the Seraskier, and the Grand Vizier himself, caused such uneasiness that General Diebitsch concentrated nearly the whole of his force and made a retrograde movement on Selimnia with twenty-five thousand men and a hundred pieces of artillery. But instead of encountering the expected army he only found a small force of cavalry posted near the town, which gave way, after a smart affair, and the place was occupied. The General left here a force to secure his line of communications, and resuming his advance forthwith, he arrived before Adrianople, in Ancient Thrace, this day week in three divisions, with the right of the army leaning on the river Tschenga. The Army has dubbed him 'Count Za-Balkanski', and every man is in the highest spirits.

I conclude this, my second letter, in confident expectation of being able to write next from Constantinople itself, since 'Za-Balkanski' carries all before him.

I remain Your Highness's Humble Servant &c, &c,

Matthew Hervey,

Lieutenant Colonel.

XVIII

TERMS OF SURRENDER

Before Adrianople

Cornet Agar had grown more animated with every mile, composing – and rehearsing – his book of travels as they rode through ancient Thrace in the footsteps of the legions. In particular he penned one arresting admonition: 'None who know the history of these parts, neither Turk nor Russian, can approach Adrianople without wariness, respecting what happened here fifteen hundred years ago.'

Hervey did know. The events of 9 August 378, by the old Julian calendar, had stood in his mind since the schoolroom at Shrewsbury: the Emperor Flavius Julius Valens, whom some called '*Ultimus Romanorum*', had met his death at the head of an army defending the Eastern Empire from the invading Goths. And one of the reasons he held the events in his mind (and much to his satisfaction, for Agar himself did not know this) was that Valens had been raised on his father Gratian's estate near where he himself was raised, on the downs of Wiltshire. But in that battle – Hadrianopolis – there had been a most shameful affair, etched deep in his mind since first he had been made to translate the page of the *Historiae* in the classical remove: Valens had been deserted by his

279

cavalry. Agar had brought with him a demy-size plan of the battle, copied in the Bodleian Library, and was sure they would be able to situate it accurately, declaring in his book of travels, and to his fellow travellers, that 'The city is a hinge on which the fortunes of empires have hung.'

Fairbrother had been equally animated by the prospect. He was much taken by the notion of the 'hinge of fortune'. Kulewtscha had been just such a battle, but Adrianople was honoured by the centuries. He had read a little of it himself, but Agar's journal was true enlightenment:

Orestes, Agamemnon's son, built the city at the confluence of the Tonsus and the Ardiscus with the Hebrus, which are rapid-flowing rivers over which magnificent stone bridges are now said to stretch. The emperor Hadrian, like Augustus in Rome, found the city brick and left it marble, whence its name of Orestias became Hadrianopolis. There, too, Licinius, Emperor in the East, was defeated by Constantine, Emperor of the West, before Valens' defeat by the Goths, and a thousand years since then has not made Thrace peaceful: it is the most contested place on earth – Bulgars, Turks, Eastern Romans, and Crusaders all coveted its pleasantness (as do now the Russians). When the Ottomans finally captured the city from Byzantium, in 1365, they made it their capital until the fall of Constantinople ninety years later.

Adrianople still had the appearance of a seat of power. From their camp on one of the few pieces of elevated ground just beyond the range of cannon shot, Hervey could see the white minarets and the lead-roofed cupolas of the mosques, and the baths and caravanserais which stood proud of the endless flat roofs of the dwelling houses and the broad canopies of the plane trees, and the gilded crescents atop the domes and towers, which seemed to stand defiant against the blue sky. Without the walls were broad meadows and fields under crop stretching as far as the eye could see, broken only by groves of fruit trees and flourishing villages. A scene of pleasantness indeed – of peace and prosperity.

It was only on the rivers that the illusion of tranquillity was exposed. Hundreds of dazzling white sails – the feluccas which bore in and out the wealth of this second city of the Porte – strained to put distance between them and the threatened walls, or else (those which put confidence in walls) made for their safety. One way or the other, those making sail knew that if Adrianople fell, what could be otherwise than the same fate for Constantinople – 'Stamboul' to them – the very seat of the Porte? A hundred and fifty miles would be nothing to an army which had accomplished so much already, nor would the walls of the Golden Horn be too formidable to men who had crossed the Balkan, the bulwark of the empire. They had heard already the invader's boast, *Za-Balkanski* ('Through the Balkan'); and those who knew of the weakness of their city's walls trembled.

When Hervey wrote to Princess Lieven of the army's high spirits, it was to the honour of the general-in-chief. He was certain, both by study and his own experience, that no army could be in such spirits unless it possessed the greatest confidence in its general. But the material condition of the army was also a factor, and in the days of their closing on the city, the contemplation of its pleasantness had been enough to make the *rekrut* forget the danger, toil and deprivations he had suffered since the beginning of the campaign, and dream only of the comfortable quarters (even, perhaps, in the Sultan's old seraglio), the abundant markets – and the other delights. The sick, of which there were yet growing numbers, hoped, too, for restoration within the city's walls (though most were destined to find only a grave).

But despite his confident assertion that his next letter would be from Constantinople, there remained a doubt – as doubt there must be in the mind of any commander who was not to be found leading suddenly with the wrong foot: was the army coming to the end of the war, or the beginning of its own destruction? They stood before the walls of Adrianople twenty thousand strong. Their intelligence – not least by secret emissaries from the Orthodox clergy tolerated within – told them the city could raise at least that number in its own defence, and that the Sultan's troops dispersed in the Balkan mountains were even now, in their scattered cohorts, marching towards them; and a fresh army was hastening from Sofia. There were reports (which General Diebitsch was inclined to believe) that Mustapha, the Pasha of Scodra in Albania, an old Janissary, was bringing forty thousand Arnauts to the fight. And even if the Turks had no mind to defend the city, willing to surrender its trophies and its stores, there was nothing to prevent the soldiers of the Mansure from marching south to Constantinople, ten or perhaps fifteen thousand strong, to join in the defence of that place. On the other hand, he, Diebitsch, could only spare two thousand cavalry to menace such a retreat. The strongest card he had to play, in truth, was the Turks' incredulity that he could have marched so far with so few, that they were indeed 'as the leaves of the forest'. His spies were already telling him that Halil Pasha, the commander of the garrison, believed the Russians stood before Adrianople with five times the number that in fact he possessed. But spies had a habit of bringing welcome news.

Since Silistria, Hervey had had almost free run of the head-quarters, and after Kulewtscha, Diebitsch had spoken with him on terms of uncommon intimacy. Now, before this *mansio*, this way-station on the road to the fabled capital of emperors, the general-in-chief confided in him that their situation demanded the greatest prudence. It was the first Hervey had heard of the word in his headquarters, and he confessed to being disappointed – until

Diebitsch revealed that their situation was so perilous that it begat a paradox: the greatest prudence required the greatest boldness.

Hervey grasped the paradox at once: Za-Balkanski's course of victories was like a slope on which it was not possible to stand still. But it did not alter the material point, he would argue. 'The final act of the campaign, if I may thus liken it to a play, General, is one which in truth requires an entirely new army. If you will permit me, it seems to me that no general, no matter how deserving, could count on the continuing good fortune of his enemy fighting in so irresolute and inexpert a manner as the Turk has so far. And we now cross the threshold of his home, so to speak.'

'I know it, Hervey,' Diebitsch had said. 'But the bones of many fine men lie whitening on the hillsides of the Balkan. I cannot turn them from my mind and surrender all now. I shall give Halil Pasha an ultimatum. If he refuses, I shall attack the city. Yet I tremble to do so, for although we should take the walls, twenty thousand men in the labyrinth of a city of four times that number, whose circumference is ten miles, would cease being an army.'

Hervey commiserated: the storming of Badajoz was an object lesson still.

Diebitsch nodded. 'The occupation of cities, without previous agreement, is a problem for the solution of which history offers few precedents.'

And so Za-Balkanski sent an ultimatum to Halil Pasha. In the afternoon of the 19th – and to his barely concealed astonishment – Turkish delegates came to the Russian headquarters to negotiate safe conduct to Constantinople. General Diebitsch expressed himself not unwilling to allow the exit of the Turkish corps – which he could hardly, in any case, prevent (not that the Turks had any inkling of the fact, evidently) – but he took a chance and imposed certain conditions, in effect a parole: they could leave the city and return to their homes, but not march to Constantinople. In return he promised protection of the inhabitants of the city, their property and religion. And he made this conditional – Hervey observed that here was the true genius – on receiving an answer to these terms by nine o'clock the following morning, a little over twelve hours. For the military, civil and religious leaders had plainly lost their heads; it would not do to give them time to collect their senses again. Moreover, if the city were not surrendered the following morning, he would be obliged to storm it, and he did not wish to risk discovery of his weakness by a longer delay.

And so what the Turk believed was a Russian army, but which did not muster more than would a corps on paper, passed that night under arms, wondering (with the *rekrut*'s simple faith in God, and his general) what the morning would bring. Their repose was not helped by the commotion within the walls, with torches and lanterns flitting this way and that all night, which gave the impression of a garrison readying for battle. An hour before daybreak, therefore, Diebitsch gave the order for what passed for – remained of – the 2nd and 4th Corps to form two columns of assault, while the equally depleted 7th Corps, with the greater part of the cavalry and horse artillery, made preparations to advance to Iskender, six miles to the south-east of the city, to cut off any retreat on Constantinople.

But Hilal Pasha did not wait on his allotted time. At seven o'clock, two hours after sunrise, when the Russians' offensive intentions were observable from the walls – if not their paucity of numbers – two envoys approached from the threatened gates to treat for more favourable terms. Hervey heard the supplication and expected Diebitsch to concede, in the customary manner of eastern bargaining, but instead he heard only the baldest refusal and the order for the assault columns to close to the advance siege-works.

His heart sank. He had seen blood enough – Russian *and* Turk.

But none had reckoned on what terms the *citizens* of Adrianople sought: before the envoys had even regained the walls, the gates were flung open and the people spilled out in a great mass, Turk, Christian and Jew alike, to tender submission, bring peace-offerings – wine, sweetmeats, fruit and bread, so that soon the *maidan* looked like a vast fairground. Then the troops themselves came out and threw down their muskets, abandoning the defence-works before any formalities of a treaty were concluded.

It was over; and Hervey could only ponder on whether, had it come to a fight, 'Valens' would have prevailed, or the Goth. 'A victory is twice itself when the achiever brings home full numbers'; Hervey felt uncommon relief, a surge like the racing tide. He was half-done with fighting.

That night they dined in the seraglio's marbled hall off gold and silver-gilt, with the choicest food of the palace kitchens and the finest wines of the Christian cellars, and slept on soft divans to the sound of tinkling fountains in the courtyard-garden. It was paradise but for the recollection that in due time, perhaps sooner than later, they would have to rise from their cushions, and leave the sound of stillness, for the siege of sieges.

Next morning, Agar begged leave to explore the Selimiye, the mosque which one of the sons of Suleiman the Magnificent had built. Hervey was content to grant it – he would have gone himself were there not despatches to write – but with Corporal Acton accompanying, for Johnson had already set the other dragoons to 'making and mending'. 'And tomorrow, if there is no movement of the army, I should like to see the ground where Valens was undone.'

Fairbrother had already declared his intention to do nothing but sit in the shade of the seraglio's courtyard, uncomprehending of all languages spoken about him and therefore able with perfect concentration to finish reading – strange as it seemed to Hervey –

Guy Mannering, which had lodged several days unopened in his small pack, with a mark at the beginning of the second part.

'What moved you to choose it?' asked Hervey when they were alone, more disposed to humour him of late.

'It was in that bundle I bought as a single lot at your bookseller's. I wanted the Hazlitt, principally, and the others looked engaging.'

'I confess I've not read it.'

'You ought to. Mannering's a colonel.'

'I imagine it is Scotch?'

'There, and Holland, and India.'

Hervey was taking his ease over yet more coffee. 'You know, I read *Waverley*, for he'd caught the rebellion very well, said those who knew about it, but I confess I was not greatly drawn to Scotland. I can't think but that its wildness is mean, or melancholy – though I wouldn't mind seeing Culloden.'

Fairbrother picked another fig from the silver dish which one of the servants of the seraglio had brought. 'Well, I must say that I'm intrigued by the place – at least as Scott portrays it.' He smiled. 'They have an abundance of laws, of which they seem inordinately proud, and lawyers enough to people the whole of Edinburgh, and yet nothing is settled but by the knife. I should rather like to see it. It makes the place of my birth seem tranquil by comparison.'

'You've no desire for the peace of English country after all these months?'

'In due season.' He looked intent, suddenly. 'Can we not see Scotland?'

Hervey shrugged. 'I have no especial desire, but neither have I objection,' he replied without looking up (he had begun renumbering the separate notes he had made in the course of the campaign). 'We would need a full month to see anything of it. The roads are abominable, by all accounts – even the ones built by the excellent General Wade.'

' "The noblest prospect which a Scotchman ever sees, is the high road that leads him to England"?'

'Dr Johnson could be cutting, but no less apt for it.'

'But all the same . . . Might we not, say, visit Drumossie Moor and advance our understanding of the military art?'

Hervey looked up at last to gauge how serious was his friend. 'You would truly wish to see Scotland? The weather's savage; you know full well you shiver as soon as the sun goes in.'

'Then we could visit in the height of summer – the Highlands; when it is by all accounts very agreeable.'

'That I must concede, for I have heard it said that so many millions of mosquitoes cannot all be wrong.'

Fairbrother laughed. 'Let no one say you are deficient in humour.'

'Does any?'

'I confess I thought you thus when first we met at the Cape, but I have long thought it otherwise, that it is merely the mask of command.'

Hervey sighed, coming to a resolution. 'My good friend, you have been the best of companions these twelve months and more. We shall go to Scotland on our return. Honours and appointments shall wait.'

Fairbrother eyed him gravely 'My dear Hervey, I shall not hold you to it, for I should never wish to have you do other than what you see as duty, but I shall, if circumstances permit, look forward to the expedition. That is all.'

And then, towards mid-morning, Hervey received intelligence that wholly changed his contemplation of the day. At Iskender with General Budberg's brigade, which had previously been sent to intercept the flight of any Turk troops, and especially messengers, towards Constantinople, was the very man whom Princess Lieven had urged him to meet – Leutnant von Moltke. That in itself might not have impelled him to act (although, in truth, he had already decided that if the occasion arose he would do as she bid), but the principal news was that he was in the company of General von Müffling, an emissary to the Porte from the King of Prussia. Müffling had been Field Marshal Blücher's *officier de liaison* with the Duke of Wellington at Waterloo, and afterwards in Paris. Hervey had once been presented to him. It might prove valuable – yielding information of use, perhaps, to Lord Hill – if he were to go at once to Iskender, and before Müffling met with Diebitsch.

'Is it so very urgent?' asked Fairbrother from deep in his book, and enjoying yet another perfectly ripe fig. 'Can we not wait until evening? Besides, I shall understand nothing. Acton will be returned in an hour or so; he will bear your armour.'

Hervey shook his head. 'I can't wait on him. If we can intercept Müffling there's a chance he might speak frankly with me.'

Fairbrother looked at his friend somewhat askance. But then, with the greatest show of reluctance, he laid aside *Guy Mannering*, carefully placed the remaining figs in his small pack, and buckled on his sword.

XIX

DIE BEIDEN FREUNDE

Later

The heat of the day was at its greatest, and the labourers of the field, if they had not fled towards Constantinople, had sought the shade. Hervey and Fairbrother saw no one in their ride to Iskender except the outlying pickets at the start and at the end. They rode at a walk and leisurely trot to spare the horses, so that what might have been covered at a gallop in half an hour took two.

General Budberg had planted his pennant atop the caravanserai on the old Justinian road, where Müffling and Moltke also lodged. Tents filled every quarter, and there were more in the pasture beyond, the bounty of a happy interception of Turk baggage bound for the capital. Budberg – *von* Budberg – was from an old Westphalian family; his father, Count Andrei, had been Tsar Alexander's foreign minister but had resigned when Alexander signed the treaty of Tilsit (for none had mistrusted Bonaparte as much as he), and had died, vindicated but in despair, a week before Borodino. The general spoke German with the accent of Riga, the family's seat, but clear enough, and he greeted Hervey with the warmth of three months' shared campaigning.

Hervey explained that he was come to meet Moltke at the request of Princess Lieven (he saw no reason to conceal the fact; indeed, he believed it would speed the meeting), but that he understood General Müffling was also here, 'And I would wish to pay compliments since I had the honour to attend on him at Waterloo.'

This latter was by no means untrue, but Hervey used the word – *bedienen* (attend) – at the extreme of its meaning to lay claim to an audience.

Budberg frowned and shrugged: he was entirely sympathetic, he explained, but Müffling was heavily dosed with laudanum, having contracted a fever in Constantinople which had very materially worsened since arriving here; 'But Moltke you may see at your leisure, Colonel. His quarters are on the other side of the courtyard.'

Hervey thanked him.

And then after a pause, in which his look turned quizzical, the general asked, 'What is this Moltke's business? Does he disguise himself in a junior rank?'

Hervey shook his head. 'I do not know the answer to either question, General, but they are exactly, I think, Princess Lieven's questions too.'

'Very well. I hope that you do not think me mistrustful; you have shown your loyalty again and again.'

Hervey smiled uncomfortably, and took his leave.

Outside, Fairbrother waited with his customary air of unconcern, though as ever it masked activity. 'Why do you suppose Müffling is come so far from Constantinople, and so ill?'

'How did you know he was ill?' replied Hervey, sensing the portents of dramatic revelation.

'His surgeon.'

'He speaks English?'

'French. He *is* French. Müffling engaged him in Paris when he was Tolly's chief of staff.'

'You mean *Blücher*'s chief of staff.'

'No, Tolly's. Müffling was at the Russian headquarters after the fall of Paris – the *first* fall. He got to know Diebitsch well.'

'Indeed? Upon my word, Müffling coming to see an old colleague. That is ripe intelligence – though it doesn't necessarily bode anything untoward. Well, I can hardly present my compliments to him when he's prostrate, so I'll go to see this Moltke instead. He is, by Budberg's reckoning, scarcely much older than Agar.'

'Then while you're attending on boys, I shall take a tour of the camp, and then I shall find a pleasant tree and sit beneath it to finish my book.'

Hervey's disappointment at finding Müffling *hors de combat* was lessened by his realizing that it might serve to his advantage, for why would an English colonel come to see a Prussian lieutenant? That he could say, in all candour, he had come to see the general would surely serve to disarm the object of the Lieven curiosity. Why a lieutenant should be such an object had puzzled him since first she had asked him to make contact, and he could only conclude, and not without sympathy, that it was Moltke's very lack of seniority that made his mission intriguing. What special expertise did he possess; what connections? It was, indeed, fortunate that Müffling's presence here provided him with the pretext for his call. Yet within a few moments of their meeting, Hervey concluded that the young Moltke was shrewd enough to take nothing at face value.

Leutnant von Moltke was a man of spare build, not very tall, his face thin but intelligent, almost hawk-like, and – Hervey supposed – a year or so short of thirty. He admitted his visitor to his room with the greatest civility rather than formality, and he did so in English – very fluent English. Indeed, Hervey found him charming. There was coffee and lemon sherbet, and a readiness to talk that was the very opposite of the taciturn Teutonic spy of his imagining.

291

His coming into the King of Prussia's service was by an unusual route, Moltke explained. He was born in the duchy of Mecklenburg-Schwerin in the year that the young General Buonaparte (he pronounced it in the Italian way) crossed the Alps and won his first great victory at Marengo. His father was in the Danish service, and five years later settled in Holstein, but was soon impoverished by the burning of his country house by the French and the plunder of his town house in Lübeck. He had grown up therefore in straitened circumstances, and at the age of eleven had been sent to the cadet school in Copenhagen. In 1818 he was commissioned into the infantry, and through the influence of his father, who was by then a lieutenant-general, he became a page to the king. Three years later, however, and for reasons he did not disclose, but which Hervey thought he perfectly understood, he resolved to enter the Prussian service.

'In consequence, Colonel, I lost seniority,' he was careful to make clear. 'I became second lieutenant once more and did not proceed to the Kriegsakademie until I was twenty-three, where I followed the three years of instruction, and passed out of there almost four years ago.'

Notwithstanding this loss of seniority, Moltke was evidently held in high regard; Hervey supposed he had been marked out at the Kriegsakademie, a thing that did not occur in England, for there was no academy of that form or distinction, but which he understood to be customary practice in Prussia. 'It is unusual, I would imagine, for an officer to be sent on detached duty so soon after commissioning,' he said, in German.

Moltke registered no surprise at Hervey's fluency (it was inappropriate that a lieutenant should compliment a superior officer), but took it as an invitation to speak in his own language. 'I think it is so. But I have for three years worked on the military survey in Silesia and Posen.'

292

Their respective service was so unalike, and in armies whose organization and method was so different, that Hervey could not begin to think what Moltke might achieve in any appraisal of the Turks (and from what he might suppose, the Porte was not in need of expertise in survey). And yet there was in this lieutenant a seriousness of manner – even for a German – that marked him as singular. It seemed to him unthinkable that Moltke could have been sent to Constantinople except for some equally singular purpose. Yet although the late reforms were far from happily settled, no Turk *ferik* (general), who had come to his rank through long years of the sword, could view with equanimity the advice of a man half his age who had never heard a shot fired in anger. Was his mission therefore one of gathering topographical intelligence under the guise of some other assignment? It would seem apt for one who had spent three years at military survey. But what possible interest could the kingdom of Prussia have in Roumelia?

Even after an hour's agreeable conversation, Hervey was none the wiser, although he did form a very favourable impression of Moltke as both an officer and a man. He found himself thinking that he would like to know him better, and hoped they would meet again soon – and not merely for the purposes of pleasing Princess Lieven. As soon as General Müffling was restored, and he and Moltke came to Adrianople, said Hervey, he would introduce him to his two fellow officers. 'You and they would have much to talk about.'

He made then to leave, and as he did so Moltke went to his travelling desk and took from it a book. '*Herr Oberst*, would you honour me by accepting this? It is a work I wrote whilst at the Kriegsakademie.'

Hervey was mystified: the work of a cadet, printed and bound . . . 'With the greatest pleasure, *Herr Leutnant*.'

He opened it at the title page, and was at once even more puzzled (as well as dispirited, as ever, on seeing the Gothic script, which he still found both a labour and strangely hostile). '*Die beiden Freunde. Eine Erzählung*. How intriguing.'

Eine Erzählung – a fiction, a novel. Not at all what he'd expected. But a charming gesture nevertheless. He slipped the book inside his tunic and put on his cap.

'I shall read it with close attention. Thank you, *Herr Leutnant*.'

'I look forward keenly to our next meeting, *Herr Oberst*,' said Moltke, bracing. And then he seemed to remember himself: 'If you are agreeable, sir?'

'I look forward to it, also, at which time I trust that General Müffling will be restored to health, and that we may discuss the campaign.'

They shook hands, and then with the accompanying click of the heels, Moltke bid his visitor *Abschied*.

'He gave me a book he'd written,' said Hervey when he had found Fairbrother and they were making their way back to General Budberg's command post. 'A novel: *Die beiden Freunde* – "The Two Friends".'

'A soldier with the sensibility to write a novel; that is *very* queer.'

'Perhaps not in Prussia. Who knows; they're a restless folk.'

'And the novel is about . . .?'

Hervey reached into his pocket and took out the book, opening it at the first page: ' "It was in the year 1762 on a fine summer's evening whose peace so often—" '

'Ah, the year Catherine became empress.'

'I believe it was.'

'Was Prussia at war then?'

'Prussia has always been at war. It is an army with a country attached to it. Let me read on: "Two young warriors were in lively discussion sitting by the pleasant Elbe—" '

'Would you count yourself a young warrior still?'

Hervey eyed his friend seriously. 'I believe . . . in my mind, yes. I don't think of the time when I was a cornet as of another world entirely.'

He took a few more thoughtful paces, and closed the book. 'And how was *your* novel? Did you finish it?'

'I did indeed. And it's given me an idea. Let me read something to *you*.' Fairbrother opened the Scott at the last page. 'Guy Mannering's returned from India a colonel, and he's resolved to give up his house and build anew: "See, here's the plan of my bungalow, with all convenience for being separate and sulky when I please".'

'It does not have the ring of great literature, so I imagine you have another purpose in reading it.'

Fairbrother smiled, grateful that his design was already half explained. 'Well, I am minded to give up my house at the Cape and build the same, a bungalow, close to your quarters at Hounslow – close enough to stroll by of an evening, yet far enough to be "separate and sulky" when I please. What say you?'

Hervey smiled broadly, and shook his head. 'I think it a capital idea. Except that you forget that I shall not be taking quarters at Hounslow. How well would your plan of building succeed in Gibraltar – or even, I might say, St Petersburg?'

General Budberg received them with the news that Müffling was now awake and that his temperature was a little lower, but that he was in no condition to see anyone. 'He begs pardon.'

Hervey was entirely at his ease. He would return to Adrianople, he said, and present himself again when the general was fit to receive him. 'I was most courteously entertained by Herr Moltke, whose mission appears to be independent of General Müffling's.'

'I was not aware of that,' said Budberg, curious.

Hervey explained what little he was able, though not his speculation.

'Why do you not stay here until the morning, Colonel? There are ample comforts thanks to the Turk.'

'I thank you, but General Diebitsch expects me to dine this evening.'

'As you will; only have a care. My Cossacks had a brush with *bashi-bazouks* before you arrived – though not on the high road. If you can wait for an hour or so, until I have finished my despatches, you may go back with my aide-de-camp and his escort.'

Bashi-bazouks had not troubled the army much. Irregulars – 'bandits' was the word the Russians preferred – were ever a nuisance to a campaign, but the Cossacks had dealt them short shrift early on, and the word had spread. 'Again, General, I'm obliged to you, but I must return without delay. We'll ride direct by the high road. We have good horses.'

But when he had taken leave of Budberg, he was astonished to find Cornet Agar waiting outside the headquarters.

'Sir, letters have arrived for you from England. I brought them at once.'

Hervey looked at him irritably. 'What in heaven's name possessed you to do such a thing? You knew I was returning before dark. Who rode with you?'

Agar looked distinctly uncomfortable. 'No one, sir. I'd given Corporal Acton and the others leave to visit the baths. And then the letters came – they were brought with the despatches from Bourgas, and—'

'Mr Agar, that was foolhardy in the extreme. But I haven't the time to speak of it now.'

He strode off to where they had stalled the horses, leaving Fairbrother to raise his eyebrows and shake his head in dismay. 'You're a damned fool,' he said. 'There are *bashi-bazouks* abroad, and they wouldn't have been interested in your telling them their history.' He put a hand to Agar's shoulder consolingly. 'Come on; we're going back. Put the letters in your sabretache.'

They took the first mile at a walk, Hervey and Fairbrother speculating on what might be Müffling's mission to the Porte, and Moltke's, while Agar rode disconsolately behind. For that piece of intelligence alone – that Müffling and Diebitsch had served together in Paris – it had been worth the ride to Iskender, said Hervey. And why did Müffling come now to see him? Prussia was no ally of Russia's in these parts: it could hardly be to prescribe the old medicine *'ran wie Blücher'* – 'on like Blücher' (old 'Marshal Vorwärts' never calculated much; 'forward' was the only way). Perhaps that was how Constantinople would be taken, though – not by prodigious numbers and scientific siege, but by just going forward; the 'slope on which it was not possible to stand still'.

'I do believe that if Constantinople falls it will fall thus. Moltke gave away nothing about the Turk, but neither did he say they would hold the walls come what may.'

Fairbrother was inclined to think that the Sultan would call back every man from the marches of the empire to defend the Topkapi.

But in truth Hervey had had enough of Prussians and the walls of Constantinople. He looked at his friend, quizzically. 'You're quite determined on building your "bungalow", aren't you?' It was not really a question, rather an observation. And he was just a little ashamed that he had not recognized sufficiently the strengthening wish to build, almost literally, upon their friendship.

'Depend upon it, *Herr Oberst*.'

But Hervey could not quite see its outcome.

So they trotted for the next mile in silence, a steady pace, in-hand, but enough to leave behind the flies that had begun to oppress the geldings. They passed a shepherd and his lop-eared flock, and an old man sitting beneath a walnut tree who raised his hand but not his head, so that they supposed he was blind. But otherwise the country was as empty as before.

They slowed to a walk in the third mile, though the horses had no need of rest, and then pressed to the trot again after ten minutes of longer rein.

Not long after, they saw the cluster of horsemen – a quarter of a mile to the right, perhaps less, by a clump of olive trees in the middle of rough grazing.

'Cossacks or *bashi-bazouks*?' said Hervey, with no great concern.

'As we have frequently observed, a bird is best identified by what it does,' replied Fairbrother, no less composed. 'If they give chase then we'd better work on the assumption that they're the latter.'

'If they're Cossacks they may still give chase. We might look like Turks at this distance.'

They shortened reins and quickened pace.

The horsemen left the cover of the trees.

The three broke into a canter.

In turn the horsemen began to gallop.

Hervey let slip the reins. There was no prospect of being caught in a straight gallop with two furlongs' lead. 'Come on. Not Cossacks – no lances.'

It was easy. All three mounts had a turn of speed, and the *bashi-bazouks* had not yet made the road.

The pair of plane trees either side of the road which marked the half-way point lay just ahead. 'A mile on and we'll be at the out-posts,' called Hervey, almost enjoying the chase. He let his gelding lengthen stride a fraction more and edged ahead of Fairbrother's again by a neck.

Neither of them saw the rope in time, or the men at each end, up from the ditches like jacksnipe, bracing the trip against the plane trees. Hervey's gelding took it at the forearm and somersaulted, throwing him twenty feet, snapping its neck in the fall and kicking wildly in the road. Fairbrother's caught it a fraction lower, stumbling sideways and throwing him into the ditch. Agar's mare ran straight into Fairbrother's and came down on top of her rider.

Hervey fought the blackness overwhelming him. He wanted to call his friend's name, but couldn't. He lay stunned, prone. He tried to move his hands and feet – *anything* rather than nothing.

Twenty yards away, in the ditch, Fairbrother did the same. His arm was broken – he knew it – but not his sword arm. He forced himself to move, to get to his knees, to begin scaling the mountainous side of the ditch. He found more breath: 'Hervey!'

No answer.

He heard hoofs behind them, pounding.

So did Hervey – or felt them. He used all his strength to roll onto his back. Where was Fairbrother – and Agar?

Fairbrother dug his fingers in the earth to haul himself another inch up the bank.

Seven wild-looking horsemen who took lives, honour and gold without a thought reined up hard. One only sprang down, for one only would be enough.

Hervey could barely see as his executioner loomed over him and drew back his knife to savour the cut.

Hervey's right hand moved across his chest.

The *bazouk* saw the pathetic gesture – *pleading*. He smiled, mockingly, tilting the blade this way and that to show what awaited his vitals.

Hervey's hand reached inside his tunic, to the Deringer pistol, primed and wadded. But he needed strength. 'Dear God . . .'

There was a great roaring in his head – like the Murom as they charged with the bayonet – and he pulled out the pistol, cocked the trigger and turned it on the looming *bazouk*.

The flame, the noise, the smoke – like the powder waggons at Kulewtscha.

The *bazouk* fell back, dazed, the ball lodged in the silvered belt at his chest. He sank to his knees, breathing heavily.

Then, gathering his strength, he began crawling to finish the job.

Another shot – louder. The *bazouk* fell dead.

'Hervey!'

Fairbrother limped towards him, dropping the pistol he couldn't re-load.

The others watched, laughing, biding their time.

'Hervey!' He sank to his knees beside him.

The moment had come; this time they couldn't cheat it. Still Hervey couldn't speak.

He heard the shots, and Fairbrother slumped across his chest.

He felt the strength given to him again – to lift his arms and pull his friend close. But still without breath to speak.

'Oh . . .'

Hervey grasped him tight. Not like this, he prayed. Not both unable to say farewells.

'Hervey . . . I'm done.' It was barely a whisper.

'No . . . hold hard, my friend.' But did he speak the words? He prayed for all he was worth.

'Hervey . . . the dark . . .'

'Fight . . . fight, my dearest friend.' Hervey's voice came in gasps.

And he could not hear the pounding hoofs of the *bashi-bazouks* – and of the Cossacks.

XX

BLEAK MIDWINTER

London, 19 January 1830

The heavy frost which preserved December's snow and kept men by their fires made Kent a dismal place through which to travel, like some vast house dust-sheeted and abandoned in death. It had been a melancholy drive without the company of passengers of stage or mail. A private chaise, a relay of horses and post-boys – a great expense for not very much greater speed, and hardly more comfort; he was intent only on the Horse Guards; all other intercourse and diversion meant nothing.

London Bridge was without its crowds – he had half expected to see it pulled down, gone – and ice languished in the hibernating Thames. Just beyond the Temple Bar one of the new policemen was keeping the peace in a dispute between pie-sellers; half-way along the Strand a piper had gathered a crowd, and at the bottom, by Charing Cross, the frosted scaffolding loomed like a giant spider's web, the men aloft like caught flies. In all its ordinariness, the familiar scene was strangely consoling.

As the chaise pulled up outside the United Service Club, he breathed (perhaps even audibly) the greatest sigh of relief. It was, so to speak, a journey of a full circle, a year almost to the day, but a homecoming without the joy of the departure. The long return – three months, almost – by way of Constantinople, steam frigate and the roads of France, had not eased much the oppressive sense of waste, of loss (and, in truth, of guilt). He had written long, condoling letters, but for all he knew they were still to arrive – and even the news itself. The committal to the earth of Ancient Thrace had been swift – too swift, but that was the only way in heat and war. He had found an obliging surgeon, though, and in the seraglio a little ivory casket, which a metal-smith had then lined with lead, and another who engraved a plate: 'Nothing of him that doth fade/But doth suffer a sea-change/Into something rich and strange.' *Cor Cordium* – it had not left his guard these six months.

The United Service at last – haven. Here he could make another beginning, though what and where he did not know. Nor would he know until he had been to the Horse Guards; and even then the answer might not come at once. The letters at Adrianople – the only ones he had received in all of the year – had contained no word. He sighed heavily. Agar's fateful ride had been needless, utterly needless.

The hall porter, an old serjeant of the Line, turned from the blazing coal fire with poker still in hand, which he brought upright to a salute and greeted him with seasonal good cheer. 'It's a pleasure to see you back, Colonel Hervey, sir. And you, Captain Fairbrother!'

The two went straight to the fire, holding out hands which felt suddenly cold.

'Will you be wanting to stay, sir?'

Hervey nodded. 'Are there rooms? I would have sent an express but thought it would not precede us by much.'

'All of 'em's free bar one, sir. No one is back from the country yet. They say as this 'ard weather's giving capital sport. But it fair makes my rheumaticky come on. 'Ave you come far, sir? I 'aven't seen you in a while.'

'Quite far, yes. Are there, do you know, any letters for me?'

The porter gave a little laugh. 'I'll say so, sir! We've 'ad to put 'em all in a cupboard.'

Fairbrother sat down on the fender-seat, his shoulders hunched. Hervey looked at him anxiously.

'Too cold. Made me light-headed. It'll pass.'

'The baths we've been promising ourselves: that's what'll do it. And a good dinner,' (he turned to the porter) 'unless, that is, the boiler's broken and the larder's bare.'

'Oh, the boiler goes like the *Rocket*, sir. Plenty of 'ot water. But I'm afraid the committee's closed the kitchen for a week to put in gas. There's the galley for coffee and such like.'

Hervey remained cheery. 'Then we'll have to go to Rule's.'

Fairbrother smiled weakly and nodded. 'Confounded ordeal, but I shall bear it manfully.'

Hervey braced himself for the last furlong. 'Meadwell, would you have our dunnage brought in? We'll find our rooms and draw the baths. And would you have brandy sent up?'

'Of course, sir. And your letters?'

Hervey shook his head. 'No, they can wait a while longer.'

When he came down an hour later the letters were arranged in three neat piles on a writing table in the smoking room. He called for coffee, lit a Turkish cigar and, quite alone, began contemplating the year's correspondence before him. But to one side was a copy of the *London Gazette* with a card bearing the royal arms attached to it. He picked it up, curious, and even with some apprehension (the *Gazette* was the government's instrument of record – every sort of official announcement, for good or ill).

The card read: *Herewith the Gazette to which I referred. V.Y.*

So Valentine Youell had written to him referring to the *Gazette* – but when, and to where?

He removed the card and began to read:

The London Gazette – 'Published by Authority'
Tuesday, October 27, 1829.

At the Court at Windsor, the 12th day of October 1829, PRESENT, the KING's Most Excellent Majesty in Council, WHEREAS by an Act, passed in the sixth year of the reign of His present Majesty, intituled 'An Act to regulate the trade of the British possessions abroad', the several sorts of goods enumerated or described in a certain table therein contained, denominated 'a Table of Prohibitions and Restrictions', are either prohibited to be imported or brought, either by sea or by inland carriage or navigation, into the British possessions in America, or into the Island of Mauritius . . .

Dull officialdom. Was he meant to read through the whole paper? He shook himself and turned the page.

The next was sidelined in red ink half-way down:

War-Office, 26th October 1829.

6th Regiment of Light Dragoons, Lieutenant-Colonel Matthew Paulinus Hervey to command, vice Holderness, who is promoted Major-General. Dated 12 October 1829.

Hervey leaned back in his chair, scarcely able to take it in. Indeed, he did not know whether to rejoice or despair.

Then he smiled. Of *course* he rejoiced. It didn't matter if it were a single troop or even a single dragoon: it was the object he had held in his mind since Spain and a cornet. 'To command', said the *Gazette*; all else was mere detail.

But had his letter not reached the Horse Guards? Had Lord Hill revoked his earlier offer of the Fifty-third? Somewhere in all these letters there would be the answer – but where to start? He thought of going to see Valentine Youell, at once, but he could hardly turn up at the Horse Guards on a matter of but his own position. He supposed he would have to report in person to Lord Hill to account for his time with the Russians, in amplification of his despatches, but that was not pressing enough reason to go now, unannounced. He must trust that there was answer beneath one of these seals. Or would Lord George Irvine be at home?

He began looking through them. Several were in hands he recognized, and he carefully placed these to one side. Some bore the impressions of coronets and other recognizable devices – congratulatory, no doubt, and these he laid aside separately too. There were three that bore the seal of the Horse Guards, and one from his agents; these he placed separately again, and would read first. The rest formed a fourth pile, which he would attend to last. There was none in Kat's hand.

The silent smoking room came abruptly alive. 'My dear Hervey!'

He turned.

'Howard!' He rose and took his old friend's hand, never happier to see him. 'When did you return?'

'A month ago.'

'The Cape pleased you?'

'Very much. But I believe I am restored to my proper station.'

Hervey's smile increased. Lieutenant-Colonel the Lord John Howard was back at his desk at the Horse Guards, where for twenty years, with brief interruptions for service with his regiment on the parade ground outside, he had exercised sound judgement and wielded a sharp pen in the service of the duke and then Lord Hill.

They were unlikely friends, perhaps, but their acquaintance went back many years, and each saw in the other the qualities that they perceived lacking in themselves.

'What extraordinary good chance you should come. I'm returned little more than an hour.'

'Not in the least good chance, I assure you. As soon as your letter reached us from Constantinople I left word here that I must be told immediately you arrived. And reminded them every week.'

'That's exceedingly gratifying. And Youell – is he replaced?'

'No. We share the duties. They'd become too much for one man. But see, tell me what occurred in Roumelia. I was very sorry to hear, by the way, about Agar-Ellis.'

Hervey sat down again, deflated somewhat. He nodded to acknowledge the sympathy as Howard pulled up a chair. 'We were trying to outrun a pack of *bashi-bazouks* on the way back to Adrianople – just the three of us. We galloped straight into an ambuscade – a rope across the road, which I didn't see, nor Fairbrother. They caught us square – toppled the three of us. Agar, so far as I can make out matters, was pinned beneath his mare, and Fairbrother broke an arm. I myself was so completely stunned I scarce knew a thing. I managed to shoot one who'd come to finish me off, but not dead, and he would have done for me had not Fairbrother at that moment shot him. But then the others began to shoot and hit Fairbrother in the back. Poor Agar must have struggled free and somehow used his pistols, but he was shot horribly through and died where he lay. We'd all be dead had it not been for a patrol of Cossacks who drove them off. They said that Agar was standing with his sword drawn. Fairbrother would have bled to death where he lay, too, had it not been for the Cossacks. They stemmed the bleeding – heaven knows how, but they say they never have a surgeon when they're ranging, so must learn to look after themselves – and got him to Adrianople, and there the surgeons worked their miracles. I thought he was dead for sure. He himself thought so.'

'And you remained there until he was fit to return?'

'Yes. The parleying started not long after. The Sultan sued for peace, which in truth was the best the Russians could have hoped for. I don't think, now, they could have taken Constantinople before the Turk reinforcements arrived.'

Howard nodded. 'Your despatches have made a considerable impression on Lord Hill. They've been copied to the duke, too.'

There was no more approbation that Hervey could have wished for. 'That is gratifying.'

Howard now brightened. 'But see, this news of command – splendid, splendid!'

Hervey smiled likewise. 'It is splendid news indeed, though it would be more so if the regiment were not reduced.'

'Oh, so you're not acquainted with recent events?'

Hervey quickened. 'As you perceive.'

'The estimates have been restored, and with interest. Such a year of trouble it's been: Ireland, the manufacturing districts even violence in the country. Not only are the Sixth and the others to have been reduced restored to full strength, an extra troop is added to the establishment.'

A year of trouble: Hervey could only be thankful – Reform, Catholics, Luddites or whatever they were. He smiled broadly as the full measure of his restoration was revealed. 'An ill wind.'

Howard smiled again. 'Quite. I raised a glass in White's to the place across the road when I heard the news.'

'Brooks's?'

'Why not? The Reformists raised their standard there.'

'An ill wind indeed!'

'Dine with me tonight – and Fairbrother. Where is he?'

'Resting after his bath. He'd be delighted to dine. At White's? The name amuses him.'

'He's a good fellow. Shall he return to the Cape?'

'I very much hope not. I tell you frankly, I'll have need of him at Hounslow.'

The coffee was brought, two cups. Howard took his, sat back and contemplated his old friend admiringly. Then he took a leather case from his pocket. 'Lord Hol'ness left this in my charge for you.'

Hervey opened it. The gilt shone bright. 'You'll know what it is? The gorget worn by the Sixth's first lieutenant-colonel. It's been passed to every one since.'

'Hol'ness said it had been his greatest wish to pass it to you in person.'

Hervey smiled, but a little wryly. 'That, indeed, would have been to break with tradition rather. But it was very decent of him to say so – the major-general.'

Howard leaned back in his chair again. 'You'll have the devil of a year ahead if things go on as they are. I wonder how you'll do it; I shall watch keenly from the vantage of the Horse Guards. What first, I wonder?'

'That is very simple – promote my groom to corporal.'

Howard smiled. '*Corporal* Johnson. After all these years. How droll! He's well, then?'

'At this moment he's probably roundly cursing me atop a waggon full of baggage on the Dover road. But see, when do you think I might call on Lord Hill?'

'Tomorrow morning.'

'So soon? I'd have imagined his day replete enough with these troubles.'

'I shall arrange some respite. And you must then, of course, go and see the fellows who disburse the Secret Vote. They're much interested in your acquaintance with Müffling, and this Moltke –

and, of course, Princess Lieven. Shrewd of you to chronicle your contact with her as you did.'

'It's just that I must go and see Agar's people before I get myself to Hounslow.'

'Of course . . . You know, by the way, that Lord George Irvine is here?'

Hervey brightened. 'I did not.'

'Recalled for consultation with Lord Hill on the Irish trouble.'

This was news of the very best: he would be able to call on the Sixth's Colonel – under whom he had served since a cornet – before, so to speak, walking on to parade; as was only proper. 'Capital.'

Howard turned somewhat solemn. 'No doubt you'll want to call on all manner of people – take leave, by rights. But as far as the Horse Guards is concerned, you've been commanding for three months already. Don't tarry too long.'

Hervey frowned. 'The troubles, you mean?'

Howard laughed, put down his cup and clapped a hand to Hervey's shoulder. 'My dear old friend, I mean that I'm sure you shan't have an eternity to enjoy it. I'll wager it won't be long before the *Gazette* is printing someone else's name "vice Hervey, who is promoted Major-General!"'

HISTORICAL AFTERNOTE

Although the action of *On His Majesty's Service* takes place largely in the Balkan mountains and Roumelia, the war of 1828–9 ranged wider: there was fighting in Asiatic Turkey, and a deal of 'tidying up' in the Caucasus in the aftermath of Russia's war with Persia (1826–8). The Treaty of Adrianople (the city is now called Edirne) was eventually signed on Russia's behalf on 2/14 September 1829 by Count Aleksey Orlov, who, incidentally, would also be the Russian plenipotentiary at the Treaty of Paris in 1856, which brought an end to the Crimean War. By the treaty, Russia gained the Danube delta and virtually the whole of the eastern coast of the Black Sea, and the Porte acknowledged the annexation of Georgia and the principal Transcaucasian khanates which Persia had ceded by the Treaty of Turkmanchay the year before. Russian subjects were granted free trade throughout Turkish territory, and passage of the Bosporus and Dardanelles was conceded to Russian and other foreign trading vessels. The Porte granted autonomy to Moldavia and Wallachia, with Russia as guarantor, and confirmed the obligation under the Akkerman Treaty of 1826 to observe the autonomy of Serbia. Tsar Nicholas elevated General Diebitsch to the title Count Diebitsch-Zabalkansky.

But this was a complicated region, as of course it remains. There

311

is no shortage of books that promise to enlighten, but one of the most recent and thought-provoking is from the pen of that most entertaining of contrarians, Norman Stone, whose *Turkey, A Short History* (Thames and Hudson, 2011) is a corrective to the attitude of Hervey's time, that, in Professor Stone's words, 'Being anti-Turkish [was] "tone"'. In large measure this anti-Turk sentiment was on account of philhellenism, of which Lord Byron was leader among the European Romantics until his death at Messolonghi in 1824. Cooler heads, such as the Duke of Wellington, were more concerned about the growth of Russian power in the Levant* as the Ottoman Empire weakened (Turkey would soon be referred to as the 'sick man of Europe'). Within two years of the treaty, Mehmet Ali of Egypt, an Ottoman vassal, with French backing invaded Syria. The Sultan's army failed once again, and Egyptian troops were soon threatening Constantinople itself. This presented the Tsar with a problem: Turkey, the hereditary enemy, risked falling into the hands of an ally of France, and this he could not afford. Russian troops therefore camped outside Constantinople as allies of the Porte ('A drowning man will cling to a serpent,' said the Sultan). In May 1833 the Egyptians withdrew from Turkish soil, but kept control of Syria, Palestine and Arabia. In July a further Russo-Turkish treaty was concluded, that of Unkiar Skelessi – as once every schoolboy spelled it, but which now must be rendered as Hünkâr İskelesi (in the same unpoetic way that Bombay is now rendered unhistorically and ultra-nationally as Mumbai, and, worse, Madras as Chennai). The treaty was one of mutual assistance in the event of attack by a foreign power, which in the case of the Porte was limited to closing the Dardanelles to all non-Russian ships.

*Although now applied almost exclusively to the eastern shores of the Mediterranean – Syria, Lebanon, Israel, Jordan – the term 'Levant' referred originally (as here) to all Mediterranean lands east of Italy. It derives from Middle French ('rising') – 'the land where the sun rises' – and could be qualified by 'near' and 'far'.

Britain (and France) was suspicious, even alarmed, that the treaty gave Russian warships passage through the Bosporus and the Dardanelles, and her efforts to clarify the status of these two narrow stretches of strategic water culminated in the (London) Straits Convention of 1841, which closed them to warships of any nation except those of the allies of the Porte in wartime.

War between Russia and Turkey broke out again in 1853 for reasons that Professor Stone calls 'surreal' (these, he writes, 'lay ostensibly in Jerusalem, and concerned the guardianship of the Holy Places of Christianity'). In 1854 Britain and France, and later Italy (Sardinia), joined the war on the side of the Porte. The Russians occupied Moldavia and Wallachia, and in the spring of 1854 invested Silistria once again and crossed the Danube into the Dobrudscha. An Anglo-French force (an astonishing innovation) landed at Varna in June, and the Light Brigade, under the command of Lord Cardigan, made a three-hundred-mile reconnaissance of the Danube and its environs, including Silistria and Shumla, in seventeen days (the 'Sore Back Reconnaissance'). It found no Russians – they had evacuated the Dobrudscha – but killed a hundred of the two hundred horses taking part.* So within a mere twenty-five years of the *Spectator* article quoted in the foreword, British troops were operating in that 'very obscure portion of Europe . . . [where] there is very little reason why we should trouble our heads with its geography'. And, strange to relate, the cavalry, consisting of Cardigan's Light Brigade and Sir James Scarlett's Heavy Brigade, were under the command of no less a man than Lord Bingham – by then 3rd Earl of Lucan – who had preceded Hervey in the mission to the Russians in 1828.

---

*The second of the two regiments of the brigade, the 13th Light Dragoons, was one of the antecedent regiments of that which the author had the honour to command.

*

There are two principal sources in English for the war of 1828–9. First is *Russo-Turkish Campaigns 1828–1829* (London, 1854) by Francis Rawdon Chesney, a colonel of the Royal Artillery who had carried out surveys of Mesopotamia, and would later be involved in the survey of the Suez Canal. The second, *The Russians in Bulgaria and Rumelia in 1828 and 1829* is by Baron von Moltke – the same Moltke whom Hervey met at Iskender. It was published in German in 1845 after his several years' secondment to the Turkish army. It was then published in English by John Murray, in the same year as Chesney's volume, 1854 (war then, as now, was evidently a good publishing opportunity). The translator was Lady Lucie Duff Gordon, although Moltke could undoubtedly have made his own translation, for his English was fluent; he had translated Gibbon's *Decline and Fall of the Roman Empire* into German, for which he received very little money (nor, it seems, did *Die beiden Freunde* make him much), and he had married an English woman – girl, indeed, for Mary Burt, his step-niece, was only sixteen when they wed. He rose to be field marshal and chief of the Prussian general staff (for thirty years), the architect of Bismarck's victories. There is, however, a question as to whether he did in fact witness the campaigns. Certainly Lucie Duff Gordon believed he did: he 'was despatched to the Turkish army by his own sovereign', she writes in her preface, 'at the express request of Sultan Mahmoud [sic], and served with it through the campaigns here described.' But then she also states that he was dead at the time of her writing.* It is, nevertheless, a very fine work, with superlative maps and diagrams.

Of Lord Bingham's time with the Russians there is no written trace. Neither the Public Record Office nor the National Army Museum has any account or reference to an account. Nor does the

---

*He died in 1891, aged ninety.

family. Or rather, it must be supposed they do not; following the disappearance of the 7th Earl of Lucan in 1974 after the murder of the family's nanny, access became difficult. But when Cecil Woodham-Smith was researching for her celebrated work on the charge of the Light Brigade, *The Reason Why* (London, 1953), she made a full inventory of the Lucan archive at the family seat in Castlebar, Co. Mayo. There is nothing in that inventory relating to Bingham's time with the Russians. Princess Lieven's remarks in the letters to her brother are in fact the best contemporary references.

There is a footnote, so to speak, to the action at Pravadi, which Hervey and Fairbrother witness from a prone position in the forest, as 'through a glass darkly' – the horseman's throwing his cloak at the feet of the Vizier. Moltke relates the story. The Turk batteries had pounded the Russian defences for hours, and the Vizier sent a *dehli*, a fanatic, to examine the effect of the fire. The *dehli* galloped to within fifty yards of the walls, and although hundreds of rounds were apparently fired at him he returned unhurt to report that 'everything was as it was' (*bir schei yok*). The Vizier, who had expected a report of several breaches at least — indeed that the walls had been entirely battered down – would not believe that the garrison was still within and resisting, and accused the *dehli* of not having ridden close enough. The *dehli* answered by throwing down his bullet-riddled cloak as proof that he had.

Finally, to obviate letters of enquiry or complaint to the publishers: Rule's serves very fine steak and oyster puddings still, but at number thirty-five, not, as in Hervey's day, at number thirty-eight.

MATTHEW PAULINUS HERVEY

BORN: 1791, second son of the Reverend
Thomas Hervey, Vicar of Horningsham
in Wiltshire, and of Mrs. Hervey; one
sister, Elizabeth.

EDUCATED: Shrewsbury School (praepostor)

MARRIED: 1817 to Lady Henrietta
Lindsay, ward of the Marquess of Bath
(deceased 1818). 1828 to Lady
Lankester, widow of Lieutenant-Colonel
Sir Ivo Lankester, Bart, lately
commanding 6th Light Dragoons.

CHILDREN: a daughter, Georgiana,
born 1818.

MILITARY HISTORY:

1808: commissioned cornet by purchase in His Majesty's 6th Light
Dragoons (Princess Caroline's Own).

1809~14: served Portugal and Spain; evacuated with army at
✗ Corunna, 1809, returned with regiment to Lisbon that year:
Present at numerous battles and actions including
✗ Talavera, ✗ Badajoz, ✗ Salamanca, ✗ Vitoria.

1814: present at ✗ Toulouse; wounded. Lieutenant.

1814~15: served Ireland, present at ✗ Waterloo, and in Paris
with army of occupation.

1815: Additional ADC to the Duke of Wellington (acting captain);
despatched for special duty in Bengal.

1816: saw service against Pindarees and Nizam of Hyderabad's
forces; returned to regimental duty. Brevet captain; brevet
major.

1818: saw service in Canada; briefly seconded to US forces, Michigan
Territory; resigned commission.

1819: reinstated, 6th Light Dragoons; captain.

1820~26: served Bengal; saw active service in ✗ Ava (wounded
severely); present at ✗ Siege of Bhurtpore; brevet major.

1826~27: detached service in Portugal.

1827: in temporary command of 6th Light Dragoons, major;
in command of detachment of 6th Light Dragoons at the
Cape Colony; seconded to raise Corps of Cape Mounted
Rifles; acting lieutenant-colonel; ✗ Umtata River;
wounded.

1828: home leave.

1828: service in Natal and Zululand

SOUTH-EAST EUROPE
and the NEAR EAST after 1815
EMPIRE
Munich
BAVARIA
Bern
SWITZERLAND
Vienna
Pesth
AUSTR
Hun
R. Drave
Venice
Venice
Tyrol
Lombardy
Mantua
Modena
PAPAL
STATES
TUSCANY
Florence
Elba
Rome
Naples
ADRIATIC
SEA
Bosnia
Servia
Dalmatia
Monte-
negro
Albania
SARDINIA
Cagliari
KINGDOM
OF NAPLES
AND SICILY
Ionian Islands
(Under British Protection)
Malta
(To England)
Tunis
Munich
R. Danube